M000191973

UNNATURAL SELECTION

THOMAS PRYCE

www.cenozoicpublishing.com

This book is a work of fiction. Any names, places, characters, businesses, organizations, events and/or incidents portrayed in this novel are a product of the author's imagination, and as such, fictitious. Any resemblance to real people, living or dead, or actual events is entirely coincidental.

Acknowledgements

A list of people in the contiguous US who *have not* helped with this book might be a shorter list than those who have. Given the fact that it's been a convoluted two decade journey to bring this novel to print, any attempt to cite each name would simply be impossible. And forgetting a single name would be a far greater sin, in my estimation, than the decision not to post a specific roll.

To those folks who have lent effort to this project, you know who you are, and I thank you profusely. From editing, support, elucidation, opinion, and beta reading, this book could not have come home without you. For your effort, you've earned a free copy of the book. Or if you'd prefer, and don't live too far away, I'll come over and cut your lawn. It's the least I could do to thank you for taking on such a thankless task.

I'd like to express a special thank you to my loving parents, sister and brother; you've always been there, and I could be no more grateful. Your lifelong guidance and support has been as vital to me as water to a weed. The comfortable synergy of such a tight-knit nuclear clan has allowed this wayward mammal to achieve far beyond the bind of my DNA. Thanks for being there, thanks for being my teacher, and thanks for never allowing the strange young man living under the stairs typing in trance to ever feel strange.

And finally, thanks to Beth Smith for your gracious eleventh hour contributions.

For more about the story behind the story visit:
www.cenozoicpublishing.com

Contact: info@cenozoicpublishing.com

Appetizers

- To be built off the coast of Dubai, Hydropolis hotel and resort will be the first underwater luxury resort in the world. The facility will be constructed of concrete, steel, Plexiglas walls and a curved roof to allow guests to see fish and other sea creatures. (worldresortholiday.com, 6/8/2011)

- Reported in the journal of *Nature* an unprecedented ozone hole opened in the Arctic during 2011. (Thinkprogress.org, 10/9/2011, Dr. Jeff Masters)

- "The World Meteorological Organization (WMO) recommends that people living in far northern latitudes pay attention to local UV forecasts. Exposure to UV radiation can lead to cancer, cataracts, and damage to the immune system." (Smithsonian.com, 4/6/2011, Sarah Zielinski)

- "Scientists have discovered a previously unknown virus and strongly linked it with the most aggressive form of skin cancer. The cancer, Merkel cell carcinoma, tends to occur most often on the sun-exposed areas of the body like the face, the head and the neck." (NYTimes.com, 1/18/2008, Lawrence K. Altman)

- "Gene therapy is the addition of new genes to a patient's cells to replace missing or malfunctioning genes. Researchers typically do this using a virus to carry the genetic cargo into cells, because that's what viruses evolved to do with their own genetic material." (Scientificamerican.com, 5/13/2008, Arthur Neinhuis)

Contents

Prologue

Pacific beach, San Diego
(Nighttime)

It was an odor that triggered the memory.

Despite a strong sea breeze, the smell seemed to be everywhere, the night sky thick with the stink of burnt flesh—burnt human flesh.

In the memory, Clarence was a boy. Together with his brother Martin, they sat in the basement watching the Discovery Channel; *Showdowns of the Serengeti,* being their favorite. The images of lions and hyenas chasing zebra, gazelle, and wildebeest through golden savannas came alive in his mind. The memory may have also been sparked by the fact that, at the moment, he too was running for his life.

On occasion, one of the herbivores would manage to escape, he remembered; keep the game interesting with a timely juke or a hoof slammed against a slavering jaw. But most times fang and claw would triumph. Clarence remembered one of those scenes now: the image of an old wildebeest being dragged down in a dusty heap, bleating loudly in protest.

Clarence remembered how he often felt bad for the Serengeti bovine. Even as a child he understood basic ecology, and the politics of the hunt. *Eat or be eaten.* Animals must feed, as much to survive as recycle the weak; to maintain the balance of power in nature's evolutionary arms race. Wildebeest were not cute or cuddly, or even very smart, but he still felt for the gangly critters.

Now, as he raced across the beach with his wife Vanessa and son Reni by his side, he felt a sudden kinship with the herbivores. He realized that they were now players, trapped in some bizarre Discovery Channel special. And no timely commercial or remote control could help them to escape. This was survival of the fittest at its best.

Killer Cannibals of the California Coast.

Reaching the edge of the Pacific Ocean, Clarence brought them to a stop and turned to his wife and son. They both panted and gasped. He shook his head and chastised himself; he should've brought them back with him during his last shore leave. But he had no authorization; and besides, who could've expected such rapid global metastasis, hell rising seemingly overnight.

Clarence swung around and mopped his brow. He scanned the shoreline for a place to hide. Nothing—just plastic bags and frags of rubbish pinwheeling across a highway of quartz crumbs. Gnarled palms and ravaged beach shops lined the dark boardwalk. But they were at least a quarter mile away, and beyond anything else, their only *real* safety lay due west. Somewhere out in the Pacific Ocean.

Clarence swept the beach, trying to get a read on the hunters that shadowed them. Distant fires warped the San Diego skyline into a mile-wide lava lamp, the glare blinded him. He squinted, shielded his eyes. And what he saw was not good—not good at all.

They were still out there, and they were still coming.

He turned to his wife and son, their face's wet with tears and saltwater spray. He grabbed them by the hand and pulled. "Let's go!"

They splashed into the frigid surf, scanning the vast ocean before them.

"Dammit!" he breathed. "Where the hell are you?" A dark wave moaned and crashed. Fighting the thickening swells, they waded deeper.

This is it his mind cried *this is the spot!* They'd planned this rescue to the nth degree. The sub *should* be there. Clarence stuffed his hand into his pocket, fumbled with the small homing beacon. It blinked red. He sighed in relief but cursed under his breath. To have come this far and not make it was simply too much to fathom.

Before the next wave broke, he snapped around again. The image that greeted him nearly caused his heart to flat-line. A living nightmare came rushing into focus; a pack of spindly figures emerging from shadow and out onto the beach.

"There it is!" Vanessa suddenly gasped, jabbing the air with a finger. "I see it."

Clarence whirled, looked out to sea. *Yes!* The sub was there, its yellow acrylic torso bobbing some forty yards beyond the breakers.

The hatch to the mini-sub hinged open and a dark figure appeared.

"Martin!" Clarence yelled above the bickering waves. "Bring er in a little closer!"

Martin spun around in the pulpit. The sub lurched and began to advance. Still thirty yards away, they struggled to reach it. Winds gusted and kicked up a biting spray, making it even that much harder to breathe.

Another storm of biblical proportion was on its way in that night. Global physiology had changed profoundly in recent years. Volatile climate and schizophrenic seismology brought famine, storm, and sweeping tsunamis with ever-greater frequency.

Mother Nature had taken quite enough. As far as *She* was concerned, the human race was getting exactly what it deserved—a ruthless demise. It was perfectly natural, just part of her job; ninety-nine percent of all species to ever live on earth had already taken the very same death-trek. But this time the act was perfectly warranted.

Karmageddon.

Martin stood on deck and clung to the rail. Clarence could see his brother waving and shouting, encouraging them to hurry. The small vessel rocked violently and Martin turned and yelled down the open hatch to his friend Jesse piloting the sub. "Keep it steady!"

"I'm doing the best I can!" Jesse yelled back, his voice shrunk to murmur by the riotous sea. "We're bouncing off the bottom!" And the controls are jammed!"

The water was chest deep as they reached the sub. Clarence pushed Reni and Vanessa up on deck, then glanced back toward shore. *Shit!* Their chance of making a clean getaway had faded from slim to none.

"What's wrong with the sub?" Clarence coughed.

"Seaweed!" Martin pointed aft.

Clarence looked back and saw the problem immediately. *Damn!*

Thick green straps entwined the prop and rudders like a giant sargassum squid. It would take several minutes to clear, and they'd be lucky if they had half that. As it was, the current nudged the small sub toward shore. The vessel was not designed for this kind of task. It would be damaged if the seaweed wasn't cleared. Hiding inside was not an option. With the prop fouled, the light-weight rig could be dragged on shore and shucked like an oyster.

That left only one option, and Clarence wasted no time putting it into action.

"Get them inside and clear the prop!" he barked. "Then take it out beyond the breakers!" Clarence then found his brothers eyes, nodded knowingly. "I got this."

Martin stared back mutely, then moved to speak.

But Clarence had already turned toward shore. He knew Martin would do the right thing. He was a scientist too; he'd run the equation, conclude that this was the only logical option. Someone had to buy time if the herd was to be preserved. And it only made sense that that someone be Clarence. He was the oldest, he was the strongest, he was the fastest. And he was already wet.

Clarence charged toward shore, the oceans momentum now in his favor. From behind, he felt the air fill with his wife's scream. "No! No! No!" The words pierced his ear drums, but were drowned out by the hollering ocean, and a strange electric buzz rising in his brain.

Clarence set his jaw, rage jacking him up for impact. He was no timid herbivore grazing the Serengeti, turning its horns to make a few gratuitous swipes before rolling over to become hyena shit. *No-sir-ee.* His inner animal throbbed with single-minded slaughter. And that's what he sought; and that's how he'd fight.

Like a wild animal.

Clarence hunkered down even more, legs churning. A feral growl began to purr from his lungs. The three lead hunters lifted and slowed, as if curious. As if to think...

Wildebeest aren't supposed to act like this.

Before they realized his intent, he sprang from the surf. The cannibals tried to stop; but it was too late. His stiff frame hurtled and crashed, and he felt the snap and surrender of bone.

Then the screaming began.

Clarence rolled, found his knees. He spit blood and teeth into the shallow surf, minerals returned to the primordial soup from which they were loaned. He surveyed the scene. One cannibal rolled and shrieked, trying to reset a dislocated knee. Another floated face down. But the third was back up and already wading out toward the sub.

Clarence moved to pursue, but was slammed down from behind. Seawater filled his lungs, his body tangled amid seaweed and wiry limbs. He tried to get up but couldn't, his left arm having snapped from the inertia of impact. The dislocated limb now flapped haphazardly, puppeteered by the rushing undertow, waving *bye-bye* in heedless pantomime to his future, his family, his life.

In and out of consciousness, he realized he was being dragged across the beach like a sack of manna. The distant crash of waves gave way to the crackle of combustion and songs of euphoria. Nearing a freshly lit bonfire, he could see dozens of stick figures dancing around the fire as it sparked and sent cinders skyward. The flames allowed him to see his captors. Scarred and rawboned, they were concentration camp thin, many cankered with melanomas. Most wore only rags. By contemporary standards, they were dressed to kill.

A pile of corpses lay beside the fire like cord wood. The hunters dropped Clarence unceremoniously on top. Then they too joined the parade, slowly circling and singing, all elbows and knees. Clarence understood their elation.

Tonight they'd get to feed.

Flickers of light came from the parade. He squinted and saw knifes and machetes swirling in a menacing metallic merry-go-round. Thoughts of the lion's claw and the crocodile tooth came unbidden in his mind.

A scene from the Discovery Channel suddenly filled his inner picture; *a pack of ravenous hyenas tearing at the husk of a zebra, its spindly limbs pawing the air with waning escape instinct. Triangular canine muzzles then disappearing into raw bloody gaps, returning with steamy pink ribbons of Serengeti Alpo.*

As much as he enjoyed those old programs, he'd be damned if he was going to witness his own evisceration. He was dying, he knew, but not fast enough. He looked down and saw a broken rib bone protruding from his chest. Mustering strength from where there was none, he lifted his head and gazed out to sea. Through hazy vision he could see the sub bobbing on the dark distant horizon. He felt his anxiety ease by degrees knowing that his family would be safe.

A future Kodak moment filled his mind; the wonderful image of his family by his side. Knowing the image would never be, he sighed and closed his eyes. With his arm that still worked he rolled his body off the mound of corpses. His calculation had been dead on, the rib stabbed right through his heart.

Part One

PACIFICA

Chapter 1

(Five Years Later)

Taking time to gaze upon rainbows or sunsets or the likes was never very high on Jesse's priority list. Today, however, was a different story. Any minute the sun would peek above the dark eastern horizon, and he could be no more eager—for it had been months since he'd seen the sun. Absence truly does make the heart grow fonder, he mused.

Jesse stood atop a massive platform that towered eighty-five feet above the Pacific Ocean. From this vantage point, he knew the view of the rising sun would be spectacular. In the dark, he visualized the image; the sun edging above the earth's crust to beam pioneering rays across miles of ocean. The very thought brought him calm. As beautiful as he knew it'd be, the pageantry took a back seat to the forecasted pleasure of warmth against his dark skin. Jesse shivered in the cool twilight, felt his anticipation rise.

It wouldn't be long now.

But he had work to do first. Several gears still needed to be lubricated and a few more solar panels needed to be polished. *Five minutes*, he figured, if he hustled. With birds no longer busying the skies at least he wouldn't be slowed by having to scrape poo.

Turning back to continue his work, he slid on a gob of lubricant. He flailed and grabbed a support stanchion to brace himself, but not before slamming his shin against the railing. He yelped and cursed, directing the invective at the railing for being so darn hard, and the algae based lube for being so darn slick. As much as it hurt, the railing prevented him from falling off the narrow catwalk and into the ocean below, or even worse, slamming into one of the slowly rotating wind turbines on the way down. He grimaced, reached down and rubbed his shin.

The fall ripped his wet suit and gashed his skin. He inspected the wound. As he did he took note of the yellow shark POD (Protective Oceanic Device) strapped to his ankle just beneath the injury. The shark POD was designed to help prevent shark attack by emitting a low level electrical halo around the diver. He'd need it in short order for the dive back down to his home. Fortunately the shark POD was undamaged. The irony of blood right next to a device intended to repel sharks did not escape him.

Jesse tied a rag around his calf to stop the bleeding, grabbed the grease gun and picked up where he'd left off. As he worked, he reflected back to the most recent shark attack. It had taken place about a month ago, the details still fresh in his mind. There had been a handful of other shark attacks over the years, but only one other had been fatal—as this one had. This most recent incident had sent shockwaves through the community; the unease less a product of the carnage, than the discovery of the cause.

Parts of Ben Grimsley turned up in the waters around Pacifica soon after he'd gone missing. Along with frags of SCUBA gear, his head, right hand, and left leg had been discovered adrift in the kelp fields. Although discolored and festooned with noshing little critters, the remains had been intact, the shark POD still strapped around his leg.

The unit still worked, but curiously, had been switched off. Turning the unit off was a two step process, so it wasn't likely that it had occurred as a result of the attack. Equally as peculiar, Grimsley had been out in the water during a fishing campaign, a time when the water was filled with bait, a time when everyone knew better than to be out-side. The physical evidence, along with Grimsley's well documented battle with depression, had left little doubt as to motive. The diver had encouraged the attack.

It was suicide by shark.

The incident had affected Jesse deeply. Although not close friends, Jesse knew Ben. Living in such a small isolated community for such a long spell, he knew every-body, at least to some degree. But it was more than the fact that a man he knew had been killed in such a grisly fashion that had Jesse so troubled. It was because the de-pression Ben Grimsley fought was of the same origin as his own.

Jesse took a deep breath, tasted salt and autumn in the fresh morning air. Postcard blue began to wash the last stars from the sky. He moved to the next solar panel and picked up the pace. The time allotted him to sit in the sun was limited, and he didn't want to waste even a second of it. The strict schedule had nothing to do with timecards or clocks, but was in heed to a calling far more fundamental.

With daylight came danger.

"Yo Jess," a voice suddenly came, wresting him from his reverie. Jesse turned. It was Alberto Cruz, a friend and fellow worker assigned to the detail. Along with two other workers, Cruz was positioned on a parallel catwalk some thirty yards away. Throughout the wee hours Jesse had strayed to the outside edge of the massive alternative energy platform, intentionally distancing himself from the other workers. He wanted no distraction during his moment in the sun.

"What?" Jesse replied, shouting above the whirr of a hundred huge wind turbines.

"You playin' hoop tonight?" Cruz shouted.

"I'll be there." Jesse nodded and flashed a thumbs up. He wasn't sure if he'd be there, or not. Quite frankly, it was about the last thing on his mind. But he knew if he said *no*, or even *maybe*, Cruz would then inquire *why*, and then do everything in his power to change his mind. He might even mosey over to do so. A great guy in general, Cruz was just wired a little tight—a five-foot six inch Latin tinderbox with raging ADD—and Jesse simply wasn't of the mind to deal with that kind of energy, at least not at the moment. Because as he looked upon the last solar panel he just finished polishing, he saw the first cilia of sunlight stretching skyward in the reflection.

His assignment complete, Jesse shed his work shirt. He wanted nothing to come between him and virgin sunlight. Along with the shirt, he stowed his tools in the nearest watertight locker. He then paced to the edge of the ALEN platform, sat down and waited for the sun to fully rise. An unusually dark cloud came into view above the coastline a few degrees to the south, the only blight to an otherwise pristine sky. Fortunately it would not interfere with his view.

Like a striptease, the sun slowly disrobed from twilight. *Ahhh…how magnificent.* The arriving warmth was every bit as beautiful as the view. He felt his soul begin to thaw and his muscles melt like polar ice on a fevered planet. But despite the swell of harmony, it was difficult to silence his mind. He couldn't help but dwell upon his ongoing dilemma. He just wasn't sure how much longer he could live under these conditions. He sighed and closed his eyes, tried to back burner his thoughts.

Just as he started to drift off, he was startled by a sharp whistle.

"Yo Jess," Cruz shouted, followed by another whistle.

Jesse stirred and slowly turned. Cruz and the rest of the team were heading down an open stairway, back to the ocean. It was time to leave.

"On my way," Jesse replied and waved. Knowing it'd likely be a while till he got topside again, he took one last look at the sunrise. Wisps of sunlight now shimmered atop the vast Pacific Ocean. The distant horizon bisected the glorious panorama, the California coastline like a thin magic marker separating earth and sky. Jesse found the view achingly exquisite, and only served to underscore his torment.

Jesse then stood and checked his dive gear. Most of his equipment—tanks, mask, regulator, and fins—were still down below on the wet deck. Before moving off he reached down and removed the rag from his calf. The wound had stopped bleeding at least. He looked down at the shark POD. For an instant the notion of turning the unit off during the dive to Pacifica flashed through his mind, but he dismissed it. Sucking it up and continuing on another day had to be better than the alternative. Jesse thought of Ben Grimsley, and wondered.

Chapter 2

Jesse left the lab as soon as his shift was finished. Ordinarily, he'd stick around for a while and tinker with his side experiments. It was a device he used to keep his mind occupied, and at one time even enjoyed. Today, however, tinkering held no appeal. And even with the crew over in bio-fuel close to breakthrough, their improvements to the algae-based petrol just being put through the final paces, there was no part of him that didn't wish to make quick exit.

Like many living in the small community, Jesse Baines was a scientist, marine biology his chosen discipline. And like most scientists, he loved discovery. The new fuel was the result of an improved rendering process. Jesse recognized the feat as more inspiring than important, and would likely add more octane to the psyche of the isolated community than it would to the back-up generators. There was a time when he'd have stayed and participated in the coming high-fives and celebration, no matter how trivial the discovery. But today's version of biologist Jesse Baines was a pitiful one. Two years of anger and frustration would put a crimp in anyone's disposition.

Jesse left the lab in a flash, saying goodbye to no one. He wasn't being rude; he'd be seeing everybody again in short order, if not at dinner then at the community meeting later that night. Punching a time card was equally unnecessary. Although he was required to log forty hours a week, it was all on his honor. After all, nobody in Pacifica got *paid* in the traditional sense, money no longer a world turning imperative; certainly not down here, certainly not anymore.

Work details were the fundamental life blood of Pacifica, as essential as hunting and gathering were to hominids of Paleolithic yore. In this unique setting the link between struggle and survival was unambiguous. Most seemed to recognize the connection, and did their fair share with little complaint. It was all S-O-P anymore, an apparent knee-jerk lower brain function hard-wired into the human survival circuitry.

By the standards of former times, the idea of such a smooth functioning state was unheard of. A colony of ants would be the only governing entity that could be used for fair comparison from that bygone era. It was socialism by necessity in this snug world, an impromptu extended family of cooperation and efficiency.

Jesse stripped off his lab coat and picked up the pace as he turned down a long vacant corridor. As important as the community's duties were, at the moment they were no longer of concern. He was now tuned to *his own* need...

Find a way out of Pacifica.

Jesse was on his way to the dive chamber. He was to speak at the board meeting later tonight, and he wanted to check out one last thing beforehand. The damage report.

The divers would be returning soon, his friend Martin was in charge of the detail in fact, and he wanted to be there when they surfaced. Maybe he'd get lucky, he found himself hoping. If they'd found any damage to the facility during their inspection, it would add support to his cause.

Truth be told, he had little new to go on. Just the same stuff he'd used during the last vote for expansion. Sure, he'd rework his arguments; maybe elasticize the facts a bit. What could it hurt? All they could do is reject him again, like they had the last time…

And the time before that.

And the time before that.

Just a little damage, Jesse thought as he power-walked down the Plexi-tubed corridor. How about a compromised cross brace or a hairline crack in the hull? Almost anything would do. From there he could enhance—whip up some story about structural fatigue or potential leaks—just enough to scare the isolationists off their asses and get them to finally act.

Jesse was pinning his hopes on the recent spike in seismic activity to give him something to work with. Engineering may not have been his forte, but he'd studied the blueprints of the facility carefully, and he always felt that most branches of science bled together. The architecture of a giant clam had similar physical issues to overcome as the structure of Pacifica. If the divers should find something, he'd find a way to use it to his advantage.

He had to admit, as much as he hated living there anymore, he was impressed by the facilities durability. Even after all these years, the immense pressure and acidic lick of the sea had managed little more than an occasional zit of corrosion. By all accounts, the facility had actually grown stronger. With legions of corals and encrusting algae gluing themselves to the outer hull over the years, the facility was almost entirely encased in a protective shell—a natural suit of armor cast in calcium plaque and benthic goop. Exactly how it'd been designed. Jesse frowned, *damn engineers*.

Overhead, the corridor lights dimmed, casting a twilight blue wash through the quiet hall. The lighting was programmed to save energy and subdue straying biorhythms. Jesse found the illusion ineffective anymore. If anything, the strict automation only served as another reminder of how unnatural this environ had become. To him, the light personified the hallway and all that it touched with the vapid glaze of rigor mortis, and even seemed to tarnish his brown skin to cadaverous ash.

He remembered how living in Pacifica once thrilled him. What twenty-four year old Marine Biologist wouldn't love living in what amounted to a massive upside-down inside-out aquarium? After graduation, he'd applied for and nailed down a research position at Pacifica, the ink not yet dry on his MA. The fact that both of his parents already worked there went a long way to him getting such a coveted assignment. Back in the beginning, whenever possible, families were kept together. Jesse remembered hearing something or other about *emotional homeostasis* and *isolation fitness* as to the reason why.

His father was a commercial diver, his mother a computer tech. It'd been nice having the clan together; Pacifica was so vast and well-designed that living there wasn't all that different from the suburban San Francisco home he grew up in. Back then, living in Pacifica wasn't so bad. But that was then, this is now.

His parents were both gone now. Tomorrow would be the two year anniversary of his mother's death, and in a few months, the two year mark of his father's disappearance. The fact that he lost them so close together left a chasm in his soul as cold and gaping as the Marianas Trench.

Not long after losing his parents, the walls of Pacifica had begun their inexorable squeeze, the resultant anxiety causing chronic pains and panic-attacks. He tried every-thing to self medicate—weight training, meditation—nothing helped. Even jogging through the tubes late at night could not stem the ongoing decay of his essence.

He looked fine on the outside: a lean six foot 180 pound physical specimen. Only last month he scored thirty points and hit the game winning shot in a basket-ball game, his friend Martin making the pass to get the assist.

Jesse turned a corner and headed down an arched acrylic corridor that exposed the ocean naked around him. He'd been down this path a million times before, and never once had he not stopped to marvel. Outside, spot lights colored the dark Pacific in shafts of Caribbean blue-green. To call the view magnificent was an understate-ment, like describing the Grand Canyon as a ditch.

Despite his current quest to get to the dive cham-ber; he stopped again, leaning his arm against the cool acrylic to gaze out. Right away, the aquatic view sparked his memory, sending his thoughts back to land, search-ing for the pictures that brought him calm. But it was an Alzheimer's reflection, fragmented and fuzzy. Palm trees, the smell of a barbeque, and the faces of old friends were all dulled by a mindscape fettered in gloom. He felt his emotional index dip further, looked down and realized his fists were clinched. *Breathe*, he told himself, *relax*. He knew he was about at the end of his rope.

The prospect of being at the end of a rope, literally, hanging gleefully, doing the suicide swing, had more than once crossed his mind. He feared that one day his depression might decay to insanity, and he'd actually kill himself. Like others had over the years. Like his mother had.

Asshole, he chided himself. Why'd you go and exhume that memory again? Now was no time to be emotional, no time to be weak. He needed his mind to be as clear as the wall he stood before if he was to be any good tonight. But as hard as he tried to stop the thought, it was impossible, the memory still vivid and raw.

He'd been the one to find her, hanging by a heavy duty electrical cord from the main girder in their quarters, her body as still and lifeless as a side of beef in a butcher's walk-in freezer. Her neck was bruised and crooked, her skin ashen and dotted with melanoma sores. She'd chosen her favorite dress for the occasion, he remembered; a flowery, tea-length number that she wore for only the most special events.

Even though it'd been almost two years ago, he remembered it like it was yesterday, and he suspected he always would. He couldn't understand, at least at the time, why she'd done it—why she'd take her life and leave him. She probably would've only lived another month or two anyway, given her cancerous condition, but it was still no excuse. Lately, however, he'd begun to understand.

Jesse knew that the only cure for his misery was to get out of Pacifica. Escape the haunt of claustrophobia and personal ghosts, hope that fresh air and freedom might ease the pain. Only problem, leaving was illegal. For one, there were only a few operational subs. Over the years, most had been lost to storm, mechanical failure, and botched missions. The second reason for the banning of missions back to land, Jesse knew, was fear. Anonymity was like a sacred golden calf in Pacifica, paramount and revered. God only knew what was going on up top these days. And a person leaving could become a potential trail back, where over a hundred human hors d'oeuvres hid.

Since swimming to the coast was not possible, that left only two options: getting a mission pushed through or stealing a sub. Jesse was no thief, and respected the rules at Pacifica. But if all else failed, and push came to shove, he'd be forced to jack a sub.

Standing alone in the hall, Jesse sighed and shook his head. The memory of his parents returned and his vision blurred with tears. A laugh escaped that had nothing to do with happiness. He gazed back out into the infinite Pacific—a world where rainbows of fish replaced soaring birds, spiny urchins stood in for quizzical rodents, and stalks of seaweed swayed in liquid winds instead of trees in breezes. Off to the left several divers worked on a mini-sub. The dark silhouette of the OTEC towered beyond that. OTEC stood for ocean thermal energy conversion, and was one of four alternative energy plants that powered Pacifica. Even from distance, the monolith grew huge and foreboding, the shimmering light creating the illusion of a lurking leviathan amid dark waters.

Out of the blue, a school of juvenile Jack mackerel fish darted into frame, a single-minded shimmer that swam with nomadic harmony. Moving as one, he tracked their theatrics. Negotiating razor sharp crags of basalt and coral he found himself mesmerized by the acrobatic anchovies, as he'd been many times before. He could actually feel his breathing begin to ease. Beyond the OTEC a second shimmer suddenly caught his eye and pulled him from the moment. He turned and scanned the waters, thinking it might be a large shark. But he saw nothing. Whatever it was, it was gone. He figured it must've been a flash of light from a sub or maintenance crew.

Jesse then pushed off from the wall and continued down the hall, mumbling to himself like a schizophrenic with a bone to pick, resuming his journey to see Martin in the dive chamber. But he was stopped in his tracks. He quickly grabbed the handrail as the ground started to tremble. He held on tight to keep from falling. Despite the potential damage the quake could cause to Pacifica he couldn't help but smile.

Maybe he wouldn't have to steal a sub after all.

Chapter 3

Somewhere back on terra firma a radio coughed and a voice followed. "This is search team bravo, over."

In the near darkness of an unusual office a figure reached for the two-way radio sitting on the desk before him. "Where the hell have you been?" the figure asked evenly, but with the distinct air of authority. The lack of radio protocol that he insisted on from his subordinates was equally telling of his status. Having to waste time uttering the word *over* was not necessary on his end. The rules of deference had been well established. Those that served him knew when they were to speak. Likewise, they knew when to listen. If he were to tell them to jump; they'd only ask *how high,* even as they took flight, then make the necessary adjustments while airborne, gravity being a far easier force to defy than he was.

"We went up north to follow a lead," the incoming voice explained in the monotone conspicuous to all of his minions, "we tried to call earlier when we moved out of radio range, but got no answer…sorry." The robotic voice carried the emotion of cardboard. The pregnant pause between explanation and apology spoke volumes, however, broadcasting the distinct tenor of respect inspired by fear.

"Did you find anything?" The figure asked, leaning into the radio.

"We got one. One female, over."

The figure shifted in his opulent office chair, the news inspiring an embryonic smile as anticipation edged toward fulfillment. "What is her status?"

"Not bad. A little run down, but alive, over." Again the answer came in the timbre of submission one might associate with a slave.

"Her skin condition, please?" The use of the word *please* had nothing to do with being polite, but was added as sarcasm to whip the underling for providing a reply deemed incomplete.

"There's some damage. But it's minor. Nothing you can't fix, over."

The figure removed the handheld radio from the desk caddy, leaned back in his office chair, his tension easing, but only by a few degrees. "How far out are you?"

"We just crossed the I-5. One of the workers suffered a pretty deep cut during the hunt, so we're just gonna make a quick stop to look for something to use as a dressing. Plus we can use a break. I know a place on the way back that's usually safe and hasn't been overly picked through. We should be back in a few hours, over."

"No stops." Tension returned to the figure's expression. *Dammit,* he muttered. One of the biggest inconveniences of living during this era was the lack of certain amenities. A trip that would've taken twenty minutes in a mechanical conveyance of the past would take far longer by human drawn cart. On the upside, he mused absently, at least he didn't have to worry about them getting stuck in traffic. "Use your shirt to wrap the wound, you don't need it. I've provided you with enough protection; the sun should be behind the buildings shortly anyway. And tell the team that if that female doesn't make it back here as quickly as possible and in good order, being a little tired will be the least of their trouble."

"Ten-four," the monotone voice replied without hesitation or rancor. This was an order that would be followed without question.

"Has there been any sign of Frederick?"

"No sign. It's been pretty quiet out here. Not much going on at all."

"Good," the figure said. "Bring her straight in as soon as you arrive. And be careful, it's getting late. Frederick has instincts second to none, and he was trained to operate in close quarters."

For an instant the figure thought to commend the workers for a job well done, but it was fleeting. Pleasantries were not his strong point, and in this case, completely unnecessary. There was no need to say thank you to a hammer or a drill bit. Moreover, the workers knew that if they did their job and returned with quarry intact, they'd receive appropriate reward.

Returning the radio to its holster, the figure leaned back in his chair. Along with the positive report he'd gotten moments ago from alpha team, this was very good news indeed. The smile on the figure ripened to full blown as he began to slowly rock in his comfy high-back office chair and think—*tonight is going to be a good night.*

Chapter 4

Reni sat slouched on the couch nibbling on a piece of dried nori. The boy aimed the remote control and pressed play; the frozen scene on the large flat-screen came to life. The program he was watching was part of his education plan. Today it was a documentary on the American justice system.

What fun.

He suppressed a yawn and squirmed further into the cushions.

The living quarters in Pacifica were located in the resort area. As part of the whole underwater endeavor a major player in the hotel industry had been enlisted to flesh out an exotic aquatic resort. The resort marked the hub of the complex, and was easily accessible by Plexiglas tentacles to all sectors of the facility. Built to accommodate well-heeled eco-tourists, the original intent was to use the revenue from the resort to help defray operating costs. Although never officially opened, occupancy was high these days; the rooms filled to the gills with many of the original scientists and workers and those fortunate enough to make it down as conditions on the surface had degraded. The resort was a clever fusion of elegance and efficiency, as far removed from Sealab as a hobo's cardboard condo was from The Four Seasons.

Like most rooms in the resort, the Jacksons' suite was modest in size, a sleek post modern fusion of neutral tone fabrics and contemporary furnishings, a small slice of human history preserved in plastic and stainless steel. To Reni, the split-plan two-bedroom suite was warm and comfortable, just perfect for him, his mom, and his step-dad. And with the clear back wall providing perennial views to the largest aquarium on the planet, what more could a ten-year-old boy ask for?

To this point, Reni found the criminal justice program nothing but boring. He fidgeted, occasionally nibbled on the piece of seaweed, adjusted his position on the couch again and again. He'd tried keeping notes. But it was kind of hard to do when you were half asleep. He'd already nodded off once this afternoon, but was awoken by the minor earthquake.

The program took a sharp turn, however, and Reni straightened as a chronicle of historic criminal cases began a parade of file footage: a man getting battered by a swarm of angry cops; a crime scene with two chalk out-lines and a bloody glove; a hulking pro athlete being led away in cuffs for running over another motorist with his SUV. *Road rage meets roid rage* the scrolling subtitle. But as cool as the images had been, they were only an appe-tizer for what came next.

The account had started innocently enough; a video pan of an old warehouse followed by a look at the labora-tory inside. The video was not the greatest, the images rendered fuzzy by a shaky camera and poor focus. Much to Reni's frustration, a pretty blonde woman in a box blocked part of the screen as she narrated. Reni grabbed a small scrap of paper. He didn't understand many of the words she used; writing them down would allow him to find out their meaning later. And he knew just who to see for such an assignment—his friend Jesse. He was like a walking Wikipedia.

He began scribbling;

Genetic engineering
Stem cells
Transfection...

The words came fast and he missed as many as he got. He could always rewind, he knew, but that would just have to wait—because the scene that started to enlarge as the blonde in the box shrunk out of sight, was off the charts.

Reni's eyes grew wider as the camera panned the lab to show a series of tall aquariums sitting atop a long wood-framed support stand, a delicate spaghetti of hoses, test tubes, and flasks stretched in between. Beneath the table was a confusion of PVC pipe, plastic drums, and pumps; all part of a filter system, Reni surmised.

But it was the unusual creatures that floated in the clear cylinders that had him sitting at the edge of his seat. Some kind of fish, he guessed. The camera was still too far away to make a positive I-D, and Reni wished it'd just zoom in already.

The animals were certainly the most bizarre he'd ever seen. From stingrays to scorpion fish, and a whole host of strange invertebrates, he'd seen his share of aquatic oddities. Watching sea life was one of his favorite pastimes, in fact. A six foot green moray eel he called Spike even staked a claim to the rocks right outside his room. He'd watch him and his aquatic associates nearly every night before bed. But never before had he seen anything quite like this swim or scuttle by.

Reni peered intently at the screen. The creatures seemed unaware of the spectacle they engendered. An occasional twitch and a feeding tube of some sort jammed into their torso were the only clues to verify they were more than formaldehyde pets.

Reni felt his heart race as the camera moved in. *Finally,* he breathed. But before the view became lucid, the blonde in the box returned, shaking her head, a look of disgust twisted in her face. The woman was speaking, *blah blah blah*, but Reni didn't hear a word, because off to the side of her intruding cube, one of the creatures remained visible in close-up. *Awesome!*

An octopus was the only animal Reni could think of to compare it to. It had a bulbous head adjoined to a seg-mented trunk, the face a tiny puckered pile of thick fea-tures. Four flippers ran along a stout torso that tapered to a tail. And like an octopus it seemed to change color, shimmering in shades of pink and grey, inspired, he guessed, as much by camera as creature. Overall the ani-mal looked like an oddity from a side show pickle jar.

Reni needed answers; his curiosity itched like a chicken pox rash. But when he refocused on the audio, the narration had become intermittent. *Darnit!* This was not the first time one of the old programs lost clarity.

With the program still playing, Reni walked to the fridge and chugged a glass of kelp juice. He was way ahead of the curve with the educational programs. Given the lack of old-world activities—no Internet or school in the traditional sense, and only a handful of children his age—he'd spend a lot of time working through the tutori-als that had been cobbled together by some of the par-ents. Even today's foray into some of the more advanced programs had been as much about killing time as any-thing else. He also did it, in large part, to try and impress

Jesse. Whenever he could, and whenever Jesse wasn't too busy, he loved hanging out with him.

As he walked by the large acrylic portal on his way back to the couch he noticed some divers swimming back toward the dive chamber. Sporting full dive gear, they all looked alike, but he knew that one of them might be his step-father, Martin. He waved, but they were too far away to notice the gesture.

The returning divers reminded him that it was almost time for dinner. He tucked the list of questions in his pocket and slipped on a pair of thin moccasins. He was about to pause the program when the scene changed again and a new spectacle caught his attention. Although the audio was still on the fritz, the image was okay. He watched as several cops brusquely escorted a man out of the lab with the odd creatures. The scene wasn't unusual in itself—the cuffed criminal scenario was a common thread to virtually every criminal case so far—but there was something about this man that Reni found unsettling. His eyes stared without blinking, his face a mask of disturbing detachment. Reni shivered as a wave of the willies sped from head to toe.

Enough already. He shook his head to clear the sensation, aimed the remote and pressed pause. The picture froze just as the man had turned and looked into the camera, just as the cops ushered him into the back of a police cruiser. The man's name was frozen on the written crawl on the bottom of the screen, and Reni wrote it down on his list. This was something else he'd have to check out with Jesse.

He stuffed the paper back in his pocket and headed for the door. As he crossed the room he stared over at the image still frozen on the flat-screen. He trembled again as the man's eyes seemed to stare at him, and Reni chided himself for not just turning the darn thing off. It almost appeared as though the man was looking out through time, through the screen. And into his room! *Yikes!*

Reni fumbled for the door knob and shot through. Outside, he leaned against the door, mopped his brow, and patted his pocket again to be sure he had his sheet of notes. With a sigh, he took off down the Plexi-tubed corridor.

Chapter 5

Waiting in the dive chamber for Martin to surface with the damage report was like sitting in the doctor's office waiting for the results of a cancer test. At the moment, Jesse sat alone in the dive room listening to the echo of tiny waves carom through the cavernous chamber. As he waited he stared dumbly at the twenty-foot circle of Pacific Ocean in the center of the room and chewed on a fingernail as his mind gnawed nervously on hope.

Had it not been for the earthquake, they'd have been back at least an hour ago. He knew this because when he'd first arrived, a diver that surfaced to trade out spent air tanks informed him so. A second survey of the facilities critical workings had been ordered due to the earlier seismic disturbance.

He hadn't bothered to ask the diver if any damage had been found thus far. Anxious as he was to find out, that information was best heard from Martin. Given his volatile emotional state, Jesse wasn't sure he could be trusted to hide his disappointment if the diver had reported that no damage had been found, or worse, his elation if he reported there had. Either reaction would not likely be well received.

Martin, on the other hand, knew him well. From foibles to dreams, Martin had privileged access to the things that made him tick. Jesse knew Martin with parallel clarity; a product of sharing similar values and interests, not to mention quite a bit of time, both being trapped within the same synthetic walls of the same slender world for so many years.

Although physically imposing, six-foot-two and well muscled, Martin was introspective and tactful. More than once, Martin had played the role of therapist and listened patiently as Jesse disgorged his soul. Jesse made a mental memo not to burden him with that task today. Even the duty of a *best friend* had limits, and he didn't want to take advantage of those boundaries any more than he already had.

Jesse was up and pacing the wet deck by the time the inspection team surfaced. One by one, he assisted the divers out of the water, where they began shedding gear. Almost right away he knew that no damage had been discovered. Everyone was smiling and socializing casually as they trundled toward the locker room to stow gear and dry off. It was the theatre of *business-as-usual*; not a nervous expression or worried word to be had. Alas, all appeared normal; and as usual, the heedless masses were upbeat and contented in their *plastic* paradise.

Just to be certain, Jesse waited for the room to clear and then turned to Martin.

"Did you guys find anything?" Jesse asked, addressing his friend for the first time since his return.

Martin shook his head. "Nothing." His face took the shape one might while offering condolence at a wake.

Jesse shifted uncomfortably, felt what could only be the mental equivalent to a wince flash through his mind. He knew the news was going to impact hard, but didn't realize how hard. Squirming like his veins were filled with Tabasco sauce he figured it best to just leave. If he stayed, he might take it out on Martin, and say something he'd regret. Better to walk off the adrenalated angst by pacing the corridors. He was about to get up when Martin spoke again.

"The only thing we found that was a little odd was out near one of the kelp fields to the east." Jesse stopped squirming, remained seated, turned to listen. "Quite a bit of kelp had been shredded and was floating free in the water column."

Interesting, Jesse thought. Not exactly what he was hoping for, but interesting. "Any idea what could've caused it?"

"Nope." Martin shook his head. "Never seen anything like it before. And it was localized to just one area so it's not likely that it was dislodged by storm of current."

Jesse felt the electric rush of endorphins—this could be something he could use. It was all he could do to contain his excitement. But before excitement morphed into hope, there were other questions that needed to be asked. "What about a sub? Could an inspection team have run through there and caused the disturbance?"

"No. Nobody passed through that sector. And besides, the swath of area taken out was way too large to be caused by a sub prop. At least not one of ours."

"Hmmm," Jesse intoned, bringing his hand to his chin. That left only two other causes for the disturbance—at least two that he could think of. One, a large ship or sub had cruised through the area, which he knew wasn't very likely. Had a large vessel passed over head its signature would've probably been detected by sonar, definitely by hydrophone. And since no vessel had passed by in years, news of such magnitude would've radiated from the communication room and traveled through Pacifica with the speed of a nerve impulse.

The second possibility for the torn kelp was even less possible than the first. But that wouldn't stop him from polishing up that possibility into theory, then using the theory to support his position later at the meeting.

"Anything else?" Jesse finally asked. He chose not to share his new theory with Martin. He'd hear it at the meeting tonight, along with everybody else. Besides, sharing the theory would give Martin a chance to poke holes in it.

"Nothing else. We even did a second survey of the major structures after the tremor this afternoon, just to be safe."

"I noticed some of the guys working on one of the mini subs. A problem?"

Martin sighed. "Broken drive shaft."

"Repairable?"

"Possibly. We're thinking of trying to use a drive shaft from an old damaged unit. It's a little larger, but with some modification, we should be able to make it work."

Another sub down, Jesse mused, bad news for the community, but something else that he could use tonight. He'd already planned on speaking on the matter. Now he had a piece of tangible evidence, however small, to add credence to his idea.

"You sure you're alright?" Martin asked, the question pulling Jesse from the quiet of his own private Idaho.

"Yeah, yeah…I'm fine, I was just thinking." Jesse managed a smile.

"Okay, but I thought you'd be much more upset by all this. I know how much you were hoping for us to find some kind of damage for you to use to help in the meeting tonight."

Martin was indeed perceptive. Although Jesse shared his passion to get out of Pacifica with Martin, and did so at almost every turn, he'd never spoken of his wish for damage to be found. Frankly, he was a little embarrassed by it, given the self serving nature of such an idea. Then again, as Jesse thought further, it was really no surprise that Martin had figured it out. The basic math of human behavior would lead anyone to the same conclusion. He made a note that he'd have to be more careful with his emotions moving forward. Should the vote fail tonight, he wouldn't want to do anything that might give away his plan to steal a sub.

Staring absently at the waves flitting across the small parcel of ocean, Jesse offered a reassuring nod. "I've got plenty to work with tonight, and I'm fine."

Out of the corner of his eye he could see Martin staring at him. He could feel his eyes studying him, probing, looking for clues. Martin wasn't buying it.

"I said I'm fine," Jesse reaffirmed, turning and meeting his friend's imploring brown eyes.

"Right," Martin said skeptically, slapping a beefy hand on Jesse's shoulder, "I'll tell you what, I'm scheduled to go up top tomorrow to work on the ALEN platform. Why don't you take my spot? I can wait till next rotation."

Jesse was deeply moved, the gesture was beyond generous. The trips topside were as crucial to human health as they were to the wellbeing of the alternative energy platform. With most of the sunlamps in Pacifica burned out or weakened from use, the time spent in the early morning sun provided a vital source of energy, enough to keep bones free of rickets and other vitamin D deficiencies. Martin knew this as well as anyone. Should he miss his rotation, he'd be putting his health in danger.

Aside from reminding Jesse of his friend's selfless nature, the offer held a second implication. It meant that Martin didn't believe the vote would pass tonight. If he had, there'd be no need to make the offer. Jesse took no offense in his lack of confidence. The simple fact was; Martin was right. The chance of Jesse changing the mind of a group so deeply entrenched was only slightly less likely than him walking on water.

"Listen, I appreciate the offer, but I'm fine," Jesse said evenly so his words would be trusted as authentic. "Besides, "I'm gonna get this thing pushed through tonight, and by this time next week, I'll be on holiday."

Martin snorted a laugh. "Indeed."

Before the echo of laughter ebbed fully, an idea came, Jesse's mind making a sudden connection. Visions of solar panels and submarines collided in epiphany, and his brain began to swell with euphoria. This was a great idea, could possibly be the solution he needed to finally convince the population that a mission back could be safely achieved, and he found himself wondering why he'd never thought of it before. Armed with the new notion, Jesse stood, and hurried around the wet deck for the bulkhead door. He was so excited to leave and get the idea on paper that he almost walked across the water in the center of the room to save time.

"Alright then," he heard from behind. "Guess I'll see you later."

Jesse turned, his manners forgotten. "Oh yeah…sorry. See ya later. I just got an idea and I gotta do something quick before the meeting."

Jesse then made his way speedily through the airlock and out into the corridor. Now all he had to do was track down a sheet of paper.

Chapter 6

Jesse sat in the back of the cafeteria as it began to fill. The chairs had just been rearranged, the tables pushed to the side as the room completed the transition from cafeteria to battleground. An amphitheatre was located in Pacifica, but it seated only fifty people. With the events on tap for this evening's meeting, that number was likely to be soundly exceeded.

Jesse leaned back and breathed deep, trying to ease a screaming headache. Staring up at the massive domed ceiling might help do the trick. At the very least, it'd spare him the torture of small talk with the vacuous drones sauntering in.

The ceiling looked like a giant white umbrella; curved support girders intersected at the top and arched down all around him. The massive hemisphere was the perfect design to keep the largest rain drop that was the Pacific Ocean from pouring down, a feat accomplished by enlisting the most fundamental geometric precepts. No architect, ancient Egyptian engineer, or computer program could improve on the eons of trial and error evolution had devoted to designing the simple shape of the egg.

The vote was the primary drama on the docket. The issue of expansion back to land was a real hot button topic. And like many political issues of days past, one side simply couldn't see the other's point of view.

Aside from the vote for a journey to the surface, reproductive privileges were also up for grabs. And although a special event, especially for the lucky few selected, it was a back seat issue. Deep down, most people would rather see a multi-vehicle pileup than even the most prestigious classic car show. And the way things had been heating up lately, the Jaws of Life had better be well oiled.

People continued filing in. Jesse had sequestered himself in the last row. It was a calculated move, an attempt to hide in a crowd. He sat with fists clinched. Even armed with a few new ideas, there were no guarantees. To the congregation's credit, everyone seemed to instinctively sense the inherent peril, and wisely avoided the human land-mine, giving him wide berth as they shuffled by to find their seats.

Jesse returned his head to level, massaging his temples. To his surprise, his headache had actually improved. He looked down at the paper he had clutched in his hand, then up at the clock. Almost showtime. He shifted in his seat, glanced around. The room was nearly full; most seated and clamoring away in small human bundles. For the life of him, he just couldn't understand them. How could they all just sit around so carefree and seemingly oblivious? How could they be happy here, the notion of true freedom not even a blip on their radar? Weren't they even the slightest bit curious to find out what was out there? If this had been the mindset of ancient explorers, *The New World* might never have been discovered—although from the viewpoint of the buffalo and the trees that may not have been such a tragedy.

Most folks in Pacifica were isolationists, arrogant and witless in Jesse's opinion. Just looking around the room at them now made his viscera quiver. He could barely keep down the few bites of squid salad he'd eaten at dinner. *Settle down*, he told himself, *don't get worked up*. The headache that'd just subsided was only a few diastolic degrees from making a raging come-back.

He sighed, closed his eyes and allowed his mind to drift. Within seconds, his thoughts shuttled him back to a childhood memory—visiting the metro zoo during summer break, going to see his old friend, Captain Jack, the big old chimp that lived in the primate cage. The exhibit was huge, he remembered, replete with plastic trees, cement rocks, and dozens of other frisky monkeys. Yet for some reason, Jack always stayed to himself, sitting alone on a faux outcrop, staring and rocking in autistic rhythm, expressly ignoring his capering cage mates. Sometimes he'd nibble at the odd piece of fruit that was tossed his way; occasionally he'd fling a piece of shit at an unsuspecting patron passing by. And once in a great while, if your visit was timed just right, Jack would sit there and masturbate. Right in full view for everyone, along with all of god's creatures, to see. It was a special event when Jack spanked the monkey. Watching the crowd watch him was half the fun. Most of the civilized simians strolling by found it entertaining, occasionally even applauded. Jesse and his friends used to get a real big kick out of 'ol Jack. The chimp was a real hit at those moments, although he never seemed aware of his celebrity.

Now, as Jesse sat in his own cage, feeling sullen and alone, while those around him clamored away in detached oblivion, he wondered what might have been going through old Jack's mind. Had the chimp simply given up? Was his behavior the result of acute discontent? Did he long to once again swing freely from branch to branch in a *real* jungle, in spite of lurking predators and having to scrounge for his own food? Did he ever wonder why he was there? Or maybe he just figured he was part of some grand experiment, as Jesse often did in Pacifica, living in the bottom of a Petri dish; being observed, watched, studied. Wondering who was at the helm of it all—a superior being? Aliens? God?

Not for the first time, Jesse felt sorry for Jack. He regretted ever having made fun of the poor primate, now that he was essentially living in his shoes.

A hand landed on his shoulder and Jesse snapped back to the now. He turned. It was Michelle Mendez.

"Hey Jess," she said and flashed him a subdued smile. Without looking back she continued up the aisle to find a seat next to some friends.

"Hi Mitch," he breathed, managing a smile of his own as she swept by.

Once upon a time, he'd actually dated her. He'd always thought that she might be *the one;* their connection as strong as an ionic bond. She'd been his closest friend and lover for almost two years. But for better or worse, that saga had run its course. Now it all seemed so long ago, once upon a time.

Her lingering essence breached his inner walls as she passed by, a diffusing contrail of lavender and female pheromones. It triggered his memory, had him reflecting back to the first moment he laid eyes upon her. She had found her way to Pacifica via a rescue mission along with her mom and several others. The majority of the population at Pacifica had arrived by similar means.

Jesse had been there in the dive chamber that day. He remembered their frightened faces as he assisted the refugees up onto the wet deck. Most of them, Michelle included, had been in pretty bad shape; exhausted, emaciated, diseased. Several had advanced signs of the dreaded Merkel cell carcinoma, or the plague as it had become to be known. Although weak and thin and emotionally drained, Michelle and her mother had been two of the few spared the violation of the plague.

Watching her chat with her friends now, he began to ponder her qualities, and what he had let go. She was an angelic little spirit, kind and dedicated. Her disarming nature made her fun just to be around. Her smile alone could make you feel totally at ease. The one she'd just given him had no such effect, however.

To Jesse, she was a cinnamon skinned goddess—lithe and exquisite—almost as if she'd been hand crafted by Cupid himself, the template downloaded directly from his brain. All in all, he couldn't find one physical feature that didn't agreed with him. These days she was little more than another face in the crowd.

Deep down, beneath the emotional landfill, he knew he still loved her. But he was in no condition to tell her that, and perhaps suck her back into the volatile vortex that was his life. It just wouldn't be fair. So for her good as much as his, he had withdrawn, and threw up hard inner walls to maintain that distance during the unavoidable chance meetings of living in such a small community. Like the one that had just occurred.

Jesse noticed Martin enter and he tracked him. As one of the five board members, he'd be sitting at the head table. Jesse saw Reni trailing Martin before breaking off to find a seat on the floor in the back. Jesse leaned back, made eye contact with the boy, waved and nodded. Reni returned a half-hearted wave, no smile.

The tepid gesture was telling, and Jesse knew why. The boy was hurt, and he couldn't blame him. Jesse slouched, angry at himself. He'd run into him in the corridor right after leaving the dive chamber. All the boy had wanted was to ask some questions; reading them excitedly from the scribble on a little note.

What's genetic engineering? Who's Dr. Harris Leezak? What was in his lab?

And what had Jesse done, basically blown him off; focused as he was on *his own* agenda. The boy deserved more than a few cursory responses. Jesse was disappointed in himself; he had to be better than that. He leaned back, looked around the room. Aside from the boy, he'd managed to alienate a lot of people over the past two years, he realized, even some good friends. He wondered why anybody even bothered with him at all anymore. He sighed, shook his head. That was going to have to change.

Win, lose or draw tonight—tomorrow, things were going to change.

Chapter 7

Daniel Winslow stood at the front of the cafeteria behind a rustic oak podium. He cleared his throat and tapped the microphone. The antique lectern stood out in sharp contrast to the antiseptic motif in Pacifica. The din in the room immediately began to recede. Winslow was a large man, jovial and engaging, six-foot-three and more than a little portly. Like the antique podium he stood behind, his extra weight was out of place. Most people in Pacifica were fit and lean, the business of survival and primal diet helped see to that.

Food was not in short supply, but no longer was it a cheap commodity. The gluttony of surplus once so pervasive in some nations was long gone. Drive-thrus and supersized lifestyles were now only folklore. Gone were the microwaved conveniences of the day where a king-sized feedbag from Burger-delight could be obtained with the simple swipe of a credit card, and a short mini-van ride through the fast food assembly line. The current economics of survival had restored balance in Pacifica; calories reaped were once again on par with calories spent on the harvest.

Winslow was the board chair. The board was in place only to organize meetings and work schedules, and to make fast decisions in cases of emergency. The tiny government made for a truly naked democracy. And although simple, the system worked.

Jesse had been listening with a perfunctory ear as Winslow went through his opening. "And since tonight's agenda might be a little longer than usual," the talking sloth said, "I'll try and keep my remarks a little shorter than usual." They were the first words Jesse actually heard. He had trouble even listening to the guy. Winslow was a well known isolationist.

A conservative chorus of laughter followed Winslow's remark, the tension in the room dipped, but only by a degree. Winslow, if nothing else, was good with a crowd.

"At this point I'd like to turn it over to Dr. Sanders." He said and nodded to a woman sitting In the front row. "Before I depart, I'd just like to wish everybody in the reproduction lottery good luck, from me and the board." He paused, smiled. "And remember, if you don't happen to get selected this time, it doesn't mean you can't keep practicing for next time." Winslow winked and stepped aside, this time the laughter in the room was near unanimous.

Dr. Diana Sanders found her way to the lectern, much of the laughter turned to applause as she stepped up. "Thanks Dan." she said with a nod, smiling out at the crowd.

Dr. Sanders was a genetics expert in charge of reproductive strategies, inheriting the position from her father. He'd been a molecular biologist assigned to Pacifica at the start, although now retired, ushered off to the afterworld by a massive coronary. He'd trained his daughter over the years, passing on his knowledge before passing on himself. Though she never attended grad school, she was recognized as a PhD, albeit an honorary title. Many others had done the same.

Dr. Sanders cleared her throat; let her smile fade. Her hair was up and professional, her face classic and attractive, although not stunning. A pair of old reading glasses rested on her nose giving her face the conservative suggestion of a librarian. Her body on the other hand, was phenomenal. And according to locker room banter, she was *bootylicious*. Unlike Winslow, she was tight and shapely. She wore a navy blue dress with a high neck line, revealing very little of her flawless olive skin, but tight enough to hourglass every inch of her killer body. Jesse and Martin had often joked how there was no one in all of Pacifica more appropriate to be in charge of reproduction.

"I'll try to be short as well; I know there are other important matters to attend to this evening," she said, her tone professional yet relaxed. "Let me assure everyone that I have done a statistical analysis of our population curve, and it is definitely time to add to our family." The room hummed with enthusiastic murmur.

Her job was as essential as any. Quantity and quality of population were under her supervision. Given their limited space and resources, too many simultaneous births could cause a strain down the road. And with such a limited pool of potential mates, she was also concerned with genetically linked disorders. She pre-screened each pair for the prospect of inbreeding, a condition that could magnify deleterious effects or even generate new ones. Most people seemed to instinctively grasp the need for the practice. And since very few red-necks had made Pacifica their home, no complaints were ever lodged.

She was also responsible for performing vasectomies on the males as they reached puberty, and subsequently reversing the surgery, temporarily, if granted reproductive approval. As hot as she was, it was maybe *the only* circumstance where a guy *would not* be pleased that she was holding his balls in her hands. The practice was the only way to be sure to maintain genetic health and keep their numbers in check. It had been adopted early on as growing necessity outweighed initial reluctance.

Dr. Sanders dropped a folded paper into the wire-mesh hopper on the table. "Before conducting the drawing, I'd like to add Florence Walsh to the pool. She and her prospective mate, Andrew Lee, recently applied for privileges and have been approved."

With the new ticket in the tumbler, she spun the crank, mixing them like bingo balls. The buzz in the room turned to breath-held silence, everyone seemingly hypnotized. The women by the wonderful promise it yielded—the men by the wonderful bounce of her tits.

She asked a young girl from the audience to come up and select the winners. The girl gleefully complied, reached in and grabbed two pieces of paper, then handed them to Dr. Sanders and returned to her seat with a proud smile.

Dr. Sanders unfolded the two tickets, leaned in to the mic. "Authorization to reproduce is granted to Laura Watts and Alexander Hankin." A small group in the crowd jumped up and cheered. A young woman grabbed the stunned man next to her and hugged him hysterically.

Not waiting for the commotion to recede, Dr. Sanders leaned close to the mic again. "And the other winners are…Sheena Mills and William Fuller." The room erupted with elation which gave way to a harmonious applause. After allowing an appropriate moment to pass, Dr. Sanders offered her congratulations as well as that of the board. She then glanced over at Winslow, he nodded and she returned to the mic. "Mr. Winslow has asked me to introduce the first speaker for tonight," she said, the relaxed tone no longer evident in her voice. The mood in the room had also turned, dead serious silence replacing the cloud-nine clamor. "He has also asked me to remind everyone to please listen carefully to both sides and try and stay objective. As you know this has become some-what of an emotional issue." She looked up, surveyed the crowd. Her eyes then stopped as she seemed to locate who she was looking for.

She leaned into the mic. "Jesse...you're up."

Chapter 8

Somewhere back on the streets above sea level, the events of an entirely different drama began to play out.

From his position alongside a slowly moving box wagon, Derrick Black glanced around as he and a small hunting party trundled through the fallen city. It had been a long mission and Derrick was dog tired. But according to orders, a break was out of the question. Despite his effort to stay focused, exhaustion set his mind to wander. And as they traveled down a windswept street, he found himself absently looking upon the city that once inspired dazzling postcards by the landfill.

Years ago, Derrick and his wife lived in a townhouse not far off; closing on the place only a month after they were married. They had even put their honeymoon on hold, using the money instead as a down-payment on their dream home. But that had all been long ago; back before everything went to shit, back before his wife had been taken by the plague, back when he was a different person entirely.

These days, the memories of their home and even his wife were dusty and faded, stagnant images that played in his mind like scenes from an old insignificant movie he'd once seen. It should have bothered him he knew—a dead wife, a dead city, a dead planet—but none of it did. One had to be sane to register such feelings, and that commodity had long been torn from his soul.

In the sky above, a ripening moon had begun the spread of welfared watts from a wandered sun. A steady sea breeze whistled through the crumbling architecture, metaphoric meteorology of the winds of change. Ahead, a single cloud hung dark in a darkening sky; the only smudge on the epilogue to what had otherwise been a bright blue day. The evening sky was otherwise sterile; no birds, planes, or buzzing insects blotting out specks of the heavens. Beyond the sphere of their slow moving entourage, there wasn't much scurrying about the surface environs either. Most life forms found the exposed biomes pitiless; the earth's affection for seed these days was only marginally more favorable than a crematorium kiln.

Yet somehow some managed.

Mustaches of Purple Needlegrass and other sturdy weeds emerged from cracks in the streets, while a faded rainbow of lichens hued the concrete in between, evidence of ecological succession sewn in pioneering carpets, and living testament to life's ability to adapt. Viewed in snapshot from the past, it was an odd picture indeed. These days, Derrick knew it all as simply part of the survival-of-the-fittest meat grinder of this era.

He shook his head to try and flush the fatigue and return to the moment. Along with Derrick, three of his peers walked alongside the makeshift wooden chariot, their movements strategic, traveling like a secret service team pacing a presidential limo, one spotted off each corner. Two other men pulled the cart. They too were large, well muscled, but not of the same cause. Their status was much farther down on the life-work food chain; the sum of their ambitions decided for them, chosen by the single supreme force that reigned in this area these days. The surrender of their will had occurred long ago, achieved by the most sinister means, reinforced by the biting dint of switch and whip. And at the moment, Derrick had a six-foot length of PVC flex hose close at hand, just in case the pace should slow to unacceptable, and the sting of reminder be required.

Like Derrick, they once lived among the free. Today, the two pulling the cart were no more than bipedal equine lashed to cart by leather strap, their lives beholden to the same one that employed Derrick and the other three hunters that walked on their perimeter. Derrick could tell that neither man was pleased with the arrangement. Nowhere was their discontent any more obvious than in the blank stare of surrender in their eyes, an ocular emptiness born of soul rot and the toxin of resignation.

At one time, seeing men abused in such fashion would've set Derrick off; make him see red with rage. Especially since members of *his own* bloodline had once been exploited as slaves. Back in the day, he'd have marched and protested and even gone to war to see this kind of injustice overturned. But like the raped environment all around him, the atrocity hardly registered on his inner map. The person that cared so much of such matters was long gone from his identity, rudely evicted by the prick that he knew he'd become; the prick that now ruled the roost of a mind grown callous. *Besides*, his inner prick reminded him, *if it weren't for them, it might be me pulling the cart.*

The two human oxen were not the only ones in shackles on this day. Because struggling in the bed of the cart they pulled was the prized catch of the day, the well earned end result of a long hunt.

A teenage female.

Bound and gagged, the young woman wormed without relent. She struggled to break free with a body near as thin as the ropes that gripped her. But like the fluid lost from her eyes, her effort to escape was a waste. The thrashing only sapped her strength, the shed tears only dehydrating her further.

The entourage moved at a deliberate pace as they traveled down the center of the eroded street. With no concern of oncoming traffic or the nuisance of street signs, they had the road all to themselves. The only obstacles were the numerous pot holes and abandoned vehicles, and the occasional frag of trash tumbleweeding by, which they deftly swerved to avoid, like a well practiced game of apocalypse slalom. The street no longer had the charm of animation or the bustle of commerce, lacked the simple recognition of even a name, was now just a drab ribbon of eroded asphalt, not unlike the countless other barren roads that crisscrossed the devastated dead zone once known as San Diego.

It had been a long hunt. The concrete jungle was vast and intricate, and the prey was always wary. But today they'd gotten lucky, and the four hunters couldn't be more content with their catch. The one who was in charge would be pleased. The young girl was a little lean and sprinkled with disease, but with the proper attention she could be restored to full function. Maybe even achieve a normal life span.

Although nine months would do just fine.

This could mean reward, Derrick knew. Many times successful hunts were given the gift of positive reinforcement. Still several blocks from the compound, by no means were any of them celebrating just yet. They all knew that danger was like an insomniac, sleeping very little in this new world. One of their own had been taken down during a similar campaign just last week. Knowing that, their weapons were at the ready, hackles high, sensory radar on full alert.

Vigilant as they'd been, the men were unaware that they were being watched, and had been for some time. Their every movement monitored, tracked from the second-floor shadows of the burned out concrete husks that lined the streets of the fallen city. And the eyes that were hot upon them were more than just curious orbs. The creature behind these eyes had other intentions entirely.

Unknown to the quartette, the script had been flipped, no longer were *they* the biggest and baddest on the block, not at the moment, not any more. Because at this very instant…

The hunters had become the hunted.

Derrick clutched his crossbow like a lifeline, ready to be brought to bear at the first flicker of trouble. Given the strength of the team, he felt certain they could deal with any problems, should any arise. Besides, the *problem* they feared most had yet to ever attempt an open attack, ambush its chosen M-O. And according to the most recent reports, the creature was not armed. Had a firearm in fact fallen into its possession, from what Derrick knew, the capacity to operate the weapon was beyond its DNA pay-grade.

The one problem the team *couldn't* help with was the fact that Derrick had to piss like a racehorse. Only a few hundred yards from the security of the compound walls, there was simply no way he was going to make it. As close as they were, he knew the team would not stop.

The welfare of his bladder, or even the ongoing beat of his heart, was of little concern to the other three hunters. This he knew from past experience, and telepathy empathy. Because the fact was, he could give two shits and a kernel of corn about any of them either. He had no true friends among these ranks; the others were no more than a means to an end. A cartel united only by similar purpose and burden.

Adding to the anxiety of the moment, the woman in the cart, fragile as she'd been when they found her, had degraded further during the long return journey. They hadn't planned on traveling so far outside the city, but that was where the information had led.

Collecting the information of her whereabouts had proven difficult as well. It had taken them all morning just to extract the information from the skull that embraced it, a task that in the past usually took all of a minute. But the young man they tortured to get the info on the girl had been a tough nut to crack.

Derrick had been right there, an active participant in the forced extraction. In this day and age inflicting pain was as common as cell phone calls once were; as well as a minimum requirement of survival, at least for Derrick and others of his ilk. Where they lived, screams of one sort or another were routine, post modern ring tones in shrill and whimper and tears.

The cries uttered earlier today had not come easily, nor did the stored secrets. The young man had held his tongue like a champ; Derrick had been duly impressed by his resolve. Even cutting off his fingers and toes reaped no useful info. The teen was strong indeed, hypnotically indifferent to the pain it had seemed, his spirit fortified with morphine grit. Even a lanced eyeball had not the desired outcome. All of which had frustrated the hunters. Although Derrick had to admit, the sound and squirt the eye made as it popped was really cool, and alone worth the effort. The spritzing gore never failed to bring a smile to his face.

Only when they'd found his younger brother hiding in a trashcan did his attitude change, suddenly *oh so* cooperative. The mere threat of torture to his little brother got him talking. And following the promise that they'd let his brother go free, he even agreed to lead them to the hiding place of his girlfriend.

The same girl who lay bound and fetal in their cart at this very moment.

With the girl secured, the informant had been summarily executed. Derrick had done it himself. He actually felt he'd done the poor lad a favor, an act of mercy to spare him from further suffering. So Derrick had gone and smacked him in the back of the head with a wooden plank. He knew from experience that the soft hollow just below the occipital worked best, bringing death quick and painless. On top of that, the lethal blow allowed prompt emancipation of the soul, giving his spirit a head start in search of final destiny. Derrick had weighed this all out carefully, just before leaning back and T-balling the young man's head into the dark hereafter.

The allocation of torture was a two-way street, Derrick knew. And if the girl up and croaked before they got her home, the punishment turned on the team would be swift and severe; just another reason for them to beat a hasty return. Negative reinforcement had as much motivational thrust as positive. The one in charge had an ample arsenal of both carrots and sticks, and metered out each with equal indifference.

Stretch receptors were now screaming for relief. At the moment, a ruptured bladder sounded every bit as painful as any torture his mind could conjure. Leaving the safety of the herd had its risks. But if he didn't release the pressure soon, he felt like he was going to die anyhow from the toxic cocktail of a hemorrhaging bladder.

And so the decision was made. He'd *go* at the very next opportunity.

Besides, he thought, reassuring himself *it'll only take a minute.*

As if on cue a narrow alley appeared up ahead, pillared by an old warehouse and the ravaged remains of a convenient store, still always open 24 hours.

Oh thank heaven.

He could duck in there, keep an eye on the convoy while spying down the alley, use the walls on each side as protection. As powerful as the creature was, it was still only flesh and blood. As far as he knew, it possessed no gamma ray green afterglow of comic book lore, couldn't smash through brick walls.

So Derrick broke formation and jogged ahead, figuring by the time the group passed, he'd be done and slip right back into position. No harm, no foul.

"Where you goin'? He said no stops!" one of the other men barked, his voice deep timbre, vague of emotion. And the tiny hint of concern it did carry seemed more along the line of *his own* concerns. A man breaking ranks would leave one corner of their treasure unprotected.

"Don't worry about me," Derrick growled in standard *fuck off* tone.

The narrow alley was darker than the street, the moonlight squeezed to shadow by proximity of architecture. Before he even reached the corner he had his dick out, the neural okay issued, sending impulses to release the hounds. He stepped to the edge of the building, glanced down the alley. Best he could see, the coast was clear, his worry all for naught.

But as bad as he had to go, the hounds were not forthcoming. Anxious as he was the pressure of time and circumstance had his system momentarily frozen, locked up like a laptop on the fritz. *Shit*! Stage freight.

Come on, come on, he encouraged himself, trying to concentrate and focus on nothing. He glanced down the narrow alley again. All quiet, as still as a mausoleum, and aside from a few decaying dunes of trash, utterly empty. Even the stiff breeze was coerced to static. The dark silence gave off an eerie spell. Derrick shuddered, fear or a preemptive pee shiver, it was hard to tell. Probably both.

He glanced back at the street, the posse now right beside him, slowly edging beyond his position. The man who had questioned him looked over as they passed, shook his head with a scowl, then returned his gaze to the street, continued his surveillance.

Just as Derrick was about to let fly, he was startled by a heavy thud, the shock of the moment effectively severing the thin stream that had only just begun to trickle free. Even before he turned, he knew *exactly* what had landed next to him.

There were no 300 pound squirrels living in the area.

The creature had dropped from somewhere above, a window, an old fire escape—it hardly mattered. And Derrick hadn't the time or inclination to look up and check.

Derrick turned to face his destroyer. Aside from the added scabs and bubbling napalm sunburn, the abomination that stood facing him looked very much like he'd remembered—a seven-foot gargoyle; part man, part beast, part Brundle fly. At one time the creature had actually been a member of the same dysfunctional community. Only back then, he was a gentle giant, his retard strength rendered benign by kindness. But the present incarnation panting in front of him possessed an all new and utterly terrifying quality. *Rage.* The emotion twisted menacingly in his features.

The assault came quickly. Derrick didn't have time to aim the crossbow, or even lift his hand from his dick. The short scream that managed to escape served no purpose. It did nothing to deter the creature's violence, and even less to persuade the other hunters to turn and help. With the lightning twist of a gator death roll, the creature he once knew as Frederick snapped his neck like a number two pencil, and Derrick felt his every atom fill with the numbing amperage of forthcoming death.

As he fell to the ground, urine began to flow freely in final irony, no longer impeded by inhibition. In a last call of nature his bladder emptied the rest of its contents as he fell to the concrete sidewalk, his body mass rupturing the organ like a tossed water balloon, his own poison spilling into his guts.

His death came quickly. It would seem that Frederick too was philanthropic when it came to killing, sparing his victims the suffering of a drawn-out demise.

Before slipping back into the concrete catacombs of his turf, Frederick hefted the lifeless husk of Derrick Black over his massive shoulder. After all, it was only proper to eat what you kill.

Chapter 9

Sitting at the head table, Martin was yanked from his daydream as Dr. Sanders called Jesse to the podium. Hearing his friends name struck him like the incandescent jolt of an anemone sting. Martin knew this moment would eventually arrive, he'd been thinking about it all day. He knew very well how important getting a mission to the surface pushed through meant to Jesse, and although not entirely on board with the idea, he still felt for him—his nervousness arising from the keen empathy shared by only the closest of friends.

He shifted in his seat, glanced over at the other four board members beside him and waited for Jesse to make his way to the podium.

These days, Martin found himself conflicted by the idea of a journey topside. The argument for expansion and isolation both had merit and, in Martin's mind, it was about as close a call as you could have on an issue. But he had family to consider—Reni and Vanessa—an element that did not factor in when Jesse ran the equation.

From the moment his brother Clarence had been killed five years ago, he stepped in to help. Over time, obligation developed into bond and then ultimately feelings of an even deeper nature. Last year, he married Vanessa; they even had a small service. With the responsibility of a wife and step-son, everything changed, and he no longer felt the potential rewards of a mission outweighed the risks. He understood Jesse's position, but couldn't agree, at least not as things stood now. So in the final analysis, despite his friend's impassioned efforts—for the time being and for the greater good of the community, he felt it best to stay put. A notion he was careful to never share with Jesse.

During the first part of the meeting, Martin had tried to keep his mind preoccupied, lest his brain short circuit from worrying about his friend. Dredging up thoughts of another era was a tactic he'd often use to gain distance from the moment. Tonight, he allowed his gaze to drift through the sea of faces before him, as he found himself replaying the prelude of fate that had brought them here.

Here in Pacifica.

Pacifica was inspired by the green revolution and a progressive American culture that had blossomed in the new century. Two massive oil spills in the early 21st century provided the final kick in the ass, tangible rationale in devastated wetlands, lost revenue, and oil embalmed wildlife to significantly sway public opinion that it was time to explore other energy options with more than token vigor. The Pacifica project was a collaborative effort spearheaded by the US government, fortified by private industry, and designed by the greatest geeks and scientists around the world. A few of those inspirational minds were still alive, several sat out in the audience before him.

Pacifica was not a self-contained biosphere, nor was it designed to be. Power, water, oxygen and foods were endowed by external works. Aside from oceanic research the original mission of Pacifica included the development of algae based fuels, mariculture studies, prospecting for natural resource, as well as the chance to test human durability in such an environment. The latter had certainly been a raging success.

To help offset global warming, a program to grow carbon dioxide sequestering algae had also been part of the original plan. Above all else, alternative energy R & D was the core goal of Pacifica. The location lent itself as perfect test ground for such ambitions. Four prototypes had been built, all still fully operational. Solar, wind, geothermal and the OTEC; an experimental gadget installed by a Japanese firm to tap energy from the prevailing thermal gradients in the water-column. Sitting in the audience not far from Martin was one of the original OTEC engineers, Haruto Mishoki. Kudos to the nerdy inspirations from the Far East.

Pacifica was humankind's greatest aquatic undertaking, built when man was at his technical apex. As Martin sat waiting for his friend to speak, he couldn't help but wonder grimly if anyone could've imagined that this undersea Eden would someday provide one of the few places where mankind *was not* sleeping with the fishes.

Martin's attention was drawn by movement. In the back of the room his friend stood up and began walking toward the front of the room. Martin sighed, slouched in his seat and thought—*here we go.*

Chapter 10

If there were some kind of magic meter to measure anxiety, and it was strapped to Jesse at the moment, the needle would be pegged against the post, maybe even smithereened from the stress. As his moment to speak approached, he tried to meditate, quiet his mind and focus his thoughts, but it had very little effect.

As his name was called by Dr. Sanders, he felt his mind unravel and his composure go Kevorkian, injected with lethal panic. Then he remembered, looked at the paper in his hand. *Whew*…at least he'd been smart enough to write it all down. If worse came to worse, all he had to do was read. Thank god for safety nets.

The pressure he felt as he made his way to the podium was not of the stage freight variety. Not that Jesse was beyond irrational fears. The gnawing nightmares he had nearly every night were a testament to that. But the fear of speaking in public was trivial compared to the fear of being trapped in Pacifica any longer.

Despite his anxiety, he continued toward the podium, nothing short of a massive chest gripper would prevent him from seeing this thing through. If anyone could persuade the population that a trip back to land was warranted, it was him. And if it all went belly up again, struck down by the empty-headed opposition, so be it. One thing was for certain, it wasn't going to be from lack of effort.

Jesse stepped behind the podium, looked out at the faces before him. Most were soured with frowns; he could actually sense the negative vibe sucking at his confidence like a greedy tapeworm. But just as he thought his brain would go zit-spray, his mind snapped back, as he conjured the image that brought him peace.

The sun.

He centered the golden orb in his mind's eye, bright and warm. It was effective, calming, centering; was even better than envisioning the audience naked. The angry faces before him turned to insignificant blurs; he was now ready to go, hyper-clear.

A heartbeat later, he spoke.

"I am here tonight to ask everyone to vote for an expedition back to the surface for the following reasons." His words were quick, crisp, scientifically unbiased. "First off, it'd give us a chance to investigate the cause of our recent drinking water shortage. I've studied the system and I believe the problem is at the main water station. Chances are all we need to do is a quick remediation of the source well. It's a gravity feed system, and if cleared, it should flow freely once again." Now into it, Jesse felt great, no trace of his earlier anxiety. So absorbed, he didn't even look down at his notes.

"I'm also concerned with our safety here. Our very lives could be in danger. According to the seismograph I built, a disturbance that took place last week was the largest since we've been here. And as I see the data, the quakes have increased in frequency and magnitude. We all felt the tremor earlier today. Any damage to our oxygen/ CO_2 exchange system or to one of the power plants could cause serious harm. And should living here ever become a problem; we haven't even explored other habitats.

"Even though Pacifica hasn't shown signs of fatigue yet, we *should still* be seeking alternative habitats. If we ever have to leave in a hurry, it will be disastrous; we don't have enough transportation to evacuate in one trip. Just today, I learned that another sub went down with a broken drive shaft, and it's uncertain whether it can be repaired. A trip to land would give us a chance to search for submarines lost in the past. Even if no longer functional, they could be used for spare parts."

Jesse paused, took a breath. The last remark shook him a bit. His father had been lost on the last mission. He knew talking about the lost subs would remind him of his dad, but he also knew that he had to bring it up; it was a strong argument for making the journey. Nobody could deny that. He pushed the unbidden image of his father's corpse rotting in a sub from his mind and continued.

"Last time we had this debate we were told our mini-subs lacked the capability to reach the bay and back. That's true. At best, we could make the coastline and back. But I have recently come up with a new idea, a means to recharge the subs using a solar panel. We could keep the vehicles docked safely underwater in the calm of the bay, thus eliminating the hazard of a beach landing. I have sketched a blueprint.'" He held up a sheet of paper with the schematic he had drawn less than an hour ago. "I'll pass this around the room."

He glanced at his notes. "We are also running out of a lot of resources that we simply can't replace or manufacture. Clothing, fabric and shoes are all in short supply. We might also be able to find some medicines or raw materials to make them. We could look for back up rechargeable batteries, and we are almost out of light bulbs. I had to look high and low just to track down a sheet of paper to make my drawing."

Jesse shifted his weight, pondered; time to introduce a new notion, toss out a little old fashion scare tactic. "In my opinion, we've simply been living down here in isolation too long; it's just not natural. I believe it's creating a chronic low grade stress that most of us are not even aware of. How come no one has ever lived past sixty years old? How come there've been so many heart attacks and suicides over the years? It's because we are not designed to live in such a confined habitat.

"Wouldn't it be great to breathe unfiltered air, see the moon, or even hold a fistful of dirt? For all we know, the environment is back to normal. And since our UV meter was destroyed by storm, we have no way to know. And what about Cascadia? We've all heard the rumors of a safe zone being established in the caves of the mountains of Oregon. Shouldn't we at least investigate that?"

With the mention of earth, he felt his inner tide suddenly ebb. Visions of things he might never see flitted across his mindscape—*trees, moon, soil, sky*—but he quickly revived the image of the sun to boost his spirit. He still had one more point to make. It was a bit of a reach, but so be it. No point leaving any bullets in the chamber.

"I'd like to cite a theory known as the Gaia hypothesis. It says that the earth itself is a living organism, capable of self healing. Look around outside. The sea life has shown significant recovery as of late, especially some of the larger species. Earlier today, it was reported that there was a disturbance in one of the kelp fields. Based on the description, the only logical explanation is that it was made by a whale."

Jesse knew he was stretching it, vulcanizing the facts in the name of freedom. In this case, however, he felt it warranted—a Robin Hood rationalization for his wrongdoing.

"I've seen a dozen sharks myself in the past two weeks, one was a great white. If there are large predators around, then there have to be smaller animals to support them. To some degree the aquatic food chain is linked to the terrestrial systems, so if one has improved, it only makes sense that the other has. And improved ecosystems could only take place if atmospheric conditions have improved.

"It's time to pull our heads out of the sand. It's time to crawl out of our shell of isolationism. Exploring the surface is our inalienable responsibility; not only to ourselves but to our children and to the human race." He stared and panned the room. "Thank you, and please vote *yes* for the journey."

Jesse left the podium confident that he'd given his all, but not so confident that *his all* would be good enough: even with the addition of his new arguments. He felt he'd made some headway, but the crowd was hard to read. They seemed to be moved, but maybe they were just being polite. Maybe they simply felt sorry for him. He'd just have to wait and see. He returned to his seat in the back. He wanted to just cast his vote and leave, didn't really want to be there for what was coming next. But there was a Q and A afterward, and he was supposed to be there. So he'd sit and wait, do the right thing.

And very likely suffer acutely in the process.

Chapter 11

Daniel Winslow returned to the podium. "Thank you for your efforts, Jesse," he said, keeping it as neutral as his bias would allow. "I'd now like to introduce Mr. Horace Ewell to deliver the other side of this argument."

Ewell got up from behind the dais and moved toward the podium, nodding at Winslow as they passed. Ewell was a board member and, like Winslow, a hardcore isolationist. Wearing an expression that always seemed to reflect a holier-than-thou attitude, Ewell had a face that Jesse flat out despised. A former scientist for the government, Ewell had made it down to Pacifica as party to the same rescue mission that brought Michelle. With the good came the bad. As much as Jesse disliked him, he was an effective adversary.

Jesse slouched in his seat, braced for the bullshit.

"Hello and good evening." Ewell smiled, nodded to the audience. In a church like chorus, many returned his greeting. "I don't even know where to begin…" He shook his head, rolled his eyes—tactics of the consummate politician. "Before I present my case, I'd just like to remind everyone what happened *the last* time we sent a group to the surface." He paused, shuffled his notes. Details were not required. Everyone knew the story. The last crew had never returned or been heard from again. It was generally assumed that they were all dead.

Ewell found Jesse's eyes and stared. *What a fucking scumbag*, Jesse simmered, the gesture was targeted. Jesse's father had been part of that crew, and Ewell knew it. He wanted to take the mic and cram it down his throat. That might teach the prick to be a little more careful where he tread. Ewell was the same person who'd argued against a rescue mission for his father and the missing crew two years ago. The fact that no search party had ever been approved only added to Jesse's resentment toward him, and nearly everybody else in the room.

"Irrespective of that tragedy," Ewell finally continued, "and the many misfortunes before that, there is still no reason to risk a trip to the surface at this time. We are perfectly safe, and have everything we need, right here." He pointed emphatically to the ground. "Mr. Baines has done an excellent job presenting his point of view on this matter." Ewell found Jesse's eyes once again. "But now I will correct his subjective and misleading remarks."

This guy could go straight to hell, Jesse fumed. He wanted to go totally Tourettes, scream out at the son-of-a-bitch like a madman. But he repressed his urge and bit his tongue, turning his anger inward to ferment in his organs, as he usually did.

"I've checked with our hydrologist, Mr. Marrison, about our recent water shortage and he assures me that the drop in water pressure is most likely due to abatement at the source aquifer. Only by drilling a new well could it be fixed. And of course we don't have the means for that kind of undertaking."

Jesse squirmed, his emotions doing cartwheels. That was blatant misinformation. Marrison may be a hydrologist, but Jesse had researched the problem thoroughly, and he knew he was right—the well could be fixed. Marrison was an isolationist piss-ant, as ignorant as he was weak. He couldn't believe how easily people would sell out principle for their political views. Some things, it would seem, never changed.

"We have to realize that we are simply living a different lifestyle down here, and have to make the necessary adjustments. Increased desalination projects may be one of them. With effort, it could be accomplished.

"As for the assertion that we could be in danger from an earthquake…" He shook his head, eyes closing. "Let me assure you that that is no more than an unfair scare tactic." He added a skeptical smirk. "It's complete *seismic fiction.*" Several people in the crowd laughed. "All inspections, including the one earlier today, have turned up no significant damage. Everyone knows that this site had been selected with great care; there are no major fault lines within miles. On top of that, the superstructure is reinforced and the hull double walled. The foundation was built with a shock absorbing system designed to withstand storms and seismic disturbances far greater than anything we have experienced."

The statements were all fact.

"Any good scientist knows that you cannot evaluate seismic data over such a short period of time. What we are likely seeing is a random blip in the earth's natural cycles. It'll all average out. We'll probably go years without another seismic event. So please disregard the self serving statements you heard on this earlier."

Jesse felt his face flush, felt like everyone was thinking about him right now, and they were thinking—*what a fool.* He wished it would be over all ready; he wanted out of there. *Where's an alien abduction tractor beam when you need one.*

Ewell shifted behind the podium. "The reason we've been seeing more sharks lately is simple. It's because they've learned to adapt. With their main food sources gone, particularly seals, they've turned to hunting fish, squid, and even us. If anything, their behavior is an indicator that things have *not* improved. Seals, dolphin and killer whales would be true indicator species. But as you all know, none have been seen for years.

"As for the notion that there was a whale in the area?" Ewell rolled his eyes again.

"I too heard about the disturbance in the kelp field today. But unlike my friend here," Ewell jerked a thumb in the direction of Jesse, "I went down to communications to check things out. There was nothing unusual, either on sonar or hydrophone, just a standard point-source disturbance at the time of the quake, nothing that would indicate the presence of a large mammal in the area. If there are any questions about this *whale tale,* feel free to check with Mr. Yarnik." Ewell nodded at a man sitting off to the right, three rows deep. The communications officer nodded back. Jesse shifted and sighed, Ewell had done his homework—this was going worse than expected.

"Mr. Baines mentioned the Gaia hypothesis, a theory that alleges that the earth can heal. There may be some validity to this, especially in this case. It's a known fact that ozone is generated in the upper atmosphere by lightning. The only problem is that the earth has suffered an environmental holocaust like never before. And for all we know, the processes we once knew may no longer be in effect."

Jesse laughed to himself, *looks like he wasn't the only one stretching the science.*

"The fact that we don't have a radiation detector is irrelevant. We don't need one. We only need look to

Mother Nature. The kelp growing in the farm would reach the surface if atmospheric conditions have improved. But to date, the kelp fronds terminate several feet below the water's surface, where it's safe from penetrating radiation."

Pausing again, Ewell vented a synthetic sigh, then proceeded with the drubbing.

"Regardless of anything else said here tonight, it is simply too dangerous to risk a trip back up. Every time we've sent people back in the past, the reports have been negative, and those are just the ones who've *made* it back. God help those who haven't. Moreover, given the years of looting, there's not likely to be any valuable resources left.

"And who knows what kind of wild animals or savages are still up there. We've all heard the stories." He patted his chest, nodded at the crowd. Many nodded back, their heads bobbing like partisans at a political rally. "Some of us saw the carnage first hand. It was horrible. I lost every-thing. I remember hiding in the shadows, struggling to survive. And I wasn't even there for the worst of it. Thank god I managed to make it down here." He pumped a fist, his earlier cavalier tone usurped by authentic concern.

"And what if someone was to get caught by those sav-ages up there? What if they found out about our sanctu-ary? Who knows what could happen? And even if we do find good people up there, what can we do? As Jesse sug-gested, our resources are in short supply, not to mention living space. The bottom line is, we are in no position to help anyone right now. Our responsibility is only to our-selves and our children."

Ewell was on a roll, freight training Jesse's arguments, and it appeared that the vast majority were *all aboard* the status quo express. Jesse began shrinking fetal in his seat; he could feel the sun setting very rapidly on any hope of victory.

"The earth's surface is an alien planet now. And as for the rumors of Cascadia? Hogwash. Taking a two week trek just to search for some mythical promised land is as asinine as it is impossible. Given the challenges of said journey we may as well be discussing a trip to Venus. Aside from the distance, who knows what dangers have spawned over the years—mutant animals, toxic weather, lethal new disease—not to mention the well documented cannibals, dysentery, plague, and searing radiation!" The crowd gasped, many nodding in cult-like cadence. "No thanks, not for me. I'd rather suffer a little of the supposed *chronic stress* here than be infected with some new mutant virus, just for the sake of an idea that is clearly only supported by a minority here.

"We have something precious here." He spread his arms, preacher style. "It should not be taken for granted. We must face the facts; this is where we are going to be for a very long time, perhaps the rest of our lives. Going back to the surface is dangerous, foolhardy and completely unnecessary." Ewell glowered as he panned the crowd. "Thank you, and please vote *no* on the proposed expedition."

Ewell departed to spirited applause, the faithful were pleased.

Jesse slouched in his seat, rubbed his eyes with the heels of his hands as if he could somehow massage away the pain. He sighed, then slowly straightened. He'd do the right thing, stick around and participate in the Q and A before casting his vote, as academic as he knew it would be. Besides, he didn't want to give anything away, didn't want anyone to become suspicious of his intentions. Community approval or not, he had a promise to keep to himself.

He'd wait till it was official, just to be sure. Then it'd be time to put things in motion. It was time to start planning.

Chapter 12

Deep within the sanctum of a massive warehouse the door to a curious ward suddenly swung open. A shadowed gang entered and lurched noisily through the darkened ward, their movements awkward and strained. A row of heavy-duty hospital beds lined each side of the room; a female body lay still in most. The commotion was loud enough to awaken one of the sedated females, jolting Denise Diaz to low level consciousness—no small task given the steady stream of benzodiazepines dripping into her system via I-V. As loud as the disturbance was, none of the other women stirred from the grip of drug-induced coma.

Lying in bed Denise managed to turn her head toward the advancing commotion; and immediately her heart sank. The young girl being ushered along was maybe fifteen and alarmingly small, she looked like a rag doll when weighed against the hulking men handling her. She'd probably just been captured in the city somewhere. Denise felt bad. She knew all too well the nightmare this girl was in for.

The abduction was only the beginning.

Even in the muted light Denise could see that the girl was weak and dehydrated, as fragile as a stick of cinnamon. Her exhaustion did not deter her struggle. The poor girl was so drained she looked like she could drop dead any second. The day would probably come where she'd wish that she had; a conclusion Denise drew from experience, the notion coming to her not long after her own abduction.

But Denise knew that everything would be done to keep her alive. Her second X chromosome was like a mark on a treasure map, her family jewels the mother lode in present day gold. Any minute the one who Denise truly hated would show up, eager and motivated by the arrival of his newest prize. He'd see to her care, provide the treatment needed to restore her to a state serviceable for *his needs.* Denise only hoped that by the time he arrived she'd somehow be elsewhere, dragged back under by meds or exhaustion. Even an embolism or massive stroke would do; either fate would be far less disturbing than having to see *that face* again.

The powerful men wrestled the girl down on the bed next to Denise, then strapped her in place with thick leather restraints. She fought them all the way, her spirited resistance more than laudable. Soon, even her futile rebellion would be brought to an end, halted by the pharmaceutical venom pumped into her veins, the same chemicals that Denise wished would hurry up and take hold of her own body once again. The void of sedation was far better than dealing with the memories harbored in awareness.

The door to the ward suddenly swung open again. A dark figure stood amid the open threshold, backlit by the glowing operations of the large room behind. Denise recognized the dark shape that stepped into the ward. *Shit*, she cursed under her breath. Her escape to coma had not come soon enough.

He was already here.

The dark figure found his way to the young girl just brought in. Standing by her bedside his face came into view, the jaundice glow of life support monitors distorting his features with ghoulish shadows. The face brought Denise instant pain. She felt a sudden dry heave in her psyche, the image of him searing her emotions like a cattle prod on raw nerves. And just as Denise suspected, with his arrival came the dreaded discharge of memories she fought so valiantly to keep interred. Her mind then replayed the account, skipping no detail, the agonizing images coming alive in the disturbing high-def of fresh memory, the vile associated emotions bleeding freely like a freshly picked scab.

The rape had occurred some eight months ago, a violation so horrific that Denise knew the scars would never heal. The damage had left a pockmark on her psyche that could only be erased by the grave. Because this crime went beyond the taking of flesh for pleasure, the assault an even deeper sin, one that invaded the most intimate parts of her womanhood and will. The nightmare of that day not only lived on in her mind, but in her body as well. The occasional kick or shudder in her gut, a stomach-turning reminder that something from that day was still inside her.

Denise felt her mind fill with dread, her eyes blur with tears. As hard as she tried she *could not* stop the parade of recollection. The memory of being probed and penetrated by cold phallic instruments flashed in her mind, a tiny ripe fruit then torn free from her abdomen, aspirated and sucked away by a long stainless steel straw, taking from her the one thing he could not manufacture or conjure in a test tube. Denise remembered how she pleaded and struggled against the restraint of drugs and cinched leather straps. But it was utterly impossible to stop him, like trying to stop a tsunami with a cocktail umbrella.

Hours later, the second stage of rape had taken place. This time the tool no more than a glorified turkey baster, the synthetic penis jammed unceremoniously inside her. The device squirting a warm recombinant goo into her uterine cavity. Returning her scraped seed, intertwined, she assumed, with the dank jizz of god only knew.

Denise had never been given any details of the procedure. But her natural maternal instincts told her everything she needed to know. The thing growing inside her *was not* normal, and whatever it was, it was *all wrong*. It had somehow been doctored and distorted, molded like DNA Play-Doh, reshaped for purposes unknown.

She felt a sudden shudder in her abdomen and felt her emotions ebb further. *It was moving again.* The alien germ was almost full term. The notion dredged up another round of volcanic anxiety, sent cinders of molten agony burning in her brain. The tears in her eyes intensified. She felt not a whit of motherly connection to the thing festering in her womb. To her it was a parasite, an infection, possessing the overall appeal of a malignant tumor. She wanted nothing to do with it, where's a coat hanger when you need one? But unfortunately for Denise, what she wanted didn't matter. Her choice had never been considered.

The welling tears began to blur her vision, the face that she hated turned to a fun house mirror reflection. Through her tears she could see him and his men turn and leave the ward, their quarry now stable, the body now well on its way to becoming another incubator, fertile soil for seed, another cog in the assembly line of creation that encircled the ward.

Denise noticed that one of the men had forgotten a pocket-knife on the counter. Not a thing in the world she wouldn't give if she could somehow reach it. And if she could've, she'd slit her wrists without contemplation. But the thought was no more than a cruel tease; the knife was simply miles beyond her reach.

Her vision began to wane further, this time the apparent call of narcotic. *Finally*, Denise breathed as she felt her mind start to disappear. She found herself distantly hoping that it was the terminal blur of a blood clot. Before blackness arrived fully she begged God for that to be the case.

Denise then drifted off, her prayer unanswered.

Chapter 13

Jesse's dreams were a mixed blessing in the truest sense. On the one hand, they provided splendid escape and a dearly needed emotional analgesic. But on the other hand, they were often disturbing, sometimes metastasizing into nightmares, all without warning or means to escape.

Only a few hundred eye movements ago he sat on a patchwork blanket with a beautiful dream girl taking in the majestic landscape, while watching the children playing in the valley below. They flirted in meaningless dream words beneath a perfect blue sky with a ripe golden sun. Ahhh...what a beautiful dream indeed.

But when the children suddenly started melting like wax figures in a microwave, the beauty was all but gone. The blissful backdrop was also altered, now like a Dali painting, distorted and oozing. The heat he felt, although only a figment, was as real as if he sat in a furnace duct. He tried to yell, tell the children to hide in the shade, but his voice had been suppressed, as was his attempt to run down the hill and warn them; bound and gagged by the universal dream forces of quicksand and lockjaw. The girl of his dreams lay beside him, now reduced to a twitching mound of maggot soup. Jesse let out a scream. It echoed loudly in his brain, but not a sound escaped the walls of his skull.

A voice suddenly shouted his name. He realized the voice came from the quivering remains of the dream girl he'd been about to have his way with just a few moments before. As he turned his terror shot straight to DEFCON 1. A new face was now furrowed in the meat puddle, no longer even female. Her image was replaced by another visage, a person that had recurred in his dreams before. It was no surprise that he showed up tonight, what with Reni asking all those questions about him yesterday.

The voice came again, even louder. "Yo, Jesse."

This time he recognized the voice. It was Alberto Cruz. He opened his eyes. "Yeah, yeah...I'm awake," he reported, still groggy, his heart a fibrillating fist of tissue.

The intercom next to his bed coughed again. "Alright, just wanted to make sure you didn't oversleep. We're on fishing detail today."

"I know, I know. I'll be there in a few. Thanks A-C."

Jesse lay in bed, cocooned in a sweaty sheet, and thought about the dream. Although his dreams were bizarre, they were rarely cryptic. This one had been no exception. It was the inner echo of his unsettled unconscious, a Freudian tug-o-war between superego and desires.

Most mornings, at least in recent days, he'd wake up sluggish and stiff, about as motivated as a Galapagos iguana on a cold morning. But today was different. It only took a second and he was up and about, getting dressed, his mind retooled and moving onto other things.

Far more important things.

Because tonight was the night, by this time tomorrow he'd be on his way home. He was pumped. The fact that he was scheduled to work outside today was perfect.

It would give him chance to have a final look around, be sure everything was in place. He had to be sure that he played it cool, do nothing to show his hand. He mustn't appear too elated or seem too depressed. Either one might raise suspicion, especially around Martin. His friend was no fool, and as intuitive as hell. Steering clear of him would be the safest bet. That shouldn't be a problem. Fortunately, the schedule had them on opposite ends of the compound for most of the day.

The decision was final; he'd make his move later that night, sometime after midnight. Most everyone should be asleep by then. He was psyched beyond measure, thrill and anxiety swirling in his soul, the growing anticipation tantamount to a space launch for a NASA astronaut.

Less than twenty-four hours and he'd be free. And then finally...finally his dream would be realized.

Chapter 14

At the moment school work was not the most appealing task, but Reni promised Andrea he'd help her with her lesson. And if nothing else, Reni was a boy of his word. Besides, he kind of had a crush on her.

Side by side, they sat on the couch in his quarters watching a biology program on the flat screen. But Reni found it hard to stay focused, his mind clouded with worried thoughts of his friend Jesse. As upset as he was at Jesse for blowing him off yesterday, he'd already forgiven him. After the meeting last night he could see that he was shaken. And what made matters worse, there was nothing he could do to help. You had to be sixteen to vote. Not that his one vote would've made any difference. His dad had said that the mission was rejected by a landslide.

"Are you paying attention?" Andrea scolded.

Reni jumped, realized that his eyes had closed. "Yeah, I'm watching. Go ahead, ask me anything."

Andrea shook her head and smirked. "Yeah right, just try and stay awake for the rest please." She drew out the word *please* for emphasis.

Reni sat up straight and focused on the TV. No chance of drifting now anyhow, he'd watched this program many times before, the best parts were coming up.

The narrator spoke. *"Evolution is the theory that organisms change over time in response to the environment. The case of the peppered moth is a good example."*

Cartoon moths filled the flat screen: some white, some black.

"As you will see, the population of moths actually changed from mostly white, to mostly black. This occurred over a period of years in Manchester, England." The diagram shifted as the narrator spoke, first displaying a majority of white cartoon moths, then changing to show a majority of black moths.

"I love this part coming up," Reni said and gave Andrea a nudge. He shifted position, his anticipation in hyper-drive.

"Before 1850, most of the local Birch trees had light colored bark. This provided natural camouflage from predators for the light colored moths. The darker moths would stand out against the white tree bark, however, and would be eaten in greater numbers."

The cartoon was replaced by actual footage. Squads of birds circled the sky, then swooped in procession like fighter planes attacking a battleship. Landing on branches, they quickly speared and gobbled moths. And because they stood out against the white tree bark, they ate mostly darker moths. Many times a light colored moth sat unseen right beside a darker moth as it was speared. The birds had an indelible avian smile that could be seen in their beaks as they chowed down. Reni found the embossed grin eerie.

Andrea typed notes on her computer as the scene changed again. A panoramic view of England now stretched across the screen. The footage was poor quality, filmed in black and white and pre-digital flecks. In the foreground, crowds of people walked along the streets.

Smoke billowed from the buildings in the background, filling the sky with thick smog; air pollution standing proud and tall in its historic heyday. Reni almost coughed out of reflex.

"After years of industrialization the tree bark changed from near white to almost black from the accumulation of soot. Now when the birds went hunting, the lighter colored moths would stand out and therefore be eaten more often. Over the years, this allowed the darker moths to increase in numbers. The light color varieties became almost nonexistent."

The scene changed again, and the birds returned in force, the monitor filling with an all out avian assault. Now it was the white moths that were eaten, the insects standing out dramatically against the blackened tree bark. Reni leaned forward as he watched. There was something about seeing an animal eating another while it was still alive he found riveting. He looked over at Andrea. She continued typing away. The drama seemed to have no such effect on her.

The narrator, a tall man with sandy hair and freckles, appeared on the screen. *"This is an example of natural selection. It is most often referred to as industrial melanism, sometime considered evolution in action. The changing environment is the driving force in the population change."*

Reni listened but the words didn't really register; his mind too busy replaying visions of soaring birds and clumsy moths. His reverie was cut short as Andrea started reading the follow-up questions that scrolled on the screen.

He gave her answers as she hammered away on her computer. Her hands were nimble and quick as they swept across the keyboard. She may not be the best at science, but she sure could type. Reni noted how soft her hands looked. It wasn't the first time he wondered what it would be like to hold her hand. But he never dared to try. Aside from being older, thirteen, an actual teenager; what if she didn't like it? Then he'd really be embarrassed. Better off just continuing to help out with her schoolwork. If he did a good job, she'd always come back for more help. And maybe someday he'd get up the nerve to tell her how he truly felt.

A sharp noise suddenly shot through the room. Andrea jumped as if she'd seen a spider, causing Reni to recoil. She leaned into him, stifled a scream. Her keypad fell onto the floor with a thud. His thoughts skittered, his heart thundered.

The sound continued to fill the room, a rhythmic metallic tapping that came from outside. Andrea was about to speak but Reni put a finger to his lips. "Shush… its Morse code." Jesse had taught him the cipher, and he knew exactly what the simple message said.

"Come on!" Reni said, leaping from the couch.

"What?" Andrea's eyebrows arched; her expression lush with curiosity.

"Come over and see for yourself." He grabbed her hand again and led her over to the clear viewing partition. She held his hand tightly. He liked the way it felt, warm, soft, exciting. They looked outside, the vast ocean opened up heavenly before them as they pressed against the cool acrylic. A dark figured in full wet suit hovered just outside the window. Reni waved and the figure waved back. It was Jesse, and Reni could see he was smiling behind his facemask. *Awesome.* Reni was glad to see him, and glad to see his spirits had improved.

In one hand Jesse held a large fish. Blood leaked from its flank, an oily ribbon pulsing free with each twitch of struggle. *Cool! Another animal about to be eaten alive,* Reni marveled. *Awesome!*

"What's going on?" Andrea asked tautly, squeezing his hand harder.

"Just watch, it's really cool. Promise," Reni assured her.

Jesse released the fish and it drifted down, undulating aimlessly. They both watched with bated breath, eyes wide with wonder. A green bolt of lightning shot from the rocks, conquering the few feet of seawater in the blink of an eye. Andrea jumped and this time she let out a yelp. Reni thought she was going to squeeze his hand right off.

With the fish firm in its maw, the large green moray eel slowly recoiled back into its rocky lair. Drifting back, the eel scissored the fish in two, then gulped each chunk with the haste of a creature fearing it might have to share. Spike looked like he'd just swallowed a protein barbell.

The eel eventually returned fully to its den, only its head visible between the rocks, a gasping green triangle with row upon row of tiny ivory incisors. Reni waved, mouthing *thank you* to Jesse.

Jesse waved back, and then slowly began drifting off.

Reni looked down; Andrea was still holding his hand. He liked how it felt. It made him feel connected. It was a sensation he'd never felt before. He also liked the way their hands looked entwined, the color contrast was neat, like the keyboard to a piano. He glanced at her as she stared out into the ocean; she wore a smile of enchantment. She was very pretty, he thought, the light pushing in from the window made her pale complexion positively glow. She looked every bit like an angel.

Suddenly the room began to vibrate, then shake. Reni watched as her smile turned to shock. She grabbed him to brace herself. He held her and leaned a shoulder against the wall. Panic bloomed on her face, the room dancing like an unbalanced washing machine. But he was there, he'd keep her safe. Reni looked out the window, his vision shivering. The eel had vanished into its cave. A meandering throng of tangs scattered and hid. Jesse swayed like a stalk of seaweed in strong currents.

Chapter 15

It was late-morning when Martin felt the quake. He'd just started making his descent through the water column back to Pacifica when it struck. Aside from getting sloshed around a bit, the quake posed him no direct threat. He just had to be sure none of his dive gear was jostled free. Take away the potential implications to Pacifica; riding the mini-tsunami was actually kind of fun.

He grabbed hold of the support stanchion he was hovering next to as the water returned to calm. "Everybody okay? Over." Martin said into the microphone in his facemask, checking on the rest of the dive team as he surveyed his own gear.

Three responses came back in rapid succession. "Okay here, over." "Fine, over." "All's well, wish I'd brought my surfboard though, over."

"Good. Continue descent." Martin said, adjusting his mask. He then glanced at his gauges. "I'm gonna take a little detour. I wanna check out the OTEC. Thought I saw something funny over by the condenser unit. Over."

"Want one of us to come along?" a voice asked in his earpiece.

"No need. Continue your inspection; finish checking the columns all the way down to the sea floor. I won't be out of visual, and I'll only be a minute."

His earpiece crackled again, a female voice, another member of the dive team. "What did you see over there? Over."

"Not sure. Thought I saw a flash of light." Martin replied. "Probably nothing; most likely just the lights from below reflecting off my mask, over."

"Just be safe and don't dally. Remember, fishing today, over," the same diver said.

"No problem. I'll be right behind you guys. Over and out."

The OTEC was about fifty fathoms to the east, below was the sprawling campus of Pacifica. Martin looked down upon the campus as he pushed off and swam over top, heading toward the OTEC.

From this height in the water column the view of the facility was no less than stunning. Several massive domes all connected by a vast network of tubular tunnels, encrusted here and there by the colorful aquatic life forms that encroached and made it their home. It was truly a spectacular symbiosis of synthetic and nature, the perfect living example of Frank Lloyd Wright's organic architectural philosophy. The ambient lighting colored the tableau in plush shades of turquoise, an effect that gave the campus a quality both ethereal and sublime. The man-made environ was as impressive a structure as the Pentagon or even the great pyramids. The fact that it was built on the bottom of the ocean made the technical achievement that much more amazing.

Swimming toward the OTEC, Martin checked his gauges again. Getting low, he noted, but he should have plenty of time to do what he wanted to do. It had already been a long day. He and a small dive team had been up and in the water before dawn to swim to the surface. It took them two hours to make the journey topside, swimming in the dark, pausing every so often for decompression stops. Once up top, they inspected and cleaned the ALEN platform by dawn's early light; impinging salt deposits crystallizing on gears and joints the main concern. ALEN was a nickname someone had dubbed the rig years back, an abbreviation for alternative energy.

The ALEN was massive. Four ventilated columns rose from the seafloor like an oil rig. A huge square platform sat atop the columns above the water surface. In profile, it looked like a humungous backless bar stool, big enough for King Kong to pop a squat on. The platform was nearly a hundred thousand square feet and dressed from edge to edge with solar panels. Fastened to the frame beneath the panels were hundreds of wind turbines. They collected the winds that surfed across the ocean glaze while solar panels seized upon the sunshine above, all computer controlled to maximize energy production. A truly smart design, turbines swiveled to harvest the wind and solar panels tilted to pursue the sun.

The ALEN was the main power-plant for Pacifica, and the pride and joy of the entire operation. It generated nearly four times as much energy as the OTEC and geothermal systems combined. The four alternative energy sources worked in concert, providing Pacifica with its power needs, all of which was accomplished with the carbon footprint of a frugal fiddler crab.

Martin swam at a steady pace as he approached the condenser. From fifty feet away it was an imposing sight, a hulking gray barrel that emerged from the dark benthos. He looked back at the ALEN to see how far the others had advanced. Inspecting the support stanchions was an extremely important task. Not only was it critical that the supports were structurally sound, electrical conduit and ventilation pipes also needed to be eyed. They allowed communication with the platform and, most importantly, allowed fresh air to be conducted down and foul air to be set free.

Resting on the seafloor beneath the ALEN sat an experimental mechanical gill. No matter how many times Martin viewed the contraption; it always struck him as odd. A half dozen breathing bellows sprayed seawater into a pair of slowly rotating Ferris wheels. It looked every bit like a Wile E. Coyote contrivance, something concocted on a cartoon chalk board and slapped together with assorted Acme parts. In an attempt to mimic a fish gill the unit was to pull oxygen directly from seawater; but like the Coyote's many schemes, it wasn't very successful. And despite the attempts to improve the unit over the years, even to this day it hardly gathered enough O-2 to fill a single pair of human lungs. The failure of the gill had left them with no O-2 back-up, thus making the inspections of the ALEN conduit even that much more important.

Approaching the OTEC reactor, Martin felt great, wasn't tired or even breathing hard. He'd already been working for six hours, which was a considerable undertaking when you factor in the onus of an ocean on your back. He was in outstanding physical condition, but he knew it was more than just that.

Like everyone else, he only got topside a few times a year. ALEN duty was divided among the population to mete out fresh air and sunshine equitably. He knew how important it was for his physical wellbeing, but often wondered if maybe the benefit to his psyche wasn't even greater.

While up top they'd remove gear and sit in the early morning sun for a spell. Martin cherished those few moments, and he always hated having to return to the

ocean so soon. But as the sun moved higher, so did the
danger. And unless he wanted to fry like a bug under a
mischievous child's magnifying glass, there was simply no
choice.

Martin shivered. With the arrival of autumn, he
noticed the ocean had begun to embrace its characteris-
tics. He quickly cross-referenced the chill against the dry
radiant heat he'd felt on his skin only an hour ago. As he
reflected, his thoughts turned to Jesse. Last night, he had
vanished right after the meeting. Martin really wished he
could've gotten chance to talk with him; he knew Jesse
had to be utterly distraught, his dream of a ticket elsewhere rebuffed once again. Martin wished there was
something he could've done, but as much out of duty to
family as community, his hands were tied.

He'd make sure to track Jesse down after work; sit him
down and force him to talk about it, play armchair shrink
once again. After all, isn't that what friends are for?

Martin arrived at the top of the OTEC condenser. As
soon as he descended onto the roof he saw it. His pupils
dilated with stun, his breath momentarily halted. He
floated closer to the unit to get a better look, then ran his
hand along the surface. He continued to swim across the
breadth of the hull. Toward the eastern edge he found
more, it was even a little worse there. It looked like it went
down the side.

Oh shit! Martin breathed, frowning behind his dive
mask.

He couldn't believe what he'd discovered.

Chapter 16

All things considered, it had been a good day, Jesse thought. To this point everything had gone just swimmingly. His work assignment was on schedule, his plan to escape firmly in place. He even got to stop by and see Reni for a spell, which was something he'd been meaning to do. Even the minor quake, although taking him off guard, had not soured his mood.

Along with several other divers, he'd just finished setting up the fishing nets. Everything was locked and loaded. Although Jesse had his share of differences with many at Pacifica; when it came time to get things done, they were always on the same page. A real *hive* mentality existed when it came to day to day chores; necessity being the driving force of such a unique symbiosis of human endeavor.

With the fishing net hoisted, Jesse watched as the prevailing current slowly pushed through, flexing it like the mainsail of an old ship. In a few minutes the bait would be released and the chum slick would stream through the net, luring fish by the bunch. Squid were sometime caught, occasionally a shark, and one time even a dolphin. But that had been many years ago.

They had tried to save the dolphin, but failed. Exhausted from struggle and unable to breathe, it had drowned before it was untangled. The mammal had several large ulcers on its dorsal; it probably wouldn't have lived much longer anyway. Getting trapped in the net simply hastened the inevitable, maybe even spared it a measure of suffering. At least that'd been the rationale spun at the time to help ease the guilt many felt for euthanizing one of nature's truly amazing creatures. They hadn't seen a single dolphin since—all apparently following the dodo and the dinosaur down the cold and somber rat hole of extinction.

After making a final survey of the grounds, Jesse raised both arms to give the signal to release the bait. At the other end of the sandy underwater prairie, a lone worker acknowledged his cue with a wave, then pulled a tether rope. The chum slick wafted out of the drum it was sealed in, allowing the fish guts and blood to mix with the sea water. The bait slick formed a huge opaque mass that spread like a three-dimensional oil spill as it headed toward the nets. The lone worker quickly got behind an underwater scooter and torpedoed back toward the dive chamber. Jesse looked around and watched as the last of the workers began beating their flippers toward the dive chamber.

With the release of the chum slick the arrival of sharks was inevitable. They were a nuisance at times, and due to the demise of their primary food sources, they'd go after divers on occasion. Divers wore shark PODs to help discourage attack. As effective as they were, nothing beat the common sense approach. Rule number one in the *Idiot's Guide* to shark attack—*stay away when there's blood in the water!*

Fortunately, the sharks were fairly predictable. With precaution, their predatory prowess could be greatly diminished. Setting the net up was like ringing the dinner bell. Many believed that the local sharks were actually conditioned at this point. In which case, the blood filled water was probably inciting a frenzy of salivation; the cartilaginous K-9's soon to arrive in Pavlovian droves.

Jesse turned and began to swim toward the safety of the dive chamber. As the last of the divers swam in, one by one, he helped them up the ladder that led to the wet deck. Jesse glanced back at the sushi cloud that stained a huge parcel of the Pacific. Several fish were already criss-crossing the dark cloud, picking off piscine vittles. Two small sharks joined the fray, circling excitedly around the drifting food web. He turned and scrambled up the ladder. To be outside now would be suicide.

Alberto Cruz reached down and grabbed Jesse's arm, helping him onto the wet deck. Jesse removed his mask, wiped his eyes. "Thanks A-C."

"No problem, my friend," Cruz smiled and slapped him on the back. "It's just good to have you back."

Jesse looked at him quizzically, but then he realized, *guess people had in fact taken notice of the unusual behavior lately*. He knew he'd been out of it, didn't realize it was that obvious. The point was further driven home as he looked around the dive chamber. Several others smiled and nodded their agreement.

"It's good to be back," he said, flashing a smile of his own, uncertain what else to say.

"Maybe we'll see you in the gym tonight," Cruz said as a question. "Could really use you; been taking a beating lately. Your friend Martin's gettin' old. Got dunked on last night; totally embarrassing." He shook his head in mock disappointment.

Jesse chortled, grinned. Several others laughed; the sound echoing through the cavernous dive chamber. But Jesse's smile quickly faded.

"Where's Martin?" he asked.

Everybody looked around and at each other, the laughter evaporating.

"He said he'd be right behind us," one of the divers from the ALEN detail replied nervously. "He took a quick detour over to the OTEC, said he wanted to have a look at the condenser. He said he'd only be a minute."

Jesse immediately began removing his spent air tanks. "Any chance he went inside already?" he asked as he slung down his gear.

Cruz stepped over to the decompression chamber and looked through the portal. "He's not in here," he reported. The concern in the room instantly skyrocketed, the growing tension as palpable as the damp, stale air. The thought of chastising the ALEN team for not being more careful crossed Jesse's mind, but it was fleeting. There'd be time to go over procedure later.

Jesses movements were superhuman as he hoisted new tanks and began fixing straps. Cruz and another diver instinctively began to assist him. The room instantly transformed, shifting into crisis mode. Everyone scrambled to help, the dive chamber taking on the urgent aura of a trauma ward.

Cruz moved to the fresh supplies and, with the help of another diver, began wrestling on fresh tanks. "I'm going with you, just gimme a second," he urged.

"No time," Jesse said as he grabbed a spear gun off the rack near the dive hole. He then pulled the mask down over his face and took a trial breath. Without even checking his gauges he leaned back and fell into the water. The uproar of concerned remarks was silenced by the cold splash of liquid blue walls.

"*Are you fucking crazy!*" The last drowned howl to reach his ears before the Pacific swallowed him entirely.

Chapter 17

Martin traced the crack along the top of the OTEC. The damage looked like a giant tribal tattoo, the fracture dark ink against the grey sunlit skin of the condenser. He then swam over the eastern edge of the unit, following the fracture downward. Once on the back side, the water column took on a darker cast, as the ambient glow from Pacifica was eclipsed by the massive condenser. Martin trembled out of reflex, and a wave of nervousness snaked beneath his wetsuit as he lost visual contact with the facility. It was an unsettling instant, like watching as the last sliver of land disappears from the horizon on an ancient oceanic voyage.

The crack on the OTEC hull grew wider as he drifted deeper, then abruptly spider-webbed in every direction, the pattern like that produced by a rock hitting a car windshield. This was serious, Martin knew, and could quickly get worse. He wondered why this hadn't been discovered the day before by the divers sent to inspect this area. Although, as he thought about it further, it was about the last place one would expect to find quake damage. Maybe they hadn't even bothered swimming up this way.

These days, the OTEC was more than a power producing entity. Last year it had been retooled to produce potable water from the ocean. By the purest of luck, fresh water was a natural byproduct of the system. So when their main water supply started to run low, it had been a no-brainer to make the alteration. If the system was to go down now, however, not only would they lose their safety net from an energy standpoint, they'd also lose their fresh water supply. Desalinating seawater could get them by; but was a mediocre solution at best given the toilsome nature of the task.

Based on the damage Martin had seen so far, it wouldn't be more than a few days till the unit shut down. The waterproof shell had been breached, the inner layers would begin to corrode, the seawater acting like battery acid on limestone. It wouldn't take long for the structure to cave and crack into a million pieces.

If the unit was to be saved, repairs needed to be initiated as soon as possible. Only problem was, the special epoxy resin that was used for this type of repair was in extremely short supply. At best, Martin knew they had enough to fix some of the smaller cracks. He also knew where several cases of the sealant were stored; and since it was of no use to looters, and had the shelf life of dirt, was more than likely sitting untouched and in good condition, ready and waiting for the taking. But they had only yesterday voted down a mission that would have put them right next to it.

He swam down the eastern edge of the unit, continuing his inspection. A shadow suddenly ran across his mask as he moved lower. He quickly looked up; saw nothing— just the innocent shimmer of the barren blue Pacific. Must've been mistaken, he thought. As he drifted deeper the cracks gave way to cracklets and then vanished entirely. The unit was perfectly intact from midway down to the seafloor. The foundation was sound as well. He scanned the rocky reef around the unit, nothing seemed out of place. No fractures, no evidence of landslide, no shifted rock or toppled corals.

Martin then swam up the other side of the unit. It too seemed in good condition. *Whew.* A sigh of relief escaped and bubbled skyward. At least the damage was localized. It could've been much worse, he knew.

Reaching the top of the unit, he reviewed the cracks again. The location of the damage still bothered him. He assumed that seismic damage would occur closer to the foundation. Perhaps the fractures were from the stress as the building swayed. His expertise was in seabed science, which had given him ample training in seismic theory, geology a major thrust of his coursework. But understanding how those forces affect man-made structures had been little more than a footnote in his studies. To gain the facts, an engineer would have to be dispatched.

As he hovered above the OTEC, he was startled by a tap on the shoulder. He quickly spun to see a chunk of fish drift by. Jagged serrations were all that remained where the flesh of head and tail once wiggled, gore and oily fluids leaked from the traumatic amputations. Martin looked around, saw several other fish frags float by.

Oh shit, he breathed. This time the escaping bubbles carried away exhaled panic.

He spun back toward Pacifica, was greeted by a huge greenish cloud that moved toward him with all the ominous of an incoming hurricane. He looked down at his watch. *Uh oh!* His heart ballooned, immediately began twitching with icy tachycardia. With all the excitement, his mind had drifted, and he'd lost track of time. He should've been back inside twenty minutes ago.

Dammit! He was stuck right in the middle of the chum slick.

Chapter 18

The news, when it hit home, made Martin feel foolish. The damage below him, as serious as it was, was usurped by more immediate concerns. Namely—survival.

What an idiot, he chastised himself. Diving 101 *never swim alone!* He hadn't planned on straying from the sightline of the others; he knew better, knew the cardinal rule. But the crack had lured him like a bass to a wiggly worm.

Okay, Martin thought, steadying himself. *Don't panic. Just breathe, stay calm. Don't make a bad situation worse.*

First things first, he checked his gauges—running low, but not critical. He had plenty of air to get back—if he left right now. Only problem, if he began swimming back now, he'd be going right through the massive bloody bait cloud that stood between him and his home. Not the best idea, because as he checked his gauges, he realized his shark POD was not working. The unit must've been damaged during the earlier seismic slosh. He could try and swim around the chum slick, but it would take twenty minutes. He didn't have enough air for a swim that long.

Best chance, he figured, wait it out. Allow the bait to dissipate, and then give it a try. He figured he still had a few minutes to play with; he could stretch his air a bit.

It wouldn't be the first time he pushed the limit of his tanks. Be calm and breath slowly, he reminded himself. *Conserve.*

Trying his radio was the second thing on his list. "Anybody out there, over."

No response. Just the unsympathetic hiss of the radio. He didn't really think he'd get anyone; there was little chance of someone being outside at this point. They all had to be back in the dive chamber by now, probably enjoying a nice relaxing lunch. Without invite, the thought of lunch and his present situation collided in epiphany, bringing new perspective, making him realize that a relaxing lunch depended largely upon which side of the fork one was located. The good news, his fellow crew-mates would eventually realize he was missing. Hopefully sooner than later.

Movement drew Martin's attention back to the OTEC again. A massive fusiform shadow drifted across the structure, casting an eerie specter on the damaged hull. It was the same shadow that he'd dismissed earlier. He was afraid to turn and look up, afraid to see what might be eclipsing such a huge parcel of sunlight.

Because he had a feeling, a very bad feeling.

He slowly turned his head, keeping otherwise still. He didn't want to draw any more attention to himself than he already had. His heart suddenly leapt and froze, felt like an icy anvil stuck in his throat. Hovering above was the biggest living creature he'd ever seen. For an instant he thought it was a grey whale. But that may have been the bias of hope clouding his first pictures; a hope that was quickly dashed by the sight of a gaping amphitheatre of massive white teeth.

At least you're not swimming alone anymore a pesky voice in the back of his mind then chimed in. He winced behind his mask, didn't find the sarcastic self chaff all that funny.

He tried to force himself to remain calm, knew that the worst thing he could do is exude distress. *Don't be nervous, don't move a muscle, don't even fart.* He was able to manage two out of three, but until he was safely inside Pacifica, nervous tension would be hitchhiking like hemoglobin on every circulating red blood cell.

The white shark had to be fifteen feet long, and as thick as a SUV. The damn thing was a Cadillac Escalade, tricked-out with teeth and fins instead of a chrome grill and rims. Only this machine ran on fossil fuel in the simplest form, high octane protein; red raw flesh its petrol of choice. Several remora fish hovered in its slipstream, waiting anxiously for their lions share leftovers. Although a completely horrifying sight, the serpent was also magnificent. Had he been viewing it from the safety of a metal cage, and had he not been a sphincter quiver from soiling his wet suit, the notion may have actually gotten more than fleeting consideration.

The only good thing, at the moment, the shark hadn't attacked. Odd, Martin thought, but he certainly wasn't complaining. The shark just sat there, a battleship gray and white leviathan, hovering in the middle of the chum slick, seemingly hypnotized by the seawater bouillabaisse. Maybe it hadn't even seen him, Martin hoped against hope. And with that slim hope, he stayed completely still, as frozen as a department store mannequin.

Unfortunately, he could do nothing about the stream of air bubbles that escaped and fled to the surface each time he exhaled. Nor could he stop the tiny electrical halo his body discharged, which, given the shark's acute senses, had to have the beast as curious as a fox sniffing around a hen house.

Geez! Martin thought, he couldn't have landed himself in a worse situation, it was the perfect storm of circumstance and stupidity—low on air, out of radio range, blood and guts all around, and a huge predator looming only thirty feet away.

His earpiece began beeping. He looked down at the gauge on his wrist. The needle was in the red, warning him he only had five minutes of air left. *Oh well, guess it could get worse.*

His mind quickly began weighing the prospect of dying from suffocation against being eaten alive, indexed the potential pain from each. The result came back in an instant, required about the same debate as choosing to sweat. So he stayed perfectly still, remained as paralyzed as the embalmed, and tried to meter his breathing even more.

He was not going anywhere.

He slowly shifted his gaze from his gauges back to the shark, and felt an instant influx of hope. He couldn't believe his eyes, or his luck. The shark was gone. He looked around. *Nothing*. For as far as he could see the coast was clear. The fish had apparently disappeared into thin sea.

Now was his chance, he knew, and he wasted no time. *Don't move too fast*, he reminded himself, make minimal disturbance Do nothing to instigate predatory itch, or serenade lateral lines. Swim smooth and stick close to the OTEC wall. As naked as he was out there, at least the condenser gave him some cover, the head-in-the-sand illusion that it was.

Inching slowly downward, he focused ahead on the sea bottom. Once there, he knew he'd have some real cover. Then he could slowly work his way back to the dive chamber. He quickly checked his gauges again. It was going to be close, but his chances were a trillion times better than they were a minute ago. His survival now more on par with a coin toss. At least those were odds he could live with.

A surge of seawater suddenly slammed across his back and Martin went flying.

Shit. Tails, you lose. The jolt sent him smack into the wall of the condenser, then tumbling like a toy doll in a Maytag washer. The ensuing vacuum wash sucked him out into the open ocean, it was all he could do to grab his mask and prevent it from being ripped off. Although it hardly seemed relevant, he was going to be dead in a few seconds anyway. Amid the tumble and turbulence, he caught a glimpse of the shark as it streaked away. A waning white and gray missile; a missile equipped with laser-guided radar every bit as finely tuned as a blood-hound's snout.

Martin knew the shark would be back.

Chapter 19

Martin struggled to stabilize himself. He knew he was a sitting duck, and about to become a very painful link in the endless oceanic food chain. But even with this gut knowledge, and as unequivocal as it was, he was not about to just *give up*. It was time to take advantage of the pent up panic. He slapped the hammer down and began swimming like a maniac, no longer concerned with the pretense of stealth or saving air. Any thought beyond finding cover was utterly irrelevant.

A large lopsided outcrop rose from the seabed a mere thirty feet away, and he fought to reach it, his movements frantic and adrenolated. The increasing warning beeps of his air supply were drowned out by his panting and thrashing. He was swimming as fast as he ever had, moving like Aquaman on Andro. He caught a glimpse of the shark streaking toward him from the side, a cartilaginous bolt of lightning bearing inexorably down upon him. He was almost there, the safety of the outcrop just ahead…

But it may as well have been on Mars. The shark was just too fast, no way was he going to make it. He was a fish in a barrel from the shark's perspective.

Martin instinctively turned, the shark now almost upon him, surging in for the final fatal strike. He repositioned, time to dig in and make a last stand. Taking a hit to the flank would be instant death, exposed as he was.

The shark leaned in for the kill, a two ton torpedo shoving a giant bear trap right at him. All governed by a walnut sized mind, with not a single neuron budgeted for fuzzy feelings. The bigger brain sentiments of mercy, remorse, and pity had no place in the mind of this simple stripped down oceanic meat grinder.

The jaws drifted open wider.

Martin turned to face the approaching beast, curled fetal. Operating strictly on instinct, his own primitive brain kicked in, telling him this was the only move left. He'd kick out his feet as the fish struck, try and land his heels on its nose, use its own momentum to tag it good.

The water around Martin went nova with violence, the moment turning instantly surreal, the ocean a misshapen hallucination. The beast rushed in and Martin thrashed his legs out, a final scream filling his facemask. He was right on target, timed it just right.

But somehow he missed.

Even more remarkable, so did the shark. It veered off, only angstroms before impact. The huge hydraulic wake did hit, however, and sent Martin tumbling again. His dive mask tore free in the wash, but not before he got a glimpse of the shark streaking away and twitching like it'd been stung by a horsefly, a thin stream of its own blood now coloring the water.

Martin was about to pass out, made a feeble attempt to secure his mask. But he just couldn't, too tired, lacked the ATP to even close his fingers around it. Before the buzzing gave way to blackness, he actually felt himself relax some. Because he knew he was going to be okay. He knew his friend was there. He didn't actually see him, didn't have to. Because he knew there were only a few who could shoot a spear gun with such accuracy; and of those few, there was only one stupid enough to venture out in these conditions.

Martin passed out. Jesse was there seconds later.

Chapter 20

Back in the dive chamber Jesse laid his friend out on the wet deck. Alberto Cruz and two other divers had come out to meet him on the way back. Despite the aide of buoyancy, hauling a limp hundred and ninety-five pounds plus dive gear made for a difficult swim. Cruz had brought an extra air tank and mask, which they immediately strapped on. And they could see that, although labored, Martin had started breathing.

The dive chamber was alive by the time they returned. A doctor was right there and an array of medical gear was in place. Only an instant after they laid him down, Martin began coughing out seawater. His eyes fluttered and bulged. He coughed again and the doctor instructed them to roll him on his side. Martin vomited out more seawater and shivered and wheezed. His color returned by degrees with each gasp, cold ashen skin advancing to ecru, then brown.

"He's gonna be fine," the doctor decreed. A collective sigh of relief hurried from the crowd in dive chamber. "Just give em a little room." He waved his arm to the tech behind him. "We're not gonna need that," he said, pointing to the defibrillator. "He just needs a minute, then we'll get him into the decompression chamber and let him rest."

"No!" Martin suddenly hollered and tried to get up. It was a reflex reaction, like a boxer coming to after a vicious knock-out.

"Take it easy, bro." Jesse leaned in and put a hand on his friends shoulder.

Martin spit more seawater, pushed Jesse's arm away. "The OTEC is cracked!" He managed. "Get a team out there as soon as it's clear." He fought to catch his breath, gasped again, still shaking with chill. "I need a full report; I want an engineer out there. I want it done right away. And then get that report to me." Normally very diplomatic and as polite as a bell hop, his behavior was out of character at the moment. Jesse knew he must be really shook up.

The doctor moved in. "Take it easy, Martin, you gotta settle down."

Martin ignored the order, pushed up to a sitting position, his eyes fully focused now. He pointed to the person closest to the bulkhead door. "Get on the intercom," he said. "Call the board members. Tell them I want a meeting. Have them ready as soon as I get out of the chamber."

Chapter 21

Oh how quickly Jesse's world had changed. In the mere space of a day he'd gone from the verge of stealing a sub to idling on the threshold of a dream. From utterly pissed off and depressed, to decidedly upbeat and optimistic. It was like he was going down on a doomed airplane without a parachute or prayer, only to have the captain come on the loudspeaker seconds before impact and say; *"Sorry for the inconvenience folks. Everything's okay, we were just taking a little nap up here. Sit back and relax. The flight attendants will be around momentarily with refreshments."*

But the plane wasn't on the ground just yet, he knew. The pilots could still have a sudden case of narcolepsy and his dream could wind up imploding in a fiery crash. But even *he* had to admit that things were looking good; and he had a feeling, *a really good feeling,* that this was going to be it. Because the entire vibe had changed, a fundamental shift in the population's psyche had evolved over the past eight hours. And like the chronically clammy air in Pacifica, Jesse felt the change all around him.

What he felt was fear.

The feeling had started almost right away, right after he'd dragged his friend back from the brink, and he began babbling about damage to the OTEC. He could tell by

Martin's tense words and the superhuman effort it took to cough them out, that whatever he'd seen, it must be significant. Because Martin was no wolf crier, as stable as they came. Everyone knew that.

And when the follow up inspection team corroborated Martin's story, the fear was no longer fleeting. It was set like cement, its grip all embracing. As the first major crack in the armor, it had seriously deflated the community's collective ego. But was the new found fear strong enough? Would it have the power to override the community's long held global agoraphobia?

At the moment, Jesse sat in the cafeteria, not too far from where he'd sat during the meeting the night before. The board was in an adjacent room involved in a *closed door* meeting. Pacifica had been put on emergency status. As far as Jesse could remember, it was the first time. Winslow himself had made the call after speaking with Martin.

Jesse also knew that with emergency status decisions could be made in an instant; a vote by the five-member board was all that was needed. A contingency measure for quick decisions when time was of the essence. It was well known that the board was hard-set against a journey back to land. But that could change now that one of their own seemed to have had a change of heart.

Jesse sat with a cup of tea, watching the doorknob; waiting for it to move, waiting for the news that he hoped to hear. He gnawed on a fingernail and sipped his tea—caffeine on top of all this excitement, just what he needed. He already felt like he had a Red Bull I-V jabbed in his aorta.

Except for a few stragglers, the cafeteria was empty. Across the way, he noticed his ex, Michelle, sitting and chatting with her mom. She looked up, and as he met her gaze he felt his heart crackle like a downed power-line in salt water. He waved and smiled. She waved back then returned her attention back to her conversation. Jesse felt something stir inside, somewhere near the intersection of his vital force and his soul. *That's odd*, he thought, *haven't felt that in a while.*

It was amazing how quickly his system retooled once the veil of depression was lifted. Jesse reveled in the sensation for a moment. He was definitely going to have to consider an attempt to reconnect with her when he got back. The thought led Jesse to the next natural question. Was he even coming back? There was simply no way to know at this point, no way to know until he had his feet planted firmly on terra firma. *No biggie*, he could wait. First things first…

Stop it already! He chastised himself as his mind trudged across the thin-ice of hopefulness. He didn't even know if there was going to be a journey, and he was already contemplating such a fate. For all he knew, they were in there discussing another option altogether. After all, logic was not always a guarantee where the board was concerned.

Jesse looked up to see Reni enter the cafeteria. *Good*, Jesse thought, he owed the kid some time. And besides, he could really use the distraction from his own incessant inner rambling. As it was, he almost had his fingernails whittled down to bone.

Led by a radiant smile Reni found his way to Jesse. He wasn't even to the table when he started to speak. "Did you guys really see a great white shark?" Wonder sparkled in his brown eyes.

"We sure did, and he was twice as long as this table," Jesse said, spreading his arms, knowing the visual scale would stoke the boy's curiosity. He then glanced up at the clock, suddenly curious. "Isn't it a little late for you to still be up? It's almost ten."

"My dad said its okay," Reni said as he took a seat by Jesse's side. "He said he wanted to talk to me after the meeting."

"Well…you might as well hang out here with me. They shouldn't be much longer." Jesse glanced up at the clock again.

"Tell me more about the shark, I wanna hear everything!" The boy shifted impatiently in his seat.

"Not too much to tell," Jesse replied, not wanting to disclose the *whole story*. Reni had already lost his biological father; he didn't think it was appropriate for him to hear the gory details of how close he was to losing his stepfather as well. "We got a look at him while we were out in the fishing arena, but he was pretty far away, we made sure we kept our distance."

"It must've been the coolest thing." The boy submitted eagerly.

"It was pretty cool," Jesse agreed.

"Wish I coulda seen it."

Jesse quickly leaned in and tickled the boy's ribs. "Bet he'd have loved to see you too!" The boy squirmed and parried away Jesse's mock shark attack.

A noise chirped from behind, Jesse whirled expectantly, but it was just a ventilation fan kicking on. False alarm. He turned back to the boy.

Reni had apparently picked up on his concern. "Whatta ya think's going on in there?" He pointed a small finger in the direction of the meeting room.

"Not sure." Jesse raised his eyebrows, skeptical.

"I bet they're talking about a trip back. I heard a lot of people talking about it. Everyone's acting all weird today."

Jesse nodded, thinking, *everyone's been acting weird for a long time around here*. Not wanting to even ponder it, he changed the subject. "So who was that chick I saw you with this morning? Girlfriend?" Jesse winked conspiratorially.

"You know who she is, it was Andrea. And she's just a friend. I help her with her schoolwork sometimes," Reni explained, defensive.

Jesse leaned closer. "Good tactic." He smirked. "Think it'll work?"

"Cut it out. I told you, she's just a friend," Reni declared, exasperated.

"Okay, okay." Jesse held up a surrendering palm. "I believe you."

"Thank you." Reni shook his head. "Finally."

"So what else is new?" Jesse asked, feeling he'd ribbed the kid enough.

Reni's face went pensive. "Well…this morning after we finished our work, Andrea was trying to explain what happened to us. Ya know, why we're stuck down here? How it all happened?"

Jesse nodded. "Well…what did she say?" It was no surprise that Reni would wonder about the subject. Everything happened when he was very young. It was only natural that his curiosity would eventually lead him to seek the details.

Reni adjusted in his seat. "She said the earth was ruined and we'll never be able to go back up. She said we'll all die from the plague if we do." There was a distinct tenor of paranoia in the boy's voice.

"That's yet to be seen," Jesse said in a supportive tone. "Don't worry about that stuff, kiddo. It's something we'll eventually figure out, I promise. And even if it takes a while to get back up top, we have a great place to live right here."

Jesse was actually *defending* Pacifica. The voice inside his mind got a good chuckle over that. But he was employing the old *white lie* philosophy. Although living in Pacifica may not have been for him: given the current state of the world, there was really no safer place for a child to be. He wanted the boy to feel secure. No point in turning him into an obsessed lunatic. One of those in Pacifica was quite enough, and he already had that niche on lockdown.

The boy nodded and smiled; the sermon seemingly effective.

"Now, do you understand about the earth's ozone layer?" Jesse asked, trying to find out where to begin. He was certain that the boy knew at least some of the story.

"Sure, it's up in the atmosphere. It helps filter out bad rays from the sun. The ultra-violet stuff and I think some other stuff."

"I'm impressed." Jesse nodded. "The ozone layer was actually formed millions of years ago, back before there was much life on the planet. Without it, higher life forms might never have even evolved."

"What about the dinosaurs?" Reni questioned.

Jesse wasn't sure exactly what he was asking, so he tried to cover all possibilities. "The ozone was formed way before the time of the dinosaurs. And without it, they probably would've never come into existence either."

"Oh." Reni nodded.

"Anyway, the ozone started to disappear. Scientists first noticed it in the late twentieth century. There was actually a big hole over the earth at one time. You might have seen some satellite images on the science programs."

Reni listened, eyes focused, his attention rapt.

"The ozone was being destroyed by a lot of the chemical pollutants that people were using." Keeping it age appropriate, Jesse edited the actual chemical names. "The governments of the world had actually made some changes to try and help. Only problem was, once the chemicals get up in the atmosphere, it takes many years for them to break down. And as they do, they continue to react and destroy ozone."

"So…okay…I don't understand. The government stuff didn't work?"

"Guess not." Jesse shrugged. "But nobody really knows why. Some people thought it was all the chemicals in the upper atmosphere, still reacting. At the time the sun was going through a cycle where it was strengthening, many scientists felt that was a factor. Some said the problem was made worse by the other environmental issues of that era. Others said the whole thing was part of earth's normal cycles, like ice ages. Of course there were a lot of people who thought that it was an act of God. One theory out there said aliens were responsible, making changes to suit their needs before taking over the planet." Jesse shook his head and rolled his eyes. The expression said *yeah right!*

"The whole thing kinda snuck up on people. At the time there was so much other stuff going on in the environment, global warming and weird weather patterns and such, that the ozone problem got pushed aside. Then all the sudden things started getting worse; the plague showed up, and not long after that an unusually large ozone hole formed over the arctic."

Jesse was careful not to overdo the details. After all, this was a small boy, susceptible to irrational worry and nightmares.

"So with no ozone people got sick?" Reni asked.

"Yes, UV radiation is poisonous in a sense. It causes cancer, especially skin cancer. And for people who had the plague it was even worse. The plague was actually just a harmless virus. But with overexposure to UV light, the virus can cause a kind of deadly skin disease called Merkel cell carcinoma. Excessive UV exposure also causes other DNA mutations as well as cataracts."

"Cataracts?"

"Yeah, cloudiness of the eyes, the lenses. It can lead to blindness."

"Why didn't people just stay inside?"

"As things got bad, most did. But what really caused society to deteriorate was that food supplies began to disappear, and fast. The UV killed many plants and animals. Algae and grasses died fast, and they were the foundation of most food chains. Once food started disappearing, the world fell into chaos. And for those who got sick or had skin cancer, they only got worse. Like everything else, medical facilities had shut down. The sick, weak, and elderly didn't stand a chance. Everybody was running around just trying to survive."

Reni sat in silence, eyes wide, utterly engaged. Jesse hoped he hadn't gone over the line. He did his best to tightrope through the story, keep it PG, had edited quite a bit in fact. He selectively side-stepped the brutal wars, the gory details of disease and murder. He also left out the cannibalism that had occurred in the latter days of global survival-of-the-fittest gone horribly awry. As careful as he'd tread, there was just no way around the implicit dread. No matter how he sugar coated it, the story was still horrifying; even if told by a big yellow bird or a furry purple dinosaur.

"Unbelievable." Reni said as he shook his head.

"It was, and that's what brought us here. And we were lucky in that. Your father and Martin and I were already down here when things really got bad up top."

"Yeah...thank god for this place," Reni remarked absently, his mind still off in another Zip Code.

Jesse placed a hand on the boy's shoulder trying to measure his reaction. He appeared fine, but it was time to change the subject, bring the conversation back to a lighter topic. "Any other questions, kiddo?" he asked.

"Well, actually, yes…"

From behind, the door handle groaned, and Jesse felt his body surge with thermonuclear anticipation. No mistaking it this time, the meeting was over. He could hear muffled voices. He wanted to turn, but the boy was about to frame another question. He forced himself to keep his attention with the kid. But he felt like a dog that had just been told to *stay* while a fancy house-cat strutted by.

"When me and Andrea were studying, we noticed that most people on the videos and old TV shows have white skin like Andrea." He paused, pondering momentarily.

Jesse heard the clear sound of voices spilling out of the meeting room. He nearly jumped out of his skin.

Unaware of Jesse's inner conflict, Reni continued. "But most of the people that came to Pacifica back during the rescues have dark skin like me." The boy tapped the brown skin on the back of his hand. "And we were wondering why?"

As much as Jesse wanted to swing around and find out the results of the meeting, he was stopped in his tracks. "That's an excellent question kiddo," he said, genuinely proud of the boy. "But it's gonna take a bit to explain that one, and I don't want to short change you. So let's say we put a bookmark in it for now."

Reni frowned, disappointed. "Okay," he finally conceded, then leaned to the side, looking beyond Jesse. "Dad!" He jumped up, waved, his spirit instantly revived.

Jesse turned. Martin was standing in the threshold of the door, one arm leaning against the door jamb. It was subtle, but there was no mistaking the smile on his face. And even more obvious was the message tacit in that smile. *It was on.* He pumped his fist under the table.

Martin looked around and then discreetly gave Jesse a thumbs-up. Jesse wanted to run around the room doing back flips, if he knew how. But it'd be inappropriate, from the perspective of most, this was still a crisis. He didn't want to be insensitive to that. Besides, he just realized something else. And it too was as obvious as if Martin held a neon sign; their friendship telepathy was that strong. It told him that Martin was going on the journey. That explained why he wanted Reni around after the meeting. He wanted to tell the boy before he heard it elsewhere. Jesse knew that telling Vanessa would not be easy for Martin either.

Leaving Pacifica had always been an issue for Martin. Although never discussed in great detail, an uncertainty hung in the air whenever the topic came up, and Jesse knew why. Martin didn't want to leave the boy without a dad for a second time. But apparently he'd changed his mind, and now felt the risk had become necessary.

Winslow and the rest of the board members filed quickly out of the meeting room, their faces taut with concern. Winslow made a beeline to the P-A system in the corner of the cafeteria. With the flip of a switch he could talk to the entire facility.

Jesse watched as Winslow picked up the microphone. "Attention. Attention everyone," he said and cleared his throat. "Sorry to bother you so late in the evening, but I have an important announcement to make—"

Jesse listened. What he heard was music to his ears.

Part Two

THE SURFACE

Chapter 22

From Jesse's perspective, the underwater journey couldn't be going any better. They'd just passed halfway in their crossing. He knew this based on the waypoints marked on the water main that ran along the seafloor. To this point, it had been nothing but smooth sailing for the two mini-subs and the four person team divided inside them. Once through the mouth of the bay they'd be in the home stretch, just a casual cruise through Mission Bay to the docks.

The plan was to set down beneath the pier that led to the massive warehouse on the northwestern shoreline, the original staging point used during the construction of Pacifica. Less than a mile inland would be the once well traveled I-5 interstate, La Jolla to the north, San Diego just south.

Negotiating the entrance to the bay was the only obstacle standing in their way. The rocky escarpments that guarded the bay squeezed benign tidal currents into a rushing torrent. Add rip currents and unpredictable eddies to the mix, and finding safe passage would be a true test of navigational savvy.

Breaching and sailing on the ocean surface would be a trillion times easier, but utterly out of the question. That would put them squarely in the crosshairs of prying eyes for miles around. Sounding a foghorn would be only a marginally more obvious signal of their arrival.

Originally, Pacifica had three larger subs and a small fleet of boats docked at the ALEN platform, but they'd been lost; the boats to a colossal storm, the subs to failed rescue missions that took place early on, back before the board was in place to govern such events. The two subs they used today were designed for eco-tours and shuttling around campus. Durable but small, they were vulnerable to the whims of waves and currents. They also lacked long-term power capability. Six hours of use and they'd have to be plugged back into the tethers on the ALEN to recharge.

Leading the way was the Lobster, a four-seat mini-sub piloted by Martin. Jennifer Owens sat shotgun, a stack of supplies and gear filled the rear seats. Visibility was not a problem as afternoon sunshine rained down in shimmering green shafts to help show the way. But the turbulence had started to pick up. Martin white-knuckled the Lobster's controls and held on for the ride.

Jesse skippered the second vehicle, nicknamed the Halibut, an even smaller two-seater. Like navigating a car through foggy roads, he focused straight ahead, staring through the plastic windshield and out into the infinite Pacific, using the roiling prop wash from the Lobster as a guide. Alex Hankin sat in the seat next to him; a few backpacks were jammed in the stingy cargo area. A solar panel was strapped on the roof like luggage on the family station wagon.

The sub's power issues would be addressed once docked. They were going to use Jesse's idea. He was shocked when he'd been asked for his sketched blueprint, by Winslow himself, no less. Jesse couldn't believe that anyone had actually been listening to him when he mentioned the idea during his speech the other night.

After the mission had been finalized, early the next morning a dive team had been dispatched to retrieve one of the solar panels from the ALEN. It would be rigged with a transformer and mounted to the pier, then connected by cable directly to the submarines while they were docked underwater. The panel would charge the batteries while they were out on their mission. It was a great idea in principle, Jesse knew, and he was sure it *could* work. But *would* it work, was the question. He hadn't a clue, and lacked the technical expertise to actually bring his vision to fruition. For that they needed help.

Enter Alex Hankin. Alex was a regular wiz when it came to anything electronic. When he was first asked if the idea could work, Alex had taken one look at Jesse's drawing, nodded and said, *no problem,* before turning and heading off. As curt as his response had been, it was about as much as Jesse had ever heard him say at any one time.

Jesse glanced over at his sub-mate. Alex was working on connections for the solar panel, as he'd been doing the entire trip. He was focused like a surgeon, twisting tiny wires, occasionally muttering under his breath. Jesse had no idea exactly what he was doing, didn't really worry too much about it. He just sat back, drove the sub and let him do his thing. No point micro-managing. He figured the guy knew what he was doing.

Or at least one would hope.

Alex was some kind of savant, a real Rainman when it came to electronics. Back at Pacifica he was roundly considered a geek, and that was among a population of mostly scientists. His legend as a technician was rivaled only by his reputation as a recluse. His unkempt hair and tattered clothing only added to his eccentric aura. From what Jesse knew of him he spent nearly all his time in the workshop, repairing equipment and tinkering with electronics.

Day to day, Jesse hardly ever saw the guy. He knew him mostly as the Tool Troll, a nickname someone had slapped on him years ago. Martin had used the nickname just yesterday, in fact, when he informed Jesse that they'd be riding together in the Halibut.

Looks like it's you and the Tool Troll is what he'd said. To which Jesse had responded, *Me and the Tool Troll, sounds like a children's after school special.* They both had laughed.

Despite shortcomings in the personality department, Jesse was grateful that Alex was on board. Should a technical issue arise, he knew they had it more than covered with this guy around. Bottom line, his wizardry outweighed his weirdness.

Nobody had brought it up, but Alex was the only one of the four-member team that had light skin. While on shore, they'd be operating at night. Darkness would give them cover from both potential prying eyes as well as the sun's rays, so his sensitive skin shouldn't be a problem. But if a situation did arise where they got stuck outside during daylight, Jesse knew that he could be in trouble. Alex lacked the protective pigment evolution had provided him and the others on the team. He pushed the thought from his head. If everything went as planned, it wouldn't be a problem. After all, Alex had agreed to come; he knew what he was getting himself into.

Jesse picked up the radio, thumbed the talk button. "Just checking in before we head into this wash. How's it lookin' up there? Over." The hiss of the open mic returned as Jesse released the trigger.

"Martin says to make sure you're strapped in tight," Jennifer replied. "It's gonna get a little choppy. But not to worry, just stay tight on our wake. We're gonna run it right up the middle. We'll be through it in a few minutes. Over."

"Will do, over and out."

Jesse holstered the mic and put both hands on the steering wheel. He toed the foot pedals, made a minor rudder adjustment and focused on the trailing vortex from the Lobster. On the fringe of his vision he could see dark shadows advertising the status of basalt escarpments looming on either side. The Halibut suddenly lurched as they met the turbulence instigated by the narrowing inlet. *Here we go*, he breathed.

Out of his peripheral vision he noticed Alex fidgeting as he tried to put tiny white buds in his ears. "What's that?"

Alex held up a small metallic blue rectangle. "iPod."

Jesse noticed that his hands were shaking. "You okay?"

"Just a little nervous, never felt too comfortable in these things. I'm a little claustrophobic. One time I had to fly in a plane when I was a kid, I still have nightmares about it," he said, forcing a smile.

Wow, Jesse thought, he must be nervous. It was the first time he'd ever heard the man string together more than one sentence. "Whatta ya got on that thing?"

"Some Mockingbird 187, Dred Zeppelin, and some old stuff like Pearl Jam and Blue October," Alex replied.

"I used to be more into jazz myself, but I remember Mockingbird 187, they got some good stuff, a bunch of bad-ass brothers playin' rock and roll like nobody's business. That other stuff must've been before my time."

"They were always my favorite too," Alex said with a thrill that momentarily breached his phobia. "Those guys broke all boundaries. The lead guitarist was like Hendrix reincarnated."

The Halibut suddenly shook and shifted like a white water raft in the rapids, Jesse did his best to hold on. "How the heck does that thing still work?" Jesse asked over the rising din. "Don't the batteries eventually wear out?"

"Still works fine," Alex said, his voice quivering in time with the sub. "I keep the battery chilled down, and only use it when I really need it. It helps me with stress".

"Well go ahead and turn it up, we got some rough goin' ahead of us."

He watched as Alex sighed and leaned back in the seat. With the ear buds in place he began breathing deeply, apparently trying to quell his anxiety.

Maybe this guy was okay after all, Jesse started to think, maybe he was just a little misunderstood. He even started to feel a little guilty for having referred to him as the Tool Troll over the years. *No biggie*. It's not like he'd ever said it to his face, and Alex probably wasn't even aware of the derogatory moniker.

As Jesse wrestled with the controls, navigating the aquatic potholes, he mentally commended the board for a job well done organizing the mission. He didn't think they were capable of such sound work. After the journey had been finalized, selecting the team was the first thing they'd done, and they nailed it.

About a dozen or so had volunteered for the mission, way more than needed. Several didn't have appropriate skills and were denied straight away. One guy was considered too old, another had been denied on account of a recent heart attack. Two were prohibited because they were deemed too valuable to risk, one a physician, the other an original architect of the ALEN.

After Martin had been put in charge he immediately recruited Jesse as his wing man. Jennifer and Alex had then been added to fill out the team.

Jennifer Owens was a nurse and a former marine, making her a perfect fit. Having someone along with medical background only made sense. In her mid-thirties, she was as sharp as a tack and as durable as duct tape. She even played basketball with the men sometimes. The fact that she was only an estrogenized five foot tall and a hundred and five pounds soaking wet never seemed to dampen her spunk.

One time, Jesse watched her dislocate a finger diving for a loose ball in a basketball game, call a time out, re-set the finger herself, slap on some tape and continue to play. Everyone insisted she sit out and relax. But she insisted *they* relax, and she *was not* sitting out. Beneath the grimace, her eyes broadcast a message that underscored her words; *there's no way I'm gonna let down my team*. That kind of determination didn't grow on trees, Jesse knew. She'd been on his team back then, and he was glad to have her on his team again today.

Entering the bay, the turbulence abated and the Halibut once again slid freely. Now through the underwater chop, it was Jesse's mind that began to churn. Instinctively, he began thinking of new dangers, those that may be encountered on land. It caused Jesse to recall the other important member of their crew—a nine millimeter pistol. Although few weapons had made it down to Pacifica, the nine millimeter had been issued to Jennifer for the mission. Knowing the gun was tucked in the former marines belt was a welcome security blanket to Jesse. He only hoped that they'd never have the occasion to use it.

Chapter 23

Jesse listened as Jennifer made final radio contact with Pacifica, informing them that they were through the pass and into the bay. Radio relays were fastened to the water-main pipe, and radio waves traveled poorly in water. Once they veered off path, they'd be out of range.

As Jennifer signed off Jesse felt a sudden surge of emotion. His growing anticipation was momentarily swept aside by a rush of separation anxiety; the sensation rising from the knowledge that they were now officially on their own. It surprised him. He didn't think that anything could dull his excitement.

Gliding through the calm of the bay, Jesse looked up to see the ocean's rippled roof, a shimmering looking glass to the bold new world above. Beside him, Alex removed the iPod and returned to wiring the solar panel, his anxiety dissipating as quickly as it had arrived. Jesse knew that any minute they'd reach the support pilings to the pier that stretched into the bay, and his anticipation returned in full force. He couldn't wait.

With each passing moment the water column began to take the muted shades of dusk. *Perfect,* he thought. The setting sun would give them sufficient light to dock, check the warehouse for supplies, and give Alex time to rig up the solar panel. The coming darkness would then provide cover as they traveled inland to their base of operations. The water station.

The radio chirped, followed by Jennifer's voice. "We see the dock. It's just up ahead. We're gonna throttle back and pull up on the right. Martin says to put the Halibut down off the back end. We can fasten the solar panel there. He thinks it will be less likely to be spotted. Over."

"Will do, over and out."

Jesse felt his every muscle fill with excitement as promise came face to face with impending reality. Ahead, the Lobster slowed and veered, then settled in a dust up of sediment beside a row of eroded pilings. Jesse eased the Halibut off the back edge, then nudged it aft, dropping it behind the Lobster.

Jesse sighed, stretched and turned to Alex. "You all set there? Is it gonna work?"

"It should be okay," Alex said, his tone indecisive. "I hope," he then offered fretfully, not looking up from his work.

"You hope! Whatta you mean, you hope!" Jesse said, suddenly concerned.

His question had only been conversational. He didn't expect such a dubious response. Until now Alex had given no indication that there might be a problem with the set-up.

Great, Jesse silently simmered, *just great.*

After allowing a few seconds to pass, Alex lifted his head and flashed a subtle smile. "Got ya," he said and looked back down, returning to the wiring. "In a few minutes this thing'll be ready to power up half the city. I promise you that. Or my name's not the Tool Troll." There was no mistaking the sarcasm in his smile, even in the low light.

Jesse felt his face instantly flush. He couldn't believe it, razzed by the Tool Troll. Alex had him going pretty good. He figured that he somehow deserved it. Jesse couldn't help but smile too.

Jesse could see flashes of color and distorted funhouse mirror images through the bent plastic of the Lobster. He knew they were readying to disembark, probably removing dive suits, stowing gear, gathering supplies.

Jesse and Alex began doing the same.

Jesse hustled to complete the shutdown, eager to be the first up top. The feeling that swelled in his heart was like nothing he'd ever felt. Alex moved quickly as he made ready to disembark. It seemed that he too was as anxious to get outside.

They exited through the lower bulkhead door. Using the lower hatch would allow the vehicles to remain dry and safely hidden underwater. The water was cold, a bracing contrast to the climate-controlled cabin they'd been trapped in for half a day. Carrying their provisions in watertight bags, they slowly drifted up, gravity knuckling under to the force of buoyancy. A few barnacles and a smattering of clams clung to the worm-eaten wood pilings. They did not escape Jesse's eye. *Rudimentary life*, he mused, definitely a positive sign.

Jesse was first to break the surface. He opened his mouth and sucked a lungful of cool air. Like an astronaut dropping a first foot on a new planet, the moment was glorious, and Jesse felt his entire being unhinge. A stiff wind chilled his face and whistled by with the haunting whine of an ear held seashell. Seconds later, Alex and the rest of the team breached and bobbed in place, treading water.

Nobody spoke in those first few moments. They all looked around, seemingly anesthetized by the moment, each pensively taking in the terrestrial mural that had been beyond their eyes for so many years. The anxiety linked to the task before them was momentarily back burnered, vague fears and the wind-born chill soothed by the warmth of inspiration. The sun had already set, probably only moments ago.

And Jesse knew in that first moment—right up there with the certainty of death, it was an inner Times Square moment, and flashed neon bright across his brain—*there is no way I'm going back to Pacifica.*

Martin motioned them in close, gathered them for instructions. Every step had already been carefully choreographed back in Pacifica, but there was no point in being sloppy.

"Okay, let's move quickly and quietly," Martin said, whispering above the wind. "You guys get the solar panel rigged," he nodded toward Jesse and Alex, "and we'll check the warehouse for the sealant. Any sign of danger, we retreat, then slip back down to the subs and wait. Depending on the threat level, we'll figure out what to do from there." He glanced from face to face. "Use your flashlights only if needed. And let's remember to keep conversation to a minimum, at least till we reach the safety of the water station." Staring at a trio of nodding heads, he then said, "Let's get to work. We meet back here in an hour."

Jesse watched as Martin and Jennifer clambered up an old eroded piling and onto the pier. The warehouse was less than fifty yards back along the old wooden walkway. Like the pier, the building was utterly run down, and even against a darkening sky its weathered mass was striking. Damage from erosion, time, and fire had conspired to demote it to the status of the condemned.

Jesse watched as they headed off down the pier. He looked at Alex and nodded. Without a word Alex dove beneath the surface, heading back down to retrieve the solar panel.

Jesse hesitated. He'd help in a moment, but he couldn't pull free from the view just yet. And the view was magnificent, beautiful beyond measure, more than he had expected. From the vast cobalt sky to the dark rocky outcrops that extruded along the sandy beaches. Even the distant cityscape of San Diego was a sight for sore eyes, greasy and damaged and charred as it was. A narrow thundercloud hung low over the city, well defined and ominous. He found himself hoping it didn't rain during their campaign. He'd had enough contact with water to last a lifetime.

Treading water, he glanced around again, this time looking closer, focusing on details, his practical left brain taking stock now that the initial excitement had subsided. He looked and stared, listened and scanned. Searching for movement. Searching for signs of life.

There was nothing; just a flock of trash tumbleweeding across the dusky shoreline. A dark brush-stroke of trees and shrubbery dotted the countryside, but he couldn't determine their health, details rendered ambiguous by distance and the interloping night.

The wind suddenly shifted and with it came the musk of marine decay. He tracked the odor back to its source along the shoreline where he noticed a myriad of shells and seaweeds washed up and lifeless; cauterized critters falling to the misfortune of tide, storm, and solar spoil. Had Jesse been a beachcomber in search of collectable relics, there'd be no problem finding treasure amid the trove of bones and calcified homes. But as a biologist, and at the moment searching for signs of life a little more animated, there was little to hang his hat on. Aside from the crustaceans on the pier, he didn't see any important organic effects. It was definitely a little eerie, not to mention disappointing, and it took the edge off his initial swell of nirvana.

He spun again and again, hoping to see something, anything. Even a gull or raccoon scavenging amid the seashore graveyard would do. But there was nothing. And with the others now gone from his optical frame, there was not a living soul in sight.

Chapter 24

The moon was on the rise by the time the team started the trek inland. Martin led the way and Jesse took up the rear as the small group snaked their way silently through the terrestrial terrain. The night sky afforded some cover, but the path to the water station was mostly open. They did their best to remain unseen, hugging the occasional outcrop or old abandoned vehicle, moving with the stealth of a Navy SEAL team.

Jesse could make out the outline of the water station from a quarter mile away. The small building sat part way up an earth-tone bluff located just north of the San Diego outskirts. Built into the rocky slope, he knew that more than half its mass was buried into the hillside. Under the bias of moonlight it stood out like a Maginot Line pillbox.

Way back when, a well had been drilled in the hillside to tap a local aquifer, providing water to a few local communities, as well as Pacifica. The artesian system allowed water to flow via gravity through a fourteen inch main, down the hillside and out along the sloping seabed to serve the underwater community. The system had worked splendidly until being reduced to a trickle some time last year.

Ascending the rocky hillside, Jesse continually checked the location of the water station, the building stood as a tiny dilating beacon of concrete. Although no threats were directly evident, Jesse couldn't wait to reach the water station and get walls between them and the menacing suspicion of scrutinizing eyes in the dark.

The night was quiet to the point of unnerving, and Jesse realized his ears were piqued like a Jack Rabbit leaving its borough to chew grass. So when sounds did issue forth—the clamor of an insect, the dry crack of cambium from a distant tree, or the restless sigh of winds—they crashed like thunder through the fallow atmosphere.

He found the lack of life disturbing as well. Aside from the crustaceans at the dock and the intermittent crying cricket, few signs of life were evident; although he had taken note of *one* interesting discovery. On the walk in he spotted soggy piles of chlorophyll colored wool pushing from the slender water of the inter-tidal zone. They bore a vague resemblance to stromatolites, but on the whole, were like nothing he'd ever seen before. With no time to stop for a sample, he was uncertain whether they were alive or just rotting husks; relics of a failed fledgling lifeline. If they were in fact alive, they were not very complex. Nothing to jump up and down about, certainly not enough evidence to infer that the radiation levels had returned to normal, as he had hoped.

Along the way, wild grasses and goldenrod filaments fought from the earth and swayed in confused breezes as if searching for terrain more forgiving. Shimmering ivy whiskered eroded outcrops and roads. Thin stands of trees etched the skyline on the edge of darkness. From distance they appeared petrified and bony, as if afflicted with rheumatoid arthritis. Under moonlight it was impossible to tell if they were dormant, dead or alive.

The moon was nearly full, a robust white orb that sat high in the night sky. They'd been fortunate with the timing of the lunar phase, pure dumb luck. It certainly made life easier for them. A moonless night would've meant using flashlights, which would've heightened the danger level considerably. Might as well just drop flyers from the sky; advertise to any potential cannibals that they'd arrived.

Eat at Jesse's Joint, fresh flesh from the Pacific.

Jillions of icy stars flickered pinholes of prehistoric light, adding breadth and dimension to the nocturnal tableau. As they advanced up the hillside, Jesse couldn't stop himself from gazing up at the tiny cross-section of universe. He found himself transfixed by the infinite view, especially since his sight-line had been shackled for so long; impeded at every turn by thick bulkheads and the dark quarantine of the sea.

The earth possessed a truly extraterrestrial spirit now, and Jesse felt like he had landed on another planet altogether. Embalmed in moonlight the landscape appeared to be scorched with rigor mortis, no longer plush with the vigor of ecology. It was as if the earth had undergone a complete transformation, a broad-based biome makeover; born-again, the illegitimate incarnation of a strange new age. All compliments of a perfect storm of events that had collided and catalyzed new reactions, and continued their metamorphic mojo right up till today.

Jesse too felt like he was going through rebirth. With each step he felt more and more liberated, finally free from the oppressive plastic womb he'd been trapped in for all those years. His elation was tempered a great deal by a free floating anxiety that had him more than a little nervous. Although things were going well so far, that could change in the time it took to take their next step. His mind was alive with every advance, playing previews of all the possible ugly scenarios…

A pack of savages emerging from the darkness, a newly evolved predator lurking in the shadows, a virulent virus inhaled, already gearing up to render innards to fevered red goo, or an alien suddenly beaming down to reduce them to tiny piles of elemental matter, with one sweep of a ray gun.

What the hell caused that to pop into my head, Jesse thought, annoyed with his meandering mind.

But his mind was just doing what minds do in situations like this. As marvelous a machine as the human brain was, it could be equally ineffectual when put under stress. Especially when fear and uncertainty were added to the mix.

And the fear that Jesse felt, despite their good fortune thus far, was colossal. It was the worst kind of fear, too. The same kind generated by those who push boundaries; the kind that burned inside ancient explorers as they headed out to sea, the kind that bloomed in the heart of an astronaut at the call of *throttle up*. Or the kind of fear generated by that dreaded doctor's visit where you are told that it's over, *you've only got a month to live*. The kind of fear that crushed all but the strongest of willed.

It was the fear of the unknown.

He wondered what his crewmates were feeling, how they were dealing with the obvious stress. From all outward appearances, everyone seemed to be holding it together. If there were any chinks in the armor, no signs were evident.

With the water station only a few steps away, Jesse felt his body uncoil, the old building like a security blanket sewn in cinderblock and earth. Knowing that in only seconds he'd have thick concrete between him and the night, he sighed in relief. Getting inside also meant that they could begin work on the well, which Jesse had to admit, would be a gratifying distraction; give him a chance to swap surplus adrenaline for toil.

Martin raised his hand, bringing the team to a halt just outside the water station. He then crept through the door, two rusty hinges all that remained to prevent trespass. Inside it was pitch black. Jesse waited outside with the others; he could see the sweeping beam of Martin's flashlight. A shriek and a loud clank suddenly came from inside and everything went dark. Jesse felt his blood surge, and his body shift instantly to warrior mode.

Time to kick some ass.

Chapter 25

Jesse was about to rush into the water station when Martin leaned out and waved them to follow. "Sorry about that, I stepped on a damn nail and dropped the flashlight."

"You okay?" Jennifer asked in urgent whisper.

"I'll be fine," Martin said as he gingerly put weight on the injured foot. "Come on; room's clear," he winced, "but watch your step in here."

Jesse shook his head and rolled his eyes, the expression lost in the dark. Under any other circumstances he'd have gotten on Martin for being so clumsy. But the urge took a back seat to more pressing issues, and he sucked a deep calming breath and followed the others.

Once inside, Martin gathered them in close. "Okay, so far so good." He whispered. "Even though we're inside, let's keep the conversation to a minimum. Hopefully this place is empty, but you never know. And let's remember our most important order."

They all nodded. There was no need to spell it out; the directive had been driven home at every turn during the planning process back in Pacifica—Winslow had said it a hundred times—*under no circumstances are you to make contact with any people should you encounter any.*

Martin panned his flashlight around the foyer. They all followed his lead. The room was small, a tight twelve-by-twelve foot concrete slab with random heaps of litter spread over unanimous grime. The walls were solid stacked block; most of the white paint had peeled, leaving a pattern of urban camouflage in black mold and crept stain. The air was thick and smelled of a hundred different degrees of rot.

A few cockroaches scurried for cover, incited by the sweeping flashlights. Somehow nobody seemed surprised, their ability to evolve on a dime was legendary, their superhuman survival skills well celebrated. It would seem they lived up to all the hype.

Fiberglas insulation and broken ceiling tiles were strewn about the floor. Colored wires and metal flex conduit dangled down from the exposed attic like streamers and ribbon for a surprise party never to be. Lying on the floor next to the entranceway was a rusted door. Thick dust, cobwebs, and well placed dents in the metal cross-buck indicated that it had been kicked in long ago.

Martin pulled them in close again. "First thing I wanna do is check out the entire building, just to be sure that we're the only ones in here." He directed his flashlight toward the lone dark hallway on the back wall. "Jess, why don't you take the lead, you know where the well room that feeds Pacifica is, right?"

Jesse nodded. "Well room B; it should be down the hall a ways."

"Any idea how many other rooms there are in here?" Martin questioned.

"I think there's about ten." Jesse offered, uncertain. "At least that's what Marrison told me."

"Actually there's twelve," Alex amended, whispering. "Aside from the nine well rooms, there's the foyer, a small office, a bathroom, and that doesn't include storage rooms and a dozen or so closets. The building has a total of 1863 square feet, not including the main hallway."

Jesse looked at Alex, as did the rest of the team, clearly surprised, as much by the detail of his utterance as the fact that he'd actually spoke in public.

"How do you know all that?" Jesse asked, amused.

"The original building blueprint is posted in the workshop." Alex explained. "I've got it pretty well memorized."

"Aren't there supposed to be posters of chicks in bikinis hanging on the walls of a workshop?" Jesse flashed him a good-natured grin.

"That would be a little inappropriate in this day and age," Alex replied, missing the sarcasm. "And besides, my girlfriend would kill me."

"All right fellas." Martin said, stepping in. "Didn't I just finish saying we need to keep the conversation to a minimum. Now let's back it down and get to work. We've got a lot to do here. I wanna get that well running tonight if possible," He glanced at Alex, winked. "And we've still got an 1863 square foot building to search."

As they started down the dark hallway, Jesse suddenly realized—Alex and his girlfriend had been one of the couples granted reproductive privileges at the meeting the other night. What the heck was he doing here with all that on his plate? He should've declined to come; it was certainly within his right. Definitely a little odd, Jesse's thought. The mystery of the Tool Troll continues.

Jesse led the way down the hall, the motif of post modern ruin continuing as the universal theme. Up ahead, a mound of garbage blocked half the hall. Jesse focused his flashlight on the pile. Cardboard and generic frags of trash were mortared together with wadded cloths.

Jesse suddenly stiffened. "There's something here," he whispered.

He swept aside a veil of wet cardboard with his foot, revealing what looked like a Mutter museum exhibit. Between a battered sneaker and ripped jeans, the kiln-dried chalk of tibia and fibula came alive under light, the leg bones glued and fixed by mummified tendons that looked like desiccated Slim-Jims. Based on the inferred forensic evidence, this person had died long ago. The team gathered around, an impromptu moment of silence ensued.

Martin finally spoke, resuming his role as leader. "This isn't something we didn't expect to see. Let's continue." Moving on, they all veered respectfully, careful not to desecrate the trash built casket.

A few steps further two doors appeared on the left. Jesse shined his flashlight on the first. "Well room A," he whispered, interpreting the peeling paint, then shifted his light to the right. "Well room B."

Martin motioned Alex and Jesse to enter the second door, waving Jennifer to follow him into the first. In SWAT team style, they pushed into the rooms. Both doors whooshed open. Jesse stepped inside and the reek of mold sledge-hammered his senses, even worse than in the hall. He recoiled, wincing, but edged ahead, almost wishing they'd brought SCUBA gear. Alex was right behind him, both using their flashlights to flush the darkness from the room.

Whew, Jesse breathed a sigh of relief. Nobody home. Just an old rusty tool chest and a massive metal well head jutting from the center of the room. And maybe a billion farting fungi.

Alex immediately began inspecting the well housing. "This is definitely it," he reported. "This is the well that feeds Pacifica."

Jesse sidled up beside him. The well head looked like a potbellied fire hydrant, a massive chunk of metal held upright by dedicated concrete.

"Whatta ya think. Any chance we can fix this thing?" he asked.

"I give it a better than fifty-fifty chance," Alex replied. "Looks like the handle to the manual pump is rusted in place though." He leaning his weight against the frozen cast iron lever, but it didn't budge. "If we can free this, we can use it to flush away any debris and mineral deposits around the intake screens. It's a wonder this thing has worked as long as it has without any maintenance."

Once again, Jesse found himself in awe of Alex. "Is there anything you don't know?"

"Actually, I only just learned about this process. I studied up on the system after you talked about it the other night. It's actually a simple rig, and I agree with your assessment, it should be repairable." He leaned and tugged on the handle again, looked up. "By the way, I don't know how to ice skate and couldn't carry a tune to save my life."

Jesse laughed. "Don't worry; I don't think either of those skills will come into play over the next two days."

Alex pulled out a small can of oil from his knapsack and proceeded to soak the rusted joint. Jesse looked on with amusement. Apparently sensing eyes upon him, Alex looked up. "I had a feeling this might come in handy," he explained. "With this and my Swiss Army knife, there shouldn't be anything we can't handle." He smiled, prompting Jesse to do the same.

Behind them, the door suddenly opened and the rest of the team entered. "All clear next door," Martin reported. "How's it looking over here?"

Jesse nodded. "This is definitely our well. We just gotta figure out a way to free up this lever so we can try to manually pump out the clog." Jesse pointed to the heavy gage rusted metal handle with his flashlight.

Martin moved by, grabbed the handle and gave it a cursory tug.

"This might help." Jennifer appeared behind him with a thick metal pipe.

Martin nodded approvingly. "That'll work." He slipped the pipe over the handle, reset his feet, then leaned and pulled with all he had. The weld held firm, but then slowly succumbed to mechanical advantage, rust squeaking in defeat as Martin worked the handle back and forth.

Martin then stood and mopped his brow, his dark skin varnished in sweat. "Can you two take care of this?" He looked to Alex and Jesse.

"No problem," Jesse replied. "You did the hard part."

"Good. I'm gonna take Jen and go check out the rest of the building. I don't think it should take too long. When you're finished here, head back to the main entrance. We'll meet you there. I don't want us crossing paths and accidentally scaring the hell out of each other."

Everybody nodded.

"We'll set up camp there," Martin continued. "I think it's our best bet. It'll allow us to keep a lookout by the door and give us a heads up just in case anybody comes our way. And since this place is mostly underground, with only one entrance, no one will be able to sneak up behind us."

With the game plan in place, Jesse and Alex went to work on the well while Jennifer and Martin left to search the rest of the 1863 square foot building.

Chapter 26

Alex and Jesse sat in the entrance to the water station, eating dried fish and rolled seaweed, a single flashlight jammed in a broken cinderblock like a synthetic campfire. Martin and Jennifer finally arrived at the rendezvous point and joined the party. It was kind of cozy, Jesse thought, the four of them sitting around the snug room reminded him of childhood nights staying up late with friends in his tree fort.

Martin informed Jesse and Alex that the rest of the building was empty, no living souls or evidence of such. Picking through the garbage, they'd even found a few spools of wire and several boxes of screws that might come in handy back in Pacifica. Jesse felt his anxiety ease by degrees with the news. The report from the well room was equally encouraging; Jesse explained that they felt fairly certain the backwashing procedure would be a great improvement back home, if not restore flow entirely. The collective sigh of relief was palpable.

Thus far, things had been going great; Jesse certainly hadn't expected this kind of success. Even the earlier visit to the warehouse had been a home-run, a stack of supplies waited in crates for their return, including the dearly needed underwater sealant.

Jesse thought about the earlier promise he'd made to himself, not to return to Pacifica. He noticed that the feeling was not quite as strong as the initial surge; but it was still there, still in the plan. He had not breathed a word of his intentions. There was no upside to doing so, no point in disturbing the flow of the mission. After all, these people were his friends. And the most important thing, even more so than his own cause, was to help them finish what they came to do, and then make sure they all got home safely. The fact that he wanted to stay behind was his burden alone.

They sat around the room and talked well into the night, sharing stories. Jesse found the stories Jennifer told about her days in basic training fascinating. As they talked quietly into the night, they each took turns sitting by the front door to keep watch.

The plan was to stay up as late as possible, then sleep away most of the approaching day. That would allow them to be fresh for the following night when they were scheduled to complete the last part of their mission—collecting supplies. The board had agreed that if they were going to send a team topside, then they might as well make the best of it.

As daybreak neared, Jesse agreed to keep lookout. It was almost dawn when Martin finally nodded off. The rest of the team had gone down over the last hour as the insomnia of excitement finally succumbed to fatigue.

With everyone asleep, Jesse decided to sit outside. The crisp night air would help keep him awake. It would also allow him to take in the predawn pageantry, enjoy the beauty of a nascent day before he was forced inside by the wrath of a rising sun.

Stepping outside Jesse felt a twinge of light headedness, and he had to steady himself. He found the view striking to the senses, and he knew that the vastness of an open sky had as much to do with his vertigo as exhaustion. Jesse inhaled deeply, could actually smell the chill in the early morning air. Gazing toward the east, he found the crystal blue horizon to be like visual valium. Despite his yawning fatigue, the sublime sensory input was exhilarating, better than any drink or drug. His chakras began to toke on the vibe, flutter and align, his aura shifting decidedly toward harmony.

He sat back against the concrete wall and took in the landscape. Along the hillside he watched filaments of weed and flower waltz in the morning breeze. He could see that, although more rust in color than chlorophyll green, the ground scruff was indeed alive. A bizarre button cactus stared up from the earth near his hand. Careful of its spines, he reached and gently stroked the plant as if to commend it for its success.

On a more global scale, a dust bowl brush-stroke colored the landscape; the stiff morning breeze sweeping up small cyclones of sand and debris from soil the color of scabs. Once again Jesse noticed a cloud over the city, backlit by the dawn's early light. He found it unusual, well defined and low lying, like no cloud he'd seen before. But he was not originally from this area. Maybe it was an intense localized storm. Maybe even a fundamental new weather pattern, something only inherent to the new earth. Jesse continued to observe the cloud, its distinctive outline becoming clearer with each new watt of daylight.

Jesse then turned his attention to the tree-line to the east. With the advancing light he wanted to see if he could detect the green growth of success. But as he swung his head, something else caught his eye. Movement. For a split-instant he was catatonic with shock. It couldn't be, could it? He quickly shook his head, making sure his eyes weren't playing tricks, or that he hadn't drifted off, dreaming.

Neither was the case.

Inconceivably, he was in fact seeing what he was seeing.

He cautiously moved back inside. From the cover of the doorway he leaned his head out. The creature was still there, still skulking slowly along a low path a few hundred yards to the southeast. Jesse forced his eyes to focus, wishing he had a pair of binoculars. He wouldn't be surprised if Alex had a pair in his bag of tricks. But he wasn't about to go check, mostly because his eyes were fixed like taxidermic marbles, and he simply couldn't take his gaze from the lumbering beast.

What the heck is it? Jesse flipped anxiously through his species rolodex. It simply didn't fit with any animal he'd ever seen, or any he'd ever read about, unless he considered Dr. Seuss cartoons, or the mythical push-me pull-me as possibilities.

Dammit, he huffed and thought, *if I could only get a better look.*

The animal was dark and hulking, walked on four tall legs, its torso inordinately long. The massive belly that hung from its core swayed with each halting step. Two hairy mounds mushroomed on either end like misplaced camel humps. The proportions were all wrong; the thing was way beyond odd, straight into the realm of the supernatural. It was too long to be a cow or moose, too big to be a deer or dog. And besides, this thing didn't even have a head; or at least one was not directly evident.

In its meandering, the creature had advanced a little closer, now less than two hundred yards away, nearing the tree-line Jesse had wanted to observe only moments ago. He felt no such impulse any longer.

The sun was about to peek from the horizon, he knew. The light of the new day was almost fully upon the region now...

And that new light revealed a great deal. Because in that instant, the identity of the bizarre creature suddenly became clear. As the news struck Jesse froze right down to his core, leaving him stiff and wholly iced, as if he'd been tied in a cryogenic straightjacket.

The beast was not a beast at all. Distance and lack of light had conspired to create an optical illusion.

Oh Shit! Oh Shit!

They were human, all three of them. Their unusual formation had created the illusion of a beast. The man in front and the man in back provided the legs of the illusion. A third person dangled dead on a long stick that ran from shoulder to shoulder, creating the illusion of a beast's belly as it swung in time with the cannibals' stride.

As horrifying as it all was, the next bit of information his panicked brain fed him was even more so. When he'd first noticed them, they'd been heading along a winding path perpendicular to the water station. He'd thought their direction was a random meandering. But now the trajectory of that path became clear.

And their path would lead them right where he stood.

The information, when it struck, was as distressing as it was unmistakable; next stop on the cannibal express— the water station.

The instant the information hit home he was moving. Quickly and quietly Jesse circled the room, waking the rest of the team. He whispered a terse Readers Digest version of the situation, urged them to gather their gear.

Martin was up in a shot, crept to the door. Peering around the edge, he looked out. The expression on his face when he turned told Jesse and the others everything.

They were still out there, and they were still coming.

Chapter 27

The team hid back in well room B. Martin had made the call. If the cannibals were to enter the well house, as it appeared that they would, their safety in room B would be the statistical equivalent to the roll of two dice. They could've holed up in any of the other eleven rooms, but Martin put his chips, as well as theirs, squarely on well room B. Nobody questioned the move.

Entering the room, they each secured a weapon, just in case the dice should come up craps, and battle became inevitable. Jesse grabbed a heavy-duty wrench from the tool box, Alex a large rusty screw driver, and Jennifer white-knuckle the nine-millimeter in both hands. Martin picked up the metal pipe he had used as a tool only hours earlier. Wrapped tightly in his hands, he found the weight comforting. If wielded with suitable rage the pipe could crack even the thickest of skulls. The pipe that had already proved its worth by helping them bring the flow of water might now help bring the flow of blood. More than any-thing, Martin hoped that it would not come to that.

By double timing it down the hall Martin had bought them time; he estimated they had a few minutes to play with. With any luck, the cannibals would pass by, head deeper into the building, at least that's what he hoped. They could decide to pop a squat in the foyer, he knew, carve and cook up their quarry right there. That would be almost as bad as if they decided to enter well room B, as that would leave the team effectively trapped.

And who knew how long that might be for.

Martin gathered them in tight. "Okay, first of all let's remember to keep our cool," he whispered. "We knew there was a chance we'd find ourselves in a situation like this. Let's do our best not to let things escalate out of control. If they do enter this room, we'll be ready."

He looked around, checking to be sure that everyone was sufficiently armed. "But I want all of our moves to be defensive. Only if we are physically threatened do we respond with force." He surveyed his team, making eye contact. He looked down at the nine millimeter clutched in Jennifer's hands, nodded. She returned the gesture. The ex-marine apparently understood.

"Let's hope that they go by us, down to one of the other rooms. I'm guessing that will be the case. The office down on the right was by far the only room close to habitable. It also has a small skylight. If they're familiar with this building at all, then that's probably where they'll head. I'm hoping we'll be okay in here. No way I'd wanna eat in this room with this god-awful smell," Martin explained, keeping them apprised of his logic.

"From there we'll slip out behind them, not sure exactly where we'll go after that. Chances are, we're gonna have to travel outside for a bit, maybe head back to the dock. It's still early but we'll stick to the shade as best we can until we find some cover."

They all nodded in rhythm, like a football team acknowledging a half-time speech.

The tension was as palpable as the heavy humid air that hung in the room, but the team was holding it together. Even staring straight down the barrel of a

potentially deadly situation, to a person they were remark-
ably calm, at least on the surface. Logically, they all had to
know that if things did get physical, the upper hand was
theirs. For one, they had the cannibals outnumbered two
to one. More importantly, they had a gun. They also had
the advantage of surprise. No matter how it went down,
the odds were stacked strongly in their favor.

On the flip side of the equation, however, they were
pitted against a rival that had survived insurmountable
odds. That alone assured that they were sturdy, among
the highest rank of Darwinian heavyweights, and a formi-
dable foe indeed.

And based on the obvious evidence, they were well
versed in killing; an act that nobody on the Pacifica team
could lay claim to. Not even Jennifer. Although trained to
kill, and put through the theoretical paces to do so during
basic training, that's the closest she'd ever actually gotten.
Target practice. The total sum of her military career con-
sisted of a six-month unit deployment stint in Okinawa,
followed by a two and a half year teaching gig; a veritable
country club commission as far as most members of the
few and the proud were concerned.

Actually pulling the trigger or crushing a skull with a
club was a *whole* other story. Especially for the domes-
ticated and civilized, and especially for a group that had
lived in such a peaceful communal setting for so long,
where violence had become passé over the years, as outdated as bloodletting or eight track tapes. And there was
simply no way to know who had that in them, who could
flip the switch and summon up that killer instinct, until
the essence of that moment materialized.

Martin continued his direction. "If we get stuck in
here for a while, then we'll just sit tight, ride it out till we
absolutely have to get outta here. If we have to, we can

even sleep here for a while. Whatever we have to do to avoid contact or conflict."

Martin paused. The team's silent nods prompted him to continue.

"We should still have a few minutes till they get here. They were moving pretty slow. I'm gonna sit by the door to see if they come down the hall."

"Sounds good," Jennifer agreed, speaking for the team.

"Wait a minute," Jesse suddenly said. "If these people are walking outside in the daytime that might mean that the UV levels are safe. I mean, doesn't that make sense?"

"Good point," Jennifer replied. "But keep in mind that it's still early. It could be that they only just made their kill and are hustling for cover; it might just be that they're cutting it close. Unfortunately, there's no way for us to know for sure." She shrugged her shoulders. "It's not like we can just walk up and ask 'em."

"That's for sure," Martin agreed. "But let's not even worry about that right now," he said to refocus the troops. "Remember, we'll be stopping at a few places later tonight to look for a UV meter, there has to be one around somewhere. At the very least I'm sure we could find the materials for Alex to put one together." He turned to Alex.

Alex nodded. *No problem.*

With that resolved, Martin moved over to the door. He put his ear against the metal panel, turned and put a finger to his lips. *Shhh.* He eased the door open a crack and a wedge of diffusing daylight pushed in.

Martin knelt by the side of the cracked door, but his view was eclipsed. Unless he leaned beyond the door jamb, there was no way to see down the hall to the entrance. But exposing a head to a bunch of head-hunters would be like dangling a raw t-bone in front of a starving lion, probably not the best idea. *Here kitty kitty.* Fortunately, he realized he could detect their approach without peeking out. Their stretching shadows would warn him of their movements.

He noticed dust dancing in the hallway from their recent rapid advance, smoldered like an exhaust trail yet to dissipate. He only hoped that the cannibals didn't take notice. Hopefully they'd be too busy with their quarry to make such a subtle observation.

Martin then eased the door shut. The rusty hinge squeaked and caused him to cringe. Although little more than a pin-drop, the sound squealed like a fire alarm. He turned and moved back to the team and whispered. "Okay, here they come. Flashlights off. I'm gonna keep my ear to the door and listen, maybe I can hear what's happening. Nobody makes a move till I give the word."

With his final order, he took up position behind the door.

The room went coffin quiet, reduced to basement blackness.

And then they waited.

Standing silently in utter darkness, the only noise was that of nervous respirations, and the occasional impact of a falling bead of sweat. Martin pressed his ear to the door, felt his heart thundering in his chest. The approaching footsteps grew louder by the second, the beat of his heart increasing in time.

And then they were there, the moment of truth was upon them, he knew. The rest of the team was unaware; there was no way to relay an update. All he could do is wait it out, brace for potential confrontation.

He held his breath, sweat beaded on his forehead. He was coiled like a panther, ready to spring into action, if action became inevitable.

But then the footsteps started to recede, he pressed his ear tight to the door to be sure. With one big sigh, he let out a lungful of air. They were definitely heading deeper into the building. It appeared that his guess had been correct. He felt the tension expel from his body like air hissing from a punctured Goodyear tire. He listened further; the footsteps were now out of earshot.

Whew! Crisis averted, or so it appeared.

Martin waited a moment, then turned on his flashlight. Using hand signals and exaggerated mouthing he signaled the good news. The team visibly unhinged, and tension drained as they throttled down from red alert.

Martin waved them over. "Let's get out of here right now, I don't want to stick around another second and chance getting trapped in here. They definitely went by, I'm pretty sure I heard a door down the hall open and close. I'm just gonna have a look before we move. If it's clear, I wanna move quickly down to the entrance. From there we'll take a second to figure out our next move."

Eager to move, they all nodded. Nobody had questioned any of Martin's decisions during the snap crisis. After all, he'd made all the right moves; any good leader would've played it the same. Winston Churchill, Steve Jobs, or even James T. Kirk would've managed the crisis no different. But that had been why he was selected. Martin was a natural leader, level headed and even keeled, well respected and respectful of those under his command. He had the innate ability to triage a situation on sight, and apply a ready-mix of wisdom and reason to effect resolution. The last ten minutes had been just another example of that skill.

Before Martin could open the door, Alex reached into his knapsack and removed the can of oil again. Without a word, he saturated the old corroded hinges, then returned it to his bag. Martin nodded and smiled, *good thinking*.

Martin then opened the heavy metal door with the care of a safe cracker.

Stepping into the hallway, Martin turned off his flashlight, held the door open and waved the others on. One by one, they followed. Then he too stepped out into the hall and eased the door closed behind him.

Martin stepped by and took the lead. He looked back and checked the team, then began to walk into the light, back toward the safety of the front entrance. But by the second step, they were stopped dead in their tracks by a piercing noise that rang out down the hall.

Chapter 28

The scream came as stark as the clatter of a metal fork in a garbage disposal. Frozen in their tracks, the team listened, ears cocked, unsure exactly what to do.

And then it came again, louder this time. The unmistakable sound of crying mixed with the grisly repeated howl of one word.

"No! No! No!"

The scream was loud and heart-wrenching, beelined to the foundation of arousal, uprooting emotions of fear, sympathy, and outright rage. Like a hungry baby crying, or a puppy yelping in pain, the reaction was universal, deeply penetrating. It was the kind of cry not easily ignored.

The fact that it was a woman crying only upped the implication ante a million-fold.

Martin was torn, momentarily paralyzed by the decision that fate had just tossed in his lap. His leadership ability would be put to the test once again. It was a potentially explosive moment, like he'd just stepped on a Claymore mine, the trigger lodged and ready to blow. If he made a move to go help, it would explode, shower them in the shrapnel of duty dereliction, the *no contact* rule that had been drilled into his skull would be breached. If he stood there and did nothing, he was safe.

But the woman down the hall would be human hamburger.

Only an instant passed, but it seemed like an eternity, the pressure in Martin's temples surged by diastolic degrees. The team waited, holding position, but clearly agitated. He knew he had to make the call, and make it soon. A split-second could be the difference in life or death. Could he really just sit there and allow this woman to be slain by cannibals?

No fucking way!

Screw their orders, he decided in that instant. This was *not* something he was going to have on his conscience. He could live with Winslow and company ripping him a new asshole back home, could live with any punishment they might mete out. But what he couldn't live with, *no way in hell*, was the obvious tragic outcome of inaction.

Besides that, and on an even more fundamental level, it was simply the right thing to do. Martin was about to give the order, about to break their number one directive of *no contact*. But he never got chance. That call was wrested from him the instant Alex started sprinting down the hall in the direction of the crying woman.

The rest of the team followed, instinct superseding command and consequence, a track team tandem in a race for a life. But there was no catching Alex. He was running down the dimly lit hall like Usain Bolt, a pocket-sized bleached blurred version of the one-time track star.

Another shriek blasted down the hall, louder this time.

Alex stopped at the last door on the right, panting, out of breath. There was no mistaking; the crying came from inside. It was the office, the room Martin had predicted they'd go to. The fact that the woman was still crying was actually good; it meant she was still alive.

Through bobbing heads, Martin could see that Alex had not entered. At least he was smart enough to wait for back up. But as Martin drew closer, he realized that Alex was not waiting, he was in fact struggling to open the door. It must be locked.

Before Martin arrived, and before he could even utter an order, the rest of the team closed on the scene. And without slowing down, Jesse hit the door like an NFL linebacker, apparently on the same page as Alex. The door gave way and caved with the sound of a dump truck impact, the door jamb splintering. All the lube in the world would not have silenced the rusty squeal the hinges made as the door swung inward. The door crashed against the cement wall with a grinding thunderclap.

Alex and Jesse were first into the room, weapons in hand, screw driver and pipe-wrench at the ready, both men hyper-alert, ready to bludgeon, punch, or drop-kick, whoever or whatever stood in the way of saving the sobbing woman. Jennifer rushed in next, panting and pumped for a fight, the nine-millimeter firm in her grip. Martin was last on the scene, only a half step behind.

Alex and Jesse stopped cold and lowered their weapons, recognizing immediately their miscalculation. A second later, Jennifer did the same.

Only a step into the room Martin froze and lowered the lead pipe he had fisted as he too realized the mistake they made in judgment.

Chapter 29

The small terrestrial family reeled and looked around uneasily as they searched for solution or escape. But neither was possible, the small concrete room penning them like a medieval dungeon. Jesse immediately lowered his weapon, as did the rest of the team. He stepped forward to try and soften the impact of what he now realized to be a hostile intrusion on their part.

"We're sorry." Jesse leaned and put down his weapon, the wrench clanked sharply against the concrete slab. The noise shot through the room like a clap of thunder during a funeral. He held his hands out to the side, did his best to assume a non-threatening posture. "We mean you no harm. We made a mistake." He patted his chest. "We are friendly," he assured them, speaking in the most rudimentary sentences, uncertain if they even understood English.

The two males they'd suspected of cannibalism had backed against the wall in the corner, both bristling with panic. They shielded a young girl behind them. The woman they'd heard crying remained unmoved. She was down on her knees, arched over the corpse the two men had carried in, still weeping. The hysteria was not that of a woman in danger, but that of a woman in mourning. Underneath the insanity of the moment the fact that there were two other individuals in a room they'd already searched had Jesse more than a little perplexed.

Jennifer stepped forward, joining Jesse in the peace offering. "We are so sorry. Please, please forgive us," she implored. "We mean you no harm."

"Why then do you break into our home," one of the males suddenly said. Even through the rattle of a Latin accent, his suspicion was evident. "And who are you?"

"We are from inland a ways," Martin quickly replied, stepping in before anyone else got chance. "We are in this area because we are searching for supplies."

Jesse realized why Martin jumped in, understood his concern. Even though these people appeared to be no threat, there was no point in disclosing too much. It was a good response, the perfect half truth. Jesse then looked at Martin to see if he was going to continue. When he didn't immediately do so, he took the reins.

"We thought you were someone else," Jesse said delicately. "The way you were carrying that body, we thought you were cannibals. And then when we heard the woman crying we thought…well, we just thought the worst and we over reacted, I guess. I'm very sorry. Please forgive our intrusion."

"We are not cannibals," said the same adult male shaking his head. Although still nervous, he seemed to believe Jesse's explanation. He then lowered his gaze and pointed to the corpse. "This is my son. We found him dead. We brought him back for a ceremony, and for his mother to see before we bury him."

Jesse looked down at the dead boy, he was a teenager. Even with the revisions brought about by death, the resemblance between corpse and kin was nearly spot on. Their faces all had a unique circular shape, even a generation removed the likeness was obvious. Short with dark heavy features and skin the color of earth, the family bloodline appeared to be somewhere between Mexican and ancient Mayan.

"I'm sorry," Jesse said in a consoling tone. "We all are." He spread his arms preacher-like to include his crew-mates. The crew nodded, agreeing.

"Yes," Jennifer said, "and we are sorry for your loss." She took a step closer. "Is there anything we can do to help you?"

"No," snapped the same adult male. "We can take care of ourselves. We are just fine." His manner and tone were still decidedly tuned to suspicious.

Jesse felt sorry for the small family, not only because they just lost one of their own, but by the vast poverty they were forced to live in. The fact that they were still alive was remarkable in itself, nobody could deny that, but they were a far cry from *just fine*. Not only were they emaciated and in poor health, their clothes were rags, Salvation Army throw-aways. The contrast between the two groups was stark. To the eye of an alien they'd appear to be members of different species entirely. The team had done all they could by wearing tattered clothes to try and appear indigenous. Turns out, they *did not* fit in at all. Mimicking this level of hardship was simply impossible; no way to replicate the details of disease, or simulate the cumulative wear and tear brought on by genuine animal survival.

The little girl peered cautiously from the shield of the man's thigh. Maybe eight years old, she was scruffy and thin; a sweet little stick figure with skin the color of a fawn, her brown hair windblown and wild. Her skin was dirt stained, although surprisingly free of marks that couldn't be removed with a little soap and water. The same could not be said for the two adult males. Scars and scabs graced their exposed skin like a living diary, a head to toe totem detailing a lifetime of struggle in keloid skin hieroglyphics. The little girl wore a tattered plaid dress that hung loosely from her frame, perhaps the correct size if she had and body mass to speak of. She did not have the luxury of shoes.

The quick view of the girl was truly a pitiful image, a UNICEF poster child if ever there was one. It was like a late night TV profile broadcast in the reality of the day; the image of a small sick and starving child, along with an appropriately strained celluloid star, trying to convince you to make a donation to some distant world saving charity. The only thing missing were the buzzing flies and grossly distended abdomen.

"Are you sure there isn't something we can do to help?" Jesse pressed, still adjusting to the extreme emotional shift. "Can we offer you some food?" In the space of a minute he went from the apex of anger to the abyss of absolute heartache, the effect of adrenalated fatigue only adding to the strain.

"As I said, we are fine. We do not need *your* help," the same man insisted, as he pushed the small girl back behind him. He was clearly still apprehensive, and a distinct air of pride echoed in his tone. He was not about to accept charity.

It seemed there was nothing they could say to put the frightened family at ease. On some level Jesse understood, extreme apprehension was likely an important survival trait in this world, and may well be the reason these people were even around. Maybe it'd be best if they just turned around and left. On paper, this was only a distraction to their mission. Turning around and leaving was technically the best move. He was certain that it'd be exactly what Winslow and the board would want them to do. After all, *no contact at any cost*, was the mantra they'd been sent off with. And he could hear the directive chime through his mind now, sufficiently brainwashed as he was.

But he couldn't just turn around and leave, couldn't just turn his back on these people. And he was pretty sure none of the others wanted to either, especially after seeing the little girl. He could see the fear and wonder in her blinking brown eyes as she'd momentarily leaned into view. The image made Jesse's heart melt like a glacier in the Gobi.

A quick solution came to Jesse. With words ineffective, why not try the louder voice of action. He stepped behind Jennifer and lifted the handgun from her belt. He checked the safety as he walked toward the family, his movements measured, careful to keep the gun barrel pointing down. By now it was clear which one was their leader. Jesse slowly offered him the weapon.

He heard anxious shuffling behind him, Martin or Jennifer, he guessed—someone was nervous. Jesse was too, but short of a two-week peace talk there was no other way to gain their trust. And without trust, there was simply no way to move on to helping the small tribe. Jesse knew the move was drastic, but he also knew that if détente were to be had, this would secure it quickly.

The man reached tentatively and took the weapon, accepting the olive branch. He eyed the gun for a moment then pushed the clip release to allow the magazine to fall into his hand. He looked at the clip, and his eyes grew wide as he realized that it was in fact loaded. In the same instant his posture shifted, his shoulders slackened. Exhaling plainly, he slapped the clip back home, continuing to inspect the gun, seemingly lost in thought.

A sudden smack of panic hit Jesse like a ball-peen hammer. His nerves started twittering, angst metastasizing into instant migraine. Beneath a calm game-face, he was wired like a steel trap, ready for anything as he tracked the man's every move. If the gun started to raise even a fraction, he'd be on top of him before the barrel could be brought to level. Jesse held his breath, hoping he hadn't made another mistake in judgment.

Chapter 30

As if to sense the apprehension in the room, the man holding the gun looked up and loosened. A tiny smile blossomed from his weathered features, bringing calm to his expression. Careful to keep the gun barrel down he then handed the weapon back to Jesse.

"I guess you are who you say you are," he said, nodding slowly.

Jesse sighed in relief, could feel the others relax behind him. He reached out and took back the gun. The man kept his hand extended. Jesse shook hands with the terrestrial man. And although his hand was much smaller than Jesse's, his bony grip was every bit as strong.

"My name is Santos," the man offered. The ease had even found its way to his voice, now much softer, although still fettered with the speed-bump of a second tongue. "This is my wife, Sofia." He pointed to the kneeling woman. The woman looked up, nodded once, but didn't speak, distraught as she was. "This is my brother-in-law Armand, and this is my daughter Nellie," he said as the young child again peeked out. He cradled her head with his hand, she hugged his thigh. This time the child smiled as she leaned out from behind her father's physical shield. It was a precious little smile, warm and innocent, oozing with charm.

"And this—" Santos stammered, extended a palm toward the corpse. "This was Sebastian, my son." Santos gazed down at the dead boy, agony and anger unhidden, his voice laced with the pain of the greatest loss.

Jesse again offered profuse condolences, then went on to introduce Team Pacifica. The two groups shared salutations and conversations. The team again offered food, insisting this time. No longer apprehensive, the clan accepted. Only Sofia declined as she continued to sit vigil over her fallen son.

Tired as they were, Team Pacifica did not allow their fatigue to impede the impromptu powwow. With the *no contact* rule already breached, making the best of the situation only made sense. There might be information to be gathered; the terrestrials had to have knowledge of the local goings on.

Jesse's curiosity had kicked into overdrive by this point; questions needled his brain like tiny inquisitive beetles. From the status of the sun, to the presence of others in the area, and about every topic in between, he was craving answers. He worked to get Santos alone to question him. He knew he had to be careful as he tread. Asking too many obvious questions could arouse suspicion. Breaking the no contact rule was one thing, but advertising the existence of Pacifica was a whole other story. As bad as he felt for the small clan, they couldn't take them home. Their philanthropy would have to be limited to whatever they could do while on site.

Sitting on old milk crates, he finally had Santos alone. Jennifer sat next to Sofia, a hand draped over her shoulder as she consoled the grieving woman. Martin helped Armand as he worked to repair the door damaged during the breach. Alex dug eagerly through his knapsack, giving whatever food he could find to the little girl.

With everyone seemingly occupied, the perfect opportunity had arrived. So Jesse tuned his voice to the frequency of tact and quietly asked the question that bothered him most. "I was wondering Santos, how did the boy die?"

Santos hesitated, glanced back at his dead son. Across the room, Sofia leaned to the side and made eye contact. As quietly as Jesse had spoken, she somehow overheard him. It was almost as if she'd been anticipating the question.

"El Cucuy!" she shouted, startling everyone. Her voice was raw, her Latin accent thick on her tongue. Aside from mumbling a few prayers, they were the first words Jesse had heard her say out loud. "El Cucuy!" she repeated angrily.

Conversation ceased in all corners of the room. The spot light swung upon the burgeoning drama the question had incited.

Santos shifted his body weight, hesitant. He stared at his wife, his eyes filled with molten emotion. He nodded. "Yes," he said, "the boy was killed by el Cucuy." He looked nervously to the side.

For the first time Jesse got the impression Santos was not being totally forthcoming, but he couldn't be certain. Maybe the man was off balance. Having to discuss the death of a child could certainly have that effect.

Jesse stared blankly, uncertain how to follow up. Fresh tears shined in Santos's eyes. Jesse almost wished he hadn't asked the question, but he had to. The information was vital to their safety and the success of the mission. He looked to Martin and the others for cues, was greeted with arching eyebrows and uncertain shrugs. No help there. Jesse then turned back to Santos and pressed.

"El Cucuy? We are not familiar with this person. Is this someone we should be aware of? Do we need to be careful?"

Santos stared at Jesse for a moment, eyeing him with the same curiosity he might if Jesse were to have two heads. "El Cucuy is not a person," he explained, the tense tone from earlier returning to his voice. "El Cucuy is a creature, more animal than human..."

"Hold on a sec," Jesse said, interrupting Santos, the pretense of tact gone from his tone. "You mean to tell me there's a creature of some type living in this area? Something part human and part animal?"

Santos nodded.

Jesse turned to look at the rest of the crew. From face to face they all looked as stunned as he felt, slack jawed and pie eyed. He then noticed Armand nodding in the corner, corroborating pantomime.

The implications set in as Team Pacifica pondered in silence.

Alex finally broke the spell. "I always thought that el Cucuy was a myth among the Latin community, like the boogie man or something?"

"That is true," Santos agreed. "It's myth, the boogie man as you say. But in this case, it's real. When we first found out we were shocked." Santos looked from eye to eye around the room, as if about to tell a story around a campfire. "We first noticed him a while back. He lives mostly in the city. Usually he is easy to avoid, and mostly harmless to us. Sebastian must have made a mistake and wandered into its territory. I have never got a good look at him, but Armand did once." He glanced over at his brother-in-law and Armand nodded again. "From the description, we named it el Cucuy. It just seemed to fit. Everybody around here now calls it el Cucuy."

"Everybody?" Jesse questioned. With the inroad paved, he figured he might as well ride out the line of inquiry. "Are there still many people in this area? Have you heard anything about a safe zone up the coast known as Cascadia?"

"I guess you really aren't from around here," Santos said, his face furrowing with questioning creases.

"We are from the woods, inland," Jesse insisted quickly, reaffirming Martin's earlier exaggeration.

"Sure, there are people living around here. I don't know if it's many. We never go to other areas so I cannot compare. But there are people, some here, some there. I heard rumors of Cascadia, but no more than that. If it's real, I do not know.

"Does anyone else live up here?" Jesse questioned, pointing down, indicating the well house.

"No." Santos shook his head. "We are the only ones in this area. Many people have moved away from this area—those that are left live in the outer parts of the city. Old concrete buildings and basements make for the best places."

"What about cannibalism? Is it still a problem?" Jesse asked. This was an important question. The answer would go a long way to setting the tempo for the rest of the mission. He was also curious for his own reasons. It might influence his travel decisions after the others left. Although to his surprise, the idea of staying behind continued to lose luster. Perhaps he suffered a touch of the old proverb—*the-seaweed-is-always-greener on the other side.*

"It no longer really happens around here," Santos said. "The people who did it got sick with shakes and crazies. Most died."

"Mad cow," Alex offered from across the room. "The sickness has probably had a self limiting effect."

"Yes…the mad cow." Santos nodded. "We have our problems, but cannibalism is not one of them. Last time I heard of this was many years ago."

Jesse felt his stress release by degrees. The el Cucuy mystery aside, this was good news.

"Thank god," Jennifer announced. "Listen, Jesse, don't you think it's time we let these people get some rest? I mean, enough with the inquisition already." She looked to Martin for support. Martin nodded his agreement.

"You're right," Jesse conceded. Perhaps he had let his own interests run away a bit. He should be more sensitive, he realized. After all, they were the ones who'd just lost a family member. Giving them some space to deal with that was the right thing to do. But he had one more question, one that could possible confirm a suspicion.

"Sorry, Santos," he said. "I just wanted to gather as much information as possible before we head out and search for supplies later tonight. Just want us to be as safe as possible." He paused, pondered. "Is it okay to ask one more thing?"

Santos nodded *no problem*.

"This el Cucuy creature," Jesse said tactfully. "How did it kill Sebastian?"

Santos sighed, again seemed nervous. "The creature is very powerful," he finally replied. "It is very strong. It can kill with its bare hands. I suspect that was the case here." Santos hung his head.

Jesse laid a hand on the humble man's shoulder. "I'm sorry, my friend. I'm sorry I had to ask that. I just wanted to know what to be ready for when we're out later tonight. I hope you understand."

Santos nodded, then looked up, his eyes charged with emotion. "I understand. No problem." Following a sigh his mood appeared to lift. "What kind of supplies do you need?"

"Just some general purpose stuff," Jesse said. "Things we can't get where we live. Stuff you can't find in the woods where we live." He looked over at Martin and nodded. "Let me see the list."

Martin reached into his pocket and produced the small map with the scribbled list of supplies. He walked over and handed it to Jesse, and Jesse showed it to Santos. Santos scanned the paper, pushed it to arm's length.

"You should be able to find most of this stuff," he said, nodding. "But you are better off looking over here. " He tapped a spot on the map. "There is an area not far from here that is less damaged than others. And it's safer too." Santos pointed toward the east, jabbing the air. Then he paused, seemed absorbed in thought. "And since you are not familiar with this area, I will guide you."

"We couldn't ask you to do that," Martin said, stepping in. "We'll be able to figure it out. Alex used to live around here, he can show us around."

"Let me help," Santos insisted. "It is the least we can do to thank you for the food you have shared. Besides, I know this area better than anyone. And I am concerned that you will find trouble without my help." Santos smiled, shrugged his shoulders. "What do you think?"

Jesse looked to Martin, as did the rest of the team.

"Okay," Martin finally conceded. "If you're sure you don't mind, then we accept your offer. It will be a great help to us. Thank you."

Jesse leaned in and grabbed Santos's hand, shook it and smiled. "Thank you, Santos, we really appreciate this."

"No problem."

Jesse started to feel a real connection beginning to develop with Santos. It made him feel better knowing he had someone local around he trusted. For all he knew, they might wind up being neighbors down the road.

"If we are going to be out all night tonight we should be thinking about getting some sleep," Jennifer said, looking to Martin again.

"True." Martin turned to Santos. "We were gonna sleep out in the entrance of the building. Do you think we'll be safe there?"

Santos hesitated. "It is best if we all sleep in this room," he said. "We usually sleep up in the ceiling, but there will not be enough room for all of us up there. We have extra blankets we can share."

Santos nodded to his brother-in-law. Armand snapped into action and slid an old desk into the far corner of the room. With feline agility he leapt on the desk and scampered up the wall, disappearing into a void in the ceiling.

Jesse and the rest of the team watched in amazement. That explained the presence of the two females in the room that had already been searched. They must have been hiding somewhere up in the ceiling cavity all along.

Blankets and pillows and towels began to spill from the gap in the ceiling like a Bed, Bath and Beyond deluge. Santos collected the bedding as it fell, passing it around. It didn't take long for everyone to find floor space. It'd been over twenty-four hours since the team had slept a full night, and a near lifetime of adventure had been crammed into that time frame. Jesse found that the blanket and small pillow, although dirty and dank, went a long way to foster relaxation. From the second he laid back slumber hummed through his body, overwhelming his typical insomnia.

Shifting to find comfort on the floor, Jesse heard Santos instruct Armand to stand guard at the main entrance. Alex volunteered to go with him. Martin told Alex to return in two hours and wake him, then instructed the rest of the team to do two hour shifts throughout the day.

Jesse glanced over at the corpse, still wondering why Santos had lied. Jesse had known from the minute he saw the body that the boy had drowned. Living where they did, he'd seen his share of drowning victims. The corpse had the typical wrinkled skin and bloating associated with this type of demise. And it wasn't likely an accident. The ligature marks around the boy's neck—deep and purple with bruising—had a distinctly different texture to the post-mortem lines around his ankles and wrists from being lashed to the carrying stick. The marks around the neck had likely been made prior to death.

The inconsistency didn't worry Jesse much, or slow his descent into dreamland, because his gut told him that Santos had made up the story for valid reason. He suspected the deception had something to do with Sofia. He'd be sure to question Santos later, when they were alone, and after he got some sleep. A hundred other questions still elbowed to be heard, and his mind continued reeling them off until sleep came and ended the parade.

Chapter 31

Jesse awoke from a deep dreamless sleep. An ashen shaft of light fell from the skylight above, telling him that nighttime was on final approach. The skylight tunnel was several feet long, and based on calculations made during their trek up the hillside; he could tell that the room was entirely underground.

Stretching, he realized that he'd slept surprisingly well. An aura of security permeated the small concrete room, and Jesse wondered if perhaps that wasn't the reason; although you couldn't get any more sheltered than Pacifica, and sleep had not always been such a positive endeavor there.

Everyone else was still asleep, the subtle wheeze of zee's echoed softly throughout the small concrete room. His three colleagues were lined in a tight row against the back wall, the better to share body heat and bedding. Sofia and Nellie were cocooned in old blankets in the corner. Armand slept nearby, wrapped only in a sheet of thin cardboard, his head propped on a worn truck tire, the lack of thread count and appropriate pillow ticking seemed to impede his ability to sleep not in the least. Panning further, Jesse realized that Santos was missing, as was the body of his dead son. Santos must be out front on guard duty, he thought.

But what had happened to the body?

Careful not to wake anyone, Jesse got up and moved to the door, letting the others sleep on. There was no hurry to start the final stage of their mission; they had all night. And fully charged batteries would be a decided asset to that effort.

He stepped out of the room and eased the door shut. He was surprised how well it operated given the damage done during their forced entry. *Very impressive,* he thought, kudos to Armand on the repairs. Jesse had watched him fix it with some superficial scraps and a few simple tools.

Apparently they were blessed with a Tool Troll of their own.

He hustled down the hall toward the entranceway, hoping to get the opportunity to have that private conversation with Santos, allowing him to tie up the loose ends from their earlier conversation. But as he reached the front entrance, he found no immediate sign of Santos. The sun had just set; the shadows of twilight swelling through the cool blue hemisphere. Jesse stepped outside, sucked a lungful of thin autumn air, found it all at once bracing and refreshing, like snorting a line of menthol smelling salts. Still not fully adjusted to being back on a roofless planet, he almost stumbled, still feeling a bit like a fish out of water. Once again he was struck by the boundless vista that allowed his vision to stretch for light years unfettered. Like viewing the Aurora Borealis or staring into the eyes of a beautiful woman; it was all still exhilarating, still soul stirring, an experience not likely to get old anytime soon.

A sharp noise, like the chirp of a struck match, suddenly echoed from the hillside below, and he zeroed in on it. About forty yards down along the rocky knoll, a man stood knee deep in the earth, digging. The man lifted and mopped his brow: it was Santos. On the ground beside him was a thick rolled blanket. *Sebastian.*

Geez! Jesse breathed. *What the hell!*

He quickly trotted down the hillside. "Santos." He uttered as he approached. Santos flinched, focused as he was on his undertaking. He lifted and turned. He'd already dug the perimeter of the grave. But the hole was not yet deep enough to serve its purpose. Santos wiped sweat from his face with a dirty rag. "How ya doing." He nodded, a somber undertone evident despite his effort at casual.

"Why didn't you ask one of us to help with this?" Jesse pressed. But as the question left his mouth, the answer materialized from within before it was spoken.

Santos was a proud man.

And that couldn't be any more evident when he finally replied. "This is my responsibility." Santos dropped his gaze. "And I didn't want to wake anyone up."

Jesse nodded. To some degree he understood.

"When I saw my wife had actually fallen asleep this afternoon, I took the chance to get him in the ground," Santos added.

Jesse realized that Santos must've carried or dragged the body the whole way by himself, out of the room, through the hallway, and down the hillside. Despite his diminutive stature, this was a strong man. And as Jesse addressed him now, he realized that his mental toughness had to be every bit as stout as his physical.

"Well, I'm up now," Jesse announced. "And I've got plenty of energy. Lemme take over for a bit. Sit down, take a load off." Jesse reached for the shovel. Santos hesitated, leaned it from his grasp. But when Jesse didn't bend, Santos begrudgingly relinquished the old tool, and then took a seat on a small outcrop off to the side of the hole.

Jesse jumped on the shovel, driving the blade into the hard pack, levering his body weight against the handle to maximize yield. Although mostly clay and rock, with sufficient effort, the ground surrendered. As somber a task as it was, the work itself wasn't a problem. The physical exertion actually felt good. Jesse enjoyed the way his heart pumped and his muscles responded, even the letting of sweat he found oddly delightful. It seemed like he was more alive than he'd been in years. The fact that he was dealing so closely with death may have had the effect of exaggerating the moment, making him feel more alive by contrast of fate. He found himself appreciating the privilege of his own continued existence, the fact that he was still standing a vertical six feet above ground instead of a flat fathom below. Breathing unspoiled air and his new found freedom no doubt added to the peculiar sense of grieving zen.

As Jesse wedged free a rock, Santos suddenly appeared to remove it by hand, his respite lasting all of a few heartbeats. Jesse looked at him, smiled, thought to tell him to sit back down, but realized that it'd do no good. This guy's motor had only one speed, and that was wide-open.

Each time Jesse excavated a rock, Santos was down on his hands and knees, pulling it out and tossing it into the pile on the side. They fell into a productive rhythm, the hole grew rapidly. At this rate they'd be to depth before the full ink of night winked across the sky.

Some issues still bothered Jesse, and they tingled like heat rash on his curiosity.

He tossed a shovelful of earth, stood and sighed, felt rivulets of sweat streak down his face. "Listen, Santos, I know there has to be a good reason you told us that the boy was killed by this creature, but I know that it's not true, at least not the way you explained it." He kept his tone carefully measured, not wanting to sound accusatory or insensitive.

Santos tossed a rock from the hole and looked up. Jesse half expected him to tell him to *fuck off*, or try to justify the lie. But he did neither. "You are right." He conceded without further prodding. "Armand and I figured that blaming el Cucuy would make it easier for Sofia to deal with. And we figured it would be believable."

Jesse returned a puzzled look, it prompted Santos to elaborate.

"Chances are, the reason he died was because he wouldn't give away the location of his mother and sister. I didn't think it would be good for them to know that. My wife might have trouble dealing with it. To know that her son died to save her life, that would be rough. As it is, I am not so sure how she will handle this whole thing." Santos glanced at the swaddled remains of his lost flesh and blood. "She and Sebastian were close."

"I'm not following." Jesse said, pulling up and leaning on the shovel.

"That's right, I keep forgetting. You are not from around here," Santos said with a hint of sarcasm. Jesse found the remark a little curious, but didn't pursue it. At the moment he had bigger fish to fry, a whole oceanful in fact.

"So it wasn't this el Cucuy that did it?" Jesse asked. First things first, he told himself, itemizing the issues. One fish at a time.

Santos shook his head. *Nope.*

"Does this creature even exist?" He then asked.

"Oh yeah," Santos nodded. "He's real; we didn't make that part up. But I don't think he's really a threat to us. From what we can tell, the creature as you call it might be a friend in a weird way."

"Friendly?" Jesse said, struck once again by a stab of surprise. This was all starting to get a little crazy. The strange tale of a killer creature was hard enough to swallow, now all the sudden it was a benevolent beast—*Shrek in the flesh*. At this point, he wasn't sure what to believe. The tale was heading down a whole new rabbit hole, a path he never anticipated. Realizing he had stopped digging, he returned to the task. In another twenty minutes it'd be fully dark, he knew.

"Did you ever hear the expression; the enemy of my enemy is my friend?" Santos asked.

"I guess." Jesse said, nodding, not certain he ever had. He jumped on the shovel, punched the head deep and tossed another load of earth to the side. Another foot or so and they'd be there.

"Well, that is the case here, I suppose. El Cucuy escaped from Eezak's place several years back, and Eezak is the same person that killed my son. Armand came face to face with el Cucuy once, and it did not hurt him. He said it sniffed him and made funny noises as if it was trying to talk, but then it just turned and headed off. He said it could have easily killed him if it wanted. It's as fast as a horse and just as strong. Just to be safe we still try and stay away."

Jesse's jaw dropped, was about to speak, but Santos continued before he could.

"And we know that it is capable of killing, we have heard stories of it taking Eezak's men down on more than one occasion." Santos seemed to be pleased as he made mention of Eezak's men being killed.

"Eezak, Eezak, who the heck is this guy?"

Santos didn't immediately answer.   Instead he swung and pointed southeast. "Dr. Eezak. He lives there. Everybody around here knows this."

Jesse turned, realized he was pointing toward the heart of the stillborn city, right at a cluster of buildings to the south, the area directly below the low lying cloud he'd noticed earlier. The cloud was still there, staining the gunmetal sky with billowing blight. And at that moment he realized his earlier meteorological assessment had been all wrong, the cloud was not the by-product of atmospheric physiology, but in fact man made. He could see the outline of mushrooming pollution; trace it back to its point of origin, where several tall smoke stacks belched dark smog into the heavens. Somehow the building was functional. It was difficult to believe, the notion impacted hard, and for no clear reason sent tendrils of dread burrowing into his mind, felt like icy worms eating at his brain.

"Dr. Eezak, Dr. Eezak." Jesse repeated aloud, cross-referencing it against his neural RAM, "Dr. Eezak." There was something to it...

And then it hit him with the suddenness of a Tazer gun. And a roundhouse of revelation rode in with the all those amps. "Dr. Leezak!" He said aloud. "You mean Dr. Harris Leezak!"

"Yes," Santos agreed. "This is what I said. Dr. Leezak."

It wasn't exactly what he'd said, but it hardly mattered. Whether it was his accent, or the fact that the name may have been denatured over time, like words do in a game of telephone, it just didn't matter. The information was profound, difficult to digest, added innumerable consequences to the mystery of this new world.

His mind began splicing facts, making connections based on conjecture and strife. And before the new information fully set, his thoughts were invaded by an improvised image of el Cucuy. Using dredged up memories of the unusual aquatic creatures he'd seen on old footage back in Pacifica, his mind added mass and spindly limbs, his imagination did the rest, supplying the final touch of exaggerated animation. The result was a twenty-first century Frankenstein running roughshod through his mindscape.

Geez, Jesse breathed, the image bringing him a chill. He was now certain that there *was* something out there. The creature was the real deal; a living-breathing, lab conjured ogre of unknown species or motive. Effectively eliminating Bigfoot, as well as all the other mythical cryptids he had lined up to explain away what he'd hoped to only be fable.

Jesse did his best to gather himself, unaware that he'd been digging like a mole on Meth for the last few minutes. Santos had stopped tossing rocks, watched from above as Jesse continued digging deeper.

"Then it *was* Leezak who killed your son?" Jesse asked as he finally throttled down. Using a palm he squeegeed sweat from his forehead.

The hole was now plenty deep.

"Yes," Santos nodded and pointed off toward the bay. "We found him tied to the pier. The tide came in and he drowned. Sebastian did not give up the information he wanted, so he killed him." Santos slammed his fist into his palm. "He should have been more careful." The remark seemed less directed to Jesse as his dead son.

"Is Leezak gonna be a problem tonight?" Jesse asked. "He's clearly dangerous. Are we gonna have to worry about him? This really seems to change the equation."

"As long as we are careful, there should not be problems. And I will be guiding you. I know this area, and how to get around." Santos spoke with confidence. "And besides, it's not often he works at night."

It took an instant for the inference to impact, but when it did, Jesse nearly jumped out of his skin. "Are you saying he operates during the day!"

Santos nodded casually, as if he were responding the most mundane of questions. "Mostly," he replied.

"That's great news!" Jesse said, louder than he probably should have. Forgetting for a moment that they were about to put a young man's body in the ground.

But Santos didn't get angry. Instead he leveled a curious gaze, tilted his head. Dark as it had gotten, enough light lingered for Jesse to see the expression. The literal interpretation of which was; *are you fucking kidding me?*

"The sun," Jesse offered, struggled for words, trying to explain. "It's safe outside. I mean…they work outside, so it must be safe." As the words hit air, he realized that what he was saying must sound very odd. This was information he *should* know. Unless of course he lived on another planet, or at the center of the earth, *or at the bottom of the ocean! Oh well*, he thought to himself, it was too late now. No way to cover the blunder. Hopefully Santos had missed the implications.

But that did *not* appear to be the case. Again his expression betrayed his inner thoughts—*are you crazy*—the current connotation. "As far as I know, it is not safe outside in the daytime," Santos explained, making an obvious effort to remain patient and polite. "Leezak's men use some kind of protective coating that allows them to stay outside during the day, even when the sun is shining. They can move freely while everyone else has to stick to the shade. It gives them great advantage. It makes day even more dangerous than night."

Jesse sighed, his rosy assumption had imploded, dying off as quickly as it had evolved. The earth had evidently *not* healed as he'd hoped.

Santos had been gracious beyond call, answering his questions. All the while his son lay there, cold and still, rolled up in an old blanket like a cadaverous crepe. But it was time to shut it down, his turn to return the favor. There were a million questions still to be asked, but they'd have to wait. It was time to get the body in the earth.

The waiting worms couldn't agree more.

Jesse climbed out of the hole, joining Santos on the brim. He noticed Alex and Martin exiting the water station on the hillside above. He held up a hand, waving them off. The two men stopped in their tracks, seemed to understand the situation. Putting the boy in the ground was going to be an emotional event, and Jesse didn't think a crowd would be any advantage.

Jesse leaned and grabbed one side of the cloth coffin, Santos the other. Jesse lifted and started to slowly slide the corpse toward the fresh dug grave. On his end, Santos did the same. The old blanket stretched and tore, a whiff of decomposition hit Jesse like a fermented fist. The bacteria and yeasts had been busy little beavers. The smell was hideous, foul enough to trigger Jesse's gag reflex. But they were almost there, he could make it. No way was he heaving, even if it meant swallowing it back down.

Both men struggled with the weight as they held the shrouded body over the hole. Jesse then nodded. "Okay, on the count of three, we'll let go together." He managed through clenched teeth, the corpse now as low as their trembling arms would allow.

"Okay," Santos agreed, likewise straining.

Jesse counted and together they released their grip. The body fell, hitting the hard pan with a thud and a hiss of escaping gas. Santos dropped to his knees beside the grave. For an instant Jesse thought he was exhausted. But then he realized it was sheer emotion, the sudden rush of anguish racing in to fill the inevitable vacuum of loss. Tears leaked from the man's eyes, some falling to the soil like tiny emotional comets, leaving a trail of mini impact craters to document his pain. Santos then put his hands together and began to pray, muttering an impromptu prayer in gibberish understood only by Santos and God himself.

Jesse stepped behind him; put his hand on his shoulder, attempting to comfort the terrestrial man. Still operating on instinct, he gave him a moment, but then felt it best to get his new friend some distance from the situation, before the gravity of grief sucked him into a depressive nose dive too steep to pull out of. Best bet, Jesse decided, get him back with his family.

"Let me finish this, Santos." He signaled Alex to come down. "You go inside for a while, spend some time with your wife and daughter. Maybe get a little rest. You're gonna need it if you still insist on guiding us later."

Santos didn't move, like a human headstone he remained kneeling at the side of the open grave. Tactfully, Jesse then reached down and helped him to his feet. "Let's go Santos, I've got this. Alex will walk you back inside. Later you can come out and pay your last respects. I'll have everything taken care of by then."

Santos nodded. "Okay. You're right."

Alex arrived and, sensing his role, slipped a supportive arm around the deflated man.

Santos then lifted his head and found Jesse's eyes. "Make sure you use all the rocks, put them on top so the animals can't dig him up."

Geez, Jesse mused, feeling the pound of naked compassion behind his sternum. "I'll take care of it, don't worry," he assured Santos, then turned to Alex. "Take him inside for a while. Try and get some food in him. I'll finish up here and be inside in a bit. And tell everyone there's a few things we gotta discuss before we head out later."

Alex nodded and guided Santos away, leading him back up the hill toward the water station, leaving Jesse alone by the grave.

Amid the crushing anxiety, Jesse felt an inkling of optimism. Santos had mentioned animals. Advanced life forms, that was at least *some* good news.

Jesse waited till they were inside, then turned and began the work of sealing the soil sarcophagus forever. He'd have the burial complete in no time, the dirt was loose and gravity was now in his favor. And he'd make sure the earthen tomb was exactly as Santos would want it; the cairn on top would protect and provide a lasting marker for future payments of homage.

Jesse had never met the boy, yet he was one person he knew he'd never forget.

Chapter 32

"Need any help with that?" Martin asked, arriving graveside.

"I got this," Jesse replied tersely, not looking up from his work.

Knowing his friend as well as he did, the curt response told Martin two things. One: he really didn't want help—this *was not* a case of saying one thing while actually meaning another. And secondly: he was in no mood to talk right now. Martin could see that Jesse was in a zone, focused like a Buddhist monk in chant, as he obsessively shoveled dirt back into earth.

So Martin heeded the cues and said no more. He took a seat on the outcrop where Santos had sat only moments ago, and watched quietly as his friend toiled amid the advancing nocturnal chill.

As he waited he glanced around. An anvil shaped cloud filled the sky above the city, while more elegant designs dappled the skies over the sea. The clouds reflected moonlight, giving texture and breadth to the night. A stand of pines huddled a few hundred feet down slope, marking the foot of the earthen up rise. Thin branches and wispy growth gave the trees a sinister scarecrow quality, casting the illusion of towering straw sentries guarding the dark hillside instead of corn fields, spindly limbs swaying in evening breezes, conveying a warning to all who should pass…

Tread if you dare, venture forth at your own risk!

Closer to home, goldenrod fronds mingled with scrub bush and rock, each pushing from the terrain with the vigor of tundra struggle. An opportunistic vine crawled along splits in the basalt he sat upon. The leaves were thick and tie-dyed in a swirling red and violet hippie fancy. Martin plucked one of the leaves and drew it close. The leaf seemed to fluoresce as he twirled it under the pale moonlight, like asphalt oil on a fresh rain puddle. He'd never seen this phenomenon in terrestrial plants before, although it'd been a long time since he'd seen one in natural setting. And even way back when, before all hell broke loose, he wasn't a big *smell the roses* kind of guy. Sitting on a rock to gaze at a plant under moonlight was not a customary pastime for him.

So there was a chance that he'd just never noticed before. He couldn't recall ever hearing of plants that glowed, but maybe there were. He could think of animals that fluoresced, fireflies and jellyfish came immediately to mind.

Perhaps there was another explanation, he then began to think, something unusual, something interesting. His hunch, this was some kind of adaptation to radiation, a protective SPF conjured in the laboratory of survival. Just one more solution engineered by evolution, a global governance that has always been an agent of *change*. Eons before the notion became a popular political rallying cry…

Yes we can!

Where others may have found beauty in the paisley pattern, Martin found charm in the plant's sturdy design. Respect had to be acknowledged, the determined vine survived in what was the environmental equivalent of a microwave oven. Charles Darwin would've surely been proud; the plant was nearly as resilient as the rock it grew upon. Martin found himself making the connection between the plant and Santos, their new friend the animal analogue to the hardy weed. Martin finally released the leaf and watched it pinwheel off and vanish into the night.

After tamping the soil Jesse began relocating stones. Martin helped. Together under the night sky, they piled rocks atop the grave. Neither man spoke as the cairn took shape. Only the sounds of their effort—rocks clacking and the hurry of their breath— trickled through the quiet atmosphere.

The job finished, both men stood beside the grave admiring the pile of rocks. Martin listened as his friend's breathing returned to normal. He couldn't be sure, but he thought Jesse might be visualizing a prayer, his eyes closed in apparent reflection. So Martin waited quietly beside him.

It didn't take long for Jesse to recover, the spirit of his *old self* resurrected in an instant. He gathered steam quickly as he shared the new information he'd learned from Santos. Martin listened as he went through the list, beginning with the description of the new el Cucuy— replete with his own colorful version of what it might look like, to the tale of Leezak and his minions—right up to his hair-brained theory about the dark cloud that hung over the city. Martin glanced over as he mentioned it. There was indeed a thick cloud, he'd noted it earlier, but saw no evidence of smoke stacks. At the moment, however, darkness made it impossible to be certain.

Standing beside the stone marker, Martin listened as Jesse went on and on, felt his blood pressure rising with each new fragment. His biggest concern, even more so than the new information, was what kind of impact the news was having on his friend.

Because he could see it in his eyes, hear it in his tone. Jesse was getting worked up, winding himself into an overblown cyclone, his wanderlust stoked red-hot, not unlike he'd been back at Pacifica during his quest for exodus. His mind was already taking off like a hooked marlin, and Martin knew that *he'd* be the one stuck having to reel him back in. Best to let him spin his tires for a while and wear himself out, then try to haul him back on task. Probably wouldn't be long till he started suggesting revision to the mission.

And when it did come, Martin almost laughed. He couldn't believe how accurate his prediction had been, was almost a word for word replay of his thoughts.

I think we should have a look around, Jesse suggested, pointing off toward the alleged home of Dr. Harris Leezak. *We should definitely see what we can learn, since we're already here. I think there's something fishy going on.*

"Listen Jess," Martin said, his tone firm yet supportive. "I agree that this is all very interesting, and something we may want to consider looking into down the road. But right now we need to stick to what we came here to do. Let's not forget about the damaged OTEC, we need to get the sealant back as soon as possible."

Jesse slouched, moved to respond. But Martin didn't give him chance. "Based on what you've said here, it doesn't sound like we'll be in any direct danger, and that's the most important thing. So I think it best if we just stick to the plan and get back home. You gotta remember, when I agreed to lead this mission, I assumed the responsibility for the safety of this crew. Some of these people have family waiting back home, myself included. And what you're suggesting is risky, and unfair to ask."

Jesse nodded. "I understand. Just figured I'd throw it out there—thought it seemed really important."

Martin was shocked. No argument. No follow up. Not even a huff or disdainful sigh. That was *way* too easy. He certainly didn't expect Jesse to so easily acquiesce. The hooked marlin he thought was going to be such a problem turned out to be no more than a carnival prize goldfish.

"You're right, it is important," Martin agreed, his voice tuned to the same frequency he used when lecturing his son. "As soon as we get back home, I'll recommend a return trip to explore. I promise." Although Martin would keep the promise, he knew deep down that there was *no way* the board would authorize any such journey. There just wasn't any up-side, and far too much to lose. He knew the whims and ways of the board almost as well as he knew his friend. And his friend was behaving very oddly at the moment. No way should he be so at ease, unless of course he had something up his sleeve.

"Fair enough," Jesse said with an acquiescent nod. "We'll look into it later then, when we get back."

Martin breathed a sigh of relief, glad this current crisis had been resolved, at least for the moment. To this point, there'd been no major conflict. It had been a concern of his all along. He also knew that if dissent were to rear its ugly head, it would most likely come from the friend who stood before him now. Down to the spiraled frame of his DNA Jesse was a free spirit. Martin knew that he was the one person brazen enough to break rules, if he felt strong enough cause. And for that reason, despite all of his talents, had Jesse not been his best friend, Martin would not have wanted him on the mission.

A short whistle chirped from the water station. They both turned.   Jennifer was standing in the doorway. Martin placed a hand on his friends shoulder. "Come on. Let's go fill everyone in. And then get ready to head out."

Chapter 33

It was just past ten pm when the team finally assembled in the entrance of the water station; Martin had brought everyone up to speed over dinner. If all went well, Martin hoped to be back in this spot in a few hours, regroup, and then make the journey back to the docks. With any luck, they'd be home before noon tomorrow, supplies in hand; quick, safe, and productive. At least that was the plan.

Before moving out, Martin gathered the team to issue final instructions and allow Santos to do the same, just to be certain they were all on the same page. Santos did not need any prompting.

"You mean *she* is going?" Santos questioned bluntly. Although obviously referring to Jennifer, he looked to Martin.

But it was not Martin who replied. "Of course I'm going!" Jennifer spat, clearly not happy about a remark perceived as sexist. She folded her arms, turned to Martin looking for support, the scowl on her face radiating anger like a space heater.

"This is not a good idea, not a good idea at all." Santos shook his head, turned to Jesse and chided. "I already told you, it is not safe for females to be outside."

Jesse shifted. "But I thought you said we wouldn't have a problem tonight. You said Leezak doesn't usually operate at night."

"It is not Leezak that worries me. His men are easily avoided." Santos said, then sighed and seemed to soften. "That's right, I keep forgetting, you are not from around here." Once again his sarcasm was transparent. "So I will explain. Leezak pays for information about women. He pays well. He somehow has access to crops and livestock. Most people around here would sell their soul for a good meal. I have seen it happen, family and friends traded for hams and potatoes. We have never taken as much as a leaf of lettuce from him, and never will."

The new information startled Martin, had him duly concerned. This could definitely impact their safety, not to mention the welfare of their new friends. The last thing he wanted to do was separate the team, but he was no longer so sure. He noticed Jennifer's posture drooping, her confidence no longer so obvious. For the first time the thought of giving up and heading back home crossed his mind.

Santos then pointed a prosecuting finger at Jennifer. "And if anybody sees her they will report her to Leezak. There's no doubt. And then we will all be in danger. And this could also put my family in trouble," he said, a prophetic reflection of Martin's own sentiments.

"What does he use the women for?" Jesse asked, stepping into the free fire zone.

Great, Martin frowned, something else to pique his friend's curiosity. Just what he needed. *Intrigue.* More crack for a jonesing crack head. And just when he felt he had him in check.

Santos raised his eyebrows, shrugged. "We don't know. But once they are taken, they are never seen again.

It started a few years ago. Now, there are no women to be found. Besides my wife and daughter, it has been a long time since I have seen another female in this area. I guess they have all left the area, or are in hiding, or already taken."

"Leezak was a geneticist," Alex offered out of the blue.

"What the hell does that have to do with anything?" Jennifer demanded.

Alex flinched, seemed to hedge, as if he wished he could twist the lid back on the can of worms. But it was too late, the lid was off, everyone looked at him to continue.

"Well...years back he conducted some pretty horrible experiments, from what I've read. I suspect that he may be using the women for some kind of genetic research. But then again it—"

"Wait a minute," Jennifer said, cutting him off. "I remember hearing all about this guy, but didn't it all go down decades ago? He had to be like forty or fifty then. That means he's gotta be an old man by now. I mean... what kind of threat could he really be? I can't believe he's even still alive, especially in this environment." Her confidence seemed to resurge.

"Not if he discovered the fountain of youth," Alex countered gently, careful not to trip any further sore-spot circuits. "It was one of the things he was allegedly studying when he was busted for illegal experimentation back in the day."

"Fountain of youth?" Martin stepped back in, feeling his own curiosity begin to flicker with ambition.

Alex shrugged, then replied. "The fountain of youth is a figurative phrase, of course. He was one of the many convinced that the key to life extension could be found in the genetic code. A lot of people were working on it back then. If the gene locations for longevity could be identified and appropriately manipulated, a person could live for much longer than ever thought possible. From what I've read, there was a lot of data supporting the claim. I'm pretty sure that longevity genes have been discovered in lower life forms."

"But did he ever do it? Did he find it?" Martin asked.

Alex shrugged. "I don't think so. At least it had never been reported. But remember, he disappeared after his court case was dropped. Maybe he continued his research. If he's still around, and if he's still working, he'd have had an awful lot of time to work on it." Alex then turned to Santos. "Have you ever seen him? What does he look like?"

"I have seen him, but never up close." Santos shrugged and then suggested. "Maybe it's not even the same guy."

"It's him," Jesse announced firmly. "It's him."

Martin could see that look again, hear it in his tone. Jesse had definitely latched on to this thing. First the functioning building and now the fountain of youth, even he was getting a little enchanted by it all. But it was time to shut it down, end this inquiry once and for all, and make some hard decisions.

"Okay then, as I see it, we really only have two options—"

"Wait," Alex suddenly intervened. "I have an idea."

Martin turned to Alex, his eyebrows rising. A guy who never said two words had all of the sudden became *Mr.* Congeniality. *No problem*, Martin told himself as he deferred, *let's hear what he has.*

"Give her your windbreaker." Alex said to Jesse. He then rummaged through his knapsack, pulled out a black baseball cap. "Figured this might come in handy if we were out in the sun," he explained as he stepped behind Jennifer and tucked her hair in behind the oversized windbreaker. He then adjusted the ball cap and pulled it over her head.

"Not bad," Martin said, the team nodding. Even Santos nodded his approval. The blousy jacket had effectively concealed her bust line and narrow waist, and the hat went a long way to deemphasize her long hair. She then took the hat off and, using a stashed scrunchie, tied up her hair and tucked in her bangs before refitting the hat. Martin shined the flashlight on her. *Even better*. The Tool Troll comes through again.

"Be back in a sec." Santos suddenly said as he slipped outside, returning moments later with a charred piece of wood. "This might help. We sometime use this as camouflage or sunscreen." He took Martin's canteen and poured some water onto the concrete floor, then began scraping the charred stick across the puddle. "We usually add animal fat if we have any, it works better. But this should do."

Alex quickly dug out the can of oil he had in his knapsack. "Will this help?" He asked, kneeling next to Santos.

Santos nodded and Alex added a squirt to the mix. "This will do just fine." Santos said, sounding proud of his concoction.

Santos rubbed his palms in the sticky black mixture. Jennifer flinched as he approached, but then seemed to realize what he was up to. Using his finger, Santos applied the homemade cosmetic, tracing her jaw line and neck, then working the upper lip. He stepped back to appraise his work, then leaned back for a final touch-up, feathering out sideburns.

"Not bad at all," Martin offered, appraising the gender bender. "That should work just fine."

And it was true. The homemade makeup had concealed her feminine facial features by adding the illusion of facial hair. Along with the rest of the make-over her appearance was decidedly masculine. Short of a strip search, her petite stature was the only other possible clue to her gender. And even at that, she wasn't all that much smaller than Santos. From a distance, and given the fact that it was night, she'd be fine.

Jennifer then adopted a macho swagger, grabbed her crotch and threw back her shoulders. Clearing her throat, she then spoke in the deepest tenor she could muster. "Yo man, where all the bitches at?"

The tension in the room immediately evaporated. They all laughed, even Martin. "Good one, Lenny," he said, anointing her with a new name.

"Call me Maximus, Maximus Meridius." She corrected him, using the same pseudo-male mannerisms. Then returned to her normal voice and explained. "You know, the guy from that old movie? The Gladiator. Hey if I'm gonna have to be a guy; I might as well have a cool name."

Everyone laughed again. The levity went a long way to reducing the tension in the room. It was a pleasant prelude to what they all knew could be a dangerous operation.

It would be the last laugh they'd have for some time.

Chapter 34

Led by Santos, they stepped out into the night, leaving the safety of the water station. The symptoms of autumn were alive in the breezes, and Jesse could feel the prickle of goose flesh on exposed skin. Although stoked to be outside, Jesse was pissed at Martin. He didn't appreciate being played like a child, especially not by a person he considered a close friend. And like he didn't realize he was being *managed*. How stupid did Martin think he was?

On some level he understood; Martin clearly had a lot of responsibly on his plate. But he shouldn't let that, or his stubbornness, get in the way of good judgment. In Jesse's opinion, he could learn to be a little more flexible. But it really didn't matter, Jesse reminded himself, Martin's ideas and ideals would soon be irrelevant. Soon they'd be gone and he'd have the freedom to do whatever the hell he wanted, whenever the urge should emerge. He shook his head, mothballing the thought. He didn't need any distractions right now, mental or otherwise. The part of the journey he'd most anticipated was underway. And he didn't need any nattering static interfering with the forthcoming odyssey, or his ability to take it all in.

Santos led the way down the hillside, the team trailing close behind. Jesse watched Santos as he advanced, doing his best to mimic his moves. *Just follow my lead,* Santos had stressed before they'd left. It had been like a period to every sentence during his earlier instructions. Jesse had listened, and was trying to do just that. But following his lead was a lot easier said than done.

Santos moved with a casual stealth that Jesse found amazing, smooth and silent as a hologram. Had it not been for the light of the moon, he'd be completely invisible, just a furtive soul and distant heartbeat wisping through the darkness. By contrast, Jesse's teammates were not so adept, their movements conspicuous and awkward. And he could hear their every step, a tiny concert broadcast in swooshing fabric, respired gases, and the shuffle of footfalls over loose scree.

Fortunately, it didn't really matter. Although they didn't want to advertise their business, they were not trying to hide either. Santos had told them that no matter what, they were likely to encounter people. At the very least, be observed, whether they knew it or not. Acting sneaky could draw suspicion in itself, he'd said, could make it appear as if they were hiding something. His strategy, therefore, was to act natural and try to blend in. Do what they had to do, quietly and casually, and then hightail it back to the water station.

Wending down the hillside path, Jesse glanced up at the moon. Set high in the sky, the orb was majestic, the gravity of its beauty drawing his eyes like tiny vitreous tides, hypnotizing him like the swing of a pocketwatch. And in that moment he felt a head-rush of pure excitement. Maybe it was a byproduct of the cool night, or the simple effect of finally striding through air untouched by fans and ducts once again. Perhaps it was the second-hand excitement that oozed from the fear of the unknown. Or maybe it was true what they said about the moon, maybe its mythical power over the animal anima indeed had merit.

If Jesse had been a wolf, the urge to bay would be difficult to ignore.

As they reached the bottom of the hill, the landscape leveled, slope giving way to plain. Ahead was a vast field. To the south eroded roads stretched and splintered in every direction. Beyond the flatland, dark buildings lined the serrated skyline, the leading edge of the former suburban sprawl that was once home to thousands, the bygone bundles of humanity who made up the lifeblood of San Diego.

They crossed an overgrown culvert, stepped up onto the eroded macadam of what was once the I-5 highway. Santos turned south on the old road, heading toward the denser environs of the crumbling concrete jungle.

Jesse found traveling on the highway to be a surreal sensation, like living a scene right out of the Armageddon playbook. All around were abandoned cars, weather beaten and dappled with rust, flattened tires slowly sinking in man-made tar pits; some destroyed, some askew, and some seemingly untouched, still in the proper lane, looking every bit like a museum exhibit, a life-sized diorama of the twenty-first century human commute.

Up ahead, a hulking gas guzzling SUV sat silent right alongside a petite plastic electric coupe. Green machine and glorified global toaster, both now sun bleached and relegated to the phylum of fossil, a tiny trilobite alongside a T-rex. Jesse smirked, found a pang of irony in the impromptu arrangement. Another appropriate museum exhibit, he mused, simply titled...

Design, Decide, Demise.

Out front, Santo suddenly stopped in his tracks, held up a hand and flexed it to fist. It was the signal to stop and hold position. The team speedily complied.

Jesse slowly leaned to improve his view. Santos was still frozen, a life-sized ice sculpture, staring straight ahead, thin air all that was apparent before him. Santos then turned guardedly and stared back at the team. He nodded, then opened and closed his fist to emphasize the signal. *Stay put!*

Jesse had no clue what was going on, and despite the lack of direct danger stimuli, felt his heartbeat crescendo, thumping as much from allure as alarm.

Without warning or whisper, Santos then sprang into the night sky. His body seemed to hover in mid-air, as if gravity had became suddenly irrelevant. Physics then returned and Santos crashed to the pavement with a quick thud, a hiss, and a grunt.

Rolling on the pavement Santos seemed to be struggling. It appeared like he was having a seizure, but then Jesse saw something in his hands, catching only the most fleeting flash of writhing shadow. It sent a stun-gun shudder right through him, followed by a surge of heart-halting adrenaline, then a news flash advisory that said…

Warning! Warning! Danger!

Santos apparently had no such reservations.

And Jesse knew what it was, knew what Santos was struggling with. But what could he do? Santos had been vehement about following his signals, and the signal had just been roundly issued.

Stay put!

So Jesse did just that. He stood frozen, as much from fear as following orders; and watched with hackles sky-high, as did the others…

…as Santos continued to fight.

Chapter 35

Santos continued to grapple with the large dark snake and rolled on the pavement like he was being swarmed by bees. The commotion was perceptible in shadowed pantomime and moonlit flashes, the imagery superheated by endorphins and mystery. At last Santos found his feet, the serpent seemingly secured. Both hands fisted the snake's neck while its writhing rubbery torso constricted his arms, a ceaselessly slithering knot of muscle that struggled to turn yawning mouth on attacker.

Jesse's eyes bulged half-dollar wide, as much from shock as trying to better see. *What the hell is he doing*, he wondered. Santos had obviously seen the snake in their path. Why didn't he just point it out and step around it? It certainly seemed like a much simpler solution to him.

Holding the snake, Santos then walked back toward the group. Transfixed by it all, the team could only marvel as he casually dislodged his right hand from the worming coil, his left remaining fast around its neck. Jesse felt his heartbeat petition with panic, the tempo swelling with each advancing step. He was surprised by the response. He'd always felt at ease around animals; dealing with sharks, eels, crabs and cephalopods on a daily basis back in Pacifica went a long way to foster such an affinity. And even before that—big, small, furry or slimy—he couldn't remember ever having been afraid of an animal. Even snakes, despite their malign reputation and lack of appeal to many, had never evoked such a response. But then again, never before had he been so close to a hand to handless, sapiens to serpent, melee.

In the town where he grew up, snakes would often lay upon a track of highway at sunset, drawn by the residual radiant heat. On more than one occasion, he could remember swerving his car to avoid one of the creatures, as it slithered curb-ward, only to look in the rearview and watch the next vehicle turn it into two twisting Twizzlers, stamped flapjack flat at mid-torso, a B.F Goodrich tread embossing it to the asphalt like a wad of warm a-b-c gum. He always found himself wondering why the driver would do such a thing, hoping it was accidental. He'd always glance back, of course. More times than not, the driver seemed unaware, distracted, yammering away in the most urgent posture, a cell phone plastered to their ear.

But every so often, he'd look back and detect another motive altogether.

Most times, it'd be a car-full of high school dudes high-fiving and looking back enthusiastically at their gnarly handiwork. One time it had been an angry, old truck driver crouched under a worn Lakers hat, white-knuckling his rig over the tiny speed bump, a satisfying Grinch-like grin curling forth as he steamrolled the snake into road-kill ribbon. Or even one time, he remembered seeing a well-heeled soccer mom swerving wildly, nearly two-wheeling the Range Rover to do the deed, then furtively glancing around and in her mirrors to see if she'd been busted, then casually primping her hair since she was already up in the rearview. Witnessing such acts of ignorance had always made Jesse upset, and embarrassed by the behavior of his species.

As a scientist, Jesse knew that most wild animals, reptiles or otherwise, wanted nothing to do with humans; flight their instinct of choice. And if escape was impossible, then a hiss, growl, snort or some other gesture would be employed that clearly said— *warning, stay away!* The fight option, and otherwise aggressive behavior, was reserved mostly for defensive purposes or acquiring food. Fangs and claws were shopping carts and cash to most animals deemed dangerous.

And in ninety-nine percent of cases that went bad, Jesse knew, it was not the fault of the feral critter, but the intruding human—someone stumbling into an animal's domain, startling it or disturbing a nest, an error in arrogance or ignorance, or both. Or often times, a premeditated invasion, ignoring all warnings for the sake of personal pleasure, sport, or the simple thrill of tempting fate; like surfing in shark territory at dusk, or running with bulls down narrow streets, or teasing a king cobra as rite-of-passage to *jackass* elite; prompted, in many cases, by a rolling camera or chanting crowd. Even trained tigers and ordinarily benign sting rays occasionally had enough, and in their own way would finally say; *please leave me the fuck alone!* And turn their respective daggers on their unwitting antagonists to underscore that sentiment.

But in this case, something about the snake, and the fact that it was being toted ever closer, shook Jesse's confidence. The fear wasn't completely irrational, he knew. He was unable to determine if the reptile was venomous or not, and that was a very *real* concern. Envenomation, under these circumstances, would be every bit as lethal as a potassium chloride push. He could tell it had a dark mottled texture, but couldn't get a read on the exact color pattern under the indigent moonlight; and it didn't help that the thing was still continually shifting, endlessly altering the mosaic. The skin pattern played tricks on the eyes as well, a cleaver whirl of kinetic camouflage, like liquid rainbows on a soap bubble. All of which made species I-D near impossible.

All he really had to go on was the shape of the head, which appeared to be broad and flat, and the unholy hiss that expelled from its gaping mandible. Not a good sign, he knew. A wide head was the ideal design to accommodate venom glands, a common anatomical blueprint. Nature's creator was a big proponent of the form-follows-function architectural precept.

Whatever the case, Jesse's inner debate was rendered irrelevant as Santos withdrew a knife from his belt and unceremoniously slashed it across the serpent's neck. A slick whoosh and the receding sounds of pitter-patter followed as the animal's head flew off and skittered across the pavement like a flat stone across a pond, effectively silencing the animal's incessant cries, but doing nothing to terminate its motion. The headless creature continued corkscrewing, unspent neurons fueling the post mortem death roll, unimpeded by lack of blood flow or the fact that its brain was laying in the weeds on the other side of the street.

Just when Jesse thought it couldn't get any worse, Santos stepped close to the group and uncoiled the long torso like a cold garden hose, thick muscles gradually yielding; its fight response ebbing as the diplomacy of death spread to inform lingering survival instincts that their services were no longer required.

God only knew why, but Santos then proceeded to milk the long snake with his hands, sliding them one over the other as if tugging a giant udder. Along the snakes anterior a bulge became visible in the moonlight. And then in a sickening surreal instant, a solid gray glob fell from the snake, slapping the pavement with a wet thud, the sound a slug might make if smacked with a Louisville Slugger.

Jesse looked down. A fetal fist-sized hair ball covered in blood and snake snot lay still on the pavement, a pink loop of its own gory particulars all too visible in the drab moonlight. Jesse thought he was going to hurl, distantly wondered how the others were holding up after witnessing such a nauseating event.

Santos then looked up. Jesse thought he detected a subtle smile, as if he might just be messing around with them a bit. And then he whispered in a casual *can you pass the salt* voice. "Snake is great, but we never eat rat."

Chapter 36

So far, so good, Jesse thought as they exited the electronics store, stepping back into the night. They'd spent the last hour and a half working their way down the strip mall acquiring supplies, their gains marked in the swell of their duffle bags.

The electronics store had been the most fruitful thus far, mostly because it had been the least ravaged. After all, nothing in the store could be eaten, worn, or wielded as a weapon. The food-mart they'd rummaged through, on the other hand, had been picked piranha clean, like a week-old carcass lying at the bottom of the Amazon River basin. A few pens, several scented candles and some toiletries were all that they'd been able to procure.

Not surprisingly, the food-mart had been completely devoid of food, not even a can of Friskies or a stray peanut shell to be found. If not for the human remains they'd almost tripped over in aisle seven, even the insects would find nothing to feed on.

The shoe store they'd visited had fallen somewhere between the two on the looting Richter scale. Decimated and denuded as it was, several shoes were strewn among the wreckage—mostly flip-flops, fuzzy slippers and other non-utilitarian lines. But fashion sense took a back seat to common sense, and without complaint they loaded up what they could, knowing that whatever they brought back would be *all the rage* back at Pacifica.

To this point, they'd discovered half a dozen bodies or so in varying degrees of decay. Most had clearly departed long ago, their final destination applications already filed, reviewed and realized. One of the dead, however, appeared fresh, his dark skin yet violated by scavengers. Save for the lack of vital signs and a few missing digits, the young man looked like he could've simply been catching a nap as he lay propped against the checkout counter; the representative soul likely still stuck in limbo, nibbling on a spiritual fingernail, praying that when the elevator finally arrived the operator's first words would be, *going up*. Discovering human remains had come as no surprise, the only *real* surprise was that, all things considered, they'd found so few, so far.

On the flip side of the spiritual spectrum, the only living souls they'd observed were three men hunkered around a big metal garbage can. They warmed their hands and cooked an obscure lump of meat over the fire that shimmered skyward from the round rusted can, which looked like the tip of a giant straw that had been jammed into the earth, allowing a small circle of hell to rise from the depths. They'd spotted them from a distance, as they'd crept through the city, the Spartan dinner party secluded down a barren alley in a remote industrial area. It had not been clear if the three had seen them as they passed by.

It was twenty minutes after the snake drama that they'd seen the three men; at which point Jesse's heart rate had still not returned to normal. And even now, two hours later, as they moved along the sidewalk toward the next store, his heart still hummed along at a caffein-ated clip. With all the uploading excitement, it probably wouldn't be until the sobriety of sleep came that his body would return to its default settings.

Although they'd only actually *seen* three people, Jesse couldn't help but think that there'd been far more eyes tracking them, especially as they'd skulked so closely between the old dwellings that lined the suburban streets, which looked so much like weather-worn tombstones. He could almost feel invisible eyes upon him, penetrating and suspicious, like spying eyes behind the ubiquitous framed portrait in a horror flick; following them, scrutinizing their every step. The perception only added to his acute case of paranoia.

As they approached the last store along the strip-mall, Santos held up a fist, bringing the team to a halt just outside. Although the signage had been battered by the elements to the point of illegibility, Jesse recognized the building as part of a once very popular pharmacy franchise—one of those places that sold a little bit of everything; cooked-up convenience in items of frivolity and those deemed essential, all packaged amid bright sale signs and impulse fodder, designed to siphon off as much disposable dinero from the consuming cattle that grazed aisles while their prescriptions were filled. The target market masses were no longer trundling in, however, vanished long ago to the now very popular pearly gates retirement home.

The building was twice as immense as the rest, the anchor to the small column of stores. Like the rest of the stores along the strip, the doors and windows had been smashed, a hailstorm of tempered glass lay strewn all about, each tiny cube a window to the past, archeological insight to shattered dreams and broken lives.

Santos held up three fingers and mimed. "Be back in three minutes."

And then he was gone, disappearing into the store to sweep the interior. He'd done the same for every store so far. The team complied, waited patiently. Amid the shambles, Jesse noticed an old metal sign that looked like a large license plate. *Open 24 hours*, it read. He smiled wanly to himself; at least they weren't breaking any rules, the invitation right there in red, white and rust.

Santos suddenly appeared and waved them in, deftly assisting everyone through the damaged doorway. As Jesse entered, he got another good look at the dead snake draped around his neck. The carcass swung with his movements, new age bling for the post-apocalyptic player. He marveled at his new friend again. Santos had tied the darn thing around his neck and wore it as casually as a yuppie wearing a cardigan out for an evening on the town.

Un-freekin-believable, Jesse thought to himself as he stepped into the store, *this guy is amazing*.

To no surprise, the interior looked as though a small savage twister had swept from aisle to aisle, leaving behind an aftermath of retail wreckage. The store was a certified disaster area, permeated and punctuated with the unmistakable smells of must, death and animal struggle. They fanned out, ignoring the stench and high-stepping the mess. Digging through the layers of landfill, they found a few items of value. Pens, paper, light bulbs, fabric, most still in the original package; several magazines, books and even a clock radio turned up in the first foray. Jesse found a bottle of red wine in a drawer that had been overlooked. Aged and unopened it might now be a classic, he mused, and he tucked the pre-apocalyptic vintage into his bag. He also grabbed a couple tiny toy cars, figuring they'd make a great gift for Reni. He found a small gold bracelet and some cosmetics for his ex, stuffing them in his duffel bag, as well. *Just in case*, he thought. Even if he didn't return, he'd give them to Martin to distribute on his behalf.

Next to a damaged case of Hummel knock-offs, Jesse found a series of scaled animal sculptures; endangered species commemorated in cut glass and faux-gold trim. Many were broke, some missing, but several remained. Each figurine came with an official certificate written in fancy font, assuring the purchaser that a portion of the proceeds would go to help save those animals of endangered status. He reached by a cracked polar bear to remove the manatee from the fragile crystal keepsake ecosystem. He blew off the dust and wrapped it in a piece of old paper. Trash was one thing there was no shortage of. Knowing how fond Michelle was of animals, he tucked the tiny figurine away safely in his knapsack, figuring it would go great in her room, hoping she'd love it. Before stepping away the thought of a human figurine among their ranks brought another sarcastic smile.

Overall, he was content with his take. Most important, he'd acquired a generous supply of necessities for the common good. He also scored toys for Reni and plenty of goodies for Michelle, should he return, and should he be of the mind to try and rekindle their lost romance.

All of which got him thinking, served to pipeline his mind, forcing him to finally address the billowing notion that he'd been struggling to suppress. With his wanderlust somewhat sated, he'd noticed his inner tide shifting, and was now leaning strongly toward heading back. Underneath that, the seedlings of an even stranger stirring still—one even more shocking to his inner critic than his urge to return to Pacifica. And that was the thought of making a commitment to Michelle, or at least making the offer of such. It had first surfaced earlier in the day, unbidden and without analysis, presumably by the same forces that drove salmon upstream for that final fatal passage. Maybe it was a side-effect of the well known *absence makes the heart grow fonder* phenomenon; he wasn't entirely sure. But what he did know was that the gravitational pull of Michelle and Pacifica were now black-hole strong, and he was a wayward beam of light being drawn back home, guided by the universal forces of desire and community. It was hard, but he did his best to suppress the raging debate and focus on his work. He knew he had time; he could always pick it up later. They still had several hours before crunch time.

One last item came to mind, and he figured he might as well take a quick look while he was there. So he stepped back over to the costume jewelry counter and, sifting through broken glass and garbage, found a simple gold-tone ring, then stuffed it in a zippered pocket on his knapsack for safekeeping. He then made final adjustments to his gear, and looked over at his teammates. It appeared the others had similar good fortune, their respective duffel bags stuffed kielbasa tight.

Overall, they'd done well. At the very least, they'd met expectations, vague as they may have been. Fortunately, the looters of yesteryear had much different needs than theirs. Overlooked by the hand-to-mouth survivalists of yore, a book or magazine would be well beyond their needs on Maslow's pyramid. But even mold riddled and decades old, a Michael Crichton novel was like finding the mother-lode in dust and yellowing text to Team Pacifica. Jesse found himself anxious to get back and curl up in his claustrophobic quarters, a book in one hand, the other draped over Michelle as she nestled next to him in bed. The vision summoned a relaxing rush both warm and pure, felt like shiatsu for the soul as it diffused through his body, easing his tension by degrees. Although he couldn't be more surprised by the change of heart, he found himself excited that their journey was near its close. They had just one final stop to make before heading back to the water station.

And then from there: home.

Chapter 37

Following a twenty minute jaunt through the broken city the team approached a massive warehouse. The old building stood huge and foreboding in the moonlight wash. Jesse read the cracked signage hung across the façade—*Johnson Electrical Supply*.

Based on the moon's altitude and arc, Jesse guessed they had at least two hours till the region was swallowed up by utter darkness. No problem. The electrical shop was their final stop. He knew that if everything went as planned they'd have plenty of time before moonset to finish up and travel back to the water station.

Despite having to navigate the pitfalls of a wasted city, they'd made good time getting there. Santos guided them expertly as they slipped through the concrete morass, the execution of the journey seemingly scripted down to the last step. Another slap on the back for their new friend, Jesse thought.

Santos was even better than having a trained dog, Jesse thought as the team shadowed him up the stairway to the warehouse. Man's best friend incarnate, he had the hybrid-vigor of all breeds wrapped up in one lean obedient biped; more versatile, less needy, and yet equally as loyal, or so it would seem. He'd already proven an expert guide and guard, not to mention a skillful hunter. All of which he did unconditionally, and without the promise of a treat. Although it would come as no surprise if he eagerly accepted a Milk-bone, then crunched it down as excitedly as a K-9. Anyone living under these conditions would do the same.

Stepping inside the warehouse, they fired up their flashlights. Santos grabbed a light and swept it through the cavernous building, a quick canvass to check for dangers. The fewer surprises, the better.

The coast appeared clear.

Their footsteps echoed through the building as they descended the solid concrete staircase. Almost as tall as it was wide, the interior was engineered in rust-red I-beams and poured concrete. The front wall soared to greet a ceiling so high their flashlight beams struggled to meet it. The back wall was subdivided into lofts framed with simple structural metalwork. Webbed metal girders spanned from wall to wall to carry the weight of the flat roof on tireless tensile shoulders. The ground level was a typical floor plan, perfectly laid out for its former endeavors. Although layered in dust, it was surprisingly intact, and gave off the vibe that it once may have been a nice place to work; tools and supplies still racked and stacked, miles of wire spools color coded and arranged by gauge. A squat yellow fork lift sat expectantly in its parking space, perfectly square amid faded parallel lines.

But the one glaring abnormality that otherwise betrayed the innocuous setting was the array of bodies that dotted the floor plan in doom. A stark reminder in ashen bone and moth-munched apparel that this was no longer a happy place; and it was definitely not just another day at the office.

Following a brief powwow at the bottom of the stairway, they dispersed. Jesse could see that Alex was amped to the utmost, kid-in-a-candy store anticipation gleaming behind his azure eyes. To expedite their search, Alex gave them each a simple assignment. Rechargeable batteries, cables, and tools of every sort were highest on the list. Jesse was to hunt for fuses, mostly ten and twenty amp sizes, but a few of the larger capacities as well. A relatively easy task, he had a pretty good idea what they looked like. If they were there, he'd find them.

But the search was not to be.

A single sharp dog bark rang out, and with the speed of a nervous shudder, everything changed. Although distant, it was unmistakable, and highlighted by the fact that it was the first significant sound, aside from those of their own making, that they'd heard all night. Santos had yet to get outside to stand watch; Jesse quickly turned his flashlight to see his reaction. Santos stood frozen on the staircase, still and quiet as a cryogenic corpse. When no further baying came, Santos swiveled and urgently issued two signals, a finger across the lips, and then across the neck. The message came across loud and clear.

Flashlights off, and keep quiet!

An instant later the front door edged open, Santos ducking his head out, then quickly back. He'd clearly seen something. Before Jesse knew it, he was startled as Santos appeared beside him in the darkness. Santos then took Jesse's flashlight and toggled it on, reissuing the same hand signs. Wasting no time, he then slinked to the back of the building; his speed and stealth near superhuman, the flashlight beam marking his journey. Arriving at the back wall he stopped by the rear exit, then killed the flashlight before cracking the door to look out. And again, it was a quick look, pulling his head back like a panicked turtle. Scurrying back to the pack, he wrangled them in tight.

"Leave the bags here. Keep your lights off." He said urgently, slightly winded. "And follow me."

"What's going on?" Martin whispered, matching his urgency.

Santos leered, eyebrows diving. "Just follow me. We'll talk about it in a minute. Now let's go. And keep close so you can see the path."

Without follow-up, they complied, abandoning their hard-won supplies and following Santos as he raced toward the staircase for the loft. Taking stairs two at a time he wisped upward, the team doing their best to stay in his slipstream. Atop the first loft, he slowed and panned, then hit the gas as he located the next staircase. They all kept pace, bee-lining upward till they reached an overhead roof access the size of a pizza carton. Lifting the small hatch, Santos surveyed the rooftop tentatively, like a soldier peering from a tank turret in enemy territory.

And then they were on the rooftop, Santos silently huddling them together again. It was explanation time. "Okay, everybody take a knee here, and listen up," he said, his breathing, like the rest of them, fast and halting. "We've got a bit of a problem here." He hesitated and looked from eye to eye. "It seems there's a hunting party out tonight."

"Leezak?" Martin asked, his tone scolding.

Santos nodded. "Some of his men."

Jesse could see Martin wanted to go Vesuvius, blow his stack. But Santos threw up a hand to forestall any potential interruption. "There's eight men or so and a couple dogs coming down the street from the south." He pointed toward the street they came in on. "And another two moving down the back alley. They're still two blocks down, but if we left now, we'd be spotted, and that wouldn't be good. Our best bet is to ride it out up here and hope they pass by."

"What about the dogs?" Alex asked.

Santos seemed to anticipate the question, because his answer came swiftly and with well-laid strategy. "The dogs could be a problem; they have excellent smell, of course. But there are many other smells in the area to distract them. Hopefully they won't get on to us. But just in case, I have an idea. Follow me, let's move." He pointed to the east. "Stay low so we don't get spotted."

And then he was moving, a bipedal question mark advancing quickly to the front edge of the roof. A three foot knee-wall rimmed the perimeter like a castle fringe without the traditional dentition. They all hunkered down and leaned against it, separating them from a sixty foot freefall and the eyesight of the approaching men.

Resting on one knee, Santos untied the dead snake. "This thing needs to be gutted anyway," he said as he stretched it out on the rolled-tar rooftop.

Is this really the time for that? Jesse wondered. He looked at everyone else. Puzzled expressions were all around.

Using his knife, Santos made a single long incision, unzipping the snake's abdomen. He then reached inside and ran his hand like an ice cream scoop along a flaccid inner tube. The guts came away easily, a final surgical slash was needed to convince the cellophane strings that it was time to let go.

"Okay, if you look out, move very slowly, and keep your heads down as low as possible." In front of four shocked faces Santos then started molding the snake guts into a raw meatball. "I'm gonna step back and chuck this across the street and down the alley we just came through. It might lure the dogs down that way, maybe confuse them. All we need is to get them off the road for a minute. Then we can slip out without being noticed."

Finally understanding, they all nodded approvingly, *sounds good*.

Santos then stepped back and sprinted forward, looking every bit like he was going to jump off the edge. But he stopped short and heaved the gore ball out into the night sky. The glob sailed with remarkable speed and even more impressive accuracy as it arced down the alleyway. *Bullseye*. With the bait in place, the team cautiously peered over the roof barrier to watch as the plan played out.

Leezak's men were still a block away, approaching slowly. As Santos had said, there were eight. Leading the parade were two huge dogs of obscure breed. A large man was towed behind each dog, their leads piano-string tight. The four men on the flanks wielded weapons. Two clutched high-powered rifles and two held crossbows. The men were all massive, and moved in an odd mechanical manner, their animations bordering on robotic.

The last two men plodded along ahead of the cart, pulling it like a rickshaw. And Jesse could see immediately that they were different, not a willing party to this entourage at all. They were bound to the yoke and shackled around the ankles. Moreover, they were void of vitality and moving with an underlying indifference—shoulders slouched, feet shuffling reluctantly—which told Jesse, as much as their restraints, that they were not present on their own accord. They were clearly chattel, modern-day slaves. An age-old atrocity resurrected by a new-age overlord. The insight, when it struck, made Jesse simmer.

The hunting party traveled slowly but with apparent intention, heads swiveling side to side, traveling right down Broadway, making no pretence to hide in the shadows. And with the moonlit view, Jesse noticed something that was every bit as bizarre as the hunting party itself. Just as Santos had mentioned, each of the eight men appeared to be coated in a waxy white substance. But why they needed to wear the coating at night was a mystery.

A worming bundle in the back of the cart caught Jesse's attention and he zeroed in on the movement. He quickly lifted the binoculars from around his neck, glad he'd grabbed them during their earlier shopping spree.

Anxiously, he focused the lenses. Although dulled by night the optical enhancement helped. He went right to the fetal figure in the back of the cart and his suspicion was confirmed. He felt his heart go liquid with sympathy; the petite hourglass shape was a dead giveaway. It was definitely a woman. Bound and gagged and lashed in place.

Dammit!

The image pissed him off considerably, heaped even more tinder on the fire raging within; he wanted to just run down there and go ninja wild, break limbs and crack skulls as means of a lesson taught, and then set the slaves and the poor woman free. He didn't know the girl, but the silent screams apparent in her pathetic escape effort hit him with the harshness of a baby seal bashing, needling his core and conscious with obligation, pressing him for action.

Unfortunately, there was nothing he could do but watch. His hands, like hers, were tied.

But before he could give it any more thought, something else caught his attention. First a fleeting glimpse, almost unnoticed as he'd panned the field glasses again, but then a flash of recognition hit, followed by a figurative ton-of-bricks plummeting down on his cerebral cortex.

No fucking way his mind wailed. He shifted anxiously, his mind supernova with shock, his blood surging with the lactic acid of unspent action. Even before he swung the glasses back the pieces had already begun to snap into place. He then focused the binoculars, finding him again, staring directly at the face of the slave. And Jesse nearly shit as the certainty hit home, crashing into his mind with the startling impact of an eighteen-wheeled head-on. Trying to improve the image, he pressed the field glasses to his skull till it hurt, using the pain in lieu of a reality check pinch.

But nothing changed, this was no dream, and the image remained exactly the same.

Even beneath the bizarre shrink-wrapped wax coating, the face was clear—every bit as clear as the nose on his own face. And suddenly the thought of helping the poor woman was no longer at the forefront, nor were the thoughts of returning to Pacifica, or marrying his old flame. They were all bundled and bound tight, then jettisoned off to some distant planet of despair, no longer even a blip on his inner radar. Only the face had his attention now. And along with the implications it dredged up, they burned solar-flare bright in his brain.

He would *not* be going home now or anytime soon. Happiness would simply have to be put on hold. At least until he figured this out.

Until he got some answers.

Chapter 38

It was like seeing an ArmorAlled ghost; the apparition sprayed, buffed and polished over flesh and blood. *His own flesh and blood.* The change of skin color had thrown him, and was the reason Jesse hadn't made the connection on the first pass, his once dark skin covered in blotchy chalk. But beneath that, everything was exactly like it had always been; his features perfectly intact, just like he remembered. There was no mistaking…

It was his father.

Seeing his father alive after two years was one thing, shocking in itself: but seeing him enslaved and shrink wrapped was quite another, adding immeasurable distress to a revelation that already blew the top off the shock-and-awe barometer.

Stunned as he was by it all, he wasn't really all that surprised. All along he'd had a gut feeling that his father was still alive. And now, as he kneeled on the rooftop looking at his dad through budget binoculars, he couldn't help but wonder if the force of fate, or some omniscient spirit, was the ultimate impetus behind this meeting, puppeteering this one-in-a-million chance with unseen cosmic strings.

Lord knows, he'd prayed for such an occurrence.

Jesse was unsure if the others had seen him, or if they even had the ability without binoculars. He quickly lowered the field glasses and realized that—*no*—they couldn't have; face recognition was impossible by naked eye, distance befouling details like moon craters on a hazy night.

He leaned back to tell Martin and the others of his discovery. Amped as he was, he had to remind himself to whisper. But before the words reached his mouth, a sudden disturbance erupted below, the tension all at once skyrocketing, and his attention was drawn back down.

The dogs barked violently and pulled against their leads, their attention riveted down the street, in *their* very direction. It was all their human handlers could do to keep them at bay. And if they weren't steroid-sized themselves, they'd probably be body surfing down the street, doing the road rash Iditarod right about now.

Shit! Jesse breathed. The hellhounds must've got on to their scent. He looked down the line at the others; their body language was obvious with the same nervous voltage burgeoning within him. Santos must've sensed the unease because he leaned back, and as if on cue whispered, "Take it easy everyone. Hold steady and stay quiet. And be ready to move quickly. This could be our chance."

Our chance? Jesse thought skeptically. The dogs were clearly on to them. In what possible way could that give them their chance? Although on some level, Jesse found himself hoping that the dogs *did* find them. That would bring this all to a head, incite a conflict, and give him a chance to attempt to free his father. But as he played the scenario in his head, even his overwrought mind could see that the odds were stacked severely against them. Even the best script ended Alamo brutal, with his friends all winding up hurt, captured, or killed; and that simply *was not* a price he was willing to pay. And he knew that his father would never approve such a move either, even if it meant his own freedom. That just wasn't the way he was wired.

His father's character was as fundamentally sound as they came, principled and uncompromising. No one knew that better than his son. His father had tried to instill the same qualities in him from as early as he could remember. Jesse liked to believe that he had in fact acquired those traits over the years. As difficult as it had seemed at times, the older he got, the more his father's parenting sermons made sense.

As the current noose of stress tightened around him now, he could hear his father's voice in his mind, calm and rational. A talk he'd given him, in one form or another, on more than one occasion. *Whenever you are faced with a difficult situation,* he'd say, *before anything, always stop and ask yourself—what is the right thing to do here? Not the thing that benefits you personally, or the easy way out, or the move that might bring you financial gain, or the thing that everybody else would do. But what is the right thing? And when the answer becomes clear, you do it. And your decision should never be made with the hope of fame or praise. The only recognition you should take is the personal satisfaction you get from knowing that you did the right thing.*

Jesse could hear his father's philosophy ring in his mind now, and it brought a modicum of calm to a situation that was quickly spiraling down the shit hole. He also knew that the right thing in this case was to sit tight and hope they somehow got out of this undetected. For the time being, any attempt to save his father would have to be put on hold.

With the dogs still barking madly, Jesse watched as one of the large men leaned down to unleash one of the beasts. Once free, the dog took off down the eroded street, racing in their direction. Jesse felt his body tensing again as the animal advanced—thick muscle flexing and rippling beneath lean pelt—its sheer size and maniacal gallop a genuinely frightening sight. It looked like Cujo on crack, wired extremely tight and hell-bent on flesh. It would be at the front door in seconds, barking and scratching, leading the armed posse right to them. He glanced over at Santos, like the rest of them he watched intently, but did not seem overly concerned. If he was worried, he was certainly playing it close to the vest.

Jesse took a deep breath and began to mentally prepare for battle.

Chapter 39

The dog had covered the city block in record time, and was now right below them. But instead of heading toward them, it veered down the alley across the street, the sound of keratin scraping against asphalt audible as it banked and plunged down the dark man-made canyon. Realizing he'd been holding his breath, Jesse exhaled and sighed. It would appear they were safe, at least for the moment.

But what was the dog after? Jesse then wondered. Had it already drawn a bead on the snake guts? Or was it on to their scent trail? After all, they'd just traveled down that alley only moments ago. Or was the dog after something else entirely? There was simply no way to know for sure.

A sharp yelp suddenly came from the alley. The cry was sickening, sounded like a dog getting smacked by a speeding car. Jesse listened for further clues, looked for movement down the alley. Nothing—stone cold silence and cave black the only further input. He looked back at the men below, now less than a half block away. They still advanced, their earlier confidence replaced by decided caution, their weapons at the ready, leveled and aimed at the alley. Even more telling, the other dog had stopped barking, and now circled sheepishly, its tail pinned tightly between its legs. You'd think it'd just seen the K-9 equivalent of a ghost, an apparition of Michael Vick holding jumper cables perhaps. Whatever the case, the animal clearly knew something, animal instincts almost never misled.

Another sound suddenly emerged from the dark alley, and Jesse swung back, his head pivoting in tennis-match rhythm to keep up with the changes below. He listened as a deep growl began to breathe from the shadows—strange and as threatening as thunder—like nothing Jesse had ever heard before, not in any zoo or even any manufactured Hollywood sound effect. One thing was for sure; it wasn't made by any dog.

Out of the corner of his eye, Jesse noticed Santos lean back, as if pushed by the sheer force of the unknown intonation. He turned just in time to see Santos mouth two words. And although he did not say the words aloud, Jesse could read his moonlit lips as clear as day. "*El Cucuy!*"

Geez, Jesse thought, this was getting crazy.

Two other men appeared on the street and joined the advancing entourage. Armed and alert, the men already seemed attuned to the situation. Jesse guessed that they were the two men Santos had seen in the back alley. They were probably called over, or heard the commotion. The team now reinforced, they advanced with more confidence, now only five or six car lengths away from the alley.

A flash of movement caught Jesse's eye and he swung back to the alley, just in time to see two dark masses land on the pavement, the arc of their flight originating from somewhere within the shadows. They thumped on the street and slid for several feet before coming to rest on the crumbling pavement. They looked like tattered old throw pillows with a couple of very long tassels. But of course they weren't. And by the time the dark brown lumps came fully to rest, Jesse had been able to make a positive I-D. They were not pillows, and tassels didn't have paws.

The dog had been severed at mid-torso, two wet masses lay still and lifeless on the pavement; the head was gone altogether. Blood pooled from red-raw truncations, a thin loop of pink hose still connecting the two lumps. By all evidence, the animal had been torn in two and hefted street-ward, the responsible party still in the shadows, still growling ominously, perhaps playing kick-the-can with the dog's head somewhere in the dark alley. As much as the dog was no friendly house pooch, Jesse still felt a genuine pang of sorrow for the animal. It certainly didn't deserve to go out like that.

Euthanized by el Cucuy.

With the battle lines now indelibly etched, things were about to get ugly in a hurry. The hunting posse was undeniably pissed, their pace increasing, ammo being chambered angrily and safeties thumbed off. Jesse realized he was rapt by it all, found himself rooting for el Cucuy in the clash that now appeared all but imminent on the street below, hoping the creature would do the same to the men who held his father captive, while somehow sparing his father from the mayhem. Although he didn't see how the creature could stand a chance against all that fire power.

Jesse's eyes suddenly bulged goiter wide as a dark mass became visible several feet deep in the alley. It was impossible to discern detail, but whatever it was, it was huge and misshapen, lurching furtively, the shadow more grizzly bear than human. The shadow then began to rise up a wall, apparently fleeing, or perhaps relocating to a position of advantage. The creature moved silently and without gravitational handicap, like a giant tarantula filled with helium. Jesse realized he was forcing his eyelids open wider, hoping he could somehow enhance his night vision. More than anything he wanted to get a glimpse of this thing.

A tap on the shoulder hit Jesse and he nearly had a stroke. He spun around, his nerves tweeting with electric-chair panic. It was Santos, standing and waving them away from the edge of the roof. As he'd done several times already, he huddled them in tight and spoke in an urgent whisper. "Now is our chance. The back alley should be clear. Let's move fast, try to stay close behind me. We'll grab your stuff then head out the back door." He scanned the four nodding faces before him. "Okay, let's move."

Chapter 40

Once back at the water station it didn't take long for the fireworks to begin. Martin had unknowingly lit the fuse when he began hustling everyone to make final preparations to head home. The verbal pyrotechnics occurred only seconds later when Jesse announced that he *would not* be returning with them. Jennifer and Martin immediately aligned against him, vehemently disagreeing and offering opinions to that effect. Alex, for his part, remained silent during the debate.

Jesse's return fire had been curt and consistent, replying to each argument with the same standard finish. *That doesn't matter; I'm just not going back.*

Had there been an impartial moderator scoring the debate, Team Pacifica would be ahead by a sizable margin. Right up until the moment Jesse informed them of what he'd seen while back on the rooftop.

"They have my father," Jesse said, putting it out there in its simplest form.

If the team's resultant thoughts were manifested in bubbles above their heads, they might've read. *What? Are you kidding? He's finally lost it!*

To this point, the rest of the terrestrial clan had been nowhere in sight. But with the burgeoning commotion, one by one—Armand, Nellie, Sofia—they dropped down from the ceiling. Once on solid ground, Nellie rubbed her eyes, sleep slits giving way to innocent blinking orbs, all of which put Team Pacifica in an even more awkward position. Sensitive information might be exchanged in frank and adult language. But at the moment, censorship would have to take a back seat to the urgency of the instant.

The clan greeted Team Pacifica with a polite nod, but otherwise ignored their guests and the tumult they'd brought into their home. They hurried by to welcome Santos back with enthusiastic embraces. With the locals otherwise occupied, Martin turned back to Jesse to press for details. "Are you certain it was your father," he asked.

"One hundred percent."

"How come none of us noticed?" Martin spread his hands, looking to Jennifer and Alex.

"None of you had these." Jesse lifted the binoculars he still had around his neck. "I was just getting ready to tell you when all hell broke loose. Next thing I knew we were running out of there. Besides," Jesse shook his head, his voice filled with frustration, "there wasn't anything we could've done in that situation anyway. There was just too much fire power around."

Jennifer stepped closer, laid a supportive hand on his shoulder. "I'm sorry Jess, I know this must be difficult for you," she said, her earlier argumentative edge usurped by the voice of reason. "But let's say that your father is still alive, and he's being held against his will by those men. What good does it do for you to stay behind by yourself? You just said yourself that the men were well armed. And who knows how many more of them there might be."

"She's right," Martin said. "And as much as we'd like to stay behind and help you on this one, you know we just can't. We're not prepared for this kind of task, and we need to get the supplies back to the community. That's why I think it's best if we all go back together. Once back home, we can assemble a proper team to return and do this right."

Jesse offered a contacted smile that had nothing to do with joy. "Listen, guys, I appreciate what you're saying and understand your position. I don't expect any of you to stay behind with me, never did. There was a good chance that I was gonna stay behind even if I hadn't seen my father. But now, I'm staying no matter what, no matter what any of you say. This is something I've gotta do. And if you were to put yourself in my shoes, and were truly honest with yourself, I think you'd agree with my position." Jennifer looked away as if what Jesse said hit home. "And if you think I'm gonna go back and pin my hopes on a rescue team being authorized by the board." He stammered, his internal editor momentarily overwhelmed. "That just ain't gonna happen."

"Listen, Jess—" Martin said, launching a counter argument. But before he got far, he was interrupted by a tap on his shoulder. It was Santos. In all the commotion, the terrestrial clan had seemed to fade into the background. But now Santos was standing beside Martin, inserting himself directly into the line of fire. Nellie stood close by his side. As usual, the little girl hugged his thigh like a teddy bear.

"I am sorry to interrupt you," Santos said and bowed, his manner both genuine and humble. "I see that you are in the middle of a serious talk, but I must ask you for a favor." Santos looked down, seemed to waver, looking every bit like a boy confessing to his dad that he'd been the one to spill the soda on the carpet. "When you go back to your home," Santos gently covered his daughter's ear with his hand, pressing her head against his leg to cover the other. "I was wondering if you could take my daughter Nellie with you."

As jaw dropping as it was to hear that Jesse was staying behind, and that his father was still alive, this was right up there with it—though Martin's response would require a much more delicate approach. For the time being, the dispute with Jesse was put on hold.

"What?" Sofia screamed from across the room. "We never talked about this!" She scurried over and snatched her daughter away from Santos. The little one was still oblivious to what was going on, a look of surprise swelling across her face as she was firmly led away.

"I know this is from out of nowhere," Santos said, continuing to plead his case. He remained right in front of Martin, gazing directly in his eyes, but seemed to speak to all in the room. "But she would be better off living with you. I'm sure that it's much safer there. I don't know how much longer I can protect her here, or keep her healthy and fed." He took a step closer to Martin and rolled up his sleeve, exposing his shoulder. Shielding his action from his family, he then whispered. "Besides, I am not so sure how much longer I will be around." Martin inspected the man's arm. There was no mistaking the author of the scabs—it was the plague. And even though only in the early stages, untreated it would kill him inside of a year. With no known cure, the only chance he had would be to have the spoiled skin surgically removed before it metastasized.

Martin inhaled, was about to speak, but Santos preempted. "We love her as much as any parents could love a child." He looked around, imploring eyes filling with tears. "And that's exactly why I ask for this. I cannot allow what happened to her brother to happen to her. And if that means I must let her go, send her off to know that she is safe, then that is what must be done, even if I never get to see her again." He frowned and looked down at the ground again, then lifted. "Don't you think?" Again he seemed to speak to the entire room.

Sadness permeating the room as if it had just sprayed from the old fire sprinklers in the ceiling. Martin sighed and placed a hand on Santos's shoulder. He looked around at the rest of the team. They all had to know what was coming. They understood the deal.

But it was time for the third big surprise since returning to the water station.

Chapter 41

Martin turned to look Santos in the eyes. "We will take her with us," he said, sending a shockwave through the room. From behind, Team Pacifica let out a collective sigh, a gesture carrying both surprise and universal approval. Off in the corner of the room Sofia kept Nellie close by her side. To Jesse she looked like a lone lioness shielding her cub from a hungry mob of hyenas. She stirred and appeared to be simmering, ready to blow. But before reaching hysteria, Martin continued, his voice filled with the ardor of a game-show host.

"In fact, if you want, we'll take all of you back to our home with us." Making the announcement, he extended an arm around Santos, scooping the smaller man close for a brief hug.

Hysteria then did ensue, but it was the kind fueled by heartfelt joy and utter relief. "As long as you don't mind living in a place very different from here," Martin said, exuding an I-know-something-you-don't-know smile.

The mood in the room quickly turned, the funereal vibe ceded by a party-like atmosphere. Nobody was more shocked by the move than Jesse. As compassionate as he knew his friend was, he also knew him as a man who went strictly by the book, especially when it came to matters of the community. He could be no more surprised by what just transpired had Martin announced that he was in fact a woman, and from now on preferred to be called Martina.

Jesse smiled and watched as the small clan celebrated; no way the offer could be withdrawn now. He couldn't have been more pleased by the decision, and as evidenced by the reaction of the rest of the team, the sentiment was clearly unanimous.

Following a few minutes of celebration, where the two peoples shared hugs and hopes of a future now awash with optimism, Martin spoke again to the entire room. "Okay, we still have to hustle. We have to make it down to the water before the sun comes up. We'll also need a few minutes to load up the subs with our supplies and new friends."

"Subs? Water?" Sophia said, curious.

Martin smiled, was about to explain, eager, it seemed, to finally let the clan in on their little secret.

But it was Santos who beat him to the punch. "They live underwater," he said as casually as if he were asking someone for the time of day.

"How the heck did you know that?" Martin asked as the room drew silent.

All eyes turned to Santos, collectively awaiting explanation. "It's obvious from all the clues you have given."

"Like what?" Martin asked, appearing surprised, but not upset.

"Well, first of all, there were so many things you didn't know. Not being familiar with el Cucuy or Leezak could be explained by living in another location. But even if you were from the woods as you said, you'd be aware that the sun is still harmful. Second, none of you have any signs of sun damage. Your skin is nearly perfect, even him." Santos pointed to Alex. "Except for Leezak's men, everybody has at least some sun damage. Aside from that, you are all in such great health."

"That's a pretty amazing deduction from such a small bit of info." Martin said.

"I have more," Santos offered, sounding like a detective laying out gathered evidence to a crime. "You have also been careful to keep the location of your home a secret, which means it must be very important to you. That could be for safety, but it could also be because there is a limited amount of space. Maybe both. At first I thought somewhere underground. But the final clue came from the food that you brought. It was all seafood, fish and seaweed. They may be common out in the deep ocean, but are very limited along the shoreline due to radiation."

Martin chortled, smiled. "Is that it?" he asked, seeming to have enjoyed the explanation.

Santos nodded and flashed a smile.

"Very impressive, Sherlock." Martin said. "It'll be good to have you around. I'm sure we can find something productive for you to do back home with that kind of problem solving ability." Martin paused, downshifted. "Just so you are aware, our place is not the greatest. We have issues as well. And it may take a little getting used to. But all things considered, the most important thing, I suppose, is that it's very safe. And in time, you should all feel right at home there."

"We'll be fine," Santos said, speaking for his small tribe as he often did. "We are just thankful you showed up on our doorstep, and we appreciate that you have seen it in your heart to take us with you." His manner could be no more grateful. "Should we bring anything along with us?" he then asked, still addressing Martin.

"The less you bring the better. In fact," Martin hesitated, seemed to be shifting gears, lines of concern furrowing in his brow. "I just realized something that could pose a problem."

With the mention of a potential problem, Santos stiffened, his eyebrows rising.

Martin shook his head, as if angry with himself. "I failed to realize that there may not be enough room for everyone to come. Darnnit!"

Jennifer immediately jumped in, rallying to the defense of the terrestrials. "There should be plenty of room, what are you talking about!"

Jesse could see her anger was locked and loaded, held in check by only a thin string of restraint. Another wrong move and Martin was going to get both barrels.

"The problem is," Martin explained, "that if Jesse's gonna stay behind as he says he is, then it's our obligation to leave one of the subs, in case he should find his father and they decide to return. And there's just no way we can all fit in the Lobster."

Jesse felt the spotlight pivot onto him, pinning him down like a corporate crook at a congressional inquest. But there was no Fifth Amendment clause to hide behind here. He'd have to respond. His friend had played it well. It was obvious to Jesse that he had intentionally woven the clever little scheme to put pressure on him to return. That explained why he had so easily agreed to take Santos and his family back to Pacifica. Something that, if put to him earlier, Jesse would've wagered his life against. Equally as obvious was the fact that he couldn't call him out on what *he knew* to be a contrived plot. If he were to accuse Martin of setting this up, agreeing to take the terrestrials home just to force him to come home as well, he'd only appear petty and pathetic, the delusions of an angry man. Had this been a game of chess, and if Jesse were forged of weaker constitution, it may have indeed been check-mate.

As pissed as Jesse was, he realized that there was simply no upside to anger. So when he finally spoke, his voice was steady and void of resentment.

"You don't have to leave a sub behind for me. You don't have to leave anything behind on my account. I'll be just fine. The last thing I'd ever wanna do is stand in the way of these good people getting a second chance in life."

Jesse had effectively countered Martin's action. It did nothing to reduce the rising pressure in the room, however. But before the quarrel advanced further, a solution was offered, and was issued by an unlikely source.

"I'll stay behind too," Alex said, the four words tossed casually into the chasm of tension that had developed between Jesse and Martin.

"What the hell does that solve?" Martin barked. This was clearly *not* part of his little plan.

Alex went on to explain in a levelheaded, matter-of-fact manner. "If I stay behind, for one thing, I can help Jesse find his father. As suggested, you can go ahead and leave us the Halibut. Without me on the Lobster you should be able to squeeze aboard. It'll be tight, but it's doable. There's six of you…well, five and a half. Put four adults in the four seats; put the little one on someone's lap and the other person can squeeze in the cargo area in the back. Take only the supplies that are most urgent. Fit what you can inside under the seats and on your laps. Any supplies that can get wet put in backpacks and tie them to the frame of the sub. Whatever is left, toss in the back of our sub. We'll bring them back when we return. And if something should happen and we don't make it back, the supplies will still be there. You can return anytime to pick them up. We can leave the solar panel in place so you can just hook up, recharge and return without any danger. You won't even need to surface."

The vacuum that developed in the wake of Alex's explanation was as a quiet as deep space. Martin rolled his eyes and issued a dismissive wave. Neither he nor Jennifer vocalized opposition to the plan. Santos was the one to break the silence. "I should stay too and help you guys."

"No." Jesse's answer came firm and without hesitation. "You've done more than enough for us; you belong with your family. Alex grew up not far from here, he knows his way around, and I was watching you closely last night. I think I have a good understanding of how to manage in this environment."

"Okay," Santos conceded without argument. "But at least let me show you this." Santos reached down and turned over an old sheet of plywood. On the back was a crude map that looked like a cave sketch of Clovis days. "This drawing shows where our crops are, should you get hungry. This mark is the well house, and these are the locations. We discovered several edible plants and roots that grow in this environment. The black screen draped over the plants helps protect them from the sun."

"Thank you Santos," Jesse said.

"Sleep up top, it's much safer." Santos pointed to the hole in the ceiling. "There's some food stored up there, and you already know where the water is." Santos then pointed to several chipped holes in the cinderblock wall. Hidden inside were containers that collected water from runoff, the family had shared from their secret stash over dinner the night prior.

"And don't forget, it is always best to boil the water first," Santos reminded.

"No problem Santos, and thank you again for everything." Jesse smiled, shook his hand. "Now let's get you and your family packed and ready. If I know my friend Martin, he's gonna want to get going ASAP."

Ten minutes later, Martin and Jennifer, along with their new friends, departed the water station. Jesse and Alex offered to go down and help them load up, but Martin declined and explained that, although the offer was appreciated, he was concerned that it would expose them to danger upon their return trek. During those ten minutes Martin had busied himself gathering gear and helping the terrestrial clan do the same. He seemed accepting of the decision half his team had made to remain. This came as no surprise to Jesse; he knew Martin, the man was not petty. With his attempt to keep the team intact lost, he'd moved on, his focus turned to getting the rest of the team back safely. When it came time to leave, and it was his turn to offer wishes of luck and shake hands with Alex and Jesse, the action came genuine and without rancor.

Now, as Jesse watched his friends descend the hill and vanish into the pre-dawn ink, a pang of absolute sadness struck his soul. It made him think of his parents, the feeling of loss having similar texture. He took measure of the sorrow, but just a quick dipstick so as not to cause any great emotional upwelling. He knew he had to keep his mind free of distracting thoughts, and stay as focused as a neurosurgeon if they were going to pull off the daunting operation that lay ahead. He was already beginning to worry if he hadn't bit off more than he could chew. The fact that Jennifer had left them the nine millimeter brought him some comfort.

Standing in the front door of the water station, Jesse turned to Alex. "Come on, we'd better head inside and get some sleep."

Alex nodded and toggled on his flashlight to guide them inside. Jesse followed.

Walking back through the dark building Jesse's thoughts turned to Alex, a man he hardly knew before yesterday was now a man for which he felt a strong connection; the bond formed, as bonds sometimes do, from beginnings unexpected. Whatever it was that Jesse would face in the coming hours or days, he would not have to face it alone. For what it would be worth, he'd have help and support.

And more importantly, he'd have a friend by his side.

Chapter 42

Jesse awoke to utter darkness and reached blindly for his flashlight. When his fingers finally closed around it, he turned it on to light the small earthen cave. The room was empty; Alex was gone. Jesse wondered how he had managed to exit the small cavern without waking him up.

After Martin and the others had left, Alex and Jesse returned to the deeper parts of the building to sleep the day away. Following Santos's recommendation, they'd climbed up into the ceiling to do so.

Jesse got up and began crawling out of the cave to look for Alex. He knew it would take more than a few minutes to navigate back to the ground floor. Earlier when they'd first climbed up into the ceiling they were initially perplexed; unable to find the place to sleep Santos had spoke of. Santos and his family were small, but no way even they could be comfortable sleeping amid the rafters, let alone be safe. One wrong move and you'd crash through the thin tiles and plummet to the concrete floor below. Santos was a protective father and husband, no chance he'd put his family at that kind of risk.

With that in mind, they'd crawled deeper into the compact attic, following the only possible pathway, wiggling around pipes, ducts, and wires that snaked all around like pythons and pit vipers in an overcrowded serpent exhibit. Jesse even had the scars to prove it, his body littered with small painful bites inflicted by fangs of hanging wire and hurtful metal duct.

Nearly twenty feet in, they'd found a hole chipped through the cinder-block wall. The hole led to a short tunnel which gave way to a subterranean cave the size of a mini-van. The back wall was a huge slab of ledge rock, brushed archeological dig clean to reveal every mafic mineral crystal. Stacked rocks and timbers supported the rest of the earthen excavation. Blankets and old throw pillows covered a packed dirt ledge that rimmed the sunken room like a circular couch. Although built more like a bomb shelter, the room had the overwhelming vibe of a groovy little pad, a retro fusion of seventies and Flintstonian motif. The only thing missing was a lava lamp.

The air inside was cool and damp. With every breath came the taste of grit and loam. But after a moment, the smell seemed to disappear, any residual reek offset by the inherent serenity the earthen womb seemed to ooze. All in all, it was a superb little sanctuary, and would serve as a perfect base of operations for their current quest, and for Jesse, perhaps much longer.

Gotta do something about that commute though, he thought as he finally reached the open ceiling and jumped down to the room below, dusting himself off. Although, as he pondered it further, the obstacle course was certainly enough to dissuade curiosity, maybe even attack. Jesse wondered if Santos hadn't left it *as is* for that very reason. Trying to eat a porcupine was not worth the effort in pain for most predators.

As Jesse approached the front door to the water station, he saw Alex sitting in the doorway, his back to him as he looked outside. His arms were wrapped around his knees, his body positioned just beyond reach of the ebbing sunlight.

"Good morning," Jesse said as he approached, not wanting to startle him.

"Good morning to you too." Alex turned, smiled and removed his iPod.

Jesse plopped down next to him. Side by side they filled the threshold, and together they sat like two old friends from the neighborhood chilling on the front porch, enjoying the view. The sun was just about to set, a huge crimson orb that looked like a molten ingot melting through a dark blue block of Pacific Ocean paraffin. A procession of backlit stratocumulus clouds laminated the western sky in cruel splendor. The clouds glowed with a blushing radiance so red and magnificent that they appeared to possess hidden magic. Jesse found himself lusting over the skyline; its sheer beauty filling his soul with a rich consuming buzz.

"Man, that's beautiful," Jesse remarked out of reflex, as if the very essence of the sunset reached inside to posses him.

"Indeed," Alex agreed. "Hard to believe something so beautiful could be so dangerous."

Jesse pondered the remark. *Is it really the sun that's the dangerous one?*

A spontaneous memory popped into his mind, an incident he remembered seeing on the news so many years ago. A black bear had bitten a five-year old at the zoo upstate as the boy stuck his hand through the chain link fence. Witnesses confirmed that the child had been taunting the animals. The injury was minor, didn't even require stitches. Consequently, the bear had been euthanized for simply doing what bears do. Since they were uncertain which bear had done it, all three critters living in the exhibit had been killed —*Apple, Isaac and Tinkerbelle*—their corpses then dumped unceremoniously in the local landfill. Jesse had wondered then, as he wondered now, *was it really the black bears that were the dangerous ones?*

Jesse found the analogy all too apropos, but kept his musings to himself. He knew Alex hadn't meant anything by the remark, but it didn't stop his mind from making the connection. Now fully awake, his brain was cranking, no doubt getting revved up for events upcoming.

"Did you eat anything yet?" Jesse asked, his focus back on the sunset to keep his mind in the now.

"Not yet," Alex replied.

"Here, try some of these." Jesse handed him a few small roots that looked like fat carrots with dirty purple skin. "Found these in a bag back in the cave. I assume it's the food Santos told us about."

Alex took one and eyed it curiously. "Are they any good?"

"I managed to get a couple of 'em down. Not much to write home about, but it's calories. Kinda tastes like wet tree bark."

"So they taste more or less like they look."

Jesse nodded. "It's either this or I can cook up the snake fillet Santos left for us."

Alex quickly stuffed one in his mouth and began chewing in haste.

Jesse laughed at the antic. "By the way, I just wanted to say thanks again for staying behind to help me out. It means a lot."

"No problem."

The lines on Jesse's face grew serious. "You know, you don't have to go with me tonight. This could turn out to be dangerous."

"You mean more dangerous than eating some unknown root that's been sitting in a moldy cave for god only knows how long?"

Jesse laughed again. "Well…just wanted to be sure you were up for it. And if at any time you don't feel comfortable with what we're doing, just let me know. This is a team effort. Last thing I wanna do is force you into a situation where you don't feel safe."

Alex nodded, continued to chew. "Much appreciated. But I'm pretty much on board with this. So I say we just go ahead and do it. We've got the element of surprise on our side; I think it should give us a great advantage. As long as we're careful, I think we'll be just fine."

"Okay then. I'm starting to feel good about this."

"Any idea how you wanna approach this?" Alex asked as he finally swallowed, wincing like a child being forced to eat his peas.

"Not exactly. With Santos unfamiliar with the layout of Leezak's place, I'd like to try to get as close a look at the area as possible." He pointed in the direction of the city. "Maybe get up on top of one of the tall buildings in the neighborhood and survey the lay of the land. From there, we should be able to come up with some kinda game plan."

Alex crunched another bite of the root. "Sounds good. When do you wanna head out?"

"We might as well get going in a few minutes, give ourselves as much time as we can. The more time we have the less chance of screwing up. The sun should be down any minute. But I don't want to interrupt your dinner."

Alex smiled, took another bite. "You know, this stuff actually ain't half bad. Tastes like crap, but I kinda like the texture."

"Well, I've got good news for ya, my friend," Jesse gave him a fun-loving slap on the back. "There's plenty of it. I found piles of it stuffed behind the rocks in the cave."

Alex raised his eyebrows. "Great."

A glowing thread of sun was all that lingered on the oceanic horizon; the sky in rapid transition as pioneering darkness crept in from the east. Jesse focused again on the celestial masterpiece, reveling in its beauty, the vista filling his spirit with awe. In just a few minutes they'd be able to safely exit the water station, and then they could be on their way. But before heading out, one more question needed to be posed.

"Let me ask you something." Jesse spoke with tact. "Why did you decide to come along on this mission anyway? Didn't you just win the reproductive lottery?"

Alex shifted and sighed. "Yeah, that was mostly my girlfriend's doing. I never thought we'd actually win the darn thing. Don't get me wrong, I really love her and all. But I'm just not convinced it's the best idea to bring a new life into the world the way things are. And lately, I just haven't felt all that comfortable living in Pacifica. Was never a huge fan even in the beginning, I'm not great in tight places, but I couldn't pass up the opportunity to work there.

"So I wanted to take this trip to see for myself what things are like, see what kind of hope there is for the future, if any, before I go ahead and knock her up." He snorted a laugh. "It was all I could do to convince her to let me go. I gotta tell ya, it was quite a scene. I actually told her that you guys insisted. Even told her that you said

I was an essential ingredient. I won't even tell you what she called you after that."

Jesse rolled his eyes. "Great, I'm sure she must just *love* me."

Alex laughed. "I wouldn't expect a Christmas card this year."

Jesse shook his head and grinned. He realized that he and Alex were a lot more alike than he would've ever imagined.

The conversation gave way to pause, leaving only the whisper of the late September sea-breeze in the air. Together they watched as the last cuticle of sun winked below the horizon. Keeping the sky from total darkness would soon be in the hands of the slowly ripening moon.

Jesse then stood and flexed his legs. "You ready to get going?"

"Ready as I'll ever be," Alex replied as he stood and stretched as well.

And together, the two men began walking down the hillside, away from the safety of the water station, and off into the night.

Chapter 43

The journey into town had gone off without incident. Jesse had modeled his actions after Santos's, mimicking the tactics he'd observed the night prior. From his time spent with the terrestrial man, he'd gained a general understanding of the animal politics in this new world. And when it came to safari through the streets, stealth was definitely the way to go, but not to the point of projecting desperation or fear, or even hinting of such. Any signs of weakness would be like blood in the water. That alone could inspire interest, if not outright predation. Jesse had concluded that a middle ground approach was best while wading through the alien wilderness, somewhere between the extreme strategies of fangs bared and playing possum. The distillation of that notion, along with primal brainstem instincts yielded one immutable edict.

Act like you belong.

So that's exactly what they'd done, and it had served them well during their passage through the city. Aside from a few scurrying insects, they detected no signs of animal life. Sixth-sense intimations were quite another subject, however, and filled Jesse's mind with more than a gist of paranoia. Like the night prior, Jesse couldn't shake the vibe of eyes upon them, or the vague perception of malign souls lurking in the shadows. And thus was the double-edged nature of traveling amid hostile environs at night. For as much as the darkness offered the perceived comfort of camouflage, it also bore the burden of blindness, making potential dangers all the more difficult to identify and evade.

With any luck, they'd be able to free his father tonight and bid adieu to this part of the world forever. And if that should be the case, it would be just fine as far as Jesse was concerned.

For the past two hours Jesse and Alex had sat on a rooftop across the street from Leezak's alleged compound, both men scanning the grounds from their nine-story crow's nest, scouting for signs of life, if not a way in.

"What time ya got?" Alex whispered.

Jesse lowered the binoculars and looked at his watch, "Just after twelve."

"Whatta you think? Do you wanna make a go at this tonight?"

Jesse sighed. "If you're up for it, I say we give it a shot. It's probably best if we wait a little longer till we move, maybe they'll be asleep. It's been two hours and I haven't seen one thing to detour us, I don't see any advantage to waiting. It's a ghost town down there. No guards, no movement, no nothing."

Alex nodded. "Yeah. It's like a dead zone down there. You'd think there'd been a nuclear accident or something."

"Exactly," Jesse agreed. "Of course there's no way to know what's going on inside the building with the windows blacked out the way they are." He paused, massaged his chin. "I'd love to get a closer look. I'm guessing that's black paint on the windows. If it's on the outside maybe we can scrape some off and get a look inside. Who knows? Maybe we'll get lucky and pinpoint where he is, or at least get some idea of the layout. That sure could make things a lot easier." He then pointed to Alex's trusty knapsack. "Got anything in there that can get us through the fence?"

Alex smiled knowingly as he stuck his hand in his bag and rummaged. "No problem." He pulled out a pair of wire cutters. "We make a few cuts in the chain links and the fence should spread right open."

"Excellent." Jesse lifted the binoculars and continued to scan.

The compound looked like an outdated penitentiary. The main building, which appeared to be an old factory of some sort, was surrounded by a huge empty parking lot, as barren as it was foreboding. Several smaller buildings hugged the main, a few garages and what appeared to be a greenhouse sat like satellites in close orbit. Collectively, they projected the eerie aura of an obsolete insane asylum; the kind from psychiatry's dark days where patients were often diagnosed by phrenology or other pseudo-scientific means, then locked up or lobotomized with the same civility extended to a lab rat. A tall chain-link fence topped with corkscrewing barbed-wire rimmed the entire parking lot like a prison yard. A gate was around back, probably locked. No guards were visible. A single flicker-ing street-lamp marked the northern perimeter, the only apparent sentinel.

Above all else, the strangest element was the dark smoke that belched from the huge smoke stacks, and the industrial whine that echoed from somewhere inside. Smoke streamed into the atmosphere like black crude from a ruptured pipeline, the taste in the air as unmistak-able as the smell. The dark toxin slowly diffused across the moonlit sky, smudging the stars and the moon with atmospheric char, graffiti sprayed across the celestial mural that Jesse had found so enchanting only a few hours before. The smoke must be from a power generator, Jesse surmised.

"I just can't believe how quiet it is down there," Jesse whispered, still scanning the grounds with his field glasses.

"Maybe they're out on the streets. You know, like last night."

"I suppose that's possible. But Santos said that Leezak has dozens of men. I can't believe we'd get so lucky as to have them all out tonight. And if that were the case, they probably have my father with them again, which doesn't really help us. They gotta have someone to pull their carts."

"You know, there could be others," Alex offered in a solemn tone. "There were two others on the mission with your father, and there were quite a few people lost way back in the beginning."

Jesse shifted uneasily. "I've considered that. I figure we'll play it by ear. See what we find when we get down there. If we find anyone else we know, of course we'll do our best to help get them out. Just wish I had a better idea what that place looks like on the inside."

"I was thinking, if we can locate the building department we might be able to find a set of blueprints to this place," Alex suggested. "My brother did an internship with a building department back when he was in college. He told me that they kept hard copies of just about everything, and I doubt any of the paperwork would be of interest to looters. The municipal buildings are not far from here from what I recall."

Jesse lowered the binoculars again. "That's not a bad idea. I bet we can find a directory somewhere and look up the address to the building department." He paused to ponder. "If we reach a point tonight where we hit a dead-end, we'll do exactly that. We could use the rest of the night to track down the plans, then take them back to the water station and look 'em over. If need be, we can always finish this tomorrow night." Jesse gave Alex a wink. "Nice thinking, my friend."

"No problem," Alex said, smiling. "That's what I'm here for. You certainly didn't bring me along for my looks."

Jesse suppressed a laugh, shook his head and smiled back. "That's for sure."

Alex shifted restlessly. "What time is it now?" he asked, sounding like a kid in the back seat of the family station wagon asking, *are we there yet?*

Jesse looked at his watch again, then back up at Alex. "It's showtime."

Chapter 44

Alex and Jesse stood before the tall chain link fence that rimmed the campus. Jesse felt his heartbeat thump in his ears; an escalation resulting from having rapidly descended nine flights of stairs, as well as the anxious anticipation of breaking and entering into what was, by all accounts, the castle of a madman.

Alex went down on a knee, pliers in hand, and worked to cut the fence. A metallic clack shot through the night as the cutters snapped home. Jesse flinched, looked around nervously. The sound had probably carried less than fifty feet, but under the circumstances, the noise stood out like a gunshot.

"This is a little heavier gauge than I thought." Alex whispered, flexing his hand.

"Want me to give it a try?" Jesse offered, still nervously scanning like he was standing in the middle of a busy intersection.

"I got it," Alex assured him as he angled the metal beak around another link. "Just keep a look out." *Pop.* The pliers snapped home again. "Besides," he said, latching onto the next victim. "A Tool Troll never relinquishes his tools."

Before Jesse knew it, Alex was worming his way through the fence, the breach hinging back as he slipped through. Once inside, Alex stood and waved Jesse to follow. After a final look around, Jesse was down on the ground slithering his way through, joining Alex on the inside. Jesse then stood, brushed himself off and gazed at the massive building ahead. Alex turned and waited as he gathered himself; a mere hundred yards of open asphalt was now the only thing separating them from their destination. This was definitely going well, Jesse thought, at the very least they'd gather some useful intel tonight.

But as Jesse took a step forward, Alex suddenly lunged at him like a linebacker on a goal line stand. All he could do is look on with mouth agape as Alex tackled him to the ground, hearing only a subtle swoosh in the air behind him and Alex's urgent warning. "Get down!"

The next thing he realized, he was on the pavement, Alex on top of him, both panting from the shock of action, and the instant spike of adrenaline.

"What the hell!" Jesse snapped, utterly perplexed. But Alex didn't immediately respond. And only when Jesse tried to push Alex off of him did the first inkling of understanding hit home. He didn't know exactly what had just happened, but one thing was for certain.

Something was wrong.

Alex was like a dead weight in his arms as he bench pressed him off. As he rolled him on his side, he was horrified by the moonlit image of his friend. His face was a taut mask of utter panic, eyes bulging, pupils fixed, mouth gasping like a by-catch fish flopping on the deck of a trawler.

"Alex!" Jesse shook him by the arm, both men still on the ground.

But Alex did not respond, his eyes fluttering, still panting as though the air around him was filled with mustard gas. And then he heard an odd sound, a rushing wheeze that came in sync with Alex's labored breathing.

Jesse quickly lifted from the pavement, then gently leaned his friend's catatonic body toward him. And then like an empathy transfusion, the panic that was on Alex's face rushed into Jesse, streaking like cobra venom right to his core.

No! Jesus! No!

The shaft of an arrow protruded from Alex's back, just below the scapula.

Blood had already soaked his shirt dark around the wound. A liquid rattle and rusted mist atomized with each hemorrhaged breath.

He slowly moved Alex onto his side, careful not to let him roll back on the arrow and puree his insides any further. Jesse felt sticky warmth between his fingers. Flexing his hand, he realized it was varnished with blood.

"Don't worry, Alex, I'm gonna get you outta here, you're gonna be okay," he said with all the conviction he could muster. Then movement caught his eye, a distant flash. He quickly looked up. A large dark figure stood on the second-floor balcony of the building across the street, a crossbow gripped in his hands. Jesse half expected him to reload and shoot again, but he didn't. Instead he turned and ran back inside the building. In that instant all hell broke loose, the compound springing alive like a disturbed beehive. Alarms bleated and floodlights flashed on all around the main building. And then another noise, doors banging open from the main building, releasing streams of men out into the night.

Jesse turned his attention back to Alex, took a deep breath, tried to regain his composure. If he was going to get them out of this, he was going to have to make all the right moves, and do so with lightning speed. Priority one: get Alex through the fence, even if he had to carry him. But he couldn't do that with the arrow sticking out. A thought then came: use the wire cutters to trim back the shaft of the arrow so Alex could be safely moved. He knew enough not to just pull the arrow out from the back. He'd already checked to see if the arrow had come through the front—*no dice*—so pulling it through was not an option. And jamming it forward to punch through and pull it out, although considered, was a risk Jesse wasn't ready to take.

He grabbed Alex's knapsack, sifted through, all the while keeping one hand on Alex so he didn't roll over on the arrow.

"Just give me a second buddy, I'm gonna have you out of here in no time." Jesse said as he found the wire cutters. Moving with measured haste he positioned the cutters around the arrow, getting as close to the skin as he dared. With steady pressure, he squeezed the tool and the balance of the aluminum shaft fell away with a metallic clang. *Yes*, he breathed, a clean cut. He felt the first glimmer of hope, his mind assuring him that this was going to work; everything was going to somehow be okay.

Now to get him out of here. He leaned back to Alex, ready to tell him of their next move. But Alex was no longer there, his life force gone, his eyes fixed and his tongue lolled to the side, blood-slick and swollen, a dusky one hundred and seventy pound husk was all that remained.

"Alex! " Jesse shouted, even though he knew there was no waking him from this sleep.

"Shit!" Jesse cried, feeling his insides curdle with nausea. *This isn't happening! Please let this just be a bad dream*, his mind begged. A distant fold in his brain kept radar on the approaching men from behind, likewise warning him that the man who killed Alex would be down on the street any second.

There's an instinctive reaction that often accompanies moments like these; a situation where one man falls next to another in battle. A knee-jerk emotion that wells up even before the superego has chance to suppress it. And that emotion was one of relief. An inner voice would then put words to the emotion, speaking in only whispered introspection: *whew, I'm glad it wasn't me!*

But in this case, that never took place, not even the seedlings of such a thought. Because it had been Jesse's own conduct that caused the death of his brother-in-arms. And there was simply *no way* around that fact. Had it not been for him, Alex would be alive and well right now, and very likely back in Pacifica, his most pressing concern deciding whether to have a baby with his girlfriend or not. On top of that, from all evidence, Alex pushing him to the pavement had saved his life. And in the process, the selfless secret service tactic had cost him his own, which only further turned the finger of guilt squarely back in his direction.

The sum of which generated another, and altogether rarer, thought in Jesse's mind; one that completely short-circuited his survival instincts, one that, at this very moment, repeated over and over in obsessive procession across his mind's eye.

I wish it was me instead of you, my friend!

On the edge of awareness Jesse knew that the men were closing. Amid the wailing siren, he could hear angry shouts, ordering him to *stay put*. He had no inclination to do otherwise. Even the gun tucked in his pants had no appeal. At the moment he was not of the mindset to wage war. Nor did he have the urge to move, or the will to attempt escape. Fleeing would mean that he wanted to live. But at the moment, despite the distant rallying cries in the back of his mind, his spirit had been effectively crushed, and he just wanted to die. He wasn't certain that they'd kill him when they arrived, but it wouldn't upset him in if they did.

And with that desire, Jesse leaned over his fallen friend and prepared to join him.

Part Three

A NEW ERA

Chapter 45

As consciousness returned Jesse was greeted by the faint outline of a slowly rotating ceiling fan. The room was dark and his mind woozy, but he knew right away he wasn't in the water station, or back in the cave. For an instant, he thought he might be dead; but that couldn't be. No way could this be heaven—mostly because that particular honor was no longer a consideration, now that he had the black-eye of ultimate blame stamped on his soul. The death of Alex was his fault, a fact that was as unmistakable as it was painful to address. And no way was this hell; certainly a climate controlling ceiling fan would be about the last appliance one would find there.

All of which effectively begged the question—where the heck was he?

As his mind cleared, so did the details of the prequel that led him to this point. After being shot in the back, he'd just assumed that it was over. It felt like he'd been stung by a hornet the size of a condor. He remembered his last fleeting thoughts as he wilted on the pavement next to his friend, and drifted into blackness; *they killed me just like they did you*. And at that moment, the terrifying prospect of dying had been rendered irrelevant by guilt, and an overwhelming impulse of karmic logic that he somehow deserved this, and this was his requisite pay-back for getting Alex killed.

Jesse had never been afraid of death, but always had concerns of dying. Not only the fear of physical pain but the potential panic the journey into destinies unknown might evoke. Even though his dying had been a false alarm, he didn't know it at the time, and therefore got a first-hand glimpse of the process he so feared. Thinking about it now, he realized that he had not been the least bit afraid. In fact, it was hard to think of another situation where the final journey might be any easier. One more reason he almost wished that he'd just gone ahead and checked out.

Jesse tried lifting his head up off the cot, and imme-diately regretted the move; a ring of pain squeezed his skull like a coiling constrictor. The rest of his body was also sore. He felt like a crash test dummy after a long day at the office. As bad as he felt, the physical pain was noth-ing compared to the mental anguish he felt over losing a friend, the difference as vast as a splinter to a ruptured aorta.

As he struggled to get to a sitting position, a revela-tion suddenly flashed with high-def clarity amid a mind still fogged. *Make amends.* See that Alex's death had not been in vain. Attempt to somehow, someway, settle the score—even if it should take great sacrifice to achieve, even the ultimate. It'd be blood well spent, and a more than worthwhile trade off as far as he was concerned.

With the new plan in hand, his mood immediately improved and he breathed a sigh of relief, now glad that he was still alive. Once again he had purpose; and that purpose continued to crystallize into aspiration, then a single word…

Revenge.

Jesse looked around the small room as he continued to stretch, trying to ease his sore muscles. *Damn,* he muttered, they must've really roughed him up. Did anyone get the license plate of the Mack truck?

The small room was prison-cell austere. The only amenities, a ceiling fan, a cot, and a small end table with a single glass of water resting on it. He eyed the water. Thirsty as he was, he thought about chugging it, but decided not to, his instinct of caution outweighing his urge to hydrate. A bathroom was off to the side, a mere four by four cubicle. Having no mirror or shower, it was little more than a porta-potty. A roll of *real* toilet paper sat next to the bowl, an amenity he'd not had the privilege of in quite some time. It was even the quilted brand. The notion gave him a dash of emotional gusto, his mind digging deep for any frag of optimism to be had. The only light in the room was a pale shaft that made its way in through the narrow glass panel on the door. He took note of a small vent on the wall behind him, but it was far too small to fit through.

He slowly stood; leaned gingerly against the cot. He wobbled, but otherwise held steady. He noticed his shirt was pasted to his back, crusted like dried paint around the spot where he'd been shot. It hurt like hell, stood out as the epicenter of soreness among hundreds of other muscles that proclaimed their own ache. The wound felt like it might already be infected.

He checked his watch in the frugal light. Five-thirty am. He'd been out for some five hours. It suddenly dawned to him that he'd been drugged. He'd been shot with a dart, not an arrow, the effects of the drug still slowing his body and mind.

He tried to open the door. The knob spun but the door held fast. He pressed his face against the small window, trying to see where he was. Not much to go on, just a long hallway that stretched in either direction. He assumed he'd been brought inside the main building; which, as he thought about it, he hoped to be the case. For one thing, it might give him a chance to find his father; something that would ensure, at least to some degree, that Alex's death was not entirely without upshot. And secondly, being inside might provide the opportunity to get the revenge he now sought. Track down the bastard who pulled the trigger and shatter his skull like a porcelain vase. He might also be able to find the mastermind, the one ultimately responsible for his father's enslavement and his friend's demise.

Leezak! Jesse breathed, as the name came to mind.

Exactly what he'd do to him, Jesse was not yet certain. As long as it somehow concluded with him begging for mercy and wishing he'd never been born.

The downside to his current predicament, and what kept a damper on his enthusiasm, was that at the moment, he was a prisoner; and he no longer held the element of surprise. But as he pondered those facts, and overlaid them with what he'd seen during their attempted breach; getting caught was probably the only way he could've gotten inside in one piece—a situation that, although far from ideal, might yet prove serendipitous.

Looking through the small window he noticed that the door was held shut by a propped folding chair jammed behind the doorknob. On top of that, he didn't see any guard posted in the hall, unless someone was stationed beyond his view.

Entirely possible.

He knocked gently on the door, then waited. And when nobody appeared, he felt fairly certain that the coast was clear. This was all too good to be true, he thought.

Did they really expect this to hold him? A metal folding chair. But then again, maybe they didn't expect him to be up so soon from his chemically induced coma. As it was his brain was still whirling from the tranquilizer dart.

He tried shaking the door, figuring it might rattle the chair free. No good. He knew he could break the window, then reach down and move the chair, but the noise would carry. *No*, there had to be a better way. And with that, Jesse turned to the cot and lifted the thin mattress. *Yes.* Several stiff wires were strung across the frame.

He removed one of the wire supports, then got down on the ground and fished it under the door. Peering beneath the door, he maneuvered the wire behind one of the chair legs and gently pushed. It immediately lurched free, and he could hear the chair as it slowly slid down the outside of the door. When he had enough room, he snaked his arm out and grabbed the chair before it slammed to the tile floor.

A second later he was standing in the hallway, pleased to be free of his cage.

Now let's see where this leads.

Chapter 46

Eager to press on with his mission, Jesse scanned the hallway outside his pen. Dimly lit, the hall stretched for twenty feet in either direction. He stood still and listened. Aside from the subtle hum of the building itself, no noises came. He found the effects of low light along with the distant industrial hum eerie, made him think of a morgue at midnight. His next step; decide which direction to go. This was easy, his mind mused absently, almost too easy.

But despite the initial success, it was too early to celebrate. Don't spike the football till the points are on the scoreboard, he reminded himself. It was a lesson he learned back in high school while playing in a football game. Running past the twenty-yard line on his way to a touchdown, he raised the football over his head to celebrate, only to have it slip from his hand. It had not only been embarrassing, but almost cost his team the game. And with that in mind, he knew he still had a long way to go before declaring *mission accomplished*.

Although long, the hallway had only two other doors, one at each end. To the left stood a single metal door with a push bar and a narrow windowpane colored with the twilight gray of a nascent day. A single word glowed expectantly in red above the door. *EXIT.* The sign seemed to beckon, reaching right into his emotional core, speaking directly to the soft spot touched by teddy bears and mother's hugs; *come to me*, it urged, *it's okay to save yourself, everything will be okay*.

He turned and glanced at the door at the end of the hall, and it too seemed to call out to him. He could hear the subtle hum of a living building from behind the door, adding an actual voice to the anthropomorphic debate. Door number two would no doubt lead him into the heart of the building, and as such, directly into the crosshairs of danger. Aside from being more vocal, the message door number two inspired was not so warm and fuzzy.

Enter at your own risk!

Jesse weighed his options, envisioned himself running toward the exit, slamming the push bar, and running off into the safety of the predawn. But the vision quickly waned, an evaporating fantasy; because in the final analysis, there really was only one choice. A chance like this might not come around again, and it had to be capitalized upon.

So he headed off toward door number two. He had no firm plan of action. With no clue what to expect beyond his next heartbeat, he was employing a decide-on-the-fly philosophy. The only standing orders at the moment were to stay focused and calm, allow instincts to navigate. His performance, he'd learned from past experience, always seemed to improve if, by one means or another, he could find a way to relax in the heat of the moment. He'd found it effective more than once during pressure situations, had proved particularly effective while shooting free throws or having sex, as well as other situations where over-thinking was the Achilles heel of success. His theory would definitely be put to the test today, as this was without a doubt the biggest challenge he'd ever faced. This was like scoring with a supermodel or sinking a free throw to win the NBA finals, and successfully doing so while under the worldwide media microscope.

And with that, Jesse centered his thoughts and lengthened his breathing. He then opened door number two and carefully peeked through.

The door gave way to another long hallway. A dozen or so doors ran down its length. As he stepped into the hall the mechanical whine of the building became louder. Like the moans of a haunted house in a B movie—a creaky floor, a shutter banging—the noise jangled his nerves. A dose of the willies shivered heedlessly down his spine. And even though he found the industrial hum disturbing, it would also serve as cover. A trade-off he'd gladly take.

Instinct told him to continue in the direction of the noise. As he advanced toward the end of the hall, he tried to peek into some of the rooms, but found the doors locked, leaving only the large a metal door at the end.

He took a calming breath, and then with the stealth of a safe cracker he twisted the doorknob, half expecting it to also be locked. He could hear the industrial whine on the other side. Whatever was causing the noise, it was not far off.

But the door wasn't locked. And as he quietly pushed through he gasped, felt an electric thrill similar to free-fall. Because what he saw was both breathtaking and surreal. The room was huge, the size of a commercial airplane hangar. At rest in the center, and gobbling up a considerable chunk of floor space, was a massive machine. It roared and echoed loudly off the warehouse walls. The smell of oil and hydrocarbon reflux was thick in the air, filling the room with industrial incense. The floor was poured concrete, the walls raw cinderblock. The soaring aluminum panel ceiling was supported and slightly pitched atop massive wood-webbed trusses.

Jesse scanned the interior, looking for the movement of workers or guards. To the best he could see, the warehouse was empty. *Odd*, Jesse thought, but he wasn't complaining. With the coast clear, he entered, letting the door close quietly behind him.

Once inside, he got a better look. The layout was like a mechanized museum, the entire perimeter rimmed with machines, the mother lode of high-tech instrumentation. Tiny against the sweeping concrete backdrop, the array of instruments sat like a worshiping tribe around a mechanical volcano god. Some of the devices he actually recognized. Off to the left was a PerkinElmer gas chromatograph. He'd used the exact same model many years ago back in college. Just beyond that was an electron microscope. He'd never actually used one, but had seen one once while taking a tour at UC Berkeley.

Aside from all the tech toys, at least forty doors and open halls bordered the massive open room. A series of garage doors lined the back wall of the warehouse, the gate-way to a loading dock it would appear. He realized that it was going to take quite a while to search the place. It would take twenty minutes just to circle the confines, let alone investigate each room and spy down every hall. He noticed two doors on the back wall with *exit* signs, giving him knowledge of three ways out, which at the moment helped very little, as he'd yet to scratch even a single chore off his current bucket list. But if things should go bad, which could occur in the blink of an eye, having knowledge of an extra a bolt-hole or two wasn't a bad thing. The notion inspired only a modicum of comfort.

As he moved off, he found his attention drawn once again to the huge machine in the middle of the warehouse. It was a strange apparatus to say the least, gave off a curious vibe that went beyond the whine of its gears. The massive metal shroud on the far side appeared to be the housing for a turbine, leading him to believe, as he'd predicted, that it was some kind of power plant. That certainly made sense. After all, the building had electricity, and that power had to be generated somewhere. He would've liked to take a closer look, but at present no time could be spared for such considerations.

Jesse suddenly froze, his attention piqued by movement; a dark figure ambled along down at the far end of the building. Even from a distance Jesse could see the man was huge. Jesse quickly ducked behind the nearest instrument and peered out. Only a few steps later the man turned and headed down a hallway. He waited till his shadow fully receded before emerging from his hiding place to continue his search.

The first door he tried was locked. An open hallway came next. Dimly lit and nondescript, he moved past, dismissing it as a dead-end. To his dismay, he found the same to be the case all the way down the first wall; doors locked, hallways quiet and ordinary. A storage closet stuffed with cleaning supplies had been the most compelling discovery.

But his luck changed as he turned and began his search of the adjacent wall. The very first door was unlocked. And as he turned the knob and stepped inside he was nearly floored by what he saw. His eyes swelled with amazement, he couldn't believe what he was seeing.

Chapter 47

Right away Jesse recognized the room. It was a near carbon copy of the lab he'd seen on the grainy video back in Pacifica; the same program Reni had questioned him about only days earlier. A dozen huge cylindrical aquariums lined the room, bordering three walls like a public exhibit. Each acrylic keg glimmered with soft amethyst light, and each was home to an aquatic animal of absurd proportions.

Jesse stepped inside the room for a closer look. Years back, he remembered watching news programs and even a documentary about the good doctor's work. He remembered all the swirling speculation and theories that surrounded his strange doings. The lab had burned to the ground only a day after Leezak's lab had been raided by cops, the fire consuming its secrets, which only stoked the flames of mystery and gave the whole happening a kind of Area 51 conspiracy vibe that had never been fully dispelled.

Jesse slowly circled the room. As shocking as he found it all, he also felt oddly privileged, because he now knew the answer to the age-old debate. Although asleep, the identity of the aquatic critters was unmistakable. They were not aliens or cryptids, like many had speculated. Nor was it a hoax, as the government reports eventually concluded and fed to the public. They were in fact human; altered somehow, but definitely human fetuses, at least at the core.

One had a long tail; another had ears the size of his own sprouting from a head the size of a lemur. Another had sprigs of dark fur dotting flamingo-colored skin. In almost every case, the torso was distorted; several swelled huge along the abdomen, some deformed about the chest. Could they be sick? Could they have tumors? If so, it certainly didn't make sense—all this work for a bunch of diseased experiments. Besides, Jesse thought as he continued to take it all in, the weird features aside, they looked otherwise healthy. It was all utterly compelling, and took Jesse more than a little will power to remind himself that this was only a distraction. Time was ticking, and he still had a lot of ground to cover. But as hard as he tried, he just couldn't seem to pull free. He was being held in situ by an invisible umbilicus of awe.

He leaned close to one of the cylinders, a final look before moving on. The tiny creature drifted peacefully in the column of water. Quiet and still, it had oversized eyes, thin slits across pink marbles. Its chest heaved slowly like a bellows breathing to kindle a fire. Up close, it was almost cute.

As if sensing his presence, the creature's eyes shot open. Jesse flinched and nearly shit. The creature stared, then jerked and screamed, its action mere pantomime, its cry a silent yawn flexing beneath a layer of translucent derma. Jesse felt his skin prickle with panic, a knee-jerk impulse of elemental recoil. After all, what was there really to be afraid of? The thing was about as dangerous as a house fly.

Jesse slowly backed away from the exhibit, and felt an absolute vacuum rush of pity for the tiny strange being.

He found himself wishing there was something he could do to help. But he could think of nothing. And even if he did have a clue what to do, he had no time to make it happen.

Once back outside, he did his best to shake the disturbing images, refocus his mind and continue his search. He looked at his watch, ten till six. *Shit*, he muttered, and picked up the pace.

The next twenty minutes were a blur of searching and speculation, taking him nearly around the entire warehouse. He started to get frustrated. Vacant hallways, locked doors, and a half-dozen closets filled with janitorial supplies being his only discoveries. But as he approached his starting point, coming nearly full circle, a word stenciled on a doorway drew his attention like flies to a septic spill. The word was barely legible in the wan warehouse light.

Maternity

Although it wasn't a place where he was likely to find his father, or the guard who murdered Alex, he had to check it out; his fundamental human curiosity insistent on at least a peek. To his mild surprise, the room was not locked. He eased the door open and crept in.

The room was filled with light shed only from vital sign monitors and life support machines, but it was enough to see. A row of beds lined each side of the room; it looked like an army barracks done in hospital motif. Jesse could hear the blips of heartbeats broadcast by the bedside monitors. He moved quietly down the center aisle, looking side to side. It didn't take long for him to realize that, exactly as the sign had implied, this was a maternity ward. In almost every bed was a sleeping woman, and as he moved along he could see by the distinctive belly bulge that at least some of them were pregnant. At the end of the ward he found another door. It too had a word stenciled across it. Jesse's mind swelled with implication as he read it.

Nursery

But he did not enter. He had to cut off his curiosity at some point. And if any infants were inside, as the sign implied, he didn't want to risk awakening one. Because unless they slept in aquatic cribs like the fetuses he'd seen earlier, a crying baby would be tantamount to a squealing alarm. So he turned and retraced his steps back through the ward. It was time to get out of there and back on task anyhow.

Passing the beds again, he noticed a rope burn on the wrist of one of the sleeping females as it dangled from her bed. The image nattered at a distant fold in his brain, urging investigation. Stepping closer, it suddenly hit him. She was the young woman who'd been captive in the back of the cart the night prior. Gazing down upon her now, Jesse seethed with emotional pre-vomit, anger and pity swirling in his gut. Although asleep, the woman shifted restlessly, her face varnished in sweat, her emaciated body trembling as if rapt in nightmare. Bruises and scrapes corrupted her skin everywhere. An I-V line invaded a stringy vein, wire leads from the bedside monitor disappeared beneath her hospital gown.

She moaned and quivered as if running from some demon in her dream. Jesse patted her head softly. "It's gonna be okay," he whispered. The gesture welling up entirely out of reflex, as did the precursor of a tear.

In a start the woman's eyes opened and Jesse thought she was going to cry out. He braced for impact, heart hammering. But what came out of her mouth was far more disturbing—three little words, uttered in a voice both urgent and frail. "Please help me."

Jesse leaned down and held her hand. "I will do whatever I can," he whispered. "Just hang in there. Everything's gonna be okay." He managed a smile, an attempt to offer solace. But it was a lifeline made of Silly String tossed to woman drowning in the most wicked sea.

The woman squeezed his hand as her eyes slowly closed. "Thank you," she mouthed, before the effects of fatigue or drug or coma ushered her back to blackness. He gently placed her hand down and pulled the blanket up to cover her.

Jesse shook his head as he turned and stalked off. *Goddammit! Where's it gonna end?* He sighed as he hit the door, promising himself that as long as he had strength to draw breath, he'd do what he could to help her. What else could he do? His inner constitution would allow no less. The notion that maybe he was in over his head popped into his mind, but he immediately quelled the insurgency, assuring himself he could handle it. Besides, negative thinking wasn't going to help matters. And right now he had a search to finish.

But only a step out of the ward he was stopped in his tracks, paralyzed by the sound of mock applause. He heard the noise before he saw the face.

*Shit, h*e breathed. His search was over, at least for now.

"Very impressive speech you made in there," said the man as he continued to slowly clap his hands, smiling sarcastically.

Two stoic goons stood a step behind the man, one on either flank. One held a hand conspicuously over a holstered handgun.

Jesse tried not to show shock. He wasn't sure what affected him most: getting caught, the fact that he was standing in the presence of a historic madman, or the fact that the man somehow heard what he'd just said inside.

Whatever the case, the result was panic induced vocal gridlock.

The man spoke again, his voice a fine-grained baritone and candidly smug. "You seem to be a little overwhelmed at the moment. Please relax, I assure you, you are not in any danger. Let me introduce myself. My name is Dr. Harris Leezak." The man proffered his hand.

Jesse slowly reached out; he was in no position to reject the gesture.

Chapter 48

S till stunned by the sharp turn of events, Jesse begrudgingly shook Leezak's hand and told him his name. There was really no other way to play it. Despite his lust for action, the options of fight or flight were both dead ends. Either choice came with the life expectancy of the second or two it would take the guard to aim and squeeze off a round into Jesse's chest, or his back if he opted for the latter.

Leezak smiled easily. "Ahhh…Jesse, it's nice to meet you. And welcome to my home." Leezak spread his arms, glancing around in a lordly manner. He was neatly dressed, a pressed white lab coat buttoned over a traditional white shirt and tie. The strict apparel seemed as much a product of his posture as laundry starch.

Jesse still couldn't believe it. Standing right in front of him was the mortal rendition of an antique digital image, the same image that so often hijacked his dreams. He was tall and fit, more so than Jesse would've guessed, the apparent bias of the T-V lens. His hair was jet black and tight cropped, his eyes shined like hot slag. His white skin was offset by dark angular facial features. Along with the flickering light from above, it created a weird chromatic disparity that Jesse found more than a little unnerving. Staring at Leezak in the shadowy wash was like viewing a *vase or faces* optical illusion, his expression seeming to alter the instant he focused on a particular detail, his face a shifting mask of passion and evil. Despite all he knew of the man, including the recent view of his current machinations, he found the encounter oddly exhilarating. It was a kind of curious emotional emulsion one feels when witnessing a plane crash, or meeting a serial killer—a true contrast in cause of fascination.

Looking closer, Jesse drew the inevitable comparison, carefully cross-referencing the prior to the present, and he realized that Leezak looked a little *too much* like the old video footage. He appeared to have barely aged. Then again, Leezak was at ease at the moment, a far cry from the disheveled Charles Manson look he had going on before vanishing from the public eye. Maybe he'd just cleaned himself up, Jesse speculated, he certainly had time to do so.

Jesse knew Leezak had to be close to seventy. Maybe Alex was right about his work? He began to wonder whether the mysterious machine in the room wasn't some kind of giant fountain-of-youth magical juicer. Because as he stood before him today, Leezak didn't look a day over forty, all the Grecian Formula and Botox in the world couldn't account for that kind of make-over.

Till now, Jesse's mind had been flooded with stun, but like a carbureted engine suddenly getting the right mix, it fired back up. And with the return of focus, he spoke.

"Home? Is that what you call this place? Seems more like a house of horrors to me." Something told Jesse that a spirited interplay the best tactic to keep himself alive. Jesse also thought that if he could put Leezak back on his heels even a little, it might help level the playing field some, maybe cause him to slip up and spill some useful info.

Leezak nodded. "I understand how you must feel." An undertone of pseudo sympathy filled his eyes as much as his voice. "You've seen some things that are probably difficult to process. Perhaps you might think differently if you knew the logic behind my work. I'm sure a lot of what you are feeling right now is due to misunderstanding." Leezak, for his part, remained calm; adroitly side stepping Jesse's attitude. The advantage of the upper hand it would seem.

"Oh, I'd just love to hear the rationale for keeping human fetuses bottled like goldfish, or holding people captive against their will, or killing people. I'm sure I'll understand a lot better when you explain *that* one to me."

"Everything we do here has a purpose," Leezak replied evenly. "And I assure you, I've never had anyone killed without reason."

Jesse frowned, shook his head.

Leezak's face took on a puzzled expression, but then comprehension seemed to flicker behind his eyes. "Oh… you must be upset about your friend out in the parking lot last night. That was indeed a regrettable error. My men have been instructed not to use lethal means unless absolutely necessary. It was clearly an overreaction. But your actions were quite mystifying, and apparently had my guards confused. It has been many years since anyone has ever tried to break in to my compound. Given the circumstances, you should be thankful my guards didn't make a second mistake and kill you too."

Jesse looked down, overcome by sadness as Alex's death was once again dredged from his emotional coping compost. He also realized how unusual their actions must have appeared, how contrary to logic it was from the perspective of his adversary. At some point he was probably going to have to explain that. Telling Leezak the truth was out of the question of course. With that in mind, his mind began scrambling for a suitable excuse for their behavior. Maybe Leezak would believe him if he said they were breaking it to try and steal food.

"In fact," Leezak said with a wink, "That's exactly why I allowed you to escape from your room this morning. I figured it would be the best way to find out why you and your friend were trying to break in. Plus, it was quite entertaining." Leezak's expression was ripe with arrogance.

Jesse's mouth dropped open, but not a word came out. He felt his inner walls of confidence begin to leak with blunder and worry.

Leezak did a half-pirouette, pointing around the room. "This entire building is wired; there's video surveillance throughout. Yes…I got a chance to watch your entire little adventure tonight. I must say, it was compelling television. Especially the poignant little speech you just gave to your girlfriend in there. A priceless performance."

Jesse simmered, his anger turned wholly inward. He *knew* his escape had been too easy. He should've realized he was being set up; his instincts had done everything to warn him, frantically waving the cognitive equivalent to red flags. But like an idiot he'd ignored them, blinded as he'd been by the ambition of the moment. Fortunately, there appeared to be a favorable upshot. Leezak seemed to have misread his intentions; he thought he'd come to save the girl. This could work in his favor.

"Although I must say, the pairing seems a bit odd; you in such outstanding physical condition, while your lady friend is so damaged." Leezak paused, rubbed his chin as he seemed to ponder.

Uh-oh, Jesse thought, time for a little misdirection. "Yeah…well, you know what they say, opposites attract," he tossed out, unable to come up with anything better.

"What do you plan to do with her anyway?" He then asked angrily to help vend the deception.

"All of your questions will be answered in due time." In a bipolar flash, impatience replaced Leezak's cordial disposition. When he spoke again, his irritation showed. "For now, I will be asking the questions. And the first question I need an answer to is: where are you from?"

"I'm from up north," Jesse said, keeping it neutral. The faces of his friends back in Pacifica flashed through his mind, and he felt a strong rush of duty. He could do nothing to betray their sanctuary; the protection of their secret was even greater than the ongoing beat of his heart.

Leezak's face hardened, his eyes smoldering. His ripening wrath was now moored by only a thin string of patience. "Do you think I'm a fool? I'm afraid you're going to have to do better than that. There hasn't been a person in this area in your physical condition for some time. You are strong and healthy, no trace of injury from the sun. All of which is utterly unheard of in these parts." Leezak waved an accusing hand toward Jesse. "I mean, look at you. Physically, you're almost on par with my men here, which means that you *must* come from a very unique location. And if there are any women there, I'd imagine at least some of them are in excellent physical condition too. And that, my friend…that is what I am most interested in."

Leezak then sighed, downshifted. "Now let's try this again. And I warn you to think carefully before you answer. I am not a man that is used to being fucked with. So for the last time, will you please tell me where you are from?"

Jesse knew he couldn't tell the truth, and no adequate fabrication came to mind. So he opted for the only option left: the smart-ass response. "I'm from the city of San Fran

Kiss My Ass." He curled a defiant smile, effectively adding salt to the wound.

Leezak smiled as well, but the expression bore no joy. And in that instant Jesse saw a look of pure predatory indifference flash across Leezak's features; the kind of big cat soulless emotion of the kill, an expression utterly devoid of mercy, an expression that would be unmoved by the death screams of even the cutest little animal. The image had Jesse suddenly second guessing his method, maybe the smart-aleck remark *was not* the best way to go.

"Okay Jesse. I get the point. I was hoping you'd be smarter, but it has become obvious that that is not the case. Very well. There are other ways to do this. Just keep in mind as we travel down this path that it was *you* that has chosen the direction. Remember what I said earlier, I don't do anything without reason, and it appears that you have just given me one."

A sinister shadow swept over Leezak's face. And without breaking eye contact, he barked out an order to his men.

"Take him to the atelier."

Chapter 49

Strapped down to a metal gurney, Jesse trembled with cold. He was naked. His ankles, wrists, and torso were fastened to a metal gurney with thick leather straps. So stiff were the binds that he could hardly move, let alone attempt escape. Above, a single pendant fixture funneled a shaft of bright light on his exposed body.

Earlier, the guards had used scalpels to slice away his clothes. The remnants now hung off the side of the table, leaving him exposed and shivering. A layer of fabric still remained between his skin and the cold steel gurney. Thank god for small favors.

He'd been there forty-five minutes already, although it seemed like an eternity. To try and generate heat he craned his neck, and once again scanned the room that Leezak had referred to as the atelier. The room was high-tech, and clearly purposed for medicine. The walls were painted in hospital white semi-gloss, polished stain-less steel furnishings and medical equipment lined the periphery. The room was otherwise spotless, the odor of industrial strength cleaner overwhelming, with every breath came the smell of Pine-Sol and penicillin; any stray microbe would have better odds surviving the hostile environ of Mars.

On the edge of his vision, Jesse noticed a cart beside him, and another fibrillating shiver sped through his body, this time naked *fear* the cause of his chill.

Oh crap, he breathed.

An array of surgical instruments were spread neatly atop the cart, the display looked like the work station of a dentist. The lineup of pliers and scissors and scalpels forecasted the same credible fear as root canal. He could only guess what they'd been set there for. If the tools were as sharp as they were shiny, they could filet tree bark.

His mind couldn't help but do the inevitable speculations; none of which inspired any happy thoughts. Jesse took a deep breath in an attempt to evict his paranoia; it helped very little. He also realized that he was *really* starting to feel the effects of the cold. He shook back and forth, trying again to generate some heat. Between the sight of the sharp instruments and the near arctic climate there was definitely some shrinkage going on, his confidence withering like his genitalia. Although any thought of embarrassment, should someone enter, were the least of his worries. Hypothermia and surgical mutilation were just a bit higher on his list of concerns.

The atelier was no more than a hundred feet from where they stood in the main warehouse an hour earlier. While he'd been ushered along, and even while he was being strapped down, he tried talking to the two guards assigned the duty, probing for info, doing his best to sound casual and friendly. But it was no use; they ignored him like he was a sack of grain. Jesse found their behavior more than a little odd. It was as if they were hypnotized or something; their mannerisms giving them a persona more robotic than human. The thought that maybe they'd been drugged came to mind, but he couldn't be sure. The fact that their grip was as strong as a pipe wrench only added credence to the bionic man hypothesis.

Jesse was now shivering steadily. If he didn't get some heat soon, he was really going to freeze to death. Maybe that was the plan. Maybe this was Leezak's idea of torture. It was fairly effective; certainly Jesse was suffering, and it was only going to get worse. But if Leezak thought this was going to make him talk, then he had another thing coming. He'd shiver and suffer till the freeze of rigor mortis set in before betraying his friends.

Just as he thought he was about to pass out, he heard the door open. Leezak entered. As he approached the clop of his shoes on the cold tile floor sounded like the slow tick of a time-bomb countdown. Standing over him, Jesse could see that he wore rubber gloves. A surgical mask hung loosely below a smug smile, ever the consummate mad scientist. Jesse wished that if only for an instant he could free his right hand. More than anything, he'd relish one swing, the chance to feel the gratifying crack of his fist on Leezak's chin. Bet that would wipe the smile off his overbearing mug.

Without a word, Leezak began sifting through the array of surgical tools. Jesse could hear the clang of tiny metal collisions. The sounds were like audible glass shards, sent pangs of fear cutting into his courage. Jesse suspected Leezak did it on purpose, more psychological torment. So annoyed was he that he almost wished he'd have drifted off, coma had to be far less dreadful than this B-S.

The clamor stopped as Leezak appeared to have found what he was looking for. Clutched between latex covered fingers, he held a scalpel under the light, undoubtedly another psych job. The sharp tool flashed and Jesse shuddered again as he felt the grip of raw terror. And despite his brass balled resolve, the panic button had effectively been pushed.

Leezak dangled the scalpel above Jesse's exposed body, the act of intimidation quite effective. Jesse could be no more nervous if Mike Tyson himself was reincarnated and standing before him threatening to bite his ear off and eat his children. But he certainly wasn't going to give Leezak the delight of his evoked anxiety. So he willfully stiffened, and did his best to mask fear beneath a bland expression.

With the theatrics finished, Leezak finally spoke.

"Did you ever notice how in the old movies they'd always come up with some elaborate scheme to try and gather information; electrodes, drugs, or some other silly form of torture?"

Leezak admired the scalpel, seemed to speak to it instead of Jesse. "And then some celluloid star manages to defy the approach, and then of course even escapes to save the day. " Leezak shook his head. "I always used to find those plot-lines trite and annoying. Didn't you?" He chortled, still admiring the scalpel, waving it back and forth, a deranged conductor leading an opus of evil.

Jesse felt his fear and confidence reversing fields, the former skyrocketing as the latter sagged. Between the hypothermia, the swooping scalpel, and the irritating speech, he was really starting to lose it. But he did his best to remain calm, metered his breathing and hoped for a miracle. What other choice did he have?

"When it comes to gathering intelligence, I say keep it simple. Forget all the drugs and idle threats—I say get right to the heart of the matter. Why beat around the bush; go directly for the fundamental fears. And in this case, given the palate I have to work with, there's really only one way to go."

Leezak flashed a belittling grin, then with the candor of a homily said, "I've always found that if you take a razor and begin to slowly cut off a man's balls, he will always talk." Leezak then looked down at Jesse, probing for reaction. "It's certainly gotta work better than water-boarding or asking pretty-please. Don't you think?"

Jesse found Leezak's leering countenance nearly as infuriating as the prospect of castration. Calling on every shred of fortitude, he met his glare with equal attitude. No way would he show weakness. Inside, however, his composure was quickly unraveling. Because Leezak had a point; at the moment Jesse could think of no torture worse than radical nad removal. Even freezing his nuts off was preferable to having them cut off.

"I think that might be against the Geneva convention," Jesse offered sarcastically, trying to stall, grabbing for straws that just weren't there.

"Ah…there's the spunky fella I've come to know and love. Thought for a minute you might have bitten off your tongue from shivering," Leezak said, then lifted the surgical mask into position. "I wish I could continue to chat, but right now I have a job to do."

Leezak slowly advanced the scalpel toward Jesse's all too exposed genitalia.

"If at any time you decide you'd like to give me the information I asked for Jesse, I'd be glad to take a break from my work and listen. It's entirely up to you."

Leezak lowered the scalpel, and Jesse felt his panic near detonation, his brain felt like it was about to burst, spray wet red confetti in a skull gushing aneurism. He was out of options; the only choice left was whether or not to scream.

His mind ranted with conflict; two questions colliding with thermonuclear inertia. *One*: Could he tell Leezak about Pacifica? *No.* And *two*: Could he withstand having his balls cut off? *Well...it looked like he was about to find out.*

Just as Jesse drew breath to try and buy time by uttering some fake story, Leezak rose up and lowered his mask, an expression of riddle on his face.

"Hmmm," he breathed. "Now this I find extremely interesting." He pointed at Jesse's crotch. "You have a vasectomy scar." His gaze narrowed as he met Jesse's eyes. "The only other time I've seen this was some time ago." Another revelation seemed to alight in his mind, and Jesse had an eerie feeling that whatever his new thought was, it wasn't good. "Yes...yes, it all makes sense now." He then gave Jesse a knowing smile. "Nicely played, my friend; nicely played."

Leezak patted him mockingly on the shoulder, then turned and walked away.

Jesse could hear Leezak speaking, the detail unintelligible. He was apparently speaking into an intercom by the door, his voice a garbled staccato of enthusiasm. Then he heard the door open and the sound of footsteps making hasty exit.

Jesse lay alone in the room wondering what had just happened. Although thankful there was no longer a scalpel next to his balls, he was still concerned. He was safe for the moment, but for how long. And what did Leezak mean when he said, *nicely played?*

Trying to make sense of it all, his mind raced as he lay on the cold metal gurney...

...shivering.

Chapter 50

Jesse lay alone in the atelier for some time. Although still cold, his panic had receded, allowing rational thought to return. But in this case, a rational mind wasn't any great advantage. Because reasoned thinking only served to underscore exactly how screwed he was, how dire his future looked. Naked, cold, and strapped to a gurney, while a madman ran around on the loose was not the best situation for anyone with plans on living to see tomorrow.

He was jolted from his thoughts by the sound of the door opening. He didn't immediately look over, but instead took a deep breath and began to mentally prepare for whatever madness Leezak had in store for him next. Once again his mind tuned in to the sound of footsteps crossing the room, this time more than one pair, along with another noise—the squeak of wheels thirsty for lubricant.

Jesse craned his head, and immediately his heart went glacial; congealing into a frozen fist of panic. Propped on a handcart, and wheeled by two massive guards, was Jesse's father. He was bound to the cart with duct tape to the point of near mummification; he looked like a prison inmate in full body restraints. He was also still covered in the chalky white coating. And Jesse now realized that it was not an applied coating, but in fact part of him.

Jesse watched helplessly as they wheeled him nearer.

Jesse did his best to cloak the shock running through his mind. How did Leezak know that he was his father, he wondered? He only hoped that his father would realize what was up and play it cool. There was always the chance that this was just a bizarre coincidence, maybe Leezak didn't even know who he was—wishful mind-chatter of the desperate.

The guards set his father down in full view beside the gurney. Leezak then turned to one of the guards and issued instructions. "Go look at the body of the guy shot last night, see if he has a vasectomy scar too. And bring me his backpack. I want to search it for clues to the location of their home." The guard offered a firm nod and then sped off. Leezak returned his attention to Jesse.

"Well, Jesse, aren't you going to say hello to your father?" Leezak's voice was filled with casual delight.

Shit, Jesse cursed in a racing mind. But despite the inner alarm bells, outside he kept it cool. "Whatta ya talking about? I don't know this guy."

"Oh, I think you do. I could do a DNA profile, but there's no point. I mean, look at you two, the filial resemblance couldn't be any more correct. Your skin's a bit lighter, but the facial structure is nearly dead on. At first I thought he was your brother, but given the age difference, I'm gonna say he's your father."

"I'm telling you, I don't know this person," Jesse insisted. "Besides, don't you know that *we all* look alike?" Jesse did not risk making eye contact with his father, nor did his father react to his presence on the gurney. It appeared that he was playing along.

Leezak laughed. He was clearly enjoying the game. "Very funny, nice try. I'd've never even made the link until I saw your vasectomy scar."

Jesse instantly cringed. *Dammit!* That was the connection. He couldn't believe it, what were the odds?

"A very rare practice in this day and age, almost unheard of, in fact, but not quite. I found this fellow about two years ago, along with two of his friends." Leezak jabbed a thumb towards Jesse's father. "Even invited 'em in and asked the very same questions I'm asking you today. Two of them didn't survive the questioning. I figured that this one would sacrifice himself as well, so I decided to keep him around. After all, good help is hard to find these days. Who'd've ever known that he'd prove so useful?"

Jesse felt utterly depleted; his psyche struggled to manage the onslaught of bad news. Aside from the fact that he and his father were at the mercy of a psychotic, he just realized something else. The screen saver to Alex's iPod was a picture of Pacifica. Jesse had seen it when he'd glanced over at Alex in the sub, and it was a crystal clear image. When Leezak's thug returned with Alex's knapsack, they'd find it. This was perhaps the worst news of all. *Shit! Shit! Shit!* Jesse's mind scrambled as the realization hit home—their cover was blown. Or at least it would be blown. But maybe there was an advantage that could be gained. He felt the nattering of an idea in the back of his mind and he struggled to fashion it into strategy.

Leezak rubbed his palms together. "It all makes so much more sense now. You weren't breaking in to save the girl; you're here to save your father. Well Jesse, looks like you're gonna get your chance to do just that. Some men are tough enough to resist physical abuse, but far fewer can stand by and watch while a family member is tortured, or killed."

"Go to hell," Jesse spat. "I told you, I don't know this guy."

"Then it shouldn't bother you much if I open up a vein in his wrist." Leezak grabbed the scalpel off the tray and walked around the table to where the guards had positioned his father. His father's left arm had been duct-taped at mid-forearm against a wooden two-by-four, the arm extended out like a limb on a crucifix. Leezak affixed a tourniquet at mid-bicep. For the first time Jesse looked over at his dad. Right away he knew something was off; he appeared altered, and it was more than just the opaque coating over his skin. He was listless, eyes vacant, pupils flat and staid as deep space. He appeared as if he'd been drugged or hypnotized, lacked the inner essence that once purposed his soul.

"As you may or may not know, the human body has about ten pints of blood. Once you lose a few, you pass out. A little more, you die. You might want to keep that in mind. I'll place a beaker down to help you keep track." Leezak held out a large glass beaker and tapped it with a long wicked finger. "Each of these lines is a pint."

Leezak then placed the beaker on a cart just below Jesse's father's arm. "The rules are simple. Give me the information I require, or we watch your father bleed. If at any point you decide you want to talk, I'll have the tourniquet tightened. But I will not repair the wound until I am completely satisfied with the information you have given me." Leezak raised his eyebrows. "Got it?"

Jesse stared off blindly, said nothing. He knew he couldn't tell Leezak what he wanted to know. But then again, maybe he could. The idea that had kindled just a few minutes earlier had returned. *The sub.* It didn't make sense then, but it started to now. It was the one place he'd have an advantage. If he could somehow get Leezak into the sub with him, he could drown the bastard. Getting him in the sub would require deception, and the manner in which to pull off that ruse was already crystallizing. Leezak was going to find out about Pacifica form the iPod anyway, so telling him would make no difference. But in order for it to work, the bait had to be convincing, and Leezak would have to believe the information had been gained by torture. And unfortunately for his father, that suffering would come at his expense. Making matters worse was the fact that he obviously couldn't communicate his plan to his father. Desperate as Jesse was, it was the only lifeline.

"I'll take your silence as a yes," Leezak said as he turned to face Jesse's father. Then with the speed of a cobra strike, he swept the scalpel blade across his wrist.

"No!" Jesse cried, and struggled violently against his binds. Blood gushed from his father's wrist at an alarming rate; Jesse felt his poise hemorrhage with equal vigor. *Maybe this wasn't such a good idea,* the voice of better judgment shrieked in his mind. The beaker began to quickly fill, much of the blood spit wide to spatter red red rain on the white tile floor.

Jesse looked at his father's face. His eyes had closed, seemingly accepting of his fate. Or maybe he had already passed out.

"Dad!" Jesse shouted, unable to contain the secret of their allegiance any longer. His father's eyes slowly opened. And in his eyes he saw a glimmer of his real father; the man who had raised him, the man who Jesse looked up to more than any other, the man who had given him the gift of life.

Leezak stood idly by, his demeanor unaffected. The life next to him meant nothing beyond his needs, a resource quarried in flesh and blood to provide means to his ends; muscle for the execution of labor, and mortality for the exchange of data. And based on what Jesse knew of the man, he suspected that Leezak viewed all human life through a similar sick lens.

Jesse looked back at the beaker. *Shit!* It was almost to the second line, and there was no way to know how much had spilled on the floor. It was time to end this, he could risk no more.

"Okay! Okay!" Jesse shouted.

"You'll answer my questions?" Leezak leaned in, eyebrows diving in angry demand.

"Yes, yes! Anything you want! Just stop the bleeding!"

Leezak nodded, and one of the guards twisted down the tourniquet. The bleeding immediately slowed to trickle. Leezak felt the bind for proper tension. "Hold it there," he instructed, then turned back to Jesse. "I suggest we proceed quickly. The sooner I hear what I want to hear, the sooner I begin repairing the wound."

Overwhelmed with emotion, Jesse looked up at his father. To his surprise, he was still conscious. Despite his blood loss and apparent intoxication, his gaze was hot upon Jesse, his glowering disappointment matched only by his disbelief.

Suddenly his father spoke, his voice wispy and weak, putting words to the notion that had already reached Jesse via DNA telepathy. "Don't do it."

Jesse turned away; he couldn't look at him. He couldn't explain why he was doing what he was doing. He wasn't even entirely certain that *he knew* why he was doing what he was doing. But it had to be done. There was simply no other way.

Jesse then turned and told Leezak everything.

Chapter 51

Jesse lay on the cot back in the small room he'd been locked in earlier and contemplated the events that had taken place in the atelier. It looked like he'd have plenty of time to do so. At first he was surprised when he realized they were leading him back to the same room he'd escaped from earlier. His sprit had momentarily swelled, figuring he could somehow find a way to do it again. Now that he knew about the surveillance, all he'd have to do is move with more care.

But then he saw the heavy-duty hasp affixed to the outside of the door, not only screwed but welded in place, the lingering smell of burnt oxides still permeating the hall. Once inside, he'd heard the metallic echo of hardened steel slap hastily into position, followed by the distinct sound of a pad-lock snap home. A guard had been posted in the hall as well. The new measures pretty much nixed any chance of escape; unless he could somehow find a way to circumvent a locked metal door and a hulking centurion. Not likely. He had a better chance of being struck by a meteor; and judging by the mass of his bionic babysitter, that might be an infinitely less painful experience.

With nothing to do, and escape off the table, his mind turned inward and triggered an explosion of thoughts.

He did his best to sort through the synaptic shrapnel. The first to emerge from the wreckage—a question; a question his inner critic began to contemplate with neurotic fervor…

Had he done the right thing?

Guilt ran amok in his conscience, laying down footprints of insecurity, making it difficult to be certain of anything. The underlying anxiety made it hard to focus—where's Tony Robbins when you need a little inspiration, looks like he'd have to take up his own motivational stroke job.

In an attempt to gain clarity, he replayed the events that had taken place earlier in the atelier, hoping to find affirmation. But before answers came, an image intruded to demand attention. And that was the stark look of betrayal on his father's face the moment he'd told Leezak about Pacifica. It was a haunting image. Jesse tried to push it from his mind, but couldn't—the image, along with the distressing implications, clinging to his mood like feeding leeches.

Jesse shifted in the cot, pulled the thin blanket up tight; he was still feeling the aftershock of the deep freeze, his bones yet to fully thaw. By sheer dint of will, he managed to shelve the image of his father, and refocus on the current question at hand.

Had he done the right thing?

He started by reassuring himself that there'd been no other way to play it. Leezak was going to find out about Pacifica anyway. On top of that, he was certain Leezak would have killed both him and his father if he didn't get the information he wanted. He'd been prepared to die for the cause, but once the cause was removed, dying for nothing made no sense. But even knowing all this, it was still difficult to deal with the fact that the location of Pacifica had been spilled from his flapping lips.

Furthermore, his mind continued to rationalize, if he had died there'd be nobody around to hold Leezak accountable for his atrocities; like kidnapping women, and murdering Alex and Santos's boy, not to mention his fetal penitentiary, and god only knew what else. Bottom line, if he'd been killed, there'd be nobody to stop the madman from reaching his friends at Pacifica. And that was simply unacceptable. *Case closed,* he shouted in neon thoughts to quiet the prattling voice of Mr. Second Guess?

With that settled, his mind took up the next most pressing happening from his stint in the atelier. Leezak had made a remark just as Jesse finished telling him of Pacifica. *Ah…I've been expecting you,* he'd said, with a curious leer of satisfaction.

Jesse wondered what he could've meant; the remark was more than out of place, it was downright odd. It wasn't a sarcastic jab or an off-handed remark, something Leezak clearly had a propensity for. But how could he have been expecting him? He had thought to ask Leezak then, the words on the tip of his tongue. But he quickly thought better, realizing that it would only slow him from tending to his father's arm, which was the obvious priority of the moment.

And in that the instant, Leezak had turned to do just that. The relief Jesse felt at that moment was immeasurable. He only wished he'd have gotten the opportunity to see how his dad was doing. But as if on cue, the goon squad stepped in, removed his binds, gave him new clothes, and hurried him off to his pen. As he'd been led away, Leezak turned and assured him that his father would be fine, and that he'd be allowed to see him later. At least he'd given him that courtesy. Jesse was appreciative, but not about to put in a call to the Nobel committee just yet.

As Jesse lay back in his cot, he realized that his back was really hurting. It felt like there was a hot rivet under his skin. He knew that it wasn't unusual for puncture wounds to become infected. But what was unusual, and caused him a bit of alarm, was that the infection came on so fast, and seemed to be several inches from where he'd been hit. He thought the dart had hit him in the meat between his ribs, just above his right kidney. But the welt that he felt now was several inches higher along the spine. But maybe he'd been mistaken about the strike point. Lord knows he'd been slightly distracted the moment he'd been shot.

Jesse sat up to alleviate the pain. Just as he got comfortable he heard the door being unlocked. The door then opened a crack and a plate of food slid through on the floor. On top of the plate was a hand-written note. He got up and retrieved the food and read the note:

Some food to get you through the day. Dinner with me at 8pm. Rest up.

Lee, was signed beneath in large script letters.

Jesse checked his watch. It was still early, not even nine am. It was going to be a long day stuck in his cell. He placed the plate of food off to the side, he wasn't hungry, but he was definitely getting a little stir crazy, and knew it was only going to get worse. He reached into his pocket and pulled out Alex's iPod to help kill time. He unwrapped the rubber band used to bundle the wires and slid it over his wrist.

Just before he'd been ushered from the atelier, the guard that Leezak sent to retrieve Alex's knapsack had returned. Jesse asked Leezak if he could have the iPod, claiming that listening to music helped him with stress.

Leezak had said, *okay*, and hadn't even looked up from tending to his father's wound.

Sitting on the small cot, Jesse stared at the photo of Pacifica on the screen saver. He then went in and deleted the image. No point in leaving any loose ends. Jesse took note that the battery still had half a charge. Plenty of juice for him to listen to a few tunes now, while saving some power for later.

He wasn't sure if he'd even like any of Alex's music. He recognized only some of the artists he'd mentioned on the sub ride in. Rather than pick a song, he set the device to shuffle, leaving the selection to the on-board computer. He then pressed play.

The image of a music note filled the screen and he popped in the ear buds. *Desperation*, a song by Mockingbird 187, began to fill his ears. *Lucky choice,* he thought, it was one of his favorites. He drew a deep breath, relaxed and listened. Rich and moving, the music loosened his brain with a soul soothing groove. Endorphins stirred and he felt his anxiety ease with each chord. Following a haunting guitar lead the rest of the band kicked in along with the lyrics. He smiled, realizing the words were eerily apropos. Exactly what the artist had been singing about all those years ago, there was no way to know. But it somehow still seemed to epitomize the moment as it spoke all too clearly to his current state of affairs.

He leaned back on the pillow, closed his eyes, and listened…

Desperate measures bleed of desperate times
Torn from the cracks of a dire mind
Save yourself; save the world
Screaming reasons of thoughts unfurled

Pain exchanged for once held faith
Till all that's left is a desperate wraith
   It's already over, over, over…
   Can't trade a soul that has already been sold
It's already over, over, over…over, over,
overrrrrraaaaaah!

He breathed deep, felt his body slacken as the tune jammed to conclusion. He then waited for the iPod to choose again; the next song, like his own uncertain future, squarely in the hands of fate.

Chapter 52

At ten minutes to eight two guards arrived and escorted Jesse out of his pen, book-ending him once again as they led him away; their behavior, as usual, stoic to the point of strange. Along the way, he thanked them for the food and again for the iPod, but as usual, they ignored him, making him feel about as relevant as a microscopic amoeba.

Arriving at a room on the other side of the compound, they directed him inside, then sat him at a large table with instructions to *stay put*, and that Dr. Leezak would arrive shortly to join him. Then they left the room. Although unsupervised, Jesse thought it wise to be a good little microbe and do as he was told. Besides, there was a surveillance camera mounted on the ceiling, and based on what he'd seen so far, the two trained robots were very likely standing guard outside the door anyhow.

Jesse looked around the room, trying to absorb as much as possible before his host arrived. And there was plenty to absorb. The room was a thousand square feet with space allotted for dining, reclining, recreation and office work, all wrapped up in a miniature museum of modern art.

Colorful canvas squares were everywhere, the walls thriving with abstract paintings that looked like Pink Floyd music pressed in canvas instead of vinyl. Taken together, they oozed a kaleidoscope so dizzying that if you stared too long you'd be splattering the Berber carpet in your own abstract work. Jesse found his mind wondering why the hell anyone would create a display so irritating to the senses, but maybe the display had a different impression to the mind of the insane.

Jesse was no art expert, he wouldn't know a Van Gogh from a cave painting, but he still found the works interesting, if not overwhelming. The gallery was like an oversized Rorschach test, but instead of butterflies and flowers, the ink spots were but a parade of angry faces, each print a staring image in contempt, the leering reflections of those back at Pacifica.

Across the room sat several bookshelves, two file cabinets pillared a large hardwood secretary. A computer rested on top of the desk, representing the nucleus of the office works. To the left was a custom bar made of dark wood and brass, replete with liquor and quaff related accoutrements. Several high back leather stools were tucked in along the business end. A pool table was off to one side, a stable of cue sticks stood at the ready in the corner. Set in the wall behind the bar was a huge aquarium; unlit at the moment, the occupants evident only as shifting shadows in dark water.

A sectional couch and coffee table were elegantly spaced nearby. It looked like a display from a high end furniture showroom, a post modern time capsule in tasteful teal micro-fiber and natural wood tones. And then there was the dining room table, the long table that stretched out in front of him like that used during the last supper.

The meal spread upon the table was fit for a king; roast fowl, hot rolls and various steamed greens. If it tasted half as good as it smelled it would be every bit of spectacular.

Despite all that he'd been through, his body responded. He felt his urges reflexively stir, hunger promptly shuffling aside worry and his persistent plotting, at least for the moment.

The smells instantly sparked his memory, sending him reflecting back to Thanksgiving dinner at his aunt Nancy's where the extended family and close friends would gather for the annual holiday gala. The day was always a good time, thanks to a cornucopia of good food, friends, and family. Those were the days, Jesse mused, back when everything was simple, and all was right with the world. As he pondered those days, and the litany of souls lost and forsaken, his reverie began to wither, his pleasant daydream degrading to a melancholy memory lane. Because they were all gone, their futures abruptly dead-ended, their remains now only fossil record footnotes of an era elapsed. Sadly, to the best of his knowledge, he and his father were all that remained of the Baines family tree. And based on their brief interaction, he wasn't even certain his father was of sound mind. Not too much to be thankful for.

Not for the first time Jesse found himself fuming over the past, and the ongoing aftermath. The way it had gone down was just wrong, no more than a senseless global purge. And once again his inner cynic began questioning the motives of the *Great Creator,* and by natural momentum of thought, *His* very existence.

Why? Was the question Jesse always asked, *why did it have to happen?*

Jesse was not ultra religious, but he believed in a universal force of some type. The cosmic chaos was just too perfect, the universe too grand to be a simple manifestation of chance, or some random primordial mishap, at least in his opinion.

God? Okay, if one needed to give the force a name, then that was fine with him.

These days, his faith stood severely damaged, however, his belief plummeting like a stock heading for bankruptcy. The loss of his family and friends were one thing, but nothing was more damaging than the fact that the almighty CEO sat back and allowed global meltdown to take place on his watch. That just didn't jibe with him, defied common sense. All of which added up to one hefty dose of epiphany, and a sweeping rethink of his ideology. Either somebody had been asleep at the wheel, or there was nobody at the wheel to begin with.

The door opened and Jesse snapped from his metaphysical haze. Leezak entered. Thank god, Jesse thought. He could use the break from himself. He also had a lot of questions.

"How's my father?" Jesse asked. The inquisition launched before Leezak even placed a second foot in the room.

"Doing just fine," Leezak replied, as he reached the table. "He should be back on his feet in no time." He took a seat at the table across from Jesse.

The news gave Jesse a rush of relief. "When can I see him?"

Leezak draped a cloth napkin across his lap. "I don't see why you can't have a look in on him later tonight." Jesse felt his emotional nausea ebb even further, the magnitude of his relief epochal. Leezak choking to death on a chicken bone would be about the only thing that could improve the moment.

"My father," Jesse started, paused as he worked to frame a question. "Something's different. The coating on his skin, and even his personality. Did you drug him?"

Leezak chewed noisily and worked to open a bottle of wine. "My staff has gone to great lengths to prepare this meal." He spoke around the food in his mouth, spread an open palm. "I understand that you have a lot of questions, and I'll answer them all the best I can. But first you will eat."

Jesse hesitated, but then figured what the heck. He was in fact hungry. More importantly, he knew that he should take advantage of the calories. There was a good chance he'd need the energy in the near future.

Leezak continued to eat, watched as Jesse filled his plate. And when Jesse finally took a bite, as promised, Leezak began to answer his question.

"The skin coating as you call it is known as the vernix caseosa. It's the protective coating we all have while we are in the womb. In the case of many of my men, and your father, I have simply turned it back on." Leezak stopped to sip from the wine he had poured for himself. He was right at home, seemed completely at ease.

"How, and why?" Jesse found himself sounding like his little friend Reni after watching a science program beyond his comprehension.

"The why is simple. Through experimentation I have found that the coating is particularly resistant to UV radiation. So for the members of my staff who often spend time outside, they have the benefit of natural protection, aside from clothing, and in many cases, like your father, the additional protective benefit of melanin. Operating outside during the day can be of great advantage."

Although he tried not to show it, Jesse was filled with awe; beyond the implications, the science was fascinating.

"As for the how," Leezak sighed. "I'm afraid it would take too long to explain to you. It's quite technical. Genetics and stuff."

"My undergraduate work was in biology, I'm pretty sure I can follow."

Leezak perked up visibly. "Excellent. We'll give it a try then. That background should help. Of course I'll keep it simple anyway." There was no mistaking the patronizing mirth on Leezak's face as he placed a forkful of food between his lips.

"As I'm sure you are aware, the human genome project was completed some time ago. It was a huge step in the field of genetics and molecular biology. It gave us a very powerful tool, a DNA blueprint, a kind of a road map to the human design."

Jesse nodded. "I'm aware of that."

"Once available, we could pinpoint, at least to some degree, the genetic origin of many traits. And by experimentation, find others. Some years back, I located the genetic origin that codes for the vernix caseosa." Leezak paused as he took another bite of his meal, chewed.

"That doesn't explain how you made the changes." Jesse said filling the void.

Leezak finished chewing, swallowed. He seemed annoyed by the display of impatience, but let it slide. "We use genetic manipulation. Once I located the responsible loci, I used an RNA interference technique to revive its action. Or more accurately, turn off the inhibition mechanism that prevents the formation of the protective coating, thus allowing it to be continually produced."

Jesse was stunned, continued to chew food while his mind digested the new information. "And his unusual personality change?" Jesse then queried.

"Genetic modification as well." Leezak offered. "His personality has been altered. Like many of my men, he's been retrofitted with an addictive personality—"

"Whoa! Hold on a second. How can—"

Leezak held up a palm, interrupting Jesse mid-rant. "It would be a lot easier if you waited till I was finished before asking further questions. I'll try and cover everything, if you give me a chance."

Jesse nodded, holstered his tongue.

"Way back, we found that many addicts, be it drug or alcohol or other, possessed similar genetic tendencies, at least in regard to certain genes. Some referred to it as the addictive personality, if you will. I had always hypothesized that people with this genetic makeup were weak willed. After all, what is an addict? Someone who lacks will power to overcome their urges and impulses. I knew some people like this, as we all did. And from watching them, and witnessing first hand their self destructive behavior, I knew this to be true. These people were weak, plain and simple. My examination of the scientific literature seemed to agree, although in most cases, you had to read between the lines. Back then it *was not* very politically correct to speak in such terms. In those days addiction was often referred to as a *disease*." Leezak dabbed air quotes, rolled his eyes sarcastically.

Leezak took another bite of food and washed it down with a sip of wine. Jesse continued to eat as well, remained quiet, and waited eagerly for Leezak to swallow and continue his explanation.

"It's no panacea, certainly not as good as the brainwashing or hypnosis you'd see in old movies. But for the most part, I have found somatic cell alterations to be quite effective. It seems to make people ultimately more pliable, easier to manipulate and control. It's a lot of work mind you, and the therapy must be continually maintained. And even with that, the effects are limited for some. But for others, it works like a charm.

"Over time I've been able to fine tune the system even further. I've located several other genes that if modified in the appropriated manner add considerably to the effect. And then to really enhance the end-product, a daily dose of diacetylmorphine is administered. You might know it as heroin. You'd be amazed at the resultant level of loyalty, it's quite unwavering. Along with some genetic modifications to maximize their physique, it insures that my men are as obedient and strong and durable as computer programmed robots."

Leezak took another sip of wine and leaned back in his chair. He couldn't be more comfortable. He seemed to be enjoying the opportunity to have someone other than himself around to hear himself speak. The thought of lunging across the table and trying to kill him crossed Jesse's mind, but there simply wouldn't be enough time to choke the life out of him before Beavis and Butthead arrived to save the day.

"I understand in theory how that all works." Jesse said. "But I know that environment plays a big role in personality development as well. My father had years to develop his way of thinking, and he was...I should say he *is* a strong person. There's no way he'd ever comply or become more pliable, as you say, by any genetic manipulation, forced addiction, or any other means."

"Very good." Leezak nodded, and appeared to be impressed. "And in some cases, that seems to be true. Environment is clearly a contributing factor. Your father has always been one of the difficult ones, and that's why he is only used during supervised situations." The image of his father shackled and pulling the rickshaw the other night came unbidden to Jesse's mind. Add the new nefarious details of Leezak's handiwork, and his blood began to really boil. But he bit his tongue and tamped down his anger. As appealing as the notion was, it'd do no good to implode. The acquisition of information was priority one.

"And in most cases," Leezak continued. "I also install a back-up measure to insure the behavior modifications I seek are achieved—a far more primitive, if not direct, solution. In the case of your father, and many others, there's a small device implanted along the spine. It lies next to the vertebral column, between T-1 and T-2. The devices are radio controlled and when activated emit an electric charge that induces paralysis. It's similar to a Tazer gun, or one of those shock collars used to control dogs, except it sends an impulse right into the spinal cord. In the event of undesired behavior, I can simply flip a switch and it's instant obedience by paralysis. Or if needed, I can keep it on for a more permanent, or even lethal, outcome. It's very effective, as you can imagine."

As Leezak was speaking, a notion began flickering in Jesse's mind. Then all at once, the notion crystallized, and he felt his heart thunder with rage. And in that instant, although impossible for him to believe, he hated Leezak even more.

Chapter 53

"You put one of those in me!" Jesse spat, slamming a fist on the table.

Leezak leered, eyebrows sloping in unspoken warning. *Settle down.*

Fuming, Jesse sat back, shook his head and scowled.

Leezak then smiled and shifted in his chair. His posture seemed to soften as he removed a remote control from his belt. The device was small and filled with buttons; a remote detonator, Jesse assumed. "I'm not a fool," Leezak said. "That's you right there." He tapped a button on the device. "Don't worry, there's a safety. Wouldn't want to lean on it and accidentally send a signal I didn't mean to. We've all done that back in the old days with our cell phones."

Jesse shook his head. Angry as he was, somehow the news didn't come as a total surprise. The Machiavellian tactic was all to in line with the personality profile he'd already pieced together on this madman. At least he now had an explanation for the unusual pain and inflammation along his spine.

"And just as a word of caution." Leezak said as he snapped the detonator back on his belt. "The device in your back has a thin stainless steel wire that wraps around your spinal cord. Should you try and remove it, or have someone pull it out, the wire will slice your spinal cord like piano wire through pudding."

Jesse was still simmering, couldn't bring himself to look Leezak in the eye. The bastard had violated his spirit as his much as his body. Leezak apparently sensed the negative emanation from his dinner guest.

"Don't take it so hard, it's just a precaution," Leezak explained evenly. "As long as you behave as I ask, you'll be fine. I give you my word. And if all goes well, you might even earn your freedom. The same goes for your father. I'll even have my surgeon safely remove the devices for you."

Jesse shook his head, still annoyed, but getting over it. Besides, as he considered the device, and all the other new information he'd learned so far during the course of this lovely little get together, it really didn't change the bottom line of what he knew he had to do.

"Ah…but we've digressed. I never finished explaining how the genetic changes are made. I assume you're still curious?"

Jesse looked up, nodded. "I am."

"Very good, then I shall continue." Leezak seemed glad to have Jesse's attention back. "I use a sophisticated technique based on viral lysogeny. It's a means of inserting new genes into a host genome using viruses."

"I've heard of that," Jesse offered, his curiosity fully revived. "But I never knew it was perfected. Especially on humans, and with such accuracy."

"That's true, my technique is a novel one. It, along with many of the others genetic procedures I use are unique; fine tuned at my private lab. And even today, much is being done to improve the efficacy of these techniques. By ignoring the handicap of law and regulation, I've been able to make monumental advancements. Many years ago I worked at one of the most prestigious bio-tech research labs in the world, DNAscent. They had the finest resources and equipment money could buy. But working in my private lab, and with a few carefully selected grad students, I'd make more headway in a single weekend than the entire staff would make in six months at DNAscent. With all the restrictions and red tape that they had to deal with, it was no wonder."

"That's what you got busted for?" Jesse said almost out of reflex.

Leezak nodded. "Yes, but I was never convicted." He held up a finger, wagged it sarcastically, a useless gesture for a useless point made, although the theater seemed amusing to its author.

"By your own admission, you said you broke rules. It seems you should've gotten in trouble. From what I recall, the case was dismissed. How was it you managed to get off?" Jesse asked. It was a question he'd always been curious about. Never did he expect to get the chance to ask of course, never expecting to ever meet him. Meeting Jesus Christ would've only been a little more surprising.

Leezak beamed, his face creasing with sinister lines. "Let's just say that the progress I had made did not go unnoticed by some very powerful people, in very high places. And since I'd been clever enough to keep my data effectively hidden, I had one very valuable bargaining chip. A great big get out of jail free card if you will."

"I don't understand. Who got you out?"

Leezak sighed, downshifted. "Why don't we save that discussion for another time? At the present, there are more important matters to talk about." Jesse felt his enthusiasm deflate. Things had just starting to get especially interesting. Looks like, at least for the moment, the free flow of information had come to an end.

"Like my trip to visit Pacifica." Leezak then said.

"Whatta you mean? Jesse asked, mostly for effect. Because he'd anticipated it, he was fairly certain Leezak would want to travel there. It only made sense.

"I mean my trip to visit your home. It appears that there may be some assets there that could benefit my operations here."

"By assets, you mean females." Now it was Jesse's turn to flash a sarcastic grin. "Let's just call a spade, a spade." Beneath outward animations of concern—feigned fidgeting and nervous tics—Jesse celebrated within private walls of dura. Leezak had taken the bait.

"Fine with me," Leezak agreed. "At least we are both of an understanding here."

Leezak then leaned in, eyes gleaming with the zeal of anticipation. "Now then…let's discuss the details of my journey to see your people."

Chapter 54

Two ball in the side pocket. *Clack!* Not bad, Jesse praised himself as the pool ball dropped in the pocket. It had been quite some time since he'd shot a game of pool. Pacifica had a table in the rec room, but it'd been at least two years since he'd been of mind to venture down and enjoy a game.

Moments ago, following an urgent call on the intercom, Leezak had left in haste, the meal on his plate unfinished. Before leaving, he uttered a speedy set of instructions to Jesse. *Hang out.* *Make yourself at home.* *Be back in a little bit.* The two guards entered the instant Leezak left. They now sat on the furniture nearby, two stone face sentinels watching his every move with a strip club stare that Jesse found more than a little unsettling. Jesse wasn't about to try anything, had no intentions of trying to escape or take a run at them. They were wired way too tight and simply too big to bring down without a weapon. And based on the new info, no way a pool stick would do the trick. Anything short of a bazooka would be insufficient caliber to take down the two jonesing genetic giants.

Eleven ball in the corner. *Clack!*

When Jesse'd first heard the intercom bleat, and the concerned conversation that ensued, he got nervous. Right away, he thought that maybe it had something to do with this father. Maybe he'd taken a turn for the worse. Or worse yet, died.

The intercom was over by the door, behind Jesse. The distance and blurred voice coming from the intercom made it difficult to discern particulars; it was like eavesdropping on a conversation between Charlie Brown's teacher and a Whoville denizen; all of which had made for a tense few minutes.

Eventually, he realized that it had something to do with someone named Frederick. He sighed in relief, his tension deflating by degrees. Although unable to make out any salient details, he'd heard the name enough during the exchange to assure him that whatever was going on, it had nothing to do with his father. Thank god, he thought, at least he could cross that worry off his ever expanding list of concerns.

Jesse leaned over the pool table to line up a shot and noticed the rubber band from the iPod dangling from his wrist. It revived the memory of Alex once again. He shook his head and took a deep breath. In an attempt to offset the spell of fresh guilt he promised himself that he would never forget the man. However small, he'd keep his memory alive in his mind as a tribute. He decided to keep the rubber band in place as a reminder of his personal pact.

Jesse lined up his shot again and stroked the cue ball. *Clack!* The eight ball rolled slowly and dropped into the predestined pocket. *Yes.* He rose up, surveyed the empty table. Almost a perfect game. Not bad for someone who hadn't played in a while, he thought. Of course, it was always easier to perform in the absence of opposition. He wondered how he'd do when Leezak returned and he challenged him to a game.

Jesse tossed the triangular rack on the table then circled to collect the balls. As if on cue, the door swung open and Leezak returned. Walking toward the pool table he launched into an apology for having to interrupt their meal. And to Jesse's surprise, it was authentic. Jesse found the behavior more than a little contradictory, it wasn't the first time he'd noticed the incongruity. The guy clearly had schizophrenic tendencies. One minute he was Dur Fuhrer, the next, Mister Rogers.

"No problem," Jesse said, acknowledging his apology. "How 'bout a game?"

He found himself hoping that Leezak would agree. Not only would it give him a chance to continue their conversation and quarry more information, it would also help burn unspent adrenaline. On top of that, he wasn't all that anxious to be stuffed back in his cage for the night.

"Sure," Leezak agreed. "Rack 'em up."

Jesse proceeded to rack the balls. "Straight eight ball okay?"

"It's up to you. Whatever game you want to lose." Leezak grinned.

Jesse let the remark slide. "You can break."

"You sure? You may not even get a shot. As talented as I am, there's a good chance I'll run the table off the break." Leezak again beamed condescending. So much for his modest behavior.

"I'll take my chances," Jesse said sarcastically.

Clack! Leezak shot and two balls dropped off the break, one high, one low, the rest scattering. Leezak circled, then leaned over and shot again. *Clack!* The ten ball dropped in the side pocket. "Looks like I got the big balls, and you got the little balls."

Jesse shook his head, rolled his eyes. "What…did you take the striped balls just so you could make that stupid remark?"

Leezak smiled, otherwise ignoring Jesse as he continued to circle and survey the table for his next prey.

"Everything okay around here?" Jesse asked. "Having a little trouble with Frederick?"

Leezak paused, looked up, curiosity etched in his expression. "What do you know about Frederick?"

"Nothing," Jesse shrugged. "Just heard you talking about him on the intercom."

Leezak leaned over the table and shot again. *Clack!* "Frederick has been a problem as of late. He's killed several of my men over the past year. But tonight his reign of terror has come to an end. We've finally caught him."

"El Cucuy," Jesse breathed, never dreaming that his casual inquiry would lead to this.

"Yes," Leezak nodded. "I believe that's what the locals call him"

"So where did he come from? And why is he so angry at you?"

Leezak sighed. "Frederick was once a friend, held a strong place in my heart, in fact. He's a genetically engineered fusion of simian species, one of my original experiments. A chimera if you will, although mostly human," Leezak shifted, appeared emotionally moved. "As close as we'd become, it sounds odd referring to him as an experiment. I really missed him." Leezak gazed off pensively, and for an instant seemed genuinely touched. "He was much more than an experiment to me, however. Was more like a pet dog, loyal and trusting and obedient as he was."

Just as Jesse thought he saw evidence of an actual human heart, Leezak once again displayed his callous nature by referring to Frederick as a pet. "If he was such a friend, what happened?"

"It seems he'd seen something he shouldn't have, something that upset him. Something he couldn't understand." Leezak found a cube of chalk and spun it on the tip of his pool stick. "He had a brother named Marcus. They were essentially identical twins. A while back, Marcus had gotten sick, terminal cancer. There was no hope, the disease had fully metastasized, and he was suffering terribly." Leezak shrugged. "He had to be euthanized, of course. After all, it was the only humane thing to do.

"When we did the procedure, focused as I was I didn't realize the door had been left open, and Frederick was watching. It was a big mistake. Because when he realized Marcus was dead, he just went berserk, practically destroyed the place with his bare hands. He killed two of my men before he ran off. He's been roaming around hunting us ever since." Leezak leaned down and lined up another shot.

Jesse marveled at the tale. Once again he found his attention rapt by the carnage curiosity of another train wreck. "As much as I hate to admit it, it sounds like you did the right thing. I don't understand why he'd get so upset? He had to see it was necessary."

Clack! Leezak sunk another ball, then lifted and leaned on the pool stick. "Frederick's mental abilities are very limited. At best he has the intellect of a six year old. We were shooting for something a little higher, but came up short. Sacrifices of intelligence came with increased strength. We'd missed the balance we were trying to achieve. That's why they never really worked out. The military was not pleased with the results."

Again Jesse felt there was more iceberg beneath the waters of this the story. Part of him warned not to proceed. But there was no stopping the forward momentum of his curiosity. Objects in motion want to stay in motion.

"Military? Are you saying Marcus and Frederick were sup-posed to be some kind of soldiers?"

"Indeed," Leezak replied, his voice set to the casual tone of a barber shop chat. "This goes way back, back when I worked for DNAscent. The company was working with the military on developing a genetically engineered soldier. Frederick and Marcus were prototypes. I was the lead scientist on the project. But when trouble found me on the outside, the military pulled the plug, washed their hands of it all. I never even got chance to improve the product. You know how it goes when secrets are involved. I guess I was seen as a potential trail back to DNAscent, which could've drawn the public eye to the project, and then of course, on them. The last thing they wanted was for the project to go public. As it was the military was not the most popular institution back in those days."

Jesse shook his head, his skull filled with shock and implication, the sentiments manifesting in a look of confusion.

Leezak apparently picked up the vibe. "You shouldn't be so surprised. It's not the first time this kind of thing has been done. The Russians had a similar program spear-headed by Stalin early in the last century. They were trying to mate apes with humans, but didn't have the technol-ogy to make it happen, at least not to a degree applicable to their needs. Had the science of the time been a little more advanced, things could've turned out much differ-ently. Who knows, the cold war may have had a different outcome. We might be speaking Russian right now, or worse, living on a real live planet of the apes."

Things haven't turned out all that great as it is, Jesse thought, as his mind swirled and tried to manage the rushing undertow of shock. Leezak, for his part, seemed utterly unfazed, which came as no surprise to Jesse. After all, it was *he* who was the wizard behind the curtain of craziness. What was surprising, on the other hand, was that Leezak still hadn't missed a shot off the break. Apparently he was as good as he'd so arrogantly proclaimed. Only two high balls remained plus the eight. After that, the game was over. Jesse was going down without a fight.

"What're you gonna do with him?" Jesse asked as his thoughts regained traction.

"Right now he's heavily sedated and fixed in restraints. I haven't made a final decision just yet. But he's probably going to have to be put down. He can't stay here, and I can't just let him go. Besides, he has some pretty serious skin problems from the sun. Probably not terminal, but how can I treat him if I can't get near him without worry of him literally biting my head off. Much as it pains me to say, it just may not be practical to let him live." Leezak leaned down and stroked another shot. *Clack!* The ball caromed beside the pocket and rolled off.

Yes, Jesse silently celebrated, the bastard finally missed. Given all that was going on, he was surprised by how much he wanted to win, the competitive nature hardwired in his DNA mainframe seemed to never shut down. The disturbing news of Frederick's potential demise aside, he was uplifted. Now was his chance. The table was wide open, the balls well spaced, perfectly set up for a run to the eight ball. Just remain calm, stay focused and take this chump down. Seven balls total, including the eight. Definitely doable.

Now it was his turn. He only hoped he didn't choke.

Chapter 55

Clack! Nice, Jesse breathed as the pool ball dropped home. One down, six to go. He quickly sank another two balls, picking off the easy shots, making sure to always set up the next. But before he could gain momentum, Leezak spoke.

"Care for a cocktail?" I have some excellent ports here." Leezak stood behind the bar, showed Jesse the bottle from which he just poured.

Jesse shook his head. "No thanks."

Jesse lined up another shot, was about to take it when Leezak spoke up again. The timing and tone smelled of a tactical interruption to throw off his game.

"I have considered your suggestion regarding our earlier conversation." Leezak said, now sitting casually on one of the bar stools, legs crossed, a drink balancing in his fingers. "And I have decided that I will agree to your terms. It will be just me and you tomorrow in the sub."

Jesse looked up from his next shot. "Sounds good. There's really no other way to do it. As I said earlier, there's only room for two in the sub anyway. Besides, there's no way you'd be able to make that trip without me to navigate, and the sub is not the easiest vehicle to handle." Jesse leaned and shot. *Clack!* Another ball dropped, *sweet.* Jesse was pleased. This time it was *the news* that thrilled him more so than the shot he'd just made. Had Leezak not agreed to his terms, he'd have been like a tiny Mayfly trapped beneath a steamy pile of dung—*in deep shit*.

Leezak took a sip from his cocktail. "And just a little warning about tomorrow: if you're thinking of trying anything, please don't. I assure you that I am well aware of any defiant actions you might be considering. I will have sufficient countermeasures. And remember, if for some reason I don't return in forty-eight hours, your father will be executed in a very painful and protracted manner."

Jesse stroked another shot. *Clack!* The three ball dropped in the side. "I promise you this." Jesse lifted, stared Leezak dead in the eyes, and said without a hint of insincerity. "So long as you agree to let me and my father go free, and not hurt any of my friends at Pacifica. I will not prevent you from your objective."

Leezak nodded. "If nothing else, I am a man of my word. As I mentioned over dinner, I'll need to borrow some of your female friends for nine months or so, but nobody will be physically harmed. And as long as I get the measure of cooperation I need, you and your father will be set free."

Jesse and Leezak clearly had a different interpretation of the term *physical harm*. Leezak borrowing any female, whether she be Jesse's friend or not, for his strange studies, sounded like physical harm to him. But Jesse let it slide, finding no upside to arguing the point.

For an instant, Jesse felt the impulse to ask Leezak to throw Frederick in on the bargain, set him free as well. But he squashed the idea. As noble as it may have been on some fundamental philanthropic level, it may have been pushing it. Besides, he thought with ever growing hope, if tomorrow goes as well as this game of pool, he might get chance to set him free himself.

Clack! The seven ball dropped, leaving only one. The eight. And Jesse had a clean shot. A lot of green spanned between the cue ball and the eight, but it was doable. The two remaining striped balls were off to the side, Leezak's *big balls* would be of no consequence to the shot.

But as he leaned down to complete the sweep, Leezak interrupted once again, an apparent last ditch effort to throw him off. What a surprise.

"Just remember Jesse, as I mentioned yesterday, everything I do has a reason, even when I'm shooting a game of pool. What if I missed that last shot on purpose?"

Jesse smiled, but wasn't falling for it. *Nice try*, Jesse thought, but not good enough to upend his focus. Leaning over to take the final shot his mind made a sudden connection, Leezak's remark sparking insight like crossed wires. And with the notion came a sickening sinking sensation.

Jesse lifted, the shot could wait. "Yesterday you said that you'd been expecting me." Jesse hesitated, searched for the words. "You lured us out of our home, didn't you?"

Leezak again showed teeth. It was the kind of condescending countenance that just begged to be swatted with a pool stick.

"Indeed," Leezak admitted, "I didn't know for sure, but I had a feeling there might be people alive down there. I was aware of its construction of course, figured it to be a perfect sanctuary. Finding a way down there to have a look around was beyond my capabilities, even as brilliant as I am. So I figured it would be so much easier to have you come to me. I had some of my men drop a few dynamite charges in the vicinity of the surface platform, and look at the result. It wasn't much different than a fishing excursion. I increased the number of street patrols over the past few weeks, figuring we might pick one of you up in the city. Never did I realize that you'd come to me, knock on my front door as you and you friend did."

Shit, Jesse simmered, the information pissed him off, although deep down he must've suspected it. Because beyond the initial shock, the news hadn't struck him nearly as hard as it should have.

Jesse found himself at a loss for words. He couldn't show anger or distress, and give Leezak the satisfaction of a reaction he was clearly hoping for, nor could he try to deny the story. Because it all made too much sense—the increasing seismic activity, the atypical damage on top of the OTEC, the flash of light both Martin and he had seen—it all seemed so obvious now. But at the time the clues had been blurred by his obsession to get out of Pacifica.

The light over the aquarium suddenly flickered, apparently on a timer. Jesse turned as blue fluorescent light spread through the aquarium to bring the décor alive in shimmering watts. Faux seaweed and synthetic crags of colorful coral stood out in a rainbow explosion. Much like the paintings around the room, it was a piece of abstract art itself; only not so disturbing to the senses.

Then movement; two figures drifted out from of the rocks. And as the fish swam higher in the water, and into full view, Jesse felt disbelief slam his brain like a meteoric migraine. Because the two fish were not fish, at least not entirely. Once again Leezak had outdone himself, managed to up the ante of his insanity. Jesse shook his head, but couldn't take his eyes from the unfolding drama…

Where he watched two tiny human fetuses gliding through the aquarium.

Jesse looked from the aquarium to Leezak. He wore a pasted grin. He seemed to relish these moments of revelation, ate them up like ego treats, little goodies in surprise and subtext. He seemed to understand the impact the aquatic display would have on a person of sound mind. And in that moment Jesse realized that he was wrong about his initial assessment—this exhibit was *far more* disturbing than the abstracts hanging on the walls.

"Say hello to Watson and Crick." Leezak raised his tumbler, offering a toast to the two frolicking fetuses. As if recognizing Leezak, two bulbous heads rushed forth and pressed against the glass, seemingly unaware that their world had strict boundaries.

"Great," Jesse shook his head, simmering. "Just great. Is there no depth to your madness? I mean, come on."

"Hey," Leezak shrugged offhandedly. "Technically they're not even human. I've done nothing wrong: just exercised my *choice*. And my choice is to have a couple of nice pets in my aquarium exhibit."

"What about all the other ones back in the ware-house? There had to be a dozen. How do you explain away that kind of horror?" For the first time Jesse realized that his voice had elevated. The weight of all the craziness had finally gotten to him, finally exceeding his measured attempts at suppression.

Leezak pointed to the pool table, nodded. "I tell you what, it's getting late, and from what I gather we have a long sub ride ahead of us tomorrow. Why don't I answer your question then, as well as fill you in on some other things I have a feeling you might find interesting. Why don't you take your shot so we can then finish the game?"

"This shot *is* the end of the game." Jesse said, still angry, as he leaned over and sighted down the cue, the eight ball in his cross-hairs. *Clack!* The cue hit the eight, and the eight slowly rolled toward the far corner pocket...

...caromed off the bumpers and rimmed out. He missed. Jesse dropped his head, disappointed in himself. He sighed, realized he was squeezing the pool stick nearly hard enough to grind it to saw dust.

Without hesitation, Leezak circled and sunk the remaining balls. As the eight ball dropped he lifted and sighed. Jesse expected an arrogant celebration, bracing for some kind of annoying end-zone dance to rub it in his face. But instead, in a civil manner he nodded and said, *nice game*, then turned and waved his two men over.

"My men will see you back to your room. I suggest you get a good night's sleep. We have a long day ahead of us tomorrow. They'll take you by the infirmary first. As promised, you may have a quick look in to see that your father is okay."

In the same mechanical manner the two men ushered him off. Walking through the hallway Jesse's mind reflected on the lost pool game, and pondered tomorrow. He found himself thinking of his friends back at Pacifica. The faces of Martin, Reni and Michelle came alive in his mind. The images sent his emotions into an anxious free fall. He missed them terribly. The fact that he had put them directly in harm's way had his heart quivering with concern, while 18 inches above, his brain incessantly reviewed his plan, hoping and praying that somehow, someway, tomorrow...

He'd find a way to win the game that counted.

Chapter 56

Bzzzzzzz
What the fuc—
Jesse felt the numbing grip of paralysis as high voltage pins and needles shot through his system. At first he thought *heart attack,* but then, *no,* this was much worse. He tried to breathe, couldn't. Someone had parked a Sherman tank on his chest. His vision then filled with nothingness.

And then, as suddenly as it had started, the seizure ended. The world spun, and life returned; sight, sound, and movement slowly rebooted like appliances after a power outage—the pain and funny-bone tingle receding with the flip of a switch. His lungs expanded, his heart tumbled and began to beat again, fluttering in clammy panic like a hypoglycemic humming bird in search of nectar.

"What the fuck was that all about?" Jesse spat, turning to Leezak.

Leezak sat in the sub beside Jesse, a remote control in his hand. "Just wanted to let you know what to expect if you decide to try anything funny." Leezak punctuated his remark with a sobering stare.

Geez, Jesse breathed, rubbing his upper arms to help restore circulation before returning to powering up the

Halibut. He was considerably ticked-off about Leezak's little demonstration, but what could he really do? The bastard was still holding the remote, and as a result, the upper hand.

As upset as he was by the shock, he was far more disturbed by the fact that Leezak had brought his own SCUBA gear, something he hadn't anticipated. Two tanks stood on the floor between his legs, regulator and mask on his lap. All along, his plan was to get Leezak alone in the sub so he could drown him; get to deep waters and flood the cabin, or just ram the rig into a crag of basalt. Whether he ultimately survived was of little consequence. As long as he lived long enough to see Leezak turn as cold and blue as the ocean around him. He tried to convince himself that the plan could still work, but after feeling the paralyzing power of the shock collar, and watching Leezak load on his own SCUBA gear, selling the plan to his rational mind was no easy sell.

Showing no outward concern, Jesse continued to ready the sub. He was still in his element, and would be for the next several hours. He'd just have to figure out a way around the problem.

Working his way down the control panel, Jesse ran through the start-up procedure, flipping switches, adjusting dials. He took note of the rubber band around his wrist and again thought of Alex. In silent reflection Jesse found himself asking his dead friend to bring him luck. Since he was certain that he was not deserving of help, nor did he even have the right to ask, given his role in Alex's death, he made his request in the name of those back in Pacifica.

Leezak brought his dive mask to his face and sucked a few trial breaths. "Just a little precaution," he said, removing the mask from his face. "Just in case you're stupid enough to try anything with the air in the sub, the only one you'll be hurting is yourself, my mask will be here on my lap during the entire journey. The remote will also be in my hand at all times. And just a note of precaution, the safety's off, which means just one touch'll set it off. Would you like another demonstration?" Leezak again brandished the small remote, along with a patronizing wink.

Jesse shook his head and rolled his eyes as he began to navigate the Halibut through the shallows of the bay. Leezak was even holding the remote in his right hand, as far away from Jesse as possible. Even if he did try to make a grab for it, by the time he leaned across to snatch it, he'd be rendered useless, turned into a writhing quadriplegic with the press of a button.

"I suppose it's a good time to tell you about this as well." Leezak held up a small glass ampoule. "I have several of these sewn into my cloths, and one in each pocket. Inside is a lethal airborne virus. And I should warn you, the glass is very fragile. It'll break from even the slightest struggle." Leezak pushed it toward Jesse so he could easily see. "Just another little beneficial by-product of my time working with the military, as well as working with one of the preeminent virologists on the planet at the time.

I've been inoculated, of course. The virus is hardy, infects easily, and kills quickly. And if it were ever to be released in such a small isolated area, like the one I suspect you have down there, I'd say the entire population would be dead in a day or two."

Jesse shook his head irritably, but said nothing.

"You can never have too much insurance," Leezak remarked, sounding like an old television ad as he tucked the small ampoule back in his pocket. "I think you can see now why I agreed to this trip with you. I'm as safe here as I would be if I were at home on my couch."

Leezak was a clever cat, no doubt about that. From the virus to the shock collar to wrapping the remote control in a waterproof bag, and even the forethought to bring his own dive gear—he'd left nothing to chance. And although surprised by the measure of Leezak's caution, Jesse reminded himself that the crux of his mission had not changed. He still had several hours before they reached Pacifica, and he was still confident that between now and then something would come to him.

But for the moment, his hands were tied. The bay was not deep enough for a person to drown. Even without SCUBA gear, a moderately capable swimmer could reach the surface, then swim to shore. Nor were there any large rocks to crash into. With that in mind, Jesse figured he might as well pass the time with conversation. Besides, a million questions still clamored for resolve.

"Last night you said you'd tell me about the creatures living in the aquariums."

"Indeed, I suppose now is a good time." Leezak shifted in his seat, still trying to find comfort in the tight cabin. "I assume you got a good look at the specimens in my lab when you were roaming around?"

Jesse nodded.

"Well, you probably noticed that their proportions were off. Especially when compared to Watson and Crick, the two little fellows in my den. Each fetus in the lab has been programmed to grow an organ. Some are growing a heart, some a liver, some have a full size kidney, and so on. You get the idea."

Jesse sensed what was coming, felt a surge of nausea in *his own* organs.

"They are a means to farm body parts. I turn off certain genes to inhibit growth, except, of course, for the one organ I am looking to grow out. The result is a perfectly matched organ; the fetus is a clone of the eventual recipient."

"And the ones in the lab?" Jesse asked. "Yours, I assume?"

Leezak nodded. "Just in case. Like I said a moment ago. You can never have too much insurance." Leezak wagged a finger. "But just to allay any concern you may have. I am perfectly healthy at the moment. No need to worry."

Jesse rolled his eyes, but otherwise ignored the remark. "And of course you don't see that as particularly barbaric. Maybe a little bit unethical, immoral?"

"You really need to learn to remove emotion when viewing these types of situations. Emotion clouds judgment, and in this case, progress. Reminds me of a time when stem cell research was actually frowned upon. Ridiculous." Leezak shook his head dismissively. "What I have done is practical and logical on every level. The fetuses are essentially clones of myself. No life has been taken, nobody's been hurt. And by not growing the rest of the body out, the brain never fully develops. They aren't cognizant, there's no suffering."

"How can you be so sure? And what about a soul? Did you ever consider that?"

"Again, you're viewing this through an irrational lens. If they did have a soul, whatever that might be, wouldn't they just have a piece of my soul, since they are genetic carbon copies? And if that's the case, then can't *I* decide how to divvy up my soul? As for suffering, their brainwaves are periodically monitored by EEG. At no time have

I found any activity that would indicate pain or complex emotion."

Jesse thought of the tormented image of the fetus he had accidentally awoken. It certainly had seemed to him like there was emotion behind its silent scream. "Sounds like you got it all figured out. Let's just hope someday when you meet your maker, he buys your rationale."

"I'm not a big believer, as you might imagine. And if I'm wrong, and there is a higher power, well, the good news is that I will not be meeting him for quite some time."

Jesse found himself hoping he'd be able to somehow trim down that time frame. "I guess it's safe to assume that you did in fact discover the fountain of youth?"

"Ahhh..." Leezak intoned, dragging out the sound. "You must be somewhat familiar with my work, or at least the conspiracy hype that surrounded it."

"I remember the speculation; it was all over the news for a while. Back in the day, you were a real celebrity for a while."

"I did indeed find a means to extend human life a great deal." Leezak replied, glossing over the celebrity remark. Apparently bragging of fame did not have near the appeal of boasting about his work. "Again, the answer's in the genes. There are several loci that if manipulated correctly retard the aging process a great deal. We can almost prevent telomere shrinkage entirely. The human body with the correct DNA make-over has the ability to last at least one hundred and fifty years, perhaps longer. At least that's what my algorithms indicate, based on experiments and longevity studies of other life forms. Which means I've got a good eighty years left."

"So it's all done with genetic engineering? Like the changes you spoke of yesterday?"

Leezak nodded.

"As much as it pains me to say, your resume of accomplishment is impressive. You've discovered a lot of stuff." For the first time in a while Jesse realized that his words were delivered sincere, his moral compass knuckling under to inquisitiveness and the fact that Leezak's scientific triumphs, however depraved, were mind-blowing.

"Thank you, I'll take that as a compliment. It's helped that I've had many years to work on these issues. And many of the methods involved are technically very similar. I've also been blessed with great facilities, and perhaps most importantly, the ability to ignore authority for the sake of progress. I mean, you're a scientist. You must understand. Think about it. The government telling a scientist how to behave is like a spoiled child telling you when it's okay to breathe." Leezak shifted in his seat, continued his speech. "Without any of those factors my accomplishments would've been greatly curtailed. And remember; right now you're in the privileged position of hearing about all of these techniques. Back in the day, information like this was often kept under wraps. I'm certain that other places around the world had achieved, or were on the verge of achieving many of these techniques, but for one reason or another, the news never reached the public."

Jesse nodded, pondered the explanation. The controversial nature of a lot of this work could certainly warrant secrecy. And given the fact that many other countries had less oversight, and much weaker media penetration, what Leezak had said made sense. It could be true, he guessed.

Jesse also knew that historically many scientific theories had been born from different sources at or about the same time. Co-evolution of discovery was common in many fields. It seemed that when an idea's time was right, it was right. It was as if the spirit of inspiration were bound by one all encompassing collective conscious of wisdom.

Still a few minutes from the turbulent waters of the pass leading to open ocean, Jesse figured he had time for one more question. "The females. What specifically do you use them for?"

Leezak nodded as if to acknowledge the merit of the question. "For all the capabilities and techniques I have developed, I've yet to come up with any greater incubator than the human womb."

Jesse frowned; he'd figured it was something along those lines. "So you grow the clones in the females until a certain point and then transfer them to the aquariums."

Leezak nodded. "That's the basic idea."

"It seems like you have quite a few females already. I mean, how many extra hearts do you need?" Jesse found irony in the remark as he said it, because even with all of the cloned hearts in the world, from Jesse's perspective, Leezak was still heartless.

"Now that there's such a shortage of people, some-body's gotta repopulate the planet." Leezak's manner and tone were utterly matter of fact. "It's been the focus of my most recent work."

Great, Jesse thought, a bunch of wicked Leezak spawn running around. A hundred come-backs filled his brain, equally as many follow-up questions, but they'd have to be put on hold, at least for the moment, because they were approaching the pass leading to the open ocean, and he'd need to focus his attention on that. Not to men-tion figuring out a way to exterminate the vermin sitting in the seat beside him.

"It gets a little rough going through the channel," Jesse said as he felt the sub vibrate in the first nudging currents.

"By the way," Leezak said. "When will we be in radio range?"

Jesse's eyebrows furrowed. "Why?"

"I want you to call ahead. I've got a message for you to deliver to your friends; a message of good will. You know, tell them you're bringing home a new friend, and how he's the greatest guy in the world, he comes in peace and bearing gifts. You know, that kind of stuff."

"Well, we're definitely in radio range." Jesse rolled his eyes. He had no idea exactly what Leezak would gain by such a message.

"I'm kidding about the message, of course," Leezak said mockingly. "I think it'll be better if my visit is unannounced. But I really do want *you* to call. I'm sure you have some kind of routine check-in, and it'll also give me a chance to evaluate the tone on the other side. I'd hate to come all of this way only to see the entire lot of your friends crop dusted with this." Leezak again held up the small vial containing the lethal virus. "Plus, I'm sure you have some kind of sonar. It will probably be better that they are not surprised when they pick us up."

"If that's what you want," Jesse agreed. Although unexpected, he'd make the call. He still needed to maintain the illusion of cooperation, and making a routine call back to Pacifica wasn't going to hurt anyone.

The sub shook in the current, and Jesse knew they were only a few minutes from the greater turbulence of the pass. Once again he thought of Alex, the image of him fumbling with his iPod on the sub ride in came unbidden to his mind.

Knowing that navigating through the pass would require a fair measure of attention, Jesse figured it best to wait till after they got through the wash to make the call. He was just about to explain that to Leezak when an idea struck. Was this the idea he'd been waiting for? It was crazy, but it just might work. And as he visualized the plan, Jesse began to wonder if maybe Alex's spirit hadn't indeed answered his earlier prayer; his assistance coming in the form of material intervention. Jesse's eyes immediately went to the rubber band on his wrist and he thought, *I gotta make this call right now.*

Chapter 57

Jesse flipped on the radio and turned to Leezak. "What exactly is it you want me to say?"

"I want you to call as if you were making a routine radio check. Speak casually—tell them of your return. Tell them everything went great and that your mission was a success."

"I guess I can do that." Jesse said. He fidgeted with the rubber band around his wrist, playing it cool.

"If it comes up, tell them that you rescued your father, but *do not* go into detail. And make no mention of your friend's demise."

Jesse nodded and picked up the handheld mic.

"If anyone should ask to speak to either of them, just tell them they're asleep." Leezak raised the remote to the shock collar into view. "And please don't say anything stupid. I don't want to have to use this again."

Jesse nodded, thumbed the talk button and proceeded to make the call exactly how Leezak had asked him to do. Beside him, Leezak listened intently, the remote held in clear view, a long finger hovering over the device like an itchy trigger finger.

Before concluding the call, Jesse asked. "Is Reni there?" Most of the call he'd been speaking to the communications tech, Jeff Yarnik. But about halfway through

Martin had arrived and taken over. Hearing the question, Leezak stiffened and mouthed *what are you doing?*

"Actually, he should be here any minute," Martin replied over the radio. "I sent someone to get him when I heard you had called in. I'm sure he'd love to talk to you."

As Martin was speaking, Jesse placed his hand over the mic and turned to Leezak. "Will you relax," he whispered. "He's my friend's kid. I brought him back some toys. I was just gonna tell him. You said to keep it casual." As he spoke to Leezak, Jesse carefully worked the rubber band down to his finger tips.

Leezak leaned back, lowered the remote. He seemed to buy the explanation, but his expression said he was still displeased. "Just tell them you gotta go now. Make up an excuse. The kid will have to wait to hear about his toys."

Jesse nodded just as the sub shook and shimmied again. He thumbed the mic and uttered an excuse. "Heading through the pass, gonna have to get back to you." He hesitated, acted like he was thinking what to say next. "Over and out." he finally said, just as another current hit and he steered slightly into it. The move enhanced the impact of the wave and the sub jounced. Leezak reached up and grabbed the panic bar. In the instant Leezak looked away Jesse let the rubber band unroll from his fingers and onto the handheld mic. He then quickly dropped the mic, pretending that it slipped, then brought his other hand back to the steering wheel. With both hands on the wheel, he counter-steered to bring the sub back under control.

"Damn turbulence," Jesse muttered. So as not to give Leezak a chance to remark he quickly continued, his voice filled with calculated anxiety. "I hate these currents. I always get nervous going through this part." He feigned uneasiness, shifting position, hands shaking, just as Alex had done coming through the pass during the trip in. He then reached into his shirt pocket, removed Alex's iPod. "Do you mind if I put this on until we get through the turbulence? It helps me with stress." He looked over at Leezak, set his expression to imploring. "It's only ten minutes?"

"Whatever works." Leezak offered a dismissive wave, rolled his eyes as if to demean Jesse for being beholden to such a trivial phobia.

The sub started to shake steadily, vibrating like an unbalanced washing machine. He'd timed it perfectly. Jesse fumbled with the iPod, then turned it on. Within seconds, he began nodding to the music, even began to mime and nod like he was singing along. He stared intently out the window as if hyper-focused. A peripheral glance told him Leezak was oblivious to his theatrics. And now for the most important part: the drums. You can't have a band without a drummer.

So Jesse began tapping to the tune, fingers like drum sticks on the steering wheel. Then it was time to add the bass drum. With his right foot he began tapping to the music playing in his head. As he nodded he took a quick glance down; the mic was right next to his tapping foot. *Perfect.*

Jesse felt a surge of hope. He had no doubt that the message was being received back at Pacifica. But what he didn't know; were they aware that it was a message? Jeff Yarnik most likely knew Morse code, but he was certain that Reni did; he'd taught the boy the cipher himself. Moreover, the message was very similar to one the boy had heard many times before. He only hoped that Reni had arrived at the communications room.

Chapter 58

Once through the pass, the turbulence quickly gave way to calm. The sub no longer vibrated and Jesse thumbed off the iPod. He couldn't help but wonder what his friends must be thinking back at Pacifica right about now. A few minutes earlier he'd called to tell them the good news of his return. Then only moments later, he'd drummed out a warning in Morse code. With any luck, they'd been able to deduce truth from duplicity, although there'd be no way to know for certain if his message had been received till he got much closer to Pacifica.

Leezak rummaged through his rucksack and produced a handheld radio. Flipping it on, the radio emitted static. Leezak toggled the call button. "Sigma one, are you there?" Leezak said, and waited.

No response.

"Is your radio still on?" Leezak turned to Jesse.

Jesse felt an instant spike of panic. Had Leezak figured out what he was up to?

"I think it's causing interference with my radio." Leezak then said.

Whew, Jesse felt his panic retreat. "No problem," he said, realizing that Leezak was just trying to figure out the cause of his bad connection.

Jesse casually reached over and turned off the unit. He was hoping to leave it on for the balance of the trip. With the mic open, any conversation they might've had would be broadcast for all to hear, possibly giving his friends a better understanding of what was going on. But it looked as though he was going to have to rely on the message already issued. Turning the radio back on after Leezak was done making his call might look suspicious.

Leezak tried his radio again and almost immediately got a reply. "Sigma one here, over." The voice sounded tinny and wrapped in static.

"Just wanted to keep you apprised of my progress," Leezak said. "We've just traveled through the pass. We're now out in open ocean."

Jesse found himself hanging on every word. He was enormously curious to know who Leezak was talking to.

"We are almost right above you, over," the voice said over the radio.

Jesse then recognized the robotic tone in the voice and he knew it was one of Leezak's subordinates.

Leezak brought the radio to his mouth. "Good. Head out to the platform and wait for my next call, over and out." Leezak switched off the radio and returned it to his rucksack.

Jesse let the implications of what he'd just learned filter through his brain. Anxious as he was to find out that a boat full of Leezak's men followed from above, he realized that they'd be of no consideration to his plan. Rather than remark on Leezak's call, he let it be, and resumed his attempt to relax. There was still plenty of time to kill before reaching Pacifica.

But despite his attempt to relax, Jesse couldn't. The high-octane energy that coursed through his blood like

Red Bull permitted no such luxury. Fortunately he had the perfect distraction sitting right next to him. Leezak was like a crossword puzzle in a doctor's waiting room, a means to pass time before an appointment, and maybe even learn something in the process. On top of that, Jesse knew that keeping Leezak distracted might prove advantageous, especially as they made final approach.

"So what are we looking at here, a bunch of little Leezak clones running around the city for the next hundred and fifty years all wearing wax skin?"

Leezak chuckled. "Now doesn't that sound like a delightful picture? And it may not be too far from the truth. There'll be no need for the wax skin, however."

Jesse felt himself reflexively frown. Certainly an odd remark, he thought. "Whatta you mean, you just gonna let 'em fry like bacon? Or maybe you can build a dome over the old Qualcomm stadium, turn it into a mini city."

"No need for all that. The next generation won't need any special protection. Soon enough it will be safe to go outside again."

Again Jesse felt a puzzled expression furrow on his face. What the hell was this guy talking about? "So now you're a psychic. What'd you do, clone Nostradamus?"

"I'm no psychic. But I do in fact have certain powers, powers far greater than you could probably imagine." Leezak looked over, Jesse did the same. For an instant their eyes met. And in that flash, Jesse felt a sudden shift in the universe, like the entire spirit world had just cried out in pain. Once again his casual digging seemed to have unearthed something. He could feel it coming, like an ominous cloud rolling in, the obligatory precursor before the storm; the exact agent of this storm yet uncertain. But whatever it was, Jesse sensed the devil in the looming details, a foreshadowing suspicion rooted in the deepest of evil.

Leezak shifted, settled in. "Perhaps it's best if we start from the beginning. We have time I presume. And at this point, I see no reason why you shouldn't know everything. Besides, I think you might appreciate the story I'm about to tell you."

His curiosity piqued, Jesse said nothing and stared out into the Pacific while his attention swung wholly toward the promised account.

"Back in the late 1960s studies were conducted on human population growth. And what they found was quite startling. Are you familiar with exponential growth?"

Jessed nodded. "Sure."

"Then you are probably aware that human population growth up until recently had followed a geometric rise over the years. If you were to look at a graph of global human population over the past few hundred years, you'd see that to be true. And even though exact census numbers had not been kept prior to that, it's believed the trend held true throughout human history The only time the population curve *did not* show geometric growth was during the mid-thirteen hundreds, the years of the black death; a plague that wiped out almost one-third of the entire human population at the time."

"I've heard about that."

"But it's what the population graphs forecasted about the future that had some people of the late twentieth century worried. Some of those first studies revealed some pretty startling results. Graphs of future growth showed the potential for huge increases in numbers through the twenty-first century. By 2100 it was speculated that human population could exceed twelve billion. We were more than halfway there in the early part of the century.

And that of course was the main source of concern: concerns over whether the planet had the resources to support such a massive population explosion. You were a bio major, right?"

"Yep. Undergrad."

"Then I am certain you worked with bacteria at some point. You'll remember that bacteria follow a certain pattern of growth when introduced to a Petri dish of nutritive media. Following a lag phase, the bacteria begin to feed and multiply. This is known as the log phase. During this phase the bacteria are happy and all is well. But soon the population enters a stationary phase, growth reaches a zero net, the bacteria begin to struggle for food and space, while trying to avoid toxic build up in the limited environment. But to the colony, everything still seems okay.

"Eventually, of course, things get worse, and the colony enters into what is known as the death phase. During this phase, reproduction ceases and the bacteria succumb. Their demise is caused by lack of food and habitat, cannibalism, as well as the poisonous by-products of their own misguided metabolism. All of which is a direct result of their own unchecked existence. They essentially cause their own extinction."

"If you're trying to compare bacteria to humans, it doesn't work. The planet is not finite like a Petri dish. There are renewable resources—wood, water, food—and people are smart."

Leezak laughed, the timbre came rich with sarcasm. "Water is indeed considered a renewable resource, but if the resource is consumed faster than it can be renewed, it's still a problem. You'd only have to ask the people living in southern California years ago, I think you'd find they'd agree. Truth is, there are limits to all resources. And as far as humans being smart." Leezak rolled his eyes, shook his head. "What do you think would've happened if back in the early twenty-first century you were to tell a young American couple they couldn't reproduce, even with an explanation of impending ecological disaster?" Leezak again shook his head, mocking the naiveté of Jesse's remark. "You'd get your ass kicked, my friend."

Jesse shrugged but said nothing, realizing he couldn't really refute either claim.

"Many world leaders became concerned that the same would eventually happen to the earth. The analogy's valid, after all. Despite your assertions, an exploding human population feeding off the same finite tit was no different than bacteria in a Petri dish. Many felt it was all leading to environmental disaster, a Malthusian catastrophe. And by the time the problems arise, many thought it might already be too late.

"Compounding the problem further was the fact that it was impossible to address by conventional methods. I mean, could you imagine a political figure, especially in the US, coming out and saying that new legislation was needed to limit the number of children you could have? It'd be political suicide. Although," Leezak brought a hand to his chin, pondered a notion that seemed to just come to him. "I imagine you have some idea of these dynamics, living in such a small isolated community as you have for some time." Leezak turned to Jesse.

Jesse nodded, then admitted. "We had some challenges, especially in the beginning."

"Well I'm sure you could see that there's no way that forcing vasectomies or even birth control for that matter would've been very effective back then. Any government attempts would've been met with outright anarchy. And any political figure who might suggest such efforts would be burned at the stake."

Jesse found he was nodding in agreement. He refrained from comment, however, mostly because he didn't want to interfere with an account that was, by virtue of its mystery, getting more and more interesting by the second. So he kept his lip tightly zipped, allowing Leezak to continue.

"Anyway, sometime back in the late 1960s, early 70s, one administration decided to address the issue. Of course it was all done under the most clandestine circumstances. Not only that, the program was also set up so that it would be imperceptible to investigation. It was created as a freestanding entity, with no direct links to anything. It was buried beneath so many layers of bureaucracy and red tape that you'd spend a lifetime looking, and only turn up dead ends. Funding was carefully siphoned off from an unwieldy tax system, built in as a percent of a percent in misappropriated monies from hundreds of other programs. It was all part of accepted loss as tax dollars passed through the complex apparatus of government."

Jesse found the notion utterly outrageous, but given what little he knew about government budgets, it wouldn't have surprised him if something of that nature could indeed be true.

"Seven scientists were selected from various fields and brought in to run the program. They eventually became known as the YP seven. Yersinia pestis is the scientific name of the bacteria that caused the black plague. In the beginning, the team mostly ran fairly benign misinformation programs and fear tactics to keep people doing things that advanced their agenda, which of course was anything that promoted death and prevented reproduction."

"What the heck?" Jesse spit out of reflex, a physical means of venting the PSI of growing shock.

Leezak ignored the remark. "They ran subtle campaigns supporting smoking, drinking, poor diet, and the like. Or what they found to be even more effective; interfering with any legislation or information that might have limited these behaviors. They even ran a huge counter-campaign against vitamins."

Jesse let out a skeptical snort. It did nothing to slow Leezak's discourse.

"I'm sure you remember hearing negative reports about vitamins. Didn't you ever find it a little curious that they always seemed to get more press than the positive stories? They'd take one negative study about vitamin E, let's say, and run it to death. And it wasn't hard to find doctors to use as puppets to broadcast the message. Since so many in the medical field held grudges against the alternative health industry, they relished the opportunity to dispel it as quackery and advance their own approach. If people had ever gotten the truth, without the cloud of misinformation, almost everyone would've had a good chance to live to a hundred. Everyone was *always* looking for the fountain of youth. And ironically, it's always been right there. All you had to do was limit your caloric intake, exercise, and consume the appropriate antioxidants and supplements. But the team made sure that that information was effectively muddled.

"The team also did whatever they could to support contraception and abortion rights, anything to reduce the number of new inputs to the population. I'm sure you've heard of AIDS?"

"Don't tell me they created AIDS!"

"No." Leezak shook his head. "But what they did was arrange a few liaisons to make sure that some key people in the heterosexual community got it. Once a few celebrities and athletes announced they were HIV positive, people were slapping on condoms left and right. The program had a huge reduction in pregnancy rate."

"I just can't believe all this stuff," Jesse said. "I can't believe that the government would do all this. Allowing someone to contract HIV would be a criminal act." He'd hoped for a distraction when he decided to engage Leezak. But never did he expect all this. A giant Humboldt squid crushing the sub like a tin can would garner no more of his attention at the moment.

"If that bothers you, then you better buckle up my friend, because it gets a lot worse. And as far as government involvement goes: there really wasn't any. By the end of the seventies, the program had spun off and become essentially autonomous. By then, much of the money had been invested privately, so future finance would never be a problem. The program was so secret that as administrations overturned, fewer and fewer were even aware of its existence, yet it continued on. And the seven men running the program were very committed to the cause."

Jesse again shook his head in disbelief; Leezak apparently picked up on his skepticism.

"Let me give you one more example, since you still seem unconvinced. Back in the early seventies a report came out that the use of DDT as a pesticide could save over five hundred thousand lives by preventing insect-borne disease. Well, you can imagine how big that went over with the newly formed YP team. So they went right to work. They immediately began a campaign to have DDT pulled. And within a year, it was a success. DDT was banned largely under the pretext that it was hazardous to the environment, thanks in large part to the undermining campaigns of the team. And the whole effort was hardly even questioned. Once you convince the public that something is harmful to the environment, you can pretty much write your ticket."

Jesse shook his head, a lot of this stuff made sense, except for one thing, which he immediately brought to light. "How the heck do you know all this stuff?"

Leezak turned, eyes bright with the glimmer of the privileged. "Because I eventually became one of the seven scientists."

"The fountain of youth," Jesse breathed as the connection snapped home in his brain.

"Very good. When my work was discovered, the team was there the next day, doing their thing. They essentially buried it under the guise of fraud and failure. And since my records were all hidden, aside from a shaky cell phone video, there was little evidence of what I'd done. And even though the area was sealed off as a crime scene, an *accidental* fire burned my lab to the ground that night, taking with it the physical evidence of my work, and it was like it all never happened. But of course, it did, and the YP'ers knew it.

"After a brief trial, I was later contacted by the team. By then, the case against me had been conveniently dropped. There was no evidence of any criminal activity. As luck would have it, at the time there were only six members to the YP team, as one member had passed away, leaving an opening that needed to be filled—perfect timing for me, wouldn't you say?

"Before I was told anything, I was subjected to an intense vetting process. I was tested more rigorously than an astronaut. Fortunately I fit their profile to a tee, scored off the top end of the chart on intellect and off the bottom end on the empathy scale. Plus, by bringing me on board they ensured that my data wouldn't go public."

Jesse frowned. "That makes no sense, why would you listen to them? Why didn't you go to the authorities, or the media, broadcast to everyone what they were doing? At the very least, tell of your findings."

"Because I believed in the cause wholeheartedly; to me it all made perfect sense. It was a position I was born to hold. Besides, my private work in genetics was never meant for the world, anyway. I was always working for my own benefit, was always in search of a means to distance myself from a race of people that I found appalling, and frankly, beneath me. And if I did go public, chances are I'd've been arrested for the less than legal means by which I achieved my success."

"I just don't see how anyone could do such a thing. How could you buy into it?"

"We all did: all seven. Some perhaps more ardently than others, but we were all on board. We all understood that what we were doing was for the good of the planet, and as unbelievable as it might sound, the good of the human race."

"This is all interesting stuff, crazy as it is. But at the start of this conversation you said you were going to explain how you know that the planet will soon be habitable again."

"We're almost there, promise. Without the background it wouldn't have made any sense."

Jesse couldn't imagine how *any* of this was going to make sense, at least to him, or anyone else of rational mind. But he'd started this, and he was now in it for the duration, wherever that might take him.

"Eventually a lot of the programs became ineffective. With the advent of the Internet, information was harder to control. And over the years, political sentiment and governmental attitudes changed, so much so that many policies were in direct conflict with what we were trying to do. Health care programs were enhanced. Administrations began pouring economic aid into third world countries to ease disease and starvation. Of course they were only doing it as a means to garner public opinion, and as a result, reelection.

"By the time I was brought on board a lot of the team's efforts had weakened. Not long after a major global economic recession, things really calmed down around the world. A kind of renaissance ensued amid a growing sense of new world order, and people were fucking like rabbits. At about the same time a schism developed among the YP team, and then a power struggle. Three of us wanted to get more aggressive: we had an idea to advance an existing program and counter our waning influence. The other four wanted to stick with the status quo. With no real oversight, it wasn't like it really mattered. But to me and two of the others, it did matter. We considered ourselves agents for the environment. And if somebody didn't step up and help, ultimately everything would be ruined. Not long after that, the YP seven became the YP three, as four of our collogues decided to suddenly retire."

"Which means you had them killed, of course."

"A means to an end." Leezak shrugged. "They'd become obsolete, and as such, counterproductive. They weren't as strong, weren't up to the task, lacked the stomach to advance the difficult work that was required. Sometimes an infected wound needs to be scraped clean before it can heal. And they couldn't handle the pain."

"How unusual," Jesse spat, "they weren't up for the noble goal of killing people."

"You mean the noble goal of saving the world. It's all a matter of perspective."

"Save the world? Let's hear this big idea. Please enlighten me."

"From the beginning the team ran misinformation campaigns against the efforts to save the ozone layer. But like a lot of our work, the initial success eventually eroded. In the beginning the pollutants that harm ozone flowed without regulation, and the ozone layer was being destroyed. At one point, ten to fifteen thousand were dying annually of skin cancer worldwide, and the numbers kept going up. But times started to change; treaties were signed, and dangerous emissions were reduced. And although the ozone layer never actually improved, it also wasn't breaking down as fast."

The nefarious inkling that Jesse had sensed earlier had begun to finally coalesce. And the enormity of that evil was beyond the measure of any scale. He felt his skull begin to swell with stark implication, *it just couldn't be!*

Chapter 59

Jesse took a deep breath and braced for the impending purgation he sensed coming.

Leezak shifted casually. "Of the two remaining YP scientists, one was a virologist, the other a chemist. Way back, our chemist had developed a device that when installed in the appropriate factory setting, one that generated the correct blend of heat and effluvium, would cause a reaction to create massive amounts of the very pollutants that break down atmospheric ozone."

"The machine," Jesse breathed, hypnotically staring out into the pacific, a fresh wave of shock sweeping through his mind. Had the steering wheel not been forged of hardened ABS plastic, his grip would have snapped it in two.

Leezak turned. "The generator in my warehouse is indeed outfitted with several units, if that's what you're referring to."

"Wait a second, hold on," Jesse snapped from his trance. "No way would that be large enough to cause such a global problem."

"Very perceptive, it's not even close. That's why we had to set up many around the globe. At one point we had them scattered everywhere."

"Impossible," Jesse spat, as if the force of his denial would somehow turn it all around, rearrange history; erase an insane past that has led to the grim future he now found himself living in.

"You'd be amazed what money could buy. And we had access to plenty of cash. We had enough funding to have the units built, then installed around the world, mostly third world places, South America, Asia, India; places where there was little oversight. At the time, given the problems with global warming, factories around the world were being retrofitted with large CCS filters to sequester carbon dioxide. And we got in the business. We'd simply go in; explain that the unit was a filter to help reduce greenhouse gases, and if they allowed us to install and monitor the unit, they'd even receive a stipend for their environmental philanthropy. As you can imagine, it wasn't often we were turned away."

Jesse was stunned. Fragments of information collided in his brain like ions in a particle accelerator, leaving his mind smoldering in speculation. Speculation then gelled to analysis. Leezak had mentioned that one of the other scientists was a virologist; the basis of the plague was viral. Before the thought ripened fully, the words started to spill forth. "The plague…the plague is a vir…"

Leezak was already nodding, confirming his suspicion mid-spill. "In 2008 it was discovered that a certain polyomavirus was linked to a very lethal type of skin cancer known as Merkel cell carcinoma—or the plague as it had come to be known. The virus was not easily spread and fairly benign to those who had it, unless you add ultraviolet radiation to the mix. But once stricken with Merkel cell, and without treatment, you were pretty much finished. It's a very aggressive cancer as you well know. We already had the plans in place to increase global UV, all we had to do was alter the virus, make it more easily transmitted, which wasn't all that difficult when you had one of the world's leading virologists on the team, Dr. Ewell."

Ewell? Jesse immediately recognized the name, he knew a Ewell back in Pacifica. Ewell was the bastard always on the other end of his arguments to venture to land. Could it be the same person? Jesse knew that Ewell was a scientist, and had worked for the government in some capacity. He wasn't sure of his discipline; Ewell had always kept that information conspicuously vague, in fact. Maybe he had reason to be vague. If it was the same Ewell, could Leezak know he was there? Could they still be working together? If so, then why would Leezak mention his name, show his hand? *No*, Jesse decided, that didn't make sense—they were not working together, at least not any more. But it didn't mean that Pacifica's Ewell wasn't Leezak's Ewell. Whatever the case, further investigation would have to be conducted tactfully. Jesse filed the notion away, because at the moment, there were matters of greater interest.

Jesse took his eyes from the infinite blue highway, the better to glare at Leezak. "So what you're telling me is that you and the other YP assholes are responsible for all this?"

"It was never our intent to take it as far as it has gone. Our initial goal was to tweak things a bit, maybe get a few thousand more cancer deaths a year. But what happened was even a surprise to us. We didn't anticipate how things would so rapidly degrade. Ozone depleted faster than we predicted, the plague more deadly. But it was the harmful effects to the environment that really caught us off guard. The combination of crumbling food chains and damaging weather patterns were devastating, no way could we have predicted the measure of their impact. Add that to the way people started to react—the ensuing panic and mayhem—and it made the devastation far worse than anyone could have estimated: the fact that it all happened right around the time when many cultures and prophets predicted global demise only added fuel to the fire. It was a real Petri dish panic. Plans were immediately made to end the program, of course, but again there was a schism in the team." Leezak held up a single finger. "And the YP3 became the YP1."

Jesse felt like his head was about to explode, spray the inside of the sub with ragged gray fillets and skull frags. But he needed to keep it together to further his understanding. So he took a deep breath and continued the inquest. "The other two scientists, you killed them too."

"Actually, they left the program before they were forced to *retire*. They must've seen it coming. I'm sure I could have tracked them down, but what was the point. They posed no threat. There was no way to stop what was happening. So I let them go their own way. See, I'm not such a bad guy after all."

Jesse rolled his eyes, but otherwise ignored the remark. The question had been revealing. It not only told him that the other scientists were not killed, but it seemed to confirm that Leezak and Ewell were not in cahoots, at least not anymore. If Jesse somehow managed to survive this ordeal, Ewell would have to be questioned when he got back to Pacifica.

"How many of these factories are still in operation?" Jesse asked, trying to learn the full scope of this mystery.

"Aside from the few left here on the coast, I'd imagine they're all shut down by now. I've had no contact for years. With global collapse, they've probably been off for a while. That's why, as you probably know, the UV levels have begun to improve recently."

Jesse didn't know. They'd had no access to a radiation detector for several years, was one of the main reasons he wanted to journey to the surface in the first place. The notion angered him, but he kept it in check. Worrying about it at this point made about as much sense as worrying about wearing clean underwear during a coronary.

"You mean there's others here on the coast?" Jesse asked.

"A few. A couple up north and one a ways to the south. Just enough to keep the environment maintained, at least to the extent that can be managed. They're each manned by a small team."

"Where did you find all of these men to help you anyway? I mean, how did you find so many people willing to stand by and watch what you did?"

"None of them know what the factories are for. As far as they know, they're simply power-plants to make electricity. They're just happy they have the luxury of at least some power. And as far as finding recruits, it was easy. As things started to go bad, many of the last survivors were... how should I put it...not the most scrupulous types. So when I gave them an opportunity to join the team, most were on board. Some subsequent adjustments to their personality, the availability of food and electricity, and I have the most loyal following a leader could ask for."

Jesse was at a loss for words, his brain clotted with chaos and implication.

Leezak sighed. "Soon it will be time to turn the rest of the machines off, and allow the environment to fully heal. As my children grow, I want them to have a safe environment to live in. The next generation will have all the advantages they need to create a new era of mankind."

"What about everybody else's children? Where was your consideration for them?"

"It's easy to see that you are a smart man, Jesse. But you are still missing the point of my work. You're only looking at the surface. Try and remove the emotion that clouds your mind—think like a scientist, a pure problem solver. If you do, you'll see that I have improved the environment. The earth will return to its once pristine form. There'll be no shortage of resources for the next thousand years. What you've also failed to see is that I've made the human race immeasurably stronger. Those who've survived are the fittest. As they breed, the species will be stronger than ever before. As a bio major, I'm sure you must understand the basic precepts of natural selection."

Jesse felt as though he'd just run a marathon, mental exhaustion seeped into his muscles like liquid lactic acid fatigue. Many questions still lingered. But they were questions that would likely never be asked. Because up ahead, he saw a faint radiance, a distinct clue telling him they were now on final approach.

Jesse felt his heartbeat quicken as he gazed out through the acrylic windshield, staring anxiously at the distant glowing echo of Pacifica.

Chapter 60

U p ahead, Pacifica glowed magnificently like the Emerald City of the deep. And almost right away Jesse could see that his friends had indeed received his message. *Whew*. The magnitude of his relief was colossal. With that task out of the way, he now focused on another; keeping Leezak distracted. He didn't think Leezak was a seasoned diver, but there was no way to know. Either way, he hoped that he wouldn't notice the phenomenon that, even from two hundred yards out, was as plain as day to him.

While staring out at the dilating image of Pacifica, Leezak had already remarked how impressed he was. Jesse said nothing to encourage the conversation in that direction. He quickly searched for some other topic to talk about, something amusing, something with enough appeal to redirect his focus. And then it came, a topic that might just do the trick, and perhaps quench *his own* curiosity in the process.

"Well, at least you aren't a racist. I figured for sure that *that* was gonna come up at some point in your discourse."

Leezak laughed, shook his head. "Global eugenics was a common conspiracy theory back in the day: one search on the Internet and you'd see that. I used to get quite a kick out of reading about that kind of stuff. Forced sterilization and global mind control, it was all fascinating reading to say the least." Leezak shrugged. "Although who really knows? It wouldn't surprise me if maybe there was some of that type of activity going on back then. But we certainly weren't involved in any tactics of favored selection. We were scientists; our concern was for the planet, and the good of the human species as a whole. Besides, apart from maybe politics and religion, there's really nothing more unscientific than racism." Leezak let out a short audible exhale punctuating his remark.

"Really? How so?" Interesting, Jesse thought.

"Well…just look at the recent events affecting the human race. It's the perfect example of how illogical racism is. When the environment changed, people with darker skin like yourself had a greater advantage because your skin pigmentation provided extra protection from the sun, allowing for a competitive advantage. It's proof positive that the strength of a species lies in its diversity. When you spray cockroaches with pesticide, a few almost always survive. This is because they're different; they have subtle genetic variations that make them more resistant to the poison. The next time you spray, even fewer die, because those who've survived the initial kill have passed on their genes. The resultant breed is much stronger."

"So now you're calling me a cockroach?"

Leezak laughed. "Of course not. But if I had, you should take it as a compliment. With all you've lived through, you might just be as hardy as one.

"Of course it's all irrelevant now anyway. Evolution's no longer valid. Now that I have the ability to alter genes, no longer do we have to wait for the environment to cull out the unfit. Rather than wait, I can make alterations at a somatic level as I've already explained, or, better yet, with my new techniques, I can make changes at the germ level. Changes at conception are far more effective and permanent. That's why the new offspring that I am now growing back at the nursery are superior, and will always have a leg up on any others. They will be perfect right from the beginning."

Great, Jesse thought, shaking his head. Leezak had just finished excoriating the practice of racism, and in the very next breath the lunatic brags how his offspring will be superior. Maybe he didn't realize his oversight, but in Jesse's view, being overly proud of one's own variety is racism in itself—an ego derived back-hand bias.

With the landing site only a few yards off, Jesse didn't bother bringing the point to light, his focus swinging toward docking the sub. Although, amid the insane diatribe, he realized that Leezak had made one remark that struck a positive chord: *the strength of a species lies in its diversity.* Jesse replayed the remark in his mind, filing it away. They were words he could use when he spoke to Reni. He remembered he still owed the boy an explanation on that very topic, should he somehow manage to survive to deliver that explanation.

Jesse maneuvered the Halibut into an open landing platform beside the ALEN; his ruse to distract Leezak appeared to have been effective. Leezak had yet to display any concern. Apparently he had not recognized the atypical color in the sea for what it was. Maybe he didn't realize that deep green was the resultant mix of oceanic blue and blood red.

"Okay, gear up," Jesse said as he pointed off to the building on the right. "From here we have a short swim across to the dive chamber. We enter up through the bottom into the wet deck."

"Again I must voice my compliments. This Pacifica is very impressive, a remarkable achievement. Not only the facility, but your ability to survive here for all this time."

"Yeah, well...you'll find that there's a lot of us cockroaches living here." Jesse said reflexively as he powered down the Halibut.

"Touché."

Jesse started putting on the rest of his dive equipment. Leezak did the same. Reaching for his radio, Leezak then made a call to his men. "Sigma one, Sigma one; final check. I've arrived at Pacifica."

"We're right above you, over," a voice came back immediately.

"Good. Hold your position. Next contact's in four hours. If you don't hear from me, you know what to do. Over and out."

Leezak tucked the radio back into his dive pack, then turned to Jesse. "Ready whenever you are." Leezak again showed Jesse the remote that controlled his shock collar. "And let's not forget about this." The two made eye contact, then Leezak pointed to the exit. "You first, I'll follow."

Jesse nodded and opened the lower hatch. The docks were set on elevated rails to allow easy access through the bottom of the vessel.

Jesse entered the water and felt a spontaneous shiver. The shudder came as much from cold as seeing the remote again. The shock nearly killed him the first time, and he wasn't so sure he'd survive another. And even if his physiology did reboot from the impact of a second jolt, he couldn't be sure how well he'd manage out in the open ocean.

Halfway to the dive chamber, Jesse starting getting more than a little concerned. Despite the fact that his friends had done exactly what he requested, there'd yet to be any indication that his plan was working. With each swim-step closer to Pacifica his brain scrambled for alternatives. Lunging for Leezak's airway was not a workable option. Leezak instinctively kept a safe step behind, rendering any such effort impossible. He'd be paralyzed or dead before he got even close.

Forty feet from the dive chamber, Jesse's concern began edging toward panic. His plan was not working. He now faced the very real prospect of becoming the post modern poster child for betrayal, effectively shoving aside Benedict Arnold as the textbook template. The notion dredged up a mega-dose of dread, pushing his psychic circuitry toward overload, the potential damage was beyond comprehension. He couldn't live with himself if Leezak made it to his friends. He had no choice. Another few steps and he'd have to have to turn and fight.

Out of the blue a peripheral flicker of hope materialized, and the large fleeting shadow breathed instant life into his flat-lined plan. The call of duty had apparently been answered, his unlikely associate arriving not a moment too soon, responding by virtue of primal craving.

Jesse glanced back, Leezak still seemed unaware. With the glance he also furtively monitored the *other* movements in the water. And then all at once Jesse could see that the moment was right.

Twenty feet short of the dive chamber, Jesse stopped, settled to the seabed, turned to face Leezak. Leezak stopped and moved cautiously away, a baffled expression furrowing behind his dive-mask. He raised the water-proofed remote before him, waved it in a taunting manner. The signal was clear. *Keep moving or suffer the consequences.* Jesse shook his head defiantly, his message equally as clear. *No chance.*

And then in one quick motion Jesse lunged wildly at Leezak, aiming for his core, bracing for the inevitable shock.

The jolt Jesse felt was like a thousand stinging jellyfish. Leezak had pressed the remote. His body went instantly limp, he couldn't breathe. High-voltage Novocain filled his body from head to toe. Jesse knew he was in dire straits, on the verge of losing consciousness, and only seconds from certain death. But the move had the effect he'd hoped. Leezak had scurried back as he tried to avoid the assault, pushing him beyond the range of Jesse's shark POD, while Jesse drifted like an anchor to the seabed. The fact that Jesse was sizzling from within was a small price to pay to achieve that simple goal.

Leezak then took another step back.

And when the shark hit Leezak from behind, Jesse's sense of relief was colossal, a simultaneous climax of elation and infinite triumph, and all before his paralysis had abated; because it took several long seconds for Leezak to let go of the remote, his hand holding on by sheer momentum of neural impulse.

As Jesse drifted helplessly to the seabed, he saw the great white shark swimming off; the body of Dr. Harris Leezak gripped at mid-torso between huge jaws, the shark running off like a spotted hyena clinging to a meaty wildebeest femur. The shark then twitched and the massive mandibles hinged home, the action scissoring the good doctor nearly in half. The shark swam off with a mouthful of spaghetti viscera, a coil of purple sausage-links unfurling like a fire hose being pulled to a five alarm blaze, leaving Leezak's corpse to swirl in its hydraulic slipstream, minus a gaping red raw half-moon amputation.

Although death had been instant, Leezak's body still had animation, puppeteered by hydraulic eddies and the twitching momentum of lingering essence. The image was perfectly dramatic, startling and exhilarating all at once. The corpse drifted amid a fresh dark torrent of gore, looking like a worming mosquito larva, upper and lower segments connected by a thin thorax of denuded spine.

The fact that Jesse did not pass out was a true delight, the spectacle was indeed a sight to behold; he'd have been upset had he missed it. Seconds later a school of smaller sharks streaked in to share in the feast, feeding like maggots on a carcass in time lapse frenzy.

Despite the physical pain, Jesse smiled. Amid the drama, a distant fold in his brain commended him on his success. And he'd even kept his promise, just like he'd said during the pool game—It *wasn't he* who prevented Leezak from reaching Pacifica.

At the moment, Jesse felt a kinship with all around him. It was as if nature knew, forces uniting in some strange ad hoc symbiosis, working together to stamp out a universal evil; a form of biological pest control to exterminate the mother of all villains.

Jesse felt his senses slowly returning, and not a moment too soon. Because the white shark had turned, was already torpedoing back, apparently in search of seconds. He breathed deeply and flexed his limbs, trying to gain movement. He glanced at the shark POD strapped to his leg. He noticed a wire lead had been unplugged in the action. He tried to reach it, but couldn't, his joints still soldered with paralysis.

Oh shit!

He spotted the cover of a small rock formation ten feet away and he stretched for it, but his movements were all off, his muscles still sputtering and seizing with mad cow epilepsy. And that about summed up his destiny. *A cow.* A helpless herbivore seconds before slaughter. Because the big shark had moved by Leezak's gnarled corpse, its eyes set on fresh meat. And in that instant, Jesse's kinship with the oceanic players went straight out the window, his Kumbaya moment promptly usurped by panic.

The last seconds ticked quickly away as impending tragedy streaked toward certainty. And in those last seconds Jesse was scared suitably shitless, and unlike his prior near death experience, he was angry and afraid. Not of the potential pain, or concern over a retirement home for his soul. But what bothered him was that he'd not be able to rescue his father, or ever again get the chance to sit and talk with him. Nor would he ever get to hang out with Martin, or spend time with Reni in conversation, or offer Michelle the tiny imitation engagement ring he still had tucked away in his backpack in the sub. Life as he knew it was now reduced to a handful of heartbeats, the door to his future slamming home hard with a single impact of fate, and a sad bloody aftermath. Feeding the local reef ecosystem with his pulpy remains was all he had left to look forward to, his molecules reincarnated in the flesh of the shark, crab, coral, and kelp.

Jesse managed to turn, face the encroaching predator, the power to raise a limb in defense beyond his strength. The creature was there, impact less than a blink away. And then out of the corner of that last falling eyelid, he saw another shadow. The six-foot shadow filled him with ardor and hope, and the promise of a second chance hummed through his core, filling his heart with a new kinship. The kind shared by only the best of friends.

The sea thundered as reality glitched, and the ocean's atoms seemed to come alive. A quick swoosh trailed a thin projectile dashing through the sea. Jesse watched in a haze as the bolt streaked through the sea, slamming into the shark only inches before impact. The creature was so close Jesse could see a loop of Leezak's intestine between its teeth, the pink hose hanging like dental floss for a meal well deserved.

The shark trembled and veered, delivering a glancing blow to Jesse's listless body on the way by, gritty derma rushed by like a belt sander, shredding his wetsuit and skin.

The resulting hydraulic pulse hit with the force of an F5 tornado. Jesse tumbled through the surf, his body a limp ragdoll, cartwheeling like a black diamond ski-slope flop. His air tank and mask were ripped off in the turbulence. He was unconscious long before his body came fully to rest.

Only seconds later Martin was there.

Epilogue

Back in Pacifica, Jesse lay on his back in the medical ward as consciousness returned. He glanced over at the clock on the wall. He felt a rush of relief as he realized it'd been less than an hour. He took a deep breath, knowing there'd be plenty of time to take out the men on the boat before they'd make the call to have his father executed.

Jesse realized he was smiling, a reflexive expression of celebration and inner peace. Gingerly, he turned his head and glanced around. Many of his friends stood in a huddle on the other side of the room. He was happy to see them, happy with his victory over Leezak, happy to see curved plastic walls, happy to be alive, and most of all, happy to be home.

He hurt all over, the simple act of smiling painful. And although the pain was everywhere, his body aching as if he'd just been run over by a John Deere harvester, all in all, it was a good pain, the soreness serving as reminder, the kind that says, *you're still alive, my friend*.

The closest face belonged to Reni, the boy's eyes growing wide as he realized Jesse was awake.

"You made it! You're okay!" Reni whispered, his words crammed with emotion.

"Well," Jesse heard himself saying, "I had to make it back. I still owe you an answer to the question you asked the other day, now don't I."

Reni returned a puzzled expression.

"You know," Jesse tried lifting his head again and immediately regretted the move. There'd be none of that for a while. "Why there were more light-skinned people than dark in the old video programs. Remember?"

Reni beamed. He seemed happier that Jesse had remembered his promise more so than the fact that he was going to get an answer.

"Ah," the boy waved dismissively, "don't even worry about it. Besides," Reni smiled again. "I already figured it out. The day after you guys left, I woke up and the answer was just there in my mind. I didn't even have to think about it."

"Really?" What the boy didn't realize was that although he wasn't actively thinking about the problem, his subconscious had been gnawing away at it even while he slept. On more than one occasion Jesse had awoken with a solution to a problem that had been beyond his scope as he closed his eyes the night prior. "Well, lemme hear it."

"It's simple; the same thing happened as happened to the moths in England. When the environment changed from the ozone, it became better for people with darker skin, allowing more to survive." Reni waited for the verdict, his expression expectant.

The strength of a species lies in its diversity, Jesse thought, recalling the statement Leezak had recently made. "Very good, kiddo; right on the money." Jesse said, patting the boy on the shoulder. He even linked an old lesson in basic biology to the account, a connection that Jesse himself had never made.

Reni beamed.

"How's your dad doing?" Jesse lifted a finger weakly to point at the group in the back of the room huddled in conversation over tea.

"Dad! Come'ere, he's awake!" Reni called excitedly, taking Jesse's cue.

Martin arrived quickly by his bedside, Michelle only a step behind. They both smiled, but there was no mistaking the underlying concern. Across the room Jesse saw Jennifer and others; even Santos had made it down for the occasion. The team was reunited. And even though Alex wasn't there, his spirit couldn't be any more alive.

"Thought we might've lost you there for a while," Martin said.

"You ain't getting rid of me that easily," Jesse replied wispily, as his gaze went to Michelle.

Martin laid a hand on his friend's shoulder. "It's great to have you back."

Jesse acknowledged Martin's remark with nodding eyelids but then his gaze drifted right back to Michelle. For some reason he just couldn't keep his eyes off her; her aura like an electromagnet, his eyes molten iron.

Martin looked to Reni. "Come on; let's give 'em a minute." He put an arm around the boy and led him away. Reni winked at Jesse as he moved off with his father.

Michelle moved closer to his bedside. She looked both anxious and relieved as she reached down and grasped his hand. Her chin visibly quivered and her brown eyes were bright with emotion, clues that betrayed the validity of her smile.

"I'm gonna be fine," he assured her, squeezing her hand firmly.

"Happy birthday," she managed, and leaned in and gave him a kiss on the cheek.

Jesse looked puzzled, for a second confused. "Thanks," he said, realizing that it was in fact his birthday. He was thirty-three today. What better way to celebrate, he thought. "What, no gift?"

"The kiss was for your birthday. You can unwrap the rest of your gift later," she gave him a fine-spun smile. "If you're up for it."

"Thanks," Jesse said, squeezing her hand again as his expression turned more serious. "I mean, thank you for everything, thanks for understanding." He could feel the electricity of her very essence, their entwined hands acting like a pipeline between hearts, conducting a two-way surge of understanding and love. He thought of the gifts he'd brought back in his backpack; the cosmetics, the wine, the figurine, and the ring; although it would be some time till he earned the right to even think of proposing to her. A lot of work had to be done before rekindling a full blown romantic relationship; he owed her that. But every journey starts with one step. And it was time to take that first step.

"I never stopped loving you," he whispered.

Michelle nodded and smiled. "I know."

Jesse then closed his eyes as he held Michelle's hand. He realized that he needed to report the news about Alex, and the fact that there was a boat up top that needed to be sunk. The details of Leezak and of the machines would have to be reported. He also needed to have a little talk with one Horace Ewell. In a few minutes, he'd call Martin back over and explain everything. But just for a moment, he needed to rest, and more importantly, enjoy the company of his friends, the solace of Pacifica, and the warmth of her hand.